EX LIBRIS

GIFT OF

SIMI VALLEY FRIENDS
OF THE LIBRARY

Forbidden Fruit

Books by Kerry Greenwood

The Corinna Chapman series
Earthly Delights
Heavenly Pleasures
Devil's Food
Trick or Treat
Forbidden Fruit

The Phryne Fisher series
Cocaine Blues
Flying Too High
Murder on the Ballarat Train
Death at Victoria Dock
The Green Mill Murder
Blood and Circuses
Ruddy Gore
Urn Burial
Raisins and Almonds
Death Before Wicket
Away With the Fairies
Murder in Montparnasse
The Castlemaine Murders
Queen of the Flowers
Death by Water
Murder in the Dark
Murder on a Midsummer Night

Short Story Anthology
A Question of Death:
An Illustrated Phryne Fisher Anthology

Forbidden Fruit

A Corinna Chapman Mystery

Kerry Greenwood

Poisoned Pen Press

Poisoned
Pen
Press

Poisoned Pen Press
6962 E. First Ave., Ste. 103
Scottsdale, AZ 85251
www.poisonedpenpress.com
info@poisonedpenpress.com

Printed in the United States of America

With many thanks to the indefatigable Greenwood Support Collective: Jen Pausacker, David Greagg, all the Pryors, Jean and Alan Greenwood, Miss Dawn for Diligence, and the recipe suppliers, tasters, commentators and email fans who make me feel slightly less isolated at three am on a dark morning.

Not to mention Ihr Altesse, Belladonna, Principessa di Gatti, of course. And Blackberry and Doughall the Giant Kitten.

In loving memory of Dennis Pryor, a charming and compassionate man of remarkable learning.

This book is for M.V.C.S, M.O.N.V.C.S., and all the singers of the Known World.

My fanatical vegans and my fanatical Christians are all fictional. There are no such organisations or churches and they are all a product of the author's horrible imagination. The freegans are not. They seem to have left the city, however. If they turn up in your area it would be nice to step a few paces of the Hare Wombat dance with them. And perhaps buy them an ice cream. They rarely find edible ice cream in dumpsters.

For unto us a Child is born,
Unto us a Son is given.

—GF Handel, *Messiah*

Chapter One

Four am is not an ideal time, especially if someone is trying to have a conversation with you about glacé cherries and the desirability of making our own.

I opened one eye, which was about as much as could be expected, made a broad sweeping motion with my only available arm, and grunted 'Go away!' with all the force at my disposal.

'Oh, shit,' said someone, and there was a whisking noise. When the alarm went off and I really had to wake up, I saw, in order of perception: 1) my cat, Horatio, indicating extreme displeasure by folding himself into a tabby and white pillar and twitching the very end of his tail; 2) my apprentice, Jason, looking abashed and rumpling his thick curly blond hair; and 3) my lover, Daniel, holding Jason by the shoulder with one hand and offering me a large cup of very strong black coffee with the other.

The last was the only thing I wanted at that moment and the delegation departed, led by Horatio, who was suggesting that only immediate and the fullest of full-cream Farmhouse milk could assuage his injured feelings at this disgraceful irruption into his solemn morning ritual. In fact, they might gainfully omit the milk component and go straight for the cream.

After my first coffee, I did the usual morning things in my usual morning trance, spiced with some outrage. Jason might be a feckless adolescent but Daniel knew how I felt about being awoken even a millisecond before I had to be. I treasure my hours of sleep. I grumbled as I dressed in my size 20 cotton baker's overall—the weather was warm, which meant that the bakery would be blistering until the air conditioning kicked in—and pulled back my hair and secured it in a clip. I looked at myself in the mirror, always unwise at this hour. Three chins, which would refine to two when I woke up. Hair which was now reddish since Meroe had arrived with that henna rinse and the need for a subject for her experiment. Blue blurry eyes. Corinna Chapman. Good morning, ma'am.

Jason had gone, Daniel was reading the paper, and my croissant, jam, butter and a pot of coffee were on the table, while Horatio discussed his dish of cream underneath. I ate, I drank, I contemplated the front page of Daniel's paper and it came into focus. Gradually, I became a human, instead of a grizzly bear woken up before it was even spring. I hate it when this happens because I have to apologise for whatever it was I did when I was half asleep.

Fortunately, I hadn't done much. I might have meant to clip Jason's ears, but I simply hadn't had the coordination.

'What was all that about?' I asked.

'I caught him too late,' said Daniel. 'I was just coming in when I heard him babbling about making glacé cherries. Sorry, *ketschele*. I sent him down to begin the baking so you could have a civilised breakfast.'

'And so I have,' I replied, leaning over to kiss him. Mmm. Coffee and croissant and the scent of Daniel's skin, which always smelt like cinnamon. 'No harm done—I'll just mention that if he does such a thing again I will personally put him into a pie and bake him. This must be about his Christmas cakes. He's been obsessing about them for days.'

'And enthusiasm should not be quashed,' Daniel told me, returning the kiss with compound interest.

I know about these things, because I was once an accountant, until I discarded my pantyhose forever, gave my suits and kitten-heeled shoes to the Brotherhood, and took up baking, which has brought me modest financial profit and much greater happiness than I deserve.

I dumped the bad mood. What right had I to feel grumpy when I had Daniel and Jason and the inhabitants of Insula, an eccentric but fascinating building in the middle of Melbourne, my favourite city?

I smiled. Horatio, having finished the cream and his kitty dins, decided that a thorough wash was essential before he went to meet his public in the shop, Earthly Delights, and levitated onto a suitable chair for the purpose.

'Time to close the windows,' said Daniel. 'It's blowing a gale.'

'I hate north winds,' I agreed, doing so and pulling the dark curtains across. 'I loathe summer, and I detest Christmas. It's only the start of December. Already it's hot and already the shoppers are frantic. I'm glad we're closing for January, because by the time we get to Christmas, we are all going to be knackered.'

'Hanukkah is less stressful,' said Daniel. 'Now, if you are going to the bakery, I am going to have a shower and flake out. I've had a long night in the rafters, trying to locate a poison pen.'

'Tell me later,' I said, kissed him again, and descended to the bakery.

I was half an hour late, and Jason had already set all the mixers going, a charming noise. The Mouse Police, Heckle and Jekyll, had delivered their tribute of dead vermin and had been rewarded. I came in as Jason opened the door into Calico Alley and they scrambled out, in search of endangered species of the Southern Ocean, scraps of which Kiko and Ian from the Japanese restaurant always keep for them. For former street cats, they had expensive tastes.

The coffee pot was on and so was the industrial air conditioner, which might keep us alive during the summer. It was an engineering marvel, according to the Green Tech people who installed it, using waste heat from the ovens to do something ingenious and carbon neutral. And it was blasting out a lot of cold air, which was wonderful. I stood in the jet stream and revolved slowly.

'Rye bread on, Captain, pasta douro prepared, muffin mix ready.'

'Well done, Midshipman.' I saluted. We were playing Hornblower, which Jason had taken as his manual for living. There could be worse role models. Besides, I got to be captain. 'Now, what was that about cherries?'

'Sorry to wake you, sir, I won't do that again,' he mumbled. 'But why shouldn't we make our own glacé cherries? It just needs someone to watch the syrup. It has to be cheaper than buying them in hundred-gram lots.'

'You want to try it? Go ahead,' I said, waving a Picardian hand. 'Make it so.'

He jumped up and showed me a recipe. It was handwritten.

'Where's this from?' I asked.

'Yai Yai,' he answered, meaning the matriarch of the delightful Pandamus family, who run Cafe Delicious. 'She says you can candy anything with it.'

'Yes, it's *glykos*, it's yummy,' I observed. 'Go ahead, but it's going to be a long process!'

'No problem, Captain, I'd rather stay in here with the cooler on anyway.'

'Good point,' I agreed. I was going to ask Therese Webb, Insula's expert on all things woven, tatted, knitted, spun, embroidered and stitched, to teach me some handicrafts. It was looking to be a long summer. I preferred the planet when it had more ozone layer.

I sat down to drink more coffee and compound my seed bread, a delicacy which comes to its full flower when married to blue cheese, and noticed that the Mouse Police had come back, reeking of tuna and panting. Cats generally don't like summer. Horatio, who is getting on, loves the sun, but no cat likes the north wind, which disarrays the ears and fibrillates the whiskers.

They plumped down on their flour sacks for a good grooming session in the backwash of the cool air. I could tell that the air conditioner was going to be a popular acquisition. Five in the morning and already the alley was being scoured by a hectic, invasive, dust-bearing wind which would, as soon as the sun rose, turn into dragon's breath.

Jason clanged the first of the rye loaves out of the oven and put in the pasta douro. I took a deep breath. I can only smell the scents of the bakery early in the morning. The nose gets used to smells, which is probably a survival trait for, say, Rotorua with all those sulphur lakes, but is also a pity considering that the aroma of baking bread is one of the premium scents of the universe. I let the cracked wheat slide through my fingers. Jason was reading, which was hard for the boy, as he had been thrown out of school very early. But he was teaching himself and one day he might even grasp the concept of spelling, and grammar as well. Though he was going to get that from Hornblower, not from recipes.

'Have we got a cherry stoner?' he asked.

'I expect so,' I replied. 'Go and check the second drawer from the left in my kitchen.'

I have a theory that all kitchens, if sufficiently occupied and loved, grow their own appliances. Only this can explain that that particular drawer always jams on an ice-cream scoop, which I am sure I never bought, and that I had at one time three melon ballers. Or it could be that some previous tenant was devoted to the worship of the goddess Anoia (a creation of the divine Terry Pratchett) who rules over Things That Stick in Drawers. Jason was serious about this Christmas cake project. I went over to see what he was reading.

An op shop recipe book, my favourite kind. Its pages were stained with ingredients long dried and it had the statutory sheaf of newspaper cuttings interleaved through the pages. I wondered how anyone could want to make lambs' brains in cream sauce when Jason came back with a grin and a cherry stoner, which looks like it was designed to do impolite things to cows.

'I reckon this ought to be it,' he said. 'You got a lot of junk in that drawer, Captain!'

'I know, and it is inevitable. No matter. Nice book.'

'Mrs. Dawson gave it to me. She said she wouldn't be need-ing it again, she mostly eats out. And she says she knows all her favourites by heart. I'd love that,' he said, suddenly, clutching the cherry stoner to his adolescent bosom and looking upwards in rapture. With his golden curls and blue eyes, he looked like a painting by one of the Pre-Raphaelites of The Soul's Awakening. 'To know all the recipes by heart.'

'And so you shall,' I assured him. 'I'm going to do my seed bread—can you get the muffins on?'

'Last of the rye bread on,' he said, sliding the tins into the oven. 'Muffins, aye, sir!'

I sat down by the mixer and poured the seeds into the mix, in order, heaviest to lightest. This is a lovely bread but it needs care. Most things that are worth anything do. I listened to the mixers mixing, the ovens roaring, the air conditioner breathing and the Mouse Police purring. I was a very lucky woman. Time went on. Bread got baked.

The plastic-wrapped paper hit the door and I fielded it before it could fly into a tub. That paperboy has it in for me. Leaving the very last mix to rise, I dismissed Jason to Cafe Delicious, whose Trucker's Special he can engulf in record time (three eggs, a potato pancake or hash brown, two strips of bacon, tomatoes, mushrooms, baked beans, sausages, toast and a can of Pepsi; I do not know where he puts it all in his slim frame). The Pandamus family clean up betting on how long it will take him to eat it.

I sliced ham and bread and cheese for the shop, counted out the orders and put them in their shipping cage for the courier to pick up and deliver to the restaurants in the city. It was get-ting light and fairly soon I would have customers walking down Calico Alley.

The first was my favourite witch, Meroe.

'Blessed be,' she said.

'Good morning, though I hesitate to say that.'

'The Goddess is in a mood,' she agreed. 'Seed bread? Wonderful. I intend to hole up with Belladonna until the storm comes.'

'There's a storm coming?'

Meroe has long, harsh black hair and always dresses in a black top, a long black skirt and a wrap, from the colour of which you can usually guess her mood. I don't know how old she is. When she smiles, she might be a weather-beaten forty. When she broods, she might be a youthful seventy. She takes care of all magical ritual round our way from her shop, the Sibyl's Cave. Today's wrap was a neutral purple, shot through with silver threads.

'Watch the way the Mouse Police are polishing their whiskers. Bad weather coming. Besides, I heard the early weather report,' she confessed, grinning. 'Poor Bella finds storms very trying. I need to be with her.'

Belladonna is a very sleek, plump and self-satisfied black cat. I could not imagine her finding anything upsetting. I said so.

'She's very sensitive to the electricity in the air, poor creature. I have actually got a small shock from stroking her in really stormy conditions. No cat likes to have blue sparks shooting from her whiskers.'

'Not soignée,' I agreed. 'I wouldn't like it myself.'

Meroe was replaced with Mrs. Dawson, who always went for a walk in the early morning to appease her Puritan conscience, which thereafter let her lead the life of a sybarite. She slept in 'disgracefully late'. She lunched at amusing little cafes, she dined in Chinatown or at various clubs, and she deserved it all. She had been a society hostess for most of her life and now, as a widow, she got to please herself at last.

Her clothes, as always, were a poem. She wore light cotton khaki trousers and a top hand-printed with giraffes. I appreciated the giraffes as I put a loaf of the sourdough into her willow-leaf basket. As always, she gave me exact change.

'Really, the only time that one can walk without the danger of heatstroke,' she commented, 'is early in the morning, and even so I am disagreeably hot.'

'Meroe says there is a storm coming,' I offered.

'If Meroe says so, then there will be a storm.'

I stood in the blast from the air conditioner as Heckle prowled past me, intent on something in the lane. Then there was a scuffle, a cry, and a thud. Jason fetched down the first-aid kit.

'Oh, no! Has he got another one?' I asked, dismayed.

'He's got another one,' he replied. 'Go, kitty! We've got the only attack cat in the city.'

I sighed and sallied forth to comfort Heckle's latest victim.

It all started when the paperboy, doubtless filled with name-less malice, ran over Heckle's tail. This had meant a hasty trip to the vet, who had stroked the vertebrae into place but had been forced to amputate the top centimetre or so, which had been hopelessly crushed under the unforgiving wheels. Heckle had recovered completely in body, but his animal spirit, Meroe said, was outraged and required vengeance.

So he had gone out several times, seeking it. He favoured young men and only if they were running. His method was ingenious. He waited until he could see the whites of their sports shoes then, with a sinuous wriggle, inserted himself between the running ankles.

He had never failed to bring down his prey. It was costing us a packet in bandaids and apologies, but so far no one had accused Heckle of doing it on purpose. He would sidle back into the bakery with a look of malignant satisfaction plastered all over his whiskers and then observe the process of repairing the victim with a smug smile. I could not imagine what I was going to do about him.

Meroe had promised to appeal to his better nature but I was not at all sure that Heckle, an old streetfighter, actually had a better nature. Clearly that centimetre of missing tail had to be paid for in blood.

I found the latest revengee sitting on the kerb, looking dazed, and raised him by the arm, escorting him into the bakery and sitting him down on the cook's chair.

'I'm so sorry, are you hurt?'

'Just a bit of a scrape,' he murmured. 'Hey, Jason, is that your cat?'

'Rowan,' said Jason, looking a little abashed. 'Sorry about that! This is my boss, Corinna. This is Rowan, he's a music student, got the flat opposite me, just moved in.'

'They told me that the city would be full of adventures,' said Rowan. Nice boy. I examined him as I mopped gravel and blood off his skinned knees. Thin, young, knobby as to knee and elbow, still growing into his limbs, Grandma would say. Pleasantly blue eyes, thatch of mousy hair. Private school accent. Abused. One knows another. I remember challenging Therese Webb, our resident craftsperson, when she diagnosed a portrait as 'sick as a child'. It was Robert Louis Stevenson and she was right, but she couldn't tell me how she knew. Therese spent most of her childhood in bed with asthma. One knows another, she said. Well, I spent my childhood in the mud and cold being neglected by my hippie parents. Then I spent the rest of it at a very exclusive girls' school, being bullied unmercifully. One knows another.

But he showed no signs of wanting to kick Heckle, which was encouraging. As Auden said, 'those to whom evil is done do evil in return', but that was not necessarily the case. Some to whom evil is done resolve never to inflict such pain on anyone and become very good indeed.

I plastered the knees in Betadine lotion—who knew what organic toxins lurked in Flinders Lane gravel?—and offered Rowan his choice of refreshments to beguile the time while it dried. He chose coffee and one of Jason's amazing raspberry muffins.

'You're Ferguson's son, aren't you?' asked Mrs. Dawson. 'You have the look of him.'

Rowan flinched, spilled coffee on his running shorts, and I changed the subject rapidly. The last thing the bullied want is to be told they resemble their tormentor.

'Music? So you are the source of the carols which have been echoing round the building the last few days?'

'Yes,' he said with a grateful look. 'We needed a place to rehearse and the cellar has the most beautiful acoustics. Almost as good as the underground car park at uni. We make enough money out of singing carols to finance the rest of the year's concerts. Mostly.'

'Very seasonal,' Mrs. Dawson was pleased to approve. I kept my opinion of carols to myself. I detest Christmas. Still, the singers were at least not committing the cardinal breach of taste, which is to include in their repertoire those sugary things which blight all shopping expeditions from the first of December. If I have to listen to someone crooning 'Have Yourself a Merry Little Christmas' one more time, I shall commit an indictable offence. Mayhem of some sort. And the same goes for Perry Como.

Rowan drank his coffee, ate his muffin, and got gingerly to his feet. Then he leant over Heckle and stroked his ears.

'There, poor old puss, did I hurt you?' he asked.

Jason stifled a giggle, and Heckle looked, for the first time in his piratical life, embarrassed. This boy was definitely among the good guys.

But there was bread to make as Rowan took his leave and Mrs. Dawson stayed to share some gossip.

'I met his father on many occasions,' she told me. 'Nasty piece of work. New money,' she added with unconscious arrogance. 'And my mother met his grandfather. He told her he was a self-made man. She replied, "Oh, the horrors of unskilled labour!"'

I laughed. Mrs. Dawson packed a muffin into her basket.

'So what was the elder Ferguson like?'

'A big, red-faced bully,' said Mrs. Dawson. 'Crude, loud and drunken. His son, this boy's father, was thin and scared. As was his wife, who was a school friend of mine. Poor Emily. This boy has just the look of his father.'

'Rich?'

'Oh, yes, dear, made a fortune in some agricultural pursuit. Pork, perhaps? I may be transferring the attributes of the animal to the man, which is a little harsh on the pig, whom I believe is an amiable creature. Well, I must get on. Pleasant to have some young people in the vicinity again.'

I did not agree. But there was bread to bake, so I baked it.

Chapter Two

And then they heard the angels tell
Who were the first to cry Nowell?
Animals all, as it befell,
In the stable where they did dwell!
Joy shall be theirs in the morning!'

Kenneth Grahame
The Wind in the Willows

We had finished baking and the shop was waiting, so I took the float out of the mop bucket—no teenage burglar would be able to identify a mop bucket, much less think to look in one—and unlocked the heavy doors. One of my assistants was standing outside, panting. Kylie, possibly, or Gossamer, thin, tall girls both. They changed hair and eye colour so often that I had no reliable identification since they had begun to cover up their navels. They now forgave me for this, poor senile woman over thirty that I am, and announced their names. The girl with green hair and long silver chains hung around her neck dressed in a seaweedy top and a long broderie anglaise skirt was, she told me, Goss. And, she added, she was very hot because their air conditioner had broken down.

'Trudi says the man is coming at ten,' she added, standing in the full blast of the shop cooler and letting her viridian hair blow around her. She looked like a votive offering to Poseidon. 'Kylie's taken Tori and gone to wind thread for Therese. She's making some huge big rug.'

'That ought to amuse Tori,' I observed. Tori is a very cute, well-behaved and fluffy kitten, but no kitten can resist wool. Kylie would have a busy morning unwinding Tori and preventing her from being woven into the carpet.

'Therese says she can keep Carolus amused. He likes cats.'

'I should have guessed it. He is the most un-canine dog I have ever met. Now, the muffins today are Raspberry Surprise—'

'What's surprising about raspberry?' she demanded, opening the inner door as Horatio descended to the shop. He leapt onto the counter and began to wash his whiskers, so as to appear immaculate for his public. His shirt front radiated cleanliness. He was definitely foreman material.

'They have rosewater in them,' I told Goss. 'It makes them taste more raspberry flavoured, as well as having the scent of flowers—you'll have to try one. There's no fresh breadcrumbs because I came up short for the Soup Run. The rolls are made, if Jason hasn't eaten them all. How about a cup of coffee and a muffin?' I asked, hoping as always to put a little flesh on those all-too-exposed bones. The girls fasted devotedly in the service of the goddess Anorexia.

'All right, I'll get one, and your coffee too,' she said amiably. We sipped and munched—those Raspberry Surprise muffins were spectacularly good—when Goss jumped up and grabbed the tray. 'Oops!' she exclaimed. 'Here come the hordes!'

If you cannot sleep in your furnace-like home, the sensible thing is to get to work early, buying some breakfast on the way, and perhaps getting in a little filing before the phones begin to ring. I had done this myself, when I was an accountant. Though it was barely seven thirty, haggard people were flocking into the shop, seeking ham or cheese rolls, muffins, cakes, hard crispy pasta douro shells and anything else which might cheer their underslept day. Most of them carried Cafe Delicious coffee cups in cardboard frames which Del supplies at five dollars each so they will be re-used. That was seldom a problem, because Del's son made excellent espresso. And Del made a *cafe hellenico* which could counteract anaesthesia.

I was not underslept, despite my abrupt awakening. I was cool, where the rest of the city was partially boiled. I counted my blessings and sold bread.

Then, suddenly, there was a lull. Nine o'clock and everyone who was going to work had got there, and there would be time to replenish the racks before the ten o'clock demand for morning tea. The dragon's-breath wind howled outside Earthly Delights. I wondered aloud whether it was better than a blizzard, at least.

'Nah,' replied Jason, carrying a whole tray of muffins easily on his shoulder. 'You can get warm, just put on more clothes, eat lots of sugar, stay inside. But it's bloody hard to get cool. Gimme a blizzard any time.' He rolled the muffins gently into their wire basket. 'Can I ask you something, Corinna?'

'You can,' I said, focusing my attention.

'You saw Rowan?' he asked.

'I did,' I agreed.

'His dad abused him. Beat him up. Yelled at him all the time. Made him feel like shit.'

'Yes,' I said gently. Jason's problem had been with his alcoholic mother and a succession of 'uncles', but it was the same problem. My apprentice understood abuse.

'But he's rich!' protested Jason. 'Went to one of them posh schools. Never short of anything. How does that happen?'

'Abuse is about power,' I told him. 'I used to think the same as you until I went to a posh school myself. The girls there were just the same as everywhere else. F. Scott Fitzgerald is wrong. The rich aren't different. Their only difference is that they are rich.'

'So there are bastards all over?' he asked.

'Sorry.'

'But there's Mrs. Dawson,' he went on. Clearly this subject had really been worrying him.

'Would have been a charming lovely woman if she'd been born in the gutter,' I told him. 'We just have to do the best we can with what we've got, Jason. Money smooths the way—that's all it does.'

'Hmm,' he said, and vanished back into the bakery. I finished my cold coffee, wondered if I had the strength to dive across to Cafe Delicious and buy an iced one, decided that I didn't and sat down to stroke Horatio and think about Jason. I remembered Hemingway's retort to the soppy Fitzgerald comment that 'the rich are different'. He had said, 'Yes, they're richer!' And although I could not care for Hemingway's writing, I had to acknowledge that he had hit the nail on the head with that reply. I smiled. Horatio purred. There was silence for the space of maybe ten minutes before I heard, in the lane, the sound of hoofs.

Small hoofs, yes, but hoofs, and I followed Jason into the bakery and looked out of the alley door in some amazement. Coming neatly and confidently down the steps from Centreway Arcade was a donkey. A female donkey. A jennet, in fact. She was silvery grey, with beautiful ears and a rather fetching straw hat. She had been saddled with two willow-basket panniers, which seemed to be empty. And she was heading for Earthly Delights with a determined expression, as far as donkeys have expressions. She clipped along past the Japanese restaurant and the coin shop, waited for a few astounded pedestrians to move aside, and then she was at my door, walking inside as far as the panniers would allow, and then making a soft but imperious braying noise when the object of her desire proved just out of reach.

'Holy shit!' said Jason inelegantly. 'What's that?'

'It's a donkey,' I said, trying not to laugh. Heckle and Jekyll had arisen from their sacks and were regarding the animal with interest from the far side of the big mixer.

'Well, duh, Corinna. What does it want?'

'I suspect that it's one of your raspberry and rosewater muffins,' I returned.

The donkey stretched out her neck as far as it could possibly go. The panniers creaked under the strain. The beautiful long-lashed eyes were desperate. I took one of the muffins, peeled off the paper cup, and held it out on the palm of my hand.

There was a flash of teeth and a curl of tongue. Gulp. Then the creature just stopped striving. She had found what she wanted, and eaten it. She was now at peace. I laid my hand on her forehead, between the sail-like ears and under the hat, and urged 'Back?' I was going to need my doorway again. Jason gave me another muffin and I held it up as incentive—no creature likes going backwards. 'Back you go, Jenny,' I said firmly and, obligingly, she moved back far enough to free the baskets and turn herself around. Her lips as she scoffed the second muffin were soft as silk. I helped her straighten her hat and wondered what to do. Someone must own this donkey. She was well groomed and shiny. The panniers, I noticed, had plastic buckets in them. Flowers, perhaps? Had I seen someone selling flowers from donkey-back?

There was a squeal of delight from the shop and Goss ran into Calico Alley and flung herself at the donkey.

'She's so sweet!' she cooed. She was. She was bearing Goss' half-throttling hug with commendable patience. Goss found a silver tag on the dangling rein.

'Serena!' she exclaimed. 'You're Serena!'

It was a good name for a creature with such poise. Just as Goss was securing another muffin to feed to the adorable creature, Serena shifted and tried to pull away. Shouting emanated from the lane. Someone was running.

'Sorry,' I said to Serena, hanging onto the tether. 'I'm afraid that retribution is about to set in.'

Serena gave me a sorrowful look, as though she had expected better of me. Then she seemed to plant her little hoofs as though she was not to be moved. The whole donkey seemed to have put on mass, grown heavier. The shouting and running feet resolved themselves into a middle-aged man dressed in a red silk shirt, jeans and boots, a black felt hat with flowers on it and a very red and angry face.

'Serena!' he bellowed at her, skidding to a halt so abruptly one expected sparks to shoot from his boot heels. 'Bad girl! What are you doing here?'

He glared at Goss, as though suspecting her of donkey-rustling. Goss stood her ground with her thin arm around Serena's neck.

'She came all by herself,' she retorted. 'Who are you, anyway? Can you prove this donkey belongs to you?'

He raised one hand as if minded to slap Goss, and Jason and I moved into sight. He paused with his hand in the air and slapped the donkey instead.

'Bad girl!'

Serena shifted a little on her hoofs and drooped her head, the image of a badly used beast of burden. Goss hugged her tighter.

'Jason, call the RSPCA, will you?' I asked.

'Aye, aye, sir,' replied Jason, eyeing the flower seller with disfavour.

'No, no, lady, I'm sorry.' All the rage went out of the man. 'I've run all the way from the market, I thought she might have walked under a tram, she's got no road sense, I was so worried...'

'Well, you've found her again, and she's all right. She wanted a muffin. A raspberry and rosewater muffin.'

'You the baker?' The man held out a hand. His skin was swarthy and his eyes black, hard to read. His hand was hard and wet. 'I'm Pahlevi, Tomas Pahlevi, I sell flowers—we sell flowers. She's a stubborn beast—I wouldn't let her eat the roses.'

'She eats roses?' asked Goss, still suspicious.

'Donkeys mostly eat anything,' he said, taking off the hat and wiping his forehead. 'When they get a taste in their mouths they go after it. She must have smelt your rosewater. I buy my flowers at the market, and roses are too expensive this time of year to feed them to donkeys. Still, I should have given her one. That'll be a lesson to me, eh, lady?'

His smile would have been reassuring if he had invested in fewer gold teeth. I didn't like Mr. Pahlevi, or his ingratiating manner, or his treatment of his donkey. But there was nothing I could do. She seemed to be well fed and healthy, and she hadn't even flinched under that slap.

'Come along, Goss,' I said to her. 'Give Serena back to Mr. Pahlevi. We'll be seeing her around, won't we? And I'm sure that she will be well treated,' I added.

Goss released the donkey, and Mr. Pahlevi, with a jerk of the leading rein, turned her around and led her out into Flinders Lane. She looked back, pathetically, blinking her long-lashed eyes, and Goss gave a small cry.

'Yes, I know,' I said. 'But we've got bread to sell. We shall keep an eye on Mr. Pahlevi, and if he mistreats Serena we shall call the RSPCA. Find out where he goes during the day,' I added. 'Someone will know.'

'All right,' said Goss reluctantly. 'We'll keep an eye on him okay.'

And then the morning-tea rush arrived, and we were other-wise occupied.

By the time the lunchtime crowd had cleaned out the last of the baking, I was pooped. So was Goss, though Kylie had called to say that the air conditioner in their flat was working again. Apparently it had exceeded its maximum permitted amount of cat fur in the filter and had shut down in self-defence. Goss volunteered to do the banking, though it meant going outside. But I knew there were several boutiques on her route in which she had dresses on lay-by. She liked to call in and say hello to them. For a sometime blonde, Goss was occasionally very shrewd.

I left Jason with the cleaning and the compounding of his cherry *glykos*.

'One hint,' I said as Horatio preceded me up the stairs to my apartment.

'Yes?' he asked, mopping industriously.

'Make sure that the sugar has dissolved before you let it boil,' I told him, from the depths of bitter experience. 'If you don't, it will not work.'

'Okay,' he assured me, and I continued my ascent. I had a fast shower, not wanting to waste water but really needing a wash. I donned a loose caftan made to a Therese Webb pattern. I had made it seven times, and each time I had a moment when I feared that the fabric would have to be folded into another dimension to fit the design. This möbius robe was made of a fine blue butterfly batik which Jon, our travelling conscience, had swapped for eight jars of Gentleman's Relish, for which he had an unlikely passion.

Daniel was deeply asleep, lying sprawled across my bed in the cool air. Despite serious temptation—those shoulders, that gorgeous back, those buttocks which one longed to bite—I closed the door quietly and let him slumber on.

The wind was making uncomfortable scratching noises at the panes, as though it was clawing to get in. The sunlight was falling onto my balcony at this hour. I could feel the heat radiating from the glass, and the sizzle as the bathwater I had poured on the indestructible green things vaporised. I hoped I hadn't boiled the poor plants. But Trudi had sworn that they could not be killed by anything short of direct nuclear strike, so I had hopes that they might survive the summer.

Now to make sure that Horatio and I did, too…

He was standing at the door, indicating very strongly that he wished to ascend to the roof garden, so despite my own views on glass shrines on hot days, I packed my esky with essentials (gin, tonic, ice), slung my satchel with various books over my shoulder, and picked him up. Horatio settled his nose into the hollow of my throat, purring just above audible level. It tickled.

Thus, giggling and lightly clad, I arrived on the roof, where the garden looked like it had been beaten flat with a broom and the shrine of the goddess Ceres was occupied by Rowan, two girls, and half a tonne of paper.

They looked busy and I did not want to intrude, but the shrine was the only cool place and Horatio was already intrigued and struggling to get down.

So I entered the shrine, sat down on the only spare bench, which as it happened was right under the sheaf of the goddess' corn and in the wash of the air cooler, and put Horatio down.

He gave his coat and whiskers a fast lick and a promise, then rose to his paws to meet his public, who were, I was pleased to see, gratified by his presence.

'Oh, a cat!' observed one girl, delighted. 'Hello, lovely cat!'

Horatio had heard these words before. He sniffed regally at the outstretched hand and suffered the divine ears to be caressed. This girl was short and stocky. She had dark hair dragged back into a scrunchie and very penetrating eyes, presently softened with affection. She was wearing an op shop cotton dress which had been adapted to her figure by letting out the seams. A serious contrast to the other girl, who was slim, pale, and had long golden hair confined severely in a plaited crown. Her long legs were bare under shorts matched with a T-shirt which proclaimed END ANIMAL CRUELTY—KILL A SCIENTIST TODAY! Rowan had scrambled to his feet, guilt written all over his pleasant countenance.

'I'm sorry, Corinna, are we allowed to be here? We needed to spread out the music…I hope it's all right…You don't mind?'

'It's all right, anyone can come here,' I soothed, hoping he would not upset Horatio, who did not like abrupt movements in his immediate vicinity. Rowan sat down again. I noticed that his T-shirt read NO DOMINION. Cryptic. I didn't know him well enough yet to ask whether it was a quote from Dylan Thomas. I indicated the bales of papers.

'What is all this? And would you care for a drink? I've only got two glasses, though.'

'Carol book,' he replied, accepting Horatio's offer of a chance to stroke a beautiful cat. 'Bec's assembling and Sarah's stapling and I'm…'

'Supervising?' asked the blonde, Sarah.

'Doing the covers,' he finished the sentence. 'The printer could have done it but it would have cost extra. No need for a drink, thanks anyway, we've got iced mint tea.' There was indeed a jug of something green reposing on the floor beside the assembly line.

Feeling unusually sophisticated, or possibly just old and corrupt, I poured a gin and tonic and opened my book as the workers returned to their task. Horatio, with one of those swift calculations at which cats are so adept, worked out the exact cynosure of all their attention and went and sat in it.

I was reading Beverley Nichols' *Cats' A.B.C.*, one of my favourites. Even though he did number his cats rather than give them names, because he found naming so difficult. I had always got over the problem of the same name having to apply to a little ball of fluff and a grave and elderly signor by having a kitten name—Horatio had been called Squeak—and an adult name. He had been called Squeak because he had a habit of climbing to the top of a wardrobe, then looking over the edge at the vast gulf below and making an absurd little squeak which alerted me to the need to find the stepladder and get him down. Again. It was a relief all round when he found out his height limits.

The young people were quietly conversing about some musical question as they shuffled and rustled and clunked the stapler, a soothing set of noises. Horatio had gone to sleep on the rehearsal schedule.

Beverley was talking about meeting five elderly Siamese cats sitting on Compton Mackenzie's stove in the Western Highlands when I drifted off into the light doze of one who has risen at four, done a hard day's work, and sipped away a generous gin and tonic.

I drifted up into consciousness again and lay still, with my eyes shut, listening to the wind howl outside and three young voices discussing something very earnestly.

'But he's a companion animal!' protested Rowan.

'You know humans shouldn't use animals as companions,' said the blonde—Sarah, that was the name.

'But he likes humans,' protested Bec crisply. 'You can see he's a volunteer. Equity will not assist a volunteer,' she added, revealing herself to be a law student.

'He ought to be free,' said Sarah.

'Free to do what?' demanded Bec, her voice rising. 'Free to starve? Humans bred dogs and horses and cows to serve them, granted. But cats just walked in and stayed because they liked it. Didn't you read the *Just So Stories* when you were a kid?'

'You're a romantic,' sneered Sarah.

'And you're an idiot,' responded Bec without rancour.

'ADOA has more important things to do than argue about a cat who is—look at him—clean, groomed, well fed and happy,' said Rowan.

'What do you make of the Nichols guy?' asked Bec, ruffling the pages—of my book, thank you so very much!—which must have slipped off my lap as I slept.

'Romantic,' sneered Sarah again. 'Pretty piccies of little kitties.'

'You use that word for everything you don't like,' observed Bec. 'No, he's all right. Listen to what he says about the circus.'

And she read aloud the pages on which Beverley denounces the circus, and imagines the animals in the audience and the ringmaster gagged and flogged around the ring. I particularly liked his idea of elephants in tiaras.

'Well, all right, then,' said Rowan. 'We can all approve of that.'

There was more rustling and clunking as the stapler went back into use. Charmingly, they began to sing. Rowan was a tenor, Bec an alto, and Sarah—as one might have expected—a soprano. They were singing a carol I vaguely knew, 'In Dulci Jubilo'.

I hadn't really woken up and I drifted off again, listening to the angelic voices. When I surfaced again the song had changed. They were singing to the tune of 'Twinkle Twinkle Little Star':

> *Haarmann Pearce and Soylent Green*
> *Vargas Fish and Sawney Beane.*

I puzzled sleepily over this for awhile. Vargas Fish? Somehow he didn't belong in a nursery rhyme, whoever he was, though some of the rhymes were fairly robust, not to say gruesome. After all, 'Ring a Ring o' Roses' was about the black death…

I woke up properly as Horatio landed on my lap with all four feet. It is surprising how heavy a full-grown cat can be if it wants to make a point. He indicated it was time to go back to the flat for his before-dinner sleep. Rowan seemed pleased that he had moved of his own volition.

'Now I can get the list back from the nice companion animal, we can box all the music and that's us for the day,' he announced. 'Hello, Corinna! We like your book.'

'Thank you, he is one of my favourite authors.' I wasn't going to offer to lend it, because Nichols was long out of print. 'Must go, Horatio wants his afternoon sleep.'

'Companion animals are wrong,' Sarah told me, with that self-righteous tone which always rouses my worse nature.

'Possibly they don't know that,' I informed her. 'But as you see, Horatio is in complete control of his companion human.'

I picked up my impedimenta and moved toward the door. Bec laughed then bit her lip. Sarah glared at me. Rowan said hastily, 'I'm going back to my apartment to watch *Doctor Who*. Anyone coming?'

I don't know if they followed him or not. I carried my companion animal down to Hebe in an irritated frame of mind.

Chapter Three

Two star-crossed lovers take their life

William Shakespeare
Romeo and Juliet

Daniel had awoken and was improving the shining hour by recalibrating my DVD player, which had somehow got onto the wrong TV channel or something, doubtless due to Horatio's habit of walking on remote controls.

Daniel completed his task, looked up, and held out his arms. I put Horatio down, dropped the junk and threw myself enthusiastically into his embrace. He smelt of soap and his signature smell, cinnamon.

'*Metuka*,' he said into my hair. Hebrew for 'sweetie'. 'You look flushed.'

'I feel flushed. I have just been exposed to self-righteous youth and I have been very rude to a young woman.'

'She probably deserved it,' he said comfortingly. 'Come, sit down and tell me all about it.'

'It was nothing,' I said, because it was, really. 'Militant animal-rights people.'

'This would be Rowan and his choristers?' he guessed.

'Good guess,' I told him. 'She told me that companion animals were wrong. In Horatio's hearing!'

'The insult seems to have passed him by,' observed Daniel.
He was right. Horatio had chosen his chair and curled up for
another nap.

'Indeed, and I will now stop thinking about it,' I said firmly.
'How are you?'

'All right. I'm working on an odd case and tonight I must go
out on the Soup Run. You too, I think.'

'Yes. I've got a sack of bread and some of Jason's rock cakes
which didn't entirely work to his satisfaction. What sort of odd
case?'

'A missing boy,' he said thoughtfully. 'A missing girl.'

'Did they go missing together?'

'That's the problem,' he said. 'Her father thinks yes. His father
thinks no. Each of them disapproves of the other. It's tricky.'

'You think? When you say disapprove, do you mean "mildly
dislike" or "looking up the internet for hit men as we speak"?'

'The latter. The girl is a sweet little evangelical miss from
one of the best schools. Put the kettle on, eh, Corinna? If I am
to stay awake I am going to need coffee.'

'Kettle on,' I reported, clicking the switch. 'Have you got
pictures?'

'Here she is. Brigid Mary Rosamund O'Ryan. Sixteen years
old.'

I looked at the professional photo. Dark hair, parted in
the middle. Dark blue eyes with a shade under them—'put in
with a sooty finger', my grandma used to say. Pink and white
complexion and a rosebud mouth. And a chin of uncommon
determination, if I was any judge. I put down the picture and
made the coffee. Daniel was having his hot. I moved to the fridge
for my jug of coffee and milk. In this weather iced was the only
way to go. My freezer was stuffed with ice-trays.

'Daddy is the hereditary head of a big furniture company,'
Daniel told me, sipping at his dark arabica. 'Been in the family

since the Gold Rush. They live in Caulfield. Very devout. All of the other children are good girls and boys.'

'How many children?'

'Seven. Brigid is the second youngest. Six months ago she was withdrawn from school. The family stated that she had glandular fever. Her lessons have been delivered and marked by the school. She seems to be a bright girl, she's good at maths and science. But no one's seen her outside her house since May.'

'Not glandular fever, you think?' I added some ice cream to my iced coffee. Bliss.

'Eventually the father confessed to me that she had been pregnant. Naturally an abortion was not to be thought of, so they kept her home.'

'They locked her up,' I said as indignantly as a mouthful of Charmaine's finest would allow. 'But she got out?'

'With help, it is feared. She was living in an upper-floor suite, the door of which was always locked, so that she couldn't get into the rest of the house, and of course she had no phone. But somehow she got out of a window, climbed down two storeys by way of a drainpipe and a rope, and got clean away. No one heard or saw a thing.'

'Good for her,' I said.

'She also took her rabbit with her.'

'Her rabbit.'

'Called Bunny. It's a big long-eared pedigreed rabbit.'

'And you need to find her,' I said to him.

'Well, yes, Corinna, because on the street a pregnant sixteen-year-old convent girl carrying a long-eared Dutch bunny has the survival quotient of an ice sculpture in a blast furnace.'

'True. But I bet she didn't do that jailbreak alone. Who is her accomplice and father of the said child?'

'Here he is,' said Daniel, and laid out another picture. It was a school group. Daniel put a finger on the tallest and most snaggle-toothed of what looked like the Youth Prisons Serious Offenders Outing. He had a scrubby complexion, much pimpled. He had pierced eyebrows and ears, and one could guess about the rest of him. Which would also be tattooed. Muddy brown eyes and dirty mousy hair—what there was of it, as he sported a convict haircut. He was not smiling.

'Oops,' I commented.

'This is Manny Lake. Also sixteen years old. Apprentice landscape gardener. Worked for a firm which—'

'Did the O'Ryan garden in Caulfield?'

'Yes. Old tradition, I suppose: fall in love with the gardener's boy.'

'Generally they are prettier than this one, but yes, that is a tradition. Do you think they're together?'

'I hope so. Manny knows his way around. But Manny's mum doesn't think he will have dared to go near Brigid again after Mr. O'Ryan's private detective scared the life out of him.'

'Not you, I take it.'

'No,' said Daniel absently. He was looking at the two faces. 'Brigid hasn't contacted any of her sisters, or any other relatives. I can't get a lot of information about her school friends. I've got a few phone numbers from the little sister. She might have taken refuge, but surely their parents wouldn't approve of a pregnant school friend sleeping in the spare room?'

'They might have hidden her,' I told him. 'Most of those parents aren't home a lot. It could be managed, at least for a while. How long has she been missing?'

'Ten days. Manny too. He told his boss he needed to travel, but asked him to keep his job open as long as he could. The landscape gardener told me that Manny was a good worker— "Not like most of these slack little bastards"—and he'd be pleased to have him back. The boss, by the way, thinks Manny is in jail. Occupational hazard among his workers.'

'Is he?'

'Not in Victoria.'

'Oh.' There seemed nothing else to suggest. Daniel put down his empty cup.

'Now, we are going to need a nap,' he said, 'if we are going out at midnight. Shall we lie down before dinner, or after?'

His smile should have rated XXX. My dark angel was already taking off his shirt, to show the smooth muscle and the scar where the Palestinian shrapnel nearly killed him—a sight which always affects me viscerally.

'How about an early dinner?' I said hastily, before he took anything else off. 'I've got Meroe's salad leaves and cold chicken and so on. And fresh peaches. Then we won't have to get up again until much later.'

'With a glass of chateau collapseau, a feast,' he said, smiling.

Fighting down a surge of lust, I assembled dinner. Meroe summons her salad leaves from some fairy paradise and has them conveyed by express broom. I had roasted the chicken myself, with sage, onion, lemon and butter. There were fresh tomatoes and fine asparagus and little potatoes made into salad with homemade mayonnaise.

We took the peaches to bed. It is always nice to have someone else to lick the peach juice off your breast.

◇◇◇

We woke at eleven and had begun to dress when I heard the loud mutter of approaching thunder.

'The storm!' exclaimed Daniel, grabbing the minimum of garments and the keys. 'Come on! I've been waiting for this all day!'

'Me, too,' I agreed, gathering more stuff—I am not comfortable without my backpack—and following him out the door, into the lift, and onto the roof, where we dashed into the shrine of the Mother Goddess amid the first drops of heavy, cold rain.

The mosquitos and flies whisked away like magic. The stifling air lifted like a lid. We stood at the door as the rain fell in a torrent, as though Aquarius was pouring his water jar straight down on our heads. If Guerlain could synthesise the scent of hot earth and rainwater and green grass and bruised flowers, the company would be able to buy France.

The cold air flowed over us and we laughed. Daniel was wearing green silk boxer shorts. I was wearing my old cotton caftan. We were getting wet and were scandalously underclad.

Not as underclad, however, as the figure dancing in the rain. Her black hair dampened and stuck to her laughing face. Her arms rose to curve gracefully as she looked up to the sky and the rain poured over her shoulders. Meroe was dancing to thank the Goddess for showing mercy on all thirsty hot inhabitants of the earth. She was eerie and beautiful, but I stepped back from the door and, as it happened, onto someone's foot.

They said something very rude in Dutch and I turned to apologise to Trudi and found that we had also been joined by the Prof and Mrs. Dawson. Both of them were respectably if lightly clad: a milky silk robe painted with Australian flowers at hem and sleeve (Mrs. Dawson) and a pair of shorts and a shirt (Professor Dion Monk). And, of course, Trudi, in her blue shorts and blue T-shirt, who was rubbing her foot and scowling.

'Sorry,' I said again. She shrugged and put her foot down gingerly.

'Is corn. If you have a corn, everyone always stands on it. No matter. Look at my garden! It rejoices!'

'So it does,' I agreed, wondering if she had not noticed a dancing naked woman in her anxiety about the pansies. I pointed her out. Trudi grunted in approval.

'Her, she calls down the rain,' said Trudi. Sitting on her shoulder-mounted kitten rest was her cat, Lucifer, a small demon-driven ginger creature in a strong harness, which was secured firmly to Trudi's belt, lest he should get away and happen to someone. He watched the rain, listening to the thunder with cocked ears, unlike all other cats, who would be curled up in a safe place, like my bed (in the case of Horatio) or the bakery (in the case of the Mouse Police) or inside a stout wardrobe (in the case of poor sensitive Belladonna).

There was a flash of lightning which bleached garden, buildings, witch and all, and Mrs. Dawson suggested that we sit down and have a warming drink, which she just happened to have brought along. Though now she is retired to live amongst us humble Insula dwellers, the old habits remain. She had a flask of hot coffee with an optional splosh of brandy. It was lovely.

I began to feel a chill on my skin and cast around Daniel and myself the mink blanket which I had brought.

Thunder crashed. I recalled old Grandpa Chapman telling me that thunder was the god Thor riding his chariot over the roads of Valhalla, and it sounded just like that: a long, loud, thrilling rumble.

'*Ave*, Jupiter Pluvius!' exclaimed the Professor. 'It is so agreeable to feel cool! Though I might, perhaps, just avail myself of that coat, my dear lady. May I?'

With a very pretty old-world gesture of courtesy he draped Mrs. Dawson's Indian cashmere shawl around her shoulders before he put on his coat. We sipped our coffee. It was heartshaking. The flash came so unpredictably that I forgot to count until the thunder came, but it must have been very close. Lucifer was bouncing up and down on Trudi's shoulder and squeaking with excitement. He was a well-named little cat.

And still Meroe danced. I saw that she was a crone. Her breasts were flat, her belly shrunken: an old witch as drawn by Cranach the Elder. But beautiful, elemental, powerful.

Finally she sagged and turned to the shrine. I wished Kepler, who had been photographing everyone in recent weeks, was here. Not at all abashed or surprised by our presence, Meroe walked into the shrine, water streaming from all her limbs. She picked up a towel which she must have left there. But she was not shivering: she was alight with vitality and joy. She allowed Daniel to dry her back and dragged on a loose woven black garment, then sat down to towel her hair.

'The Goddess is good!' she exclaimed.

'She certainly is,' agreed the Professor. 'I hope we shall not suffer the fate of Actaeon.' I racked my memory. Ah, yes. The poor young huntsman who spied on Aphrodite bathing and was turned into a deer, to be torn to pieces by his own hounds. Those old gods had a basic sense of humour.

'It is unwise to spy on maidens,' she told him. 'Crones do not care.'

'Oh, I do so agree,' said Mrs. Dawson warmly. 'The older I get, the fewer things are really worth worrying about. Will you have coffee, Meroe?'

'No, I will have rainwater from Trudi's tank,' she replied, crossing the shrine to the fountain and filling her cup. She drank deeply. 'Divine! Have some!' she urged.

Daniel and I drank. It tasted of earth and was wonderful, fresh out of the sky.

'My woodbine, you can smell it now,' Trudi remarked.

'Will it keep raining?' I asked. 'The storm has gone.'

'Till morning,' she said. Trudi is an oracle with weather. She has been gardening all her life. Her father was a famous grower, she says, of tulips. How she ended up at sixty, out of a failed marriage, as steward, housekeeper, fixer-upper and only person whom the freight lift obeys, in Insula, I did not know. But we were very glad to have her. She stood up, hefted her bag, checked that her kitten was still attached, and left us. The Professor and Mrs. Dawson took their leave. Meroe announced that she had to return to her own flat, Leucothea, to comfort Belladonna after her fright, and Daniel and I realised that we were due on the Soup Run, and that the storm which we had so enjoyed might not be a lot of fun if you were out on the street with no shelter.

We returned to Hebe, dressed, grabbed our stuff and went out through the bakery to carry with us the bread for the soup and a bundle of fliers with the pictures of the two missing lovers to distribute to the other lost and stolen and strayed.

Chapter Four

O, star of wonder, star of night!…
Following yonder star.

Rev. John Henry Hopkins
'We Three Kings'

The bus was waiting outside McDonald's and was already surrounded by soaked petitioners. The storm had scoured and polished Flinders Street like one of those amazing cleaners called Crash! or Zoom!—the exclamation mark particularly annoys me—every surface was light-reflecting and shiny. But our clientele were not gleaming. They were dripping, soggy lumps of misery and needed immediate attention.

Fortunately they had Sister Mary. She bustled up, a small, plump, elderly, indomitable nun with innocent blue eyes and a spirit which could have outfaced the Inquisition. And given Torquemada a good scolding. She has kept the Soup Bus running despite council opposition (they say it messes up the stopping areas and gives tourists the wrong idea about our fair city), continual crises in funding and the clients themselves, who are not reliable people and occasionally try to hold us up for the drugs which they think the nurse has in that black bag. Which is why the Soup Bus has a heavy person, to dissuade the reckless from such antisocial attempts. Ma'ani, Samoan mother and Maori father, over a metre across the shoulders and with the disposition of a large friendly dog, was scheduled for later. I heard that the kids had taken to calling him Shrek. He thought this was funny. Luckily. Ma'ani had missed out on the All Blacks by a whisker and it was not wise to trifle with him.

Tonight's heavy, Daniel, heaved his sack of bread into the bus and went to the driver's position to put the seat back. Sister Mary had been driving; she could only just reach the pedals and steered by divine guidance.

'There you are, Corinna, God bless you!' she exclaimed. 'We have already got a lot of sandwiches from our admirable friend Uncle Solly. Jules is our lawyer tonight and Jorgen is our nurse.'

A large man with long lint-white hair nodded amicably. He exuded calm. Obviously Viking stock, and Vikings just did not panic. Our clients were not going to rattle him.

'And we have Janeen as soup distributor along with you, so that's everyone. Hand out those polythene sheets to everyone who hasn't got a coat, will you, and give them a ticket to the Star—they've agreed to get everyone dry.'

'That's uncharacteristically nice of them!' I exclaimed, climbing aboard, finding a ladle, and stepping to the strapped-down soup urns. The Star is an upmarket all-night laundrette decorated with hundreds of old movie posters, which shows the said old movies and has always been very firm about not letting the homeless in unless they had something to wash. Though apparently one can gain a lot of shelter by putting twenty cents in the drier, forgetting to reload it until an attendant objects, then putting in another twenty cents.

'I had a chat with the manager,' said Sister Mary blithely. 'They can wash the clothes and dry them easily enough. They've got a dry-cleaning machine that does sleeping bags. A charitable parishioner, God bless and save him, donated enough to hire the place on rainy nights—when hardly anyone comes in anyway, as I reminded the owner—and we've agreed to clean up after our people have gone. I've hired a few of the ladies to look after the process. There won't be much business in King Street tonight.'

'No, it's wet enough to dampen anyone's ardour,' I agreed. Those ladies (of the night, in Sister Mary's delicate phrase) were tough. There would be no trouble in the Star laundrette, or, if there was, they would finish it. And make it wish it had never been born.

The smell rolled over me, the warm fug trapped under the awning. Wet unwashed people smell worse than wet unwashed dogs. God forgive me. Janeen, a small meek pious girl who had tossed up between nuclear physics, medicine and social work, and chosen medicine, gave me a small meek nod and we started handing out blue plastic groundsheets, chicken noodle soup and Uncle Solly's sandwiches, tickets to the laundrette and freebies to various restaurants and cafes which had agreed to feed a certain number of the homeless every day. At the back door, of course, but the food was excellent and would otherwise go to waste. The best of the Chinese and Malaysian had all agreed and were earning merit as we spoke. The tickets were freely swapped and bartered. Anyone who drew the Duke of Chin (three hats in the *Good Food Guide*) was able to secure at least four lesser restaurants in exchange. This crowd was mostly young and preferred the cafes. So far the fast-food outlets, with one notable example, had not been susceptible to the sister's rhetoric. But she would come back, week after week, with holy exhortations and charm and leaflets outlining our work (printed for free in Carlton by a nonplussed printer who still hadn't worked out why she had agreed), and sooner or later the most obdurate manager would crumble, give in, and offer his whole establishment if Sister Mary would only go away and stop being nice to him. The kids bargained fiercely over the General Chicken Franchise tickets. Some came to see Jorgen for clean syringes and bleach fits and condoms. No one wanted to see Jules, who was therefore cutting bread with a certain flourish and insouciance. He was handsome, with dark hair and brown eyes, a swarthy lad who surely couldn't be old enough to be a lawyer.

'You cut bread very well,' I commented.

'My papa owned a bistro in Lyon,' he replied. 'When we came here I swore I would never work with food again. But I seem to have remembered how to cut bread,' he said, faintly surprised to see a stack of perfect slices peel away from under his knife.

The crowd was wandering away, most of them going up the hill toward the Star, sheltering under the blue polythene sheets. First sitting was over.

Daniel started the engine and the bus thrummed along with the drumming of the rain. I found a seat. I also grabbed one of Uncle Solly's sandwiches. Kosher and delicious from his New York Deli. Salt beef. Yum. I refrained from taking another, as depriving the hungry would undoubtedly get me a few extra centuries in hell and I had already had dinner.

Chug, chug, the bus sounded even more spavined than usual. I hoped that we still had brakes with all this water on the road. But if it broke down Sister Mary would know a devout mechanic or two who could lash the old girl together for one more mission. After all, she had direct orders from the Highest Authority.

To distract myself from the temptation of those salt beef sandwiches, I unwrapped Daniel's bundle of pictures and showed them around the bus.

'God have mercy on them,' said Sister Mary, as I explained the plight of the runaway lovers and the girl's extreme condition. 'I'll post the picture on the outside of the bus—no, that won't do in this weather. I'll post it next to the soup, and see if we can get any news. I don't recall seeing either of them. I tend to notice pregnant girls. Anyone?'

Heads shook all round. Then Janeen ventured in her small meek voice, 'I might have seen the boy. With the freegans.'

'Freegans?' I asked. 'You mean vegans? Those austere vegos who don't eat dairy food or eggs either?'

Janeen giggled. I had never heard her giggle before. 'No, freegans. You'll probably see them tonight, you can ask them. They got moved on from Fitzroy and now they're in the city.'

'You aren't pulling my leg, by any chance, are you?' I asked, though I couldn't imagine Janeen going anywhere near anyone's leg unless she was splinting it.

Sister Mary laughed. 'You wait until you meet them,' she said.

And we had arrived at our next stop. It was still raining. There was cover and it was crammed with sopping people. No one had imagined that sleeping out in Melbourne in December could give you heatstroke and hypothermia at almost the same time. Truly, ours is a marvellous city.

Janeen and I made more sandwiches as Daniel and Jules handed out soup—this was chicken and vegetable, almost solid with barley—and sandwiches to the old alcoholics who lived in or near the boathouse. This was practically a colony. Long-established and picky about newcomers, like most small towns. One whiskered grandfather expressed this to Jules as he came back for a refill.

'We don't like them blow-ins,' he opined.

'Which blow-ins would these be, Grandpa?' asked Jules, unfazed by the gust of methanol and the stench of old cigar stubs which characterised this part of the route.

'I don't approve of long hair on men,' said the old man prudishly. 'Or them free love ways. Or them guitars all night when a man's trying to sleep.'

'No, indeed,' agreed Jules politely, as the old man was shoved away by another almost indistinguishable old man.

'Ar, shut yer trap,' said the second old man. 'The kids are all right. Give a man a few deeners for a drink, which is more'n I can say for you. Deep pockets and short arms, that's you. Thanks, mister,' he said to Jules, taking a big handful of sandwiches and a mug of soup. 'Got any chock'late ternight?'

'Yes, later,' said Jules. Sister Mary hits up Haigh's regularly for milk chocolate seconds, and those deformed bunnies and frogs go to a good home. I looked at Janeen, who was slicing cheese.

'We've got hippies in the park?' I asked incredulously.

'Freegans.' She giggled again. 'Like I said. I've finished the cheese, what's next?'

'Salami,' I said, handing over a few feet of mild Hungarian and leafing cheese into bread. Jules had a customer with one of those ominous blue forms, a summons, so I stacked and cut and stacked and cut until I ran out of bread. Jorgen relieved Daniel as the crowd began to die down. The old men were no trouble, usually. They lived the quiet life of rodents under the bushes and tried not to attract any attention. And they died, under the bushes, and were taken away and buried unidentified, because not even their brain-damaged colleagues knew who they had been. They weren't interested in drugs or sex anymore, having no need of syringes or condoms from such as Jorgen. I always felt very sorry for them.

Just as we were about to start again, there was a sound of voices singing. They were in key and in harmony, and they were singing—rats!—a Christmas carol. But it was an old one and I didn't mind it so much, coming across the rainy dark among the trees.

I saw a faire mayden
Sitten and sing:
She lulléd a litel child,
A sweeté lording.

Lullay, mine lyking,
My dear sonne, my sweetyng;
Lullay, my deare hearte,
Mine owne deare darlyng.

'Pretty,' commented Jorgen. I thought so, too. Daniel and I put on gloves and took up our rubbish bags, so that the council should not be affronted by dropped wrappings and lost plastic cups, though the old men rarely left anything, squirrelling away all manner of things in case they should come in useful.

The singers came into view as we cleared the site of a few paper bags and the odd (empty) bottle. Now they were danc- ing to a strange, off-beat drum and were rapping 'I Singe of a Mayden'. It was the very first time I had heard medieval rap. Or possibly hip hop or indie. I am an ignoramus when it comes to modern music.

'I singe! (thud) Of a mayden!' shouted the lead man, 'Who is! (thud thud) Matchless!' Thud, rattle, thud, thud.

They were a sight. Dreadlocks flying, Birkenstocks bouncing, boys in long dresses, girls in military gear. Every possible haircut from marine number one to flowing locks to shiny bare painted scalps. All happy, though not apparently stoned or drunk.

'Who are you?' I asked as they came closer.

'Freegans!' shouted the lead man. He was gorgeous. Slim, almost naked under a white caftan, Jesus hair, sandals on his feet. Happy-clappies, perhaps? I braced myself for a wave of enthusiasm and a lecture on how much God loves me.

None was forthcoming.

'We made soup,' said a stout girl in an army shirt. 'Lentil and vegie.'

Now Sister Mary is very picky about what she will accept to feed the poor, and I cast a look back at her. But she had tripped down the steps and was beaming at the strange crew.

'Nigel!' she said. 'God love you. I don't know how you manage in this heat.'

'We've got the river,' he said. Private school boy with fine diction. 'Camp down on the shore. They haven't moved us on yet. And the leftovers at the Vic market are very superior. Better than Prahran, I think. And much friendlier. I believe you have been training them, Sister.'

Two young men hauled a big aluminium pot forward and carried it into the bus to decant into the serving pots. It smelt very good, rich and meaty.

'Not just vegie, then,' I commented, stowing my rubbish bag and gloves.

'For ourselves,' said Nigel, 'we only eat vegan food. But for the poor—that is different.'

'Or if it is free!' exclaimed a small girl in a Buddhist T-shirt.

'Because we're freegans!' said several others.

They reeked of patchouli oil and wood smoke, they were clean and cheerful, and they cared for the poor. What was there to dislike? I could feel Jorgen bridling though. Their philosophy had not impressed him.

'Free?' I asked.

'We dive the dumpsters,' explained Nigel, as his sweating acolytes returned with the empty pot. 'Lots of free stuff there. We scour the markets after closing time. We dress from the rubbish bins, we eat what the world provides. Gaia is tired of users. She needs people who clean up after the wasters, like Tasmanian devils eating road kill. We are vultures, hyenas, carrion crows…'

'Maggots,' mumbled Jorgen, loud enough to hear.

Nigel was not disconcerted. 'And from our maggot form we shall hatch into creatures with wings!' he said without even a pause. I was enchanted.

Jorgen went back to the bus, mumbling under his breath. Janeen was standing next to the stout girl with her hands clasped, a picture of girlish adoration.

'But don't you get sick?' asked Jules.

The stout girl snorted. 'We don't eat the rotten stuff. We carry it back to compost. When the cupboard of the world is bare, we eat only fruit and vegetables. When it gives us a whole tray of lamb chops, as it did tonight, we build a fire and feast.'

'Bounty!' enthused Nigel. 'But we do not want to deprive the poor by our gleaning, so we make soup for Sister Mary.'

'God is well aware of what you do,' Sister Mary assured him.

'We are the only free people,' Nigel said in farewell. 'But to come along with us you must leave everything behind and worship the Goddess!'

'Nigel,' asked Daniel, 'have you seen this girl? Really pregnant. Her family wants to know how she is.'

'I don't recognise families,' said Nigel loftily.

But a young man in a heavy-metal T-shirt said, 'She was here, with a boy about the same age. Scared as hell. Wouldn't go out until after midnight. Jadis was feeding her lots of tofu and said she was too thin.'

'Too thin and too stressed,' agreed Jadis, who was dressed entirely in bright blue streamers and feathers, now rather depressed and waterlogged. 'Told her to wait to see your nurse, I reckon she was close to delivery. The boy stayed with her all the time. Then he went off for a couple of hours, came back and they both ran away. Sorry,' she said to Daniel. 'Did her parents really lock her up like she said?'

'Yes, they did,' he replied soberly. 'But I think they will be more amenable now.'

'Whatever,' shrugged Jadis. 'But if you find her, tell her Jadis is thinking of her.'

'I will. Where did they go?'

'Parted from us in Collingwood just before we got the order of the boot,' said Nigel. 'Five days ago now, as you mortals count time. Farewell!'

Then they were gone, rapping to 'I Sing of a Mayden' again.

'Well,' I said.

'They are very virtuous,' Sister Mary said, getting back on the bus.

'And I am so relieved to have escaped a rave on how I must immediately come to Jesus,' said Daniel. 'Oops, sorry, Sister.'

'God still loves you, Daniel,' she replied serenely. Nuns are very good at serene.

'That is his function,' replied my beloved. 'Rats, as Corinna would say. Five days! Where would they have gone from there?'

'They might have come into the city,' said Jules.

'We will look out for them,' said Sister Mary. Serenely.

Daniel got back into the driver's seat and the bus lumbered on.

We got to Flagstaff as Janeen confronted Jorgen, the nurse.

'What's your problem with the freegans?' she demanded. Not meekly. I was amazed.

'Beggars,' he shrugged. 'You heard that boy's voice. Good school, all the advantages. Thrown away. Disappointing his parents. He's the leader. The others would go back to the real world if it wasn't for him. Vegans are fakes. Artificially restricting their diet out of smug self-importance. I have no patience with them.'

'Jorgen!' Janeen drew a breath in outrage.

Just then we stopped at Flagstaff in the middle of a fair-sized riot and her comments remained, regrettably, unsaid. I hadn't heard a good denounce for ages.

My wish was to be gratified sooner than I had thought, however. The core of the fight—which had formed into that ring with the battlers in the middle which means that you can identify a pub fight from the air, if necessary—appeared to be two grown men, not the bunch of tearaway teenagers I had expected. The tearaways were in the crowd, cheering on both men without fear or favour. They didn't care who won. They just wanted blood.

Disliking humanity more than usual, I grabbed a ladle. Janeen did the same, in case someone took advantage of the riot to attack us directly. Daniel took off his light jacket. Sister Mary sighed and walked straight out of the bus and through the onlookers, pushing them gently aside. Jorgen took a step toward the fight and was held back by Daniel.

'What are you doing?' raged the lint-haired man. 'You can't leave an old lady alone in that!'

'We can if she's Sister Mary,' said Daniel, still holding onto his shoulder.

'You coward!' snarled Jorgen. I was beginning not to like him a whole lot.

'Just wait,' soothed Jules. 'And watch. We've seen this before. She is protected by the divine, by God himself.'

'And a really hard-working guardian angel,' I supplemented.

The crowd was falling away from Sister Mary's progress. Not only falling away but also walking away, executing a nonchalant stroll which said that whatever was happening at Flagstaff tonight they were not and never had been part of it. And had only vaguely heard of it.

'If we tried to do it, we'd be sausage meat,' commented Daniel.

'Or that paste which Mr. Selleys makes to fill the gaps between floorboards,' added Jules, with a nice sense of metaphor.

'But if it's Sister Mary doing it,' said Janeen, back to being small and meek, 'it's like a kind of magic.'

'It's divine protection,' insisted Jules. 'The padre told me about it when I was a child in Lyon. Only saints have it. And isn't Sister Mary well in line for sainthood?'

We had to agree. St Francis himself had been a rich and spoilt young man who had grievously annoyed the popes in his time. He would surely stand patron for her.

And now she was in the middle of the rapidly dissolving ring. Most of the spectators had gone. The few that remained were so comprehensively sozzled or drugged that they made no move as the diminutive nun climbed over them to reach the combatants, who were locked together in what looked to me like a death grip. She put one little hand on each arm, and pulled.

And they came apart, panting, shaking, suddenly cold, as though all their anger had been earthed through Sister Mary. They stumbled a few steps backwards, away from each other, staring, wondering what had happened to their fine killing rage.

'Now we can be useful,' said Daniel to Jorgen, and released the big man. Together they went to Sister Mary's side and took a man each. They were similar, both stocky, dark-haired men with swarthy skin. Mr. O'Ryan had a Portsea tan, obtained at a price from an indoor tanning salon. Mr. Lake had obtained his from working in the open air all his life. They stood in heavy custody, looking astonished.

'I know them,' Daniel told the sister. 'This is Brigid's father. And this is Manny Lake's father. The runaways. Though what they are doing here when they hired me to find their children, I do not know.'

'Oh, ye of little faith,' reproved Sister Mary.

'I can't just sit at home,' whined Manny's father. 'My boy's missing. And he's a good boy, no matter what this bastard says.'

'My daughter!' wailed Mr. O'Ryan.

'You are both showing a lack of faith. Not only in the admirable Daniel, but in God,' said Sister Mary severely. 'God knows the fate of your children, and if He chooses, God and Daniel may bring them back to you. Hitting each other will not help. Now go home. May the Lord bless and keep you, and may the Lord make His face to shine upon you, and give you better sense.'

They went. That wasn't the blessing as I remembered it, but it was a good one.

'Daniel,' Sister Mary called, 'take the bus around to the other side of the gardens. It's still raining, we've got people to feed, and—'

'You are rather wet,' I said. 'Have you got a spare dress or habit or whatever? Have some soup at least, Sister. Or do you want me to worry?'

This was a low blow, as she would hate anyone to worry about her. She drank the thick vegie freegan soup, which she said was excellent, changed into another plain dress, revealing that nuns wore Bonds Cottontails, and allowed Janeen to towel her short white hair dry.

Meanwhile the crowd who had emphatically not been at the fight in the gardens flocked to the bus. This was a family site, full of soaked parents and soggy wailing children. We gave out a hundred tickets to the Star laundrette, nappies, formula and bottles, tins of baby food, a lot of polythene groundsheets and almost all of the freegan soup. Little hands reached for the strangely deformed chocolate animals and I saw little faces smile. Poor people. Poor wet people.

Then we stopped at the Star, to make sure that there were no difficulties. It was stuffed with people, some of them semi-nude, all of them watching *Casablanca* in complete silence. The machines rumbled, the dry-cleaning machine chewed at soaked sleeping bags, and the faces were shadowed in black and white as the bartender played 'As Time Goes By' one more time. 'You played it for her, now you can play it for me! Play it, Sam!'

Sam played it. This is one of my favourite films but I could not stay. The Ladies of the Night were leaning against the wall, chewing gum and keeping an eagle eye on the crowd. But this site wasn't going to be a problem, as long as they had enough films noirs. One more stop, then Daniel and I would swap with

Ma'ani and Meredith. For some reason I was knackered. This might have been why I didn't immediately react when Janeen resumed her argument with Jorgen, whose temper had not been improved by being presented with three unrelated babies with summer diarrhoea.

'Those freegans?' she insinuated in her small meek voice.

'Beggars and vagrants,' he scoffed.

'I was one of them. And vegans?'

'Self-righteous neurotics,' he sneered.

'I'm one of them,' she said.

And Jorgen didn't say another word. We reached McDonald's again and Daniel and I left the bus. The last I saw of them, Sister Mary was greeting Ma'ani, Janeen was looking small and meek, Meredith was demanding the latest on the fight at Flagstaff, and Jules was chuckling.

Chapter Five

God rest you merry, merchants,
May you make the Yuletide pay!

Tom Lehrer
'A Christmas Carol'

Daniel and I went to bed and slept. I woke at four and did my favourite Saturday thing—well, second favourite, now that Daniel had arrived in my life—which was to turn over and go back to sleep. The rain got on with its task of filling the dams and Corinna got on with cashing in her sleep debt.

At ten or so we rose languidly, bathed sumptuously, ate sourdough toast and drank coffee. I was just luxuriating in the cool air coming through the open window when I remembered, dammit, I had to go to one of the big shops and buy Christmas decorations. For the shop. I was feeling conspicuous when all the others had them. Even the Lone Gunmen, our very own Geeks Unlimited, who I would have thought had not a festive bone in their collective chilli-sauce-stained bodies, had a wreath on the door neatly framing the ad for a new game, Universal Slaughter.

On cue, the sweet voices came seeping up from the wine cellar.
'And offer'd there, in his presence
Their gold and myrrh and frankincense.

Nowell, Nowell, Nowell—no, no, you're flat, sopranos! Sarah, what have you been smoking? Cigars?'

There was a shriek of outrage, and Daniel laughed, so I laughed too. But not heartily. While the voices bickered about the pitch of the soprano voices, I found clothes and reluctantly donned them. Stout sandals. Loose Indian shirt and jeans. Strong straw hat, attached by robust cord under my chin. Large cloth bag. Purse. Sunglasses. Sunscreen. Umbrella. It was coolly shiny outside but I did not trust it for a moment.

Daniel offered but I refused his assistance. Misery is supposed to love company but I wasn't taking an innocent Jewish boy into the front lines of Christendom. He might find himself a starring role in a merry Yule re-enactment of the Sack of Jerusalem by the Emperor Titus with a supporting cast, the Roman army.

Horatio had already resumed his little all-day nap on the coffee table as I went out into the street, wincing at the light and the heat. I hate summer, did I mention it?

And as I turned into the main street my ears were assailed and my patience began to evaporate. I kept my feet in the lunchtime crowd only by hanging onto the lamp-post as the grim Christmas hordes ramped past and damn near over me and the music jingled and rattled.

'Oh what fun it is to ride in a one-horse open sleigh!' declared one shop, selling DVDs of mayhem and murder. The staff of which would not know a sleigh unless someone had been slain in it…My sense of humour was degenerating. One who makes a pun would pick a pocket, as Stephen Maturin would say. Doubtless the real pickpockets were also out in force in this melee. They probably loved Christmas shopping.

Up the steps and into the biggest store in Melbourne, and up the escalator to the Christmas decorations, and they were all ghastly. Trash made by slave labour in China. Expensive trash, too. I wondered what had happened to the old blown-glass bubbles and wooden figurines from my own childhood. I had probably given them away. I found that I could indeed have blown-glass bubbles, if I felt like mortgaging Earthly Delights.

Pausing in exasperation, I noticed a sign saying TO THE CRIB and followed it, to stand becalmed in a sea of knee-high excitement. And it was rather pretty. A square had been fenced off and an open-fronted stable built. In it were the holy family, a girl in a blue mantle, an older man and a small child, which was screaming its head off. Even the baby Jesus had his off days. Surrounding them were animals. A donkey, a calf, a few sheep and goats, some chooks and ducks and a sleeping dog completed the picture. Only the goats looked comfortable. Goats always look comfortable, due to their cat-like conviction that they are masters of a universe which was built specifically for goats.

The greedy grabbing hands of the children sank into sheep's wool and snatched at feathery tails, but never got near the goats. Likewise the shrieks and tantrums of the spectators did not seem to disturb them, while the rest of the animals were looking stressed, shifting from hoof to hoof. That calf was too young to be away from its mother, I thought, and the ducks had no water.

'They die a fair bit,' said someone near my ear. He was not speaking to me. A man in shorts and a T-shirt which proclaimed him an habitué of Club Med was speaking to a man in a suit. 'Trick is to get 'em out before the kiddies notice. Ducks'd last a bit longer if you'd let me put in a duck pond.'

'Too messy,' said the suit.

'Ah well, I'll just bring in a couple more bantams. Kids yesterday mauled 'em. You don't want your Christmas crib with bald fowls, do you? And I'll pack up the deceased.'

'What do you do with them?' asked the suit.

The man in the shorts grinned. 'Roasted. With orange sauce.'

I was disgusted. Those animal-rights people would have things to say about this, I thought. On the other hand, I could approve of eating the deceased duck, since it was deceased. I have never liked waste. I beguiled my time in wondering what the freegans would make of a dead duck, and realised that they too would be hoping to find a few discarded oranges. The baby Jesus was still crying and I was not far from it. The donkey looked me full in the face and twitched her ears miserably. The baby calf lowed and tried to eat a mouthful of hay. The air was heavy with the smell of dung and humans. A child plastered his ice cream on my thigh and screamed.

At last the mob of moppets moved along and I was free and able to remove myself from the crib, the floor and eventually from the shop, having bought nothing. I did get a nice gust of Arpège on the way out, though.

I was partially deaf and very hot and there seemed nothing else to do but walk back to Insula as fast as was comfortable in the heat. My hat was drooping and so was I as I pushed open the front door and dead-heated Mrs. Dawson, looking disgustingly fresh and cool in ivory linen. All she lacked was a solar topee to be the complete memsahib.

'Corinna, dear!' she exclaimed. 'Come up to my apartment for a nice cool drink?'

'Thanks,' I muttered, dragging off the hat and losing my last hairpin. My hair fell ragged and wet around my face and I shoved at it. It was just long enough to be annoying. I briefly contemplated shaving my head.

'You look like you have been in combat,' she said, leading the way to the lift.

'I have been trying to buy Christmas decorations,' I told her. 'Behold my success.' I displayed my empty hands.

'Oh, my, you should have said.' She opened her door and ushered me into a cool parlour. 'Sit down now and I'll get us a gin and tonic. My son has just sent back to me the family box of decorations. The children don't like them, he says. Too old-fashioned. Too breakable. If you would like to take them off my hands I would be delighted. I've put up the ones I really love.'

I saw that she had. There was a little crib with hand-carved wooden figures. There was a delicate set of Viennese candle chimes, little golden angels, which would revolve and ring when the tiny candles were lit. Two tall elegant porcelain angels, one with a trumpet, one with a scroll. And there was a superb set of glass bubbles, hung from a branch of pine fixed to the mantelpiece.

Mrs. Dawson gave me an icy glass and produced a large cardboard box. It seemed rude to fall on it and rummage so I sipped my drink. Mrs. Dawson leant over me, gathered up my hair and fastened it both securely and comfortably on top of my head, something I have never been able to do. She is an example to us all.

The drink was generous and I began to feel my coiled nerves unwinding. The soft Christmas carollers through the walls were sweet, singing in perfect harmony a song about the holly and the ivy.

'There,' said Mrs. Dawson—one day I am going to be easy about calling her Sylvia. 'If you haul your hair up and coil it on the top, you can keep it out of your eyes and it looks, I must say, very good. Actually, you are doing me a favour, Corinna. I was feeling sad and lonely with the Christmas decorations returned. I have had a very long and happy life and there are memories in all of them. And now my husband is gone and my children are living their own lives and here am I. I don't often feel lonely and I really don't like the feeling.'

'You could acquire a cat,' I suggested. 'You never feel lonely with a cat. Or a particularly lovely little dog, like Therese's King Charles spaniel, Carolus. People also speak highly of birds and I have one friend who is devoted to her fish. Tetras. Little neon fish.'

'An idea,' she said diplomatically. 'I thought that I would be away from home much more than I have been.'

'Well, what say you settle for a half-share in Nox the black kitten and an unashamed wallow in nostalgia?' I offered. 'I'm not expected back for hours. Break out the gin again and let's open the box.'

'Accepted with pleasure,' she told me. She poured us another drink from a frosted jug and opened the box.

They were a representative collection, I saw, laying them out on the sofa one by one. The neon shiny fifties' balls, made of something other than glass. The plaster Indian decorations of the sixties—all animals, camels, elephants, studded with little mirrors and glittering like stars. The woven tinsel bells and wire stars of the eighties. The cool wooden and straw Scandinavian decorations of the nineties, which were the most recent. And the inherited ones, hand-blown glass and elaborate Victorian ice-drop decorations, with places inside for candles, in which Mr. Scrooge might have seen his scowling face. Beautiful silken flower wreaths and meticulously cut Chinese hanging fantasies. And the fairy in a feather skirt for the top of the tree.

Every one had a story and Sylvia—I managed it!—recalled them all as she handled each and laid it back in its wrappings. I soon got lost among the relatives and the children and the parties but she was right, it had been a long and happy life. We were both crying as the last one, the fairy, was put back in the box.

Mrs. Dawson wiped her face, laughed a little, and poured us another drink.

'Thank you, dear,' she said. 'I feel much better. Now, tell me, what are you working on at present?'

She clearly wanted something else to think about and so did I. I told her the strange tale of the pregnant girl and her descent from the second floor of her prison house. Sylvia shook her head.

'No, dear, she couldn't have. I've been that pregnant three times and, although I managed to stay fairly active, I could not have climbed down a rope. One has no sense of balance, you see—one is all belly. And she was carrying a rabbit as well? No. However she got out of the house, it wasn't like that.'

'I've never been pregnant,' I said slowly. 'But of course you are right. The rope was a decoy. She must have just walked down the stairs. But who, in that case, let her out, risking her parents' wrath?'

'A servant, perhaps, felt sorry for her. Children in those wealthy households depend more on the staff than on their parents. The housekeeper is always there, you see, when they come home from school. They tend to live in the kitchen, poor mites. I was determined that my children should not lose sight of their parents, and we made time to tell stories and play games and I was always home when they came in from school.'

'A good point. I don't know if Daniel has spoken to the staff.'

'Or there is the gardener,' she added. 'Since she fell in love with the gardener's boy. Or there is her little sister. I do hope you find her,' she added, as I stood up and she put the box into my arms. 'She could die giving birth in the street. Poor girl. Some families,' she added, opening the door for me, 'should not be allowed to have children.'

I arrived at my own apartment and rang the bell, because I could not reach around my armload to use the key. Almost like a pregnant belly, in fact, and I saw Mrs. Dawson's point.

I was a trifle woozy with gin during the day, but very pleased.

Daniel answered the door and took the box.

'I like your hair like that,' he commented. 'Have you been to a salon?'

'No, Mrs. Dawson's. Those are her family decorations. Just let me see what I actually look like,' I said, passing him on the way to the bathroom, 'and then I have a tale to unfold.'

I looked good. I had never thought of just coiling the hair up on the top of my head, or if I had, I would have assumed that I would resemble Wilma Flintstone. Instead it looked both cool and comfortable and I approved. When I went back to unfold my tale, Daniel had made me a fruit juice and ice drink. He buys all these strange juices from a bulk discount grocery store. Today's was delicious.

'What is it?' I asked, rolling it round my mouth.

'Serbian apricot,' he replied. 'With a judicious admixture of Malaysian strawberry juice and soda water. I've put the decorations on the table. What is this tale?'

'Ah,' I said wisely, and told him Mrs. Dawson's opinion of the likelihood of Brigid getting down that rope.

'I hadn't thought of that, but then, I haven't been pregnant either,' he commented. 'Time to go and talk to the household, and especially to Brigid's little sister, Dolores. Trouble is, the last time I tried to talk to her she just goggled at me.'

'Well, you are gorgeous,' I said soothingly. Daniel often forgets this.

'Thank you, but it won't help in unlocking that little parcel.'

'Don't look at me,' I exclaimed, sipping more Serbian Surprise. 'I don't know anything about girls.'

'Nonsense, you manage Kylie and Goss.'

'And we need one of them,' I told him. 'Fourteen to twenty-one is a long way, but Goss knows the dialect. Ideally we need to separate the girl from her parents.'

'Not a problem,' said Daniel. 'I happen to know that Mr. and Mrs. O'Ryan are in Canberra at some evangelical convention this weekend.'

'Leaving a fourteen-year-old home alone?' I asked.

'No, there's a housekeeper. Nice woman, brisk and sensible. Sandra? Sarah? I'll get my notes. Then we can have a briefing with Goss or Kylie. Which one, do you think?'

'Goss is more intelligent,' I shrugged. 'I think. Then again, Kylie can be surprisingly shrewd in her own way. I'll see who's home, if either. They could always do with some extra money,' I added meaningfully.

'Certainly,' agreed Daniel, rummaging in his satchel. He had a number of these, into which he could stuff all his notes, electronic equipment and lunch. This one had Tintin and Snowy on it. 'The labourer is worthy of his or her hire. Mr. O'Ryan will be paying her. I still haven't reached the end of a rather generous retainer. Shall we say fifty dollars an hour?'

'We shall,' I smiled, and went to unearth the phone from under Horatio.

As it happened, Goss was home, had washed and dried her hair, and was bored. She was also eager to earn fifty dollars an hour for talking, something she was willing to do for free.

'I'll be a detective, then?' she asked breathlessly half an hour later, as we sat down to listen to our briefing.

'Yes,' said Daniel. 'Now, this is what we know about the O'Ryan household. Mr. O'Ryan is a big, red-faced, loud sort of patriarch. Free with his hands, to judge by the way he was about to belt the boy's father last night. A violent temper, I'd say. His children are afraid of him. Not so his wife, who is just as loud and violent as he is. She was the one doing most of the shouting when I interviewed everyone for the first time.'

'Nice,' shuddered Goss. 'Usually there's, like, one nice parental unit and one nasty one. This sounds gross.'

'My view entirely. Mrs. O'Ryan is, however, as thin as her husband is fat. He's covering it with good tailoring and she probably lives on communion wine or whatever they have in the happy-clappies. She's very religious, or so her husband says. He told me that Mrs. O'Ryan made the girls go to church every day on the holidays.'

'And what did she say about him?' I asked. Couples like this always have a favourite fault with which to flay their opposite half.

'She says he bellowed at the girls and scared them,' said Daniel, raising an eyebrow at me. 'They both blame each other for not keeping a closer eye on Brigid. Mrs. says that Mr. is away most of the time and Mr. says that so is Mrs, going to all these church activities and spiritual retreats.'

'Yeuk,' commented Goss. I had to agree.

'All right, now what about the staff?'

'There is a housekeeper called Sandra Beecham. Not Irish or evangelical, oddly enough. Sensible woman of about forty. Handsome and well dressed. She has a legion of cleaners and people to assist her, but they are casual and only come in for the day. That includes the gardener and his boy. They hire a caterer for any important dinners, but usually Sandra does the cooking and runs the household. I don't get the impression that the O'Ryans are home much for meals. Typically he would be at a working lunch and an even more working dinner, and she probably exists on no-cal frozen dinners and the occasional sip of Evian.'

'You didn't take to the clients, did you?' I asked.

'I don't have to,' he responded seriously. 'My real client is that poor girl and her heavy burden. And the missing boy, who is a good boy. The sister and only child still at home is Dolores. She's fourteen. Not pretty like her sister but the same type: dark hair and blue eyes. She has spots. She didn't say a lot to me but she seems intelligent enough. Her sister is good at maths and science, while Dolores is getting very good marks for English and such. Her mother made me read the school reports. Reading between the lines I got the impression she's dreamy and disconnected and her teachers are concerned about her. Not so her mother, who says she's greedy and lazy.'

'With a mother like that, who needs enemies?' I asked.

'I gather that Brigid was the apple of the parental eyes, and poor Dolores comes in a distant second.'

'Right,' said Goss, getting to her feet. 'I know enough about her now. And we need to stop off on the way.'

'Why?' I asked.

'To pick up a few things.'

Goss refused to tell me anything more. Timbo, Daniel's driver, was waiting in the big car. It was, fortunately, air-conditioned, as the weather was getting into its stride. The coolness brought by the rain had burnt off and the sky was that achingly cloudless blue which presages heat rash before bedtime. Timbo, who is the nicest possible big fat slob, was sweating. By the evidence of the wrappers strewn all around him he had been reducing his temperature with frequent applications of ice cream.

Goss grinned at him. He smiled back. A smile from Timbo is a wonderful thing.

We sped off to Kew, stopping only at a food hall where Goss directed. She came back carrying a large bag, which she concealed in the patchwork carrier she had brought along. I sniffed. I could smell food.

At the house, we left Timbo in the car with the air conditioning running and spoke into the radio thingy at the gate. It swung open and admitted us.

A woman opened the front door. This must be the handsome and well-dressed Sandra, who was indeed well dressed, in a linen shift and jacket. And handsome, if you consider perfectly dressed hair, immaculate fingernails and immovable lipstick handsome. She smiled an exact two centimetres at Daniel, swept Goss and me with a glance which priced our clothes, shoes, makeup, hairstyles and comparative worth, and allowed us into the cold house.

Now, I like cold. In this climate, cold is becoming an indicator of wealth. Perhaps Sandra thought that too. The house was stuffed with the usual decorator furniture. I noticed that Mrs. O'Ryan was into French Provincial. Sandra led us into the parlour and stood waiting for us to explain ourselves.

'I need to look at Brigid's room,' said Daniel, 'and talk to Dolores.'

'And these are your associates?' asked Sandra, in a neutral tone which was very annoying.

'They are,' said Daniel, pointedly not introducing us. 'Now, if you please.'

'Refreshments?' asked Sandra, abruptly capitulating.

'No, thank you,' said Daniel. 'Is Dolores in her room?'

'Yes,' said Sandra.

'Then we will go there first,' said Daniel, and led the way up the stairs.

I was impressed. I had no idea Daniel knew how to be so rude. So politely rude. Goss was leading the way. The air conditioning was turned up so high that she was shivering. Then again, Goss had not an ounce of protective fat on her whole body. If she had found any she would have gone on another of her 'starve yourself thin' diets.

Dolores had a suite of rooms of her own, directly under those belonging to her absconding sister. Daniel knocked on the door, which had a pink fuzzy rabbit on it.

Dolores answered, saw Daniel, was struck afresh by his beauty, then caught sight of the rest of us and recoiled a little. This allowed us into the room.

The room was pink—very pink. It had fairies all over the pink wallpaper and pink carpet and pink curtains. Dolores had placed a pink teddy bear on the bedcoverings (pink) and through the open bathroom door we could see pink towels, pink shower curtain and tiles (pink).

Goss giggled a little and said to her, 'And you grew out of pink how long ago?'

Dolores, who was just as Daniel had described, scratched her spotty chin and croaked, 'Five years.'

'I did, too,' said Goss. 'Chill. Sooner or later they will get the idea and let you have a real room. Where are your pictures and posters and real stuff?'

'In the desk,' said Dolores, who seemed to be comprehensively enchanted by Goss.

Daniel sat down on the couch (pink) and I joined Goss. The hinged top of the desk rose to reveal a jumble of girls' magazines, flyers for bands, scribbled notes and even a string of glittery beads. Goss pounced on a picture.

'Orlando! He's a hottie!' she exclaimed.

'Dreamy,' crooned Dolores. 'Who are you?' she asked rather belatedly.

'Goss,' said Goss, sticking out a hand. 'That's my boss, Corinna—she's a baker. You know Daniel. We're trying to find your sister.'

'I don't know anything,' said Dolores flatly.

'You do,' said Goss. 'And we won't tell a soul, not one soul. And because I know what kind of mum you have, I brought some stuff. And we won't say a word about that, either.'

'What stuff?' demanded Dolores suspiciously. 'How do you know what sort of mum I have?'

'This stuff,' said Goss. She shut the desk lid and laid out the food from her bag. A foil-wrapped hamburger. A packet of chocolate biscuits. A bag of crisps. A half-litre of chocolate milk. 'And I know what kind of mum you've got because I've got one too.'

Dolores looked at the food as St Anthony must have stared at the temptations in the desert.

Goss was continuing. 'Been on a low-calorie diet for years, no rice or potatoes, only salads and grilled chicken,' said Goss. 'Hence the spots. Won't let you do any exercise because it isn't nice for girls. Locks you in here when there's company because she says you're disgustingly greedy and not as pretty as your sister. Sit down and eat,' she said, and Dolores sat down and picked up the hamburger, tearing at the wrappings with taloned fingers. As she bit into it Goss added, 'But it doesn't last forever. You can get away in the end. I live in a flat with my bestie, Kylie.'

Dolores ate the hamburger in ten bites and Daniel opened the bag of crisps for her. It was like watching a starving puppy wolf down food. What must life be like for poor Dolores, not as pretty as her sister, locked in up here in this stifling pink room which belonged to a younger girl, not allowed to grow up? How she must have envied Brigid.

We did not say anything else until she had sipped down to the last millilitre of the chocolate milk. There were tears in her eyes.

'How do you get on with Sandra?' asked Goss.

'She's all right.' Dolores wrinkled her nose. 'Sometimes she slips me a chip or two when she's cooking for the olds. She gets me books from the bookshop if I pay her for them and do the orders online.'

'You're online?' asked Goss, sounding surprised. 'Haven't they caught on to that?'

'No,' said Dolores, and actually laughed.

'MySpace or Facebook?'

'Both,' said Dolores gleefully.

'And you let your sister out?' asked Goss calmly.

'No,' said Dolores.

Goss remained unmoved. 'You did, you know.'

'No,' said Dolores.

'You let her out, didn't you?' accused Goss for the third time.

'Yes,' said Dolores. 'Because I hated her and I wanted her to die!'

And she burst into tears.

Chapter Six

For there is no friend like a sister
In calm or stormy weather

Christina Rossetti
'Goblin Market'

'Girls will be girls,' I commented, finding pink tissues and a glass of water. Dolores had flung herself into Goss' arms and the storm of wild weeping was showing signs of settling down into hiccups and sobs and dabs with a tissue. I hoped she wasn't going to be sick. She needed that meal, poor mite.

The person who had dressed her, I decided, needed a good smack in the mouth. The girl did have a certain amount of embonpoint, so to make her wear a white pencil skirt and a form-fitting (pink) T-shirt was pure cruelty.

'One day you can come to visit,' coaxed Goss. 'We can get you some better clothes. Ones that aren't pink, for starters.'

Goss herself was wearing a pair of straight-legged jeans and a really well-cut gentleman's white shirt, belted loosely over an aquamarine chemise. At least I think it was a chemise. The notable thing about her clothes is that none of them were in the least pink. The belt was a thing of beauty, decorated with heavy silver studs. It struck me as vaguely Western. The poor girl was asking about it.

'It's a concha belt,' Goss informed her. 'From the Wild West, one of my fave boutiques. I'll take you there. Now, we've gotta get some more facts. Was Brigid online, too?'

'Yes,' sighed Dolores, who was really living up to her name. 'But she hasn't…hasn't…'

'Nothing at all since she went away? Are you friended on her MySpace?'

'Yes,' said Dolores. 'On MySpace. She hasn't done blogging since she left. We talked a lot. She had lovely things. Mum won't let me borrow any of them. She doesn't like me, either. No one likes me!'

'I like you,' declared Goss. 'Now chill, and tell us all. Did you know her sweetie?'

'I thought I did,' said Dolores slowly. 'Manny used to let me help with the planting. And the weeding. I love flowers.'

'Then you can go and be a gardener too,' said Goss boldly. 'I got friends at the agricultural coll. You get to live there, too,' she said meaningfully. Dolores looked up with a wild surmise. A place to live which wasn't pink! Bliss! Then she went on, carefully. Goss was doing Dolores a lot of good.

'He was a nice boy. He loved Brigid but I would have sworn she never looked at him. I don't know when they managed to… get together. But they must've, somehow.'

'Love will find a way,' Daniel whispered to me. Dolores heard him.

'She had this major crush on Sean Reilly,' she protested. 'Or maybe it was all an act. She lied a lot,' she said matter-of-factly. 'Well, we both did. Do.'

'Only thing to do with parents like that,' encouraged Goss. 'Did she see much of this Sean?'

'He's at the college across the road from the school. He used to walk across and talk to her sometimes. She would go all gooey, it was sick. He's the captain of the cricket team, prefect, all that stuff. He's a hottie all right, but I don't like him. Too full of himself. But Manny, he was nice.'

'All right,' said Goss. 'What was it like here with Brigid locked up?'

'It was awful,' said Dolores, about to weep again. 'Dad yelling and Mum yelling and Sandra yelling.'

'What was Sandra yelling about?'

'She said that Brigie had to see a doctor. That she ought to have some exercise. That it was cruel to lock her in like that.'

'Did she win?' asked Daniel quietly.

'No, except about the doctor. He came one night and examined her and said she was healthy. He wasn't our usual doctor. Sandra was worried. Tried to feed her extra. She used to carry trays all day.'

This did not sound like the haughty woman downstairs. I said so.

'She's been with us a long time,' said Dolores, as though she was just realising this. 'I suppose she feels responsible for us. A bit. I wasn't a lot of help. I was furious with Brigid.'

'Why?'

'Because she was silly!' snapped Dolores. 'She never paid any attention to the outside world. She just did maths and science and more maths and science and she wanted to be a doctor and save the children and now…'

Dolores burst into tears again. Daniel looked at me. I looked at Daniel. The situation was not good.

'We'll have a look at her room,' I said, getting up. 'You come too, Dolores.'

Up a flight of stairs into an entirely different suite, furnished in quiet good taste, though fussy in that French Provincial way. Baskets of dried flowers. Framed flower prints on the walls, which were a quiet pacific blue. Spindly white or cane furniture.

Brigid had an office space for herself, with bookshelves and a serious desk behind a French Provincial screen pasted over with Victorian ladies in walking dress. Daniel switched on the computer and I left him to it, prowling from dressing table—sensible cosmetics, lip gloss, baby powder—to wardrobe. Mostly 'smart casual' clothes as worn by the average forty-year-old, with a couple of evening dresses of the modest kind, high necklines and long sleeves. For the pretty daughter to wear when presented to the cocktail party throng, I supposed. Dolores had a hard life, to be sure, but Brigid's might have been harder, with the weight of all those expectations on her head. An embroidered motto of the sort which usually said *Home Sweet Home* or *Bless This Mess* or—my favourite—*Never Trust A Thin Cook*, which Therese was even now embroidering for me. It merely ordered *Strive*.

Goss had pursed her lips and was obviously restraining herself from comment. I nodded at her.

'Well?' I asked.

'Her clothes are just as bad as…' She glanced at Dolores, who sighed.

'Mine,' she completed the sentence. 'But Brigie didn't mind! She'd wear whatever they told her to wear. If the girls teased her about looking like their mothers she'd just smile. She had a plan, she told me, and nothing was going to stop her. She was going to be a doctor. She'd win lots of scholarships, enough to pay the fees, and there's a trust fund from Grandma to live on. Then she'd leave home and she'd never see the parents again, never talk to them, never think of them. No more Rev Putnam, no more virginity tests, no more asking for a pad. And I used to say, *What about me?* And she'd say, *I'll take you with me, Dolly.* But now she's in trouble. She was never in trouble!'

'Dolly,' said Goss consideringly. 'That's a nice name. Better than Dolores. I know how that is. My name's Gossamer but no one ever calls me that. Was it Manny's idea about throwing the rope out the window?'

'Yes,' said Dolly, conquering tears again. 'He didn't want me to get into trouble either.'

'What's her password?' asked Daniel. 'This file is password-protected.'

'Escape,' said Dolly.

I kept wandering. There was a large metal cage, leaking straw, where Bunny presumably spent his more confined moments. Dolly flicked through a box in the bottom of the wardrobe and was showing the contents to Goss.

'No singers, no actors, just pictures of famous doctors,' she was complaining. 'She only listened to classical stuff that doesn't have a tune. Tchaikovsky. Some dude called Vivaldi. Not real music. She didn't even have an iPod.'

'Did she have a mobile phone?' I asked. I had never seen a teenager without a mobile phone.

Dolly brightened. 'Yes,' she said. 'I called it. But all I got was her voicemail. And she will have ditched it by now. She knows the parents can track her by the phone. Dad told her that when he gave it to her. Me, too. But I never go anywhere for it to track. Except to school and back. In the car. With the driver.'

'Driver? Do you have the same driver every time?'

'No, it's a firm. Most of them are all right. I don't even know their names.'

'She was bright,' said Daniel from the computer. 'Got straight A's for all her science and maths subjects—and a nice line in B's for English.'

'I used to do her creative writing,' confessed Dolly. 'She didn't like making things up. She didn't read books, you know, or watch movies, except for school. She was only interested in the real.'

'Well, it must be real enough wherever the poor girl is now,' said Goss.

'I know. You'll find her?' Dolly grabbed Goss' sleeve. 'She must be scared. She's never even been to the mall on her own.'

'We'll find her,' said Goss. 'Who were her besties?'

'She didn't really have any. The parents won't let us bring anyone home, and they don't like us going to other people's places, either. They say we have to keep ourselves as an elect. That's what God wants. I don't know why they had kids,' said Dolly. 'They don't even like us much.'

'Your father wants Brigid back,' Daniel told her. 'He's put up a lot of money.'

'That's just money,' said Dolly. 'And because she belongs to him. He doesn't like anything that belongs to him getting free. He didn't even like Bunny, because Brigie loved him.'

'This is Bunny?' asked Goss, holding out a photo. I looked. A very large Dutch rabbit, white and brown, with long ears and a slightly supercilious expression.

'That's him. She could have left him with me. I would have looked after him. But maybe she thought Dad would kill him. He used to threaten to cook him in a pie. He thought it was funny. Brigie didn't.'

'All right,' said Daniel, pressing some buttons and shutting the computer down. 'I've copied her hard disk. I'll look at it carefully at home. Here's my number, Dolly. You've got a phone? Call me if you hear anything about her. And if you hear from Brigid herself, tell her to call me. There's voicemail if I'm not there. And I won't make her go home, Dolly, not if she doesn't want to. But we'll find her. Shall we give her a message from you?'

Dolly gulped and groped for her soaked wad of tissues. 'Tell her I love her!' she wailed, and burst into further tears.

I went downstairs to talk to Sandra. Perhaps she routinely froze all her employers' guests. Perhaps she just didn't approve of Israelis or young women or fat women. I found her in the kitchen. She had donned a very becoming navy blue apron with white piping. She was vengefully kneading dough. Now this was something I knew about. I sat down, uninvited, to watch.

She had a proper action: thud, knead, pull, roll, thud, knead. She was putting a lot of muscle into it. It was a good mix, yeasty and bouncy. After about ten minutes I commented, 'I should let it rest now.'

'What do you know about it?' she snapped.

'I'm a baker,' I said. 'Corinna Chapman. I've got a shop in the city, Earthly—'

'Delights,' she finished, thudding the dough into its bowl and covering it with a spotless white tea towel. She slammed the kettle onto the stove and lit the gas. 'Coffee?' she demanded.

'Thanks,' I replied.

She sat down on the hard polished wood chair and leant her elbows on the table so that she could look into my face.

'You make good bread,' she told me, almost as if it was an accusation.

'Thank you,' I replied, a little taken aback.

'You've got your own shop and I expect you make a good living from it. Then why did you get involved in this dreadful business?' she snarled, thrusting her face closer as though she meant to bite me.

'Daniel is my lover. He's the detective. I help out sometimes. I brought Goss, my shop assistant, to talk to Dolores because I don't speak Adolescent. Why are you so angry with me?'

'You'll bring her back,' she said flatly. 'You'll bring her back to this house.'

'No,' I said, edging away a little in case she really did flesh those white teeth into my throat. 'We want to find Brigid because it is not safe for a girl like her—and in that condition—to be on the street, if she is on the street. But if she doesn't want to come home, we aren't the people to make her.'

'Her father will demand an answer.'

I shrugged and used an Uncle Solly phrase. 'Then he not get. Or as Grandma Chapman used to say, want must be his master. You've seen Daniel. He's a Sabra. He's doing his job out of conviction, backed up by some pretty powerful people, including one nun who is in line for sainthood. How vulnerable would you say he is to pressure?'

She grabbed my wrist. She was very strong. I fought down an urge to fight to get my hand back.

'You won't tell?'

'Not if Brigid doesn't want us to tell.' I took her wrist in my grip as well, and squeezed.

We sat like that for a little while. I was wondering if I was going to have to kick her in the shins when she released me, gave a sound which might have been a sob, and stood up, putting her apron hem to her eyes.

'I believe you,' she stated. Thereafter she assembled, with amazing speed, coffee in a filter pot, milk and sugar, cups, saucers and spoons, and a plate of flat cookies studded with Smarties.

I took a cookie. I was suddenly hungry with all this emotion flying around. The cookie was delicious and the coffee a lifesaver; strong, authoritative and black as the ace of spades. Sandra poured a cup for herself as well and sat down next to me.

'I don't know where she is, the poor lamb,' she whispered. 'I'd tell you if I did, now that I know you won't give her up. I've had her as my own since she was seven years old and that man sacked her nurse. Without warning, just said that the child was too old for a nurse.'

'I hate to say this,' I nevertheless said, 'but your employer is a pig.'

She grinned mirthlessly. 'So he is. I stay because the salary is huge—as is the workload—and the children need me. If only Brigie'd told me, when she first knew, I could have fixed everything. Got her to a clinic. But she was ashamed. She told her father and then there was nothing I could do. She wasn't allowed to leave the house at all. I couldn't smuggle her out. And then the baby was too far advanced, anyway.'

'So when she vanished, where did you think she had gone?'

'I thought one of her sisters or brothers. But they all swear she isn't with them and the detectives that the boss sent reported that there is no sign of her. Your Daniel is only the most recent of the private detectives he's sicked onto the poor girl. The others all failed. I wasn't worried about them. They were big strong men, ex-cops. But you might find her.'

'Any ideas at all?' I ate the rest of my cookie and took another.

'I really don't know. She didn't have any friends. She just worked. She was an obsessive little thing. She's got top marks for her maths subjects. Used to play chess with her father until she was good enough to beat him and then he didn't want to play anymore. She never learnt to allow him to win. Not flexible. All black and white, like most sixteen-year-olds. If I could capture that boy, I'd wring his neck with my bare hands.'

She could do it, too. Those were very strong hands.

'What about Mama? Would she know?'

'Not a chance. She only wanted daughters as decoration. She hated bearing them—only did it because it was God's commandment. Never let them have a private thought—they even had to come to her for sanitary pads because she wanted to know when they bled.'

'Because?' I asked, boggled.

'Because in their batty religion menstruating women are unclean and they had to take special cold baths and live on dry bread and water. She even examined them to check for an unbroken hymen—so humiliating! You can imagine how fast the others ran away; married as soon as they could. Mama only noticed them if they were pretty and she could use them to adorn her parties or impress some disgusting visiting pastor. Brigie was beautiful but she didn't flirt with the guests. She sat there like a good girl and said yes and no and passed the hors d'oeuvres. And thought about mathematics, she told me once. God, she'll be so hot and dirty, so tired!'

'We'll find her,' I soothed. 'What about Dolores?'

'She lives inside her own head,' said Sandra. 'She writes and writes, all fantasies. She isn't pretty or amenable, so at least she is let alone. Of the two, I would have thought that Dolly would run, not Brigie. They'd be all right if they were together. Dolly may be vague but she remembers to eat. Poor girl. I wish I could feed her, but her mother makes her weigh herself every week, and if she's gained anything, back she goes onto lettuce and grilled chicken.'

'It's child abuse,' I said softly.

'Oh, yes, and I can see any magistrate believing that,' flashed Sandra.

'What about this trust fund they have?'

'Enough to live on, yes, certainly, if Pig Papa would disburse it. He's one of the trustees and I can't see him letting either of the girls out of his grasp.'

'There may be ways,' I told her, determined that there would be.

Daniel and Goss came down the stairs. I finished my coffee and shook Sandra's strong, work-worn hand.

'Here's my number,' I said, grabbing one of Daniel's cards and writing it down.

'I'll call,' she promised. Goss goggled. Daniel took my arm.

Sandra made us take the rest of the cookies. Timbo woofled through them in a fusillade of Smarties as we headed back toward town.

The phone rang. Daniel answered it.

'Turn around,' he told our driver. 'We're going to Collingwood.'

'Why?' I asked, snaring the last cookie.

'That was Sandra. The Collingwood Children's Farm called. They've found Bunny.'

Chapter Seven

King Jesus hath a garden, full of divers flowers.
Trad.

'How?' I asked, brushing crumbs off my front.

'Microchipped. Like Horatio and the Mouse Police. Apparently he hopped into the farm and they ran a reader over him. He's with the vet at present.'

'She'll be devastated at losing Bunny,' commented Goss.

'Poor girl! The freegans did say that they saw Brigid in Collingwood just before they got moved on by the constabulary. I wonder if they might still be there?'

'It's a farm,' said Daniel. 'Not a lot of places to hide.'

'There speaks a man who has never been to the farm. It's huge, goes right down to the river, and behind it is Studley Park. And come to think of it, next door is the convent, which is also huge and replete with buildings. I went to a market there. Sisters of the Good Shepherd, as I recall. Sister Mary might prove our entrée, even though the nuns have gone. And maybe it will be cool,' I said, wishful-thinking, looking at the relentless blue of the sky outside the car.

We parked in the car park in St Heliers Street and wound our way down to the Children's Farm. Behind it the trees of

Studley Park rose in rank. The air was heavy with eucalyptus. It was hot and quiet. Even the little birds who lived free of care in the thick hedges were quiet. I suppose even birds can have an afternoon nap. Despite the cookies I was hungry, conscious of missing lunch, and wondering what on earth I was going to do with a bunny as big and assertive as this one. For he must not go back to the house, not if Brigid's dad had threatened to cook him. That sort of man might easily kill him. And he must not be killed.

'Not us,' said Goss, who was thinking along the same lines. 'Not anyone who already has a cat or a dog. Which lets off Therese. And the Professor has Nox and Trudi has Lucifer and we have Tori and Cherie Holland has Calico and Mrs. P has that gross little mongrel Traddles and you have the Mouse Police and Horatio.'

'Nerds?' asked Daniel.

'They'd forget to feed him.'

'What about the Cafe Delicious family?' he asked.

'They might forget and eat him. Del makes a really brilliant rabbit casserole.'

'Which leaves Mrs. Dawson and Jason,' observed Goss.

'I can't see Mrs. Dawson really taking to a rabbit, can you?' asked Daniel.

'No,' I said. 'She would look after him properly if he was foisted on her, but only out of a sense of duty.'

'How about Rowan?' asked Goss, who had rather taken to the student upstairs.

'His group disapproves of companion animals,' I told her. 'They even disapproved of Horatio—to his face! He would not be safe or suitable. In any case, he isn't in on this action.'

'No, then it's Jason, isn't it?' asked Goss, and giggled.

'Then it is Jason,' I agreed. 'Jason will cope, especially if we sling him a reasonable emolument for rabbit-sitting. After all, we are going to find this girl, so it won't be forever.'

'Not forever,' agreed Daniel.

We had been pacing down a hot, stony path between ranks of surprisingly green vegetation and had reached a hut. There we enquired of an enchantingly plump girl for the vet and Bunny. She opened the door and let us in.

The vet was a thin, wiry woman, who was concluding her examination of a really big rabbit. She lowered him into a crate.

'He's fine, Estelle, just get him some water. This is no climate in which to wear fur. Slip that frozen bottle of water in there with him. There, he's draped himself over it. That's the way, Bunny. Soon have you cool. You've come for Bunny? I've given him a calci booster. He's not injured, though he's hopped a fair way. His paws are sore. Here's an ointment for the paws and a care sheet for rabbits, since you don't look like the original owner.'

'Thanks,' I said. 'No, we know nothing about rabbits. How did he end up here?'

She shoved back her short straw-coloured hair and frowned.

'We found him this morning, scavenging the guinea pigs' food,' she told me. 'He was hungry but not starving. I'd say he hadn't come too far without a meal. Heat-affected, though. The trouble is that tame rabbits get used to a highly nutritious diet. They aren't used to eating grass. And he has a lot of rabbit to feed. Well, I am sure that you would like to leave a donation. We can sell you the carrier if you haven't got one of your own. What happened to his owner?'

'That's what we would really like to know,' said Daniel feelingly, leafing through his wallet for notes. 'Can you give me a receipt?'

'Certainly,' said the vet. 'If I was you, I'd have a look at the convent. Lots of places to hide there. A runaway?'

'A heavily pregnant runaway.'

'Ah,' said the vet, writing out the receipt and handing over the carrier. 'I saw a pregnant girl in the convent grounds, but it was a while ago. Estelle! When did the Shetland have that night of colic?'

'Wednesday,' said Estelle, who had been listening in the intervals of selling tickets and goat food to the populace.

'Wednesday last week, I was up all night with the pony. I saw a heavily pregnant girl and a boy sneaking into the convent by the back door, the one which leads to the art place. Just along the street. I was going to offer them a drink of water, but they drifted along like smoke and I lost them. And I had the pony to care for, so I went back down the hill. You're looking for her?'

'Yes,' said Daniel.

'Better find her soon or she'll drop,' said the vet with the frankness of those who deal with animals. 'Two weeks or less, I would have said, and she didn't look well. Good luck with Bunny. Keep him cool,' she said. We left, the comfortable sound of chooks foraging accompanying us up the hill.

'Convent?' I asked.

'Better send Timbo to Jason with Bunny, if we have to keep the poor creature cool,' said Daniel. 'He can come back and pick us up. I'll just write a note and tell Jason to buy a proper cage and some rabbit food. And give him his first rabbit-sitting payment, of course.'

'You write the note,' I offered, 'and I'll call him.'

Jason's first scream of outrage when he was informed of his new role was greatly reduced and his feelings of oppression assuaged by the offer of twenty dollars a day to mind the beast. Timbo chuckled and agreed to see Bunny settled in before he came back for us.

And then we were on our own with the convent.

It was vast.

The Sisters of the Good Shepherd, I recalled, were responsible for a lot of people: good girls to be educated, bad girls to be confined, orphaned girls to be turned into competent housemaids and cooks. They also looked after elderly female invalids and the insane. They ran a laundry. At one stage they had three schools. And when they acquired a new responsibility, they just built a new building. Despite the best efforts of the previous government, it had not been pulled down and turned into apartments. It was a working arts complex, with painters and dyers and sculptors and galleries and its own radio station and bakery.

It was to the bakery that my feet found themselves heading. I could smell bread. Good bread. And we had missed lunch.

The little cafe was crowded and I edged toward the front, looking at the ovens. They were wonderful, ancient bread ovens made of wrought iron, which holds the heat like nothing else can. I felt a pang of powerful acquisitiveness. Actually, it was plain greed. I wanted those ovens.

Daniel and Goss, in my wake, were amused. I tamped down the lust. These ovens weren't going anywhere and it was suffocating in the little cafe.

I bought a selection of baguettes filled with cold roast beef and salad and cheese and other things, and we sat down in the shade to drink iced tea (with insufficient ice) and eat them while Goss enthused about the market—which was carried on, it seemed, just around a few unimportant corners, no more than a few k's of convent territory, and could we have a little tiny peek at it?

Daniel was nodding. So I assented, even though I knew, with the fat woman's resigned bitterness, that there would be nothing in the market which would fit me. And if by some strange chance there was, it would be blue crimplene, in which I have forbidden Daniel even to bury me.

The convent buildings were relatively modest. An L-shaped red-brick construction was fronted by a charming (but lightly baked, now) garden under a circular concrete gazebo which proclaimed that the protection of St Joseph was requested. Modern buildings fronted onto the huge outer wall. No one but an Olympic athlete was going to get into the convent. Or, I realised with a small shudder, out of it…The nuns had run a Magdalen laundry, in which the bad girls were employed. Some of them must have seen that wall as a barrier against all hope of escape.

And we were hunting an escapee, or a pair of escapees, so this might be a good place for them.

'Bunny can't have hopped a really long way,' said Daniel, echoing my thought as he often did. 'And this place has a lot of windows which would open and a lot of niches under the bushes.'

'You've been looking at ways to break in?'

'Certainly,' he replied.

One thing to be said about the market was that it had no Christmas carols. A Peruvian band were hooting and thumping in the middle, spruiking their CD. I always listen for the Simon and Garfunkel song 'El Condor Pasa' in such music and never hear it. But at least it wasn't 'I Saw Mommy Kissing Santa Claus', for which I hope that someone will have to atone. What an evil old misanthropic bitch I am.

Goss slid into the market like a salmon into John West seas—easily, effortlessly. And she took me along with her for a demonstration of Postgraduate Shopping. Daniel shoved both hands in his jeans pockets and mooched along after us, chatting to the stall holders, the picture of a reluctant male attendee.

Clever man. I had no intention of buying anything, anyway. But it was an interesting market, and following Goss was engrossing. She would drift along, talking idly of this and that—wondering, in fact, how Jason would get on with Bunny—and then suddenly stiffen like a pointer, dive into a mass of garments, and drag one forth. And it appeared that I was going to buy things.

'Boho, that's the look for you,' Goss decided. 'Long skirt, loose blouse, maybe a big belt.'

'None of it will fit me!' I protested, veteran of many humiliating attempts to shoehorn my curves into standard garments. Goss shot me a look so loaded with scorn that I suppressed further comment.

'You're a perfect size 20,' she told me. I blinked. 'Perfect' had never been a term used with 'size 20' in my hearing before. But I continued to protest. Privately. Hell would freeze over—I spared a moment to apologise to any Sisters of the Good Shepherd who might still be around in spectral form—before I bought any of this overpriced tat, Goss or no Goss.

Actually it wasn't tat. Not all of it. There were some lovely Chinese-influenced shirts with mandarin collars and some very elegant forties' style Dior and Chanel suits, entirely unsuited to the Chapman figure. But Goss had been very helpful and I decided I could put up with some shopping once in a way. I was sure that she would be diverted into buying something for herself once she found, as she was going to find, that nothing was over size 10. And if I approved of what she was going to buy I would purchase it for her; she deserved a little present. The wind had died down, but it was still unacceptably hot, and the rows of hanging rails and little tents seemed to go on forever. The Peruvians thumped and bubbled. Daniel sidled along, looking bored.

Then I found a seller who sold shaved ice with fruit cordial, which made me feel better. And then a stone cutter. That was more like it. Crystals and polished rocks of all colours sparkled in the sun. I didn't dare buy a crystal without consulting Meroe, our local witch, but there was a large slice of opalescent shell which attracted my fingers. Goss wandered away as I bought it and hung it around my neck. Lovely.

I was just sucking down the last of my orange ice when both of my companions emerged from the crowd and grabbed an elbow each.

'I got her first,' Goss told Daniel.

'All right, but I get her next,' he grumbled.

I didn't seem to be getting a lot of choice, but I was feeling full of icy fruitiness so I went along with Goss, who conducted me into a close, hot tent and started dragging off my garments. Over my head she threw a thin, lacy petticoat and then a floaty skirt in some sort of cheesecloth, perhaps, in varying shades of blue, from indigo at the hem to azure at the waist. Then she dropped over my head a smocked white cheesecloth blouse, with puffy sleeves and ribbon ties, as worn by Prince Caspian. She fastened round my waist a heavy leather belt with an ornate silver buckle. Then she turned me toward the mirror.

Oh, my, there I was, authentically bohemian, if that is a real term, perfectly comfortable, and delighted with the contrast of my new silver and shell pendant over my white top.

'See?' demanded Goss. 'Now pay the lady, Daniel's getting uptight.'

I paid the lady a surprisingly small sum. She packed my own clothes into a string bag. I replaced my straw hat, and I was out in the sunlight again.

Daniel whistled. I curtseyed, spreading my skirts. Goss beamed.

'Now, come along this way,' Daniel ordered, and we hurried after him. The skirts were well cut and easy to manage and flared around my ankles delightfully. Daniel led the way out of the market and around the convent. Quite a long way. I could see what he meant about the windows. Several of them did not quite fill their frames and could be jemmied. But Daniel was heading for a tree, a huge old oak which, being of weeping habit, had feathery branches going right down to the ground, like a living green cage. Daniel searched for an entrance and dived in and we followed.

'It's so cool,' whispered Goss. I did not know if she referred to the air temperature or the beauty of the space under the tree but she was right about both.

'I think they were both here,' said Daniel. He scanned the ground. We all tracked around the green-walled haven.

'You can't see if anyone is here from the outside,' I remarked. 'And it is cool. And there's water nearby. And a bunny was here.' I pointed out rabbit droppings.

'Bigger than the wild rabbits,' said Daniel. 'That was Bunny. And, see, if he was left here or hopped off, there's the Children's Farm, just down the hill. Also, this grass has been nibbled really short.'

'I don't like this,' said Goss suddenly. 'Something bad happened. Look, the grass is all torn up over here, and that's blood on those leaves.'

'It's blood,' agreed Daniel calmly, collecting a sample in a little plastic bag. 'But I don't know if it's human. Not the girl, anyway, not the blood of labour, there isn't enough of it.'

Goss shivered. We had to get her out of here. The atmosphere under the great tree had subtly changed and become threatening. I looked hard to see if there was anything else.

'The bark of this branch has been cut,' I said.

'So it has,' he agreed soberly. 'What's that under your foot, Goss?'

'It's a phone,' she said, scrabbling in the thick soft leaf mould. 'Been stood on,' she added.

'The Lone Gunmen can retrieve the data,' Daniel said. 'Dig a little more around there and see if there is anything else.'

'Just some papers,' said Goss. 'They're—a maths exam.'

'Right. Out you go,' Daniel told her, pushing her through the branches. 'Go back to the market and buy yourself a present from us.'

Goss went without a backward look. I would have liked to join her.

'What do we seek?'

'Camping equipment, food bag, water bucket—all of those things are missing,' he told me, peering into the maze of branches.

'Stolen?'

'Not usual if this was one of those assaults in company,' he said. 'They come upon some poor helpless person, beat them, spit on them, destroy anything they have and keep moving, the little bastards. There's not enough blood to suggest anyone was seriously injured. I would guess that they struggled with the boy, saw the pregnant girl and took off. In the meantime, Bunny decided he had had it with a life of adventure and hopped off. Then they both packed up and left here. The phone was pressed right into the ground. Nothing else,' he said, sifting the leaf mould through his fingers. It had a fine, earthy smell.

'Nothing more,' he said sadly. I strained what Meroe calls my intuition for some trace of the lovers, but all I felt was silly. So I gathered up my fine new skirts and went to find Goss in the market. She seemed to have recovered her aplomb. She had also found a sequined T-shirt. Of course. I mobilised my credit card again. It was a rather pretty garment.

Timbo had returned by the time we made it out of the convent and into St Heliers Street. I had never heard of St Helier. Such a lot of saints in an unholy world. Who would have the heart to attack a harmless runaway and a pregnant girl? I asked Daniel this question, and he shrugged. As good an answer as any, I suppose.

Timbo giggled when asked how Jason was managing with Bunny. But he doesn't like to talk with his mouth full and we had bought him a whole packet of the convent's very good ginger biscuits, so we passed the journey home in a mist of spicy crumbs.

Arrived at Insula, Goss went up to her own apartment to have a shower and share her experience with Kylie. I went to mine for a wash, as well. I was hot and weary and disgusted, a nasty combination. But I felt better when I was clean, and my new clothes really were lovely. I swished when I moved.

'That's called a froufrou,' remarked Daniel, sliding a hand under the skirt. And encountering my sensible Cottontails. This proved no barrier and I spontaneously decided to go and see Jason later, when he and Bunny would have had a chance to form a bond.

We barely made it to the bed. Air conditioning has done wonders for my love life.

◇◇◇

Some time later we took a mutual shower and dressed to see Jason. My froufrou had gained a certain panache with practice. I had never worn long skirts in the daytime before. I liked them. Daniel departed to talk to the Lone Gunmen, our resident nerds, about retrieving all the messages from the SIM card of the ruined mobile phone. I ascended in the lift to the top floor, where Jason occupied an apartment which had been lent to Mrs. Dawson by the exceedingly rich owner. He had it on the understanding that he kept it neat and tidy, which he mostly did because one who has lived on the street appreciates a roof over their head. And has very few possessions.

Jason opened the door. He had an armful of rabbit. It was attempting to disembowel him with its strong clawed back feet. He was holding it very tightly.

'Gimme,' I said, taking Bunny and supporting him by his body. His feet fitted nicely into my hands. He stopped struggling instantly. I could feel his little heart racing against my sensitised breast.

'What were you trying to do, Jason?' I asked my apprentice.

'Put the bloody ointment on his feet,' said Jason sulkily. There had clearly been an imperfect fusion of souls between Jason and Bunny.

'Two-person job,' I told him. 'Let me in.'

The apartment was, as usual, tidy. It had been augmented by a large, even luxurious bunny cage. It had a water bottle, a litter tray and a retiring room, and was heaped with hay. Jason had cut up a substantial salad for the rabbit, despite his scowl. I sat down with Bunny on my lap and stroked him on the forehead. His fur was as soft as down. His heart slowed down and he did not struggle as Jason applied the ointment to his sore feet. Then I fed him a handy bit of lettuce and put him back into his cage with the salad. He settled down to nibble. I did like the way his little brown nose whiffled. I could tell I wasn't going to be able to eat rabbit again. Not that I had eaten it much anyway.

'Apart from that, how has your day been?' I asked, and Jason cracked and laughed. He ruffled his blond curls.

'Not bad. I got a righteous serve from that thin chick for having a companion animal, when Timbo was carrying the cage inside. She was real loud until Rowan shut her down. What's her problem?'

'She's a fierce animal-rights person.'

'Then she ought to be glad that I'm not turning Bunny into a nice *ragoût de lapin*,' said Jason hotly. His fluency is directly proportional to the culinary use of the word. 'Not that I didn't think of it when he was trying to scratch me guts out.'

'Your restraint does you credit,' I told him.

He grinned at me. 'I could mind any number of rabbits for you, Corinna,' he told me with an unexpected, brief, throttling hug. I wondered what had brought on this rush of affection. I asked.

He looked away.

'Since we've been looking for that girl I been remembering what the street's like,' he confessed. 'Nightmares. But,' he told me, standing up and shaking himself, 'then I wake up and I'm here in this grouse flat and I've got bread to bake and it's all down to you, Corinna. Anyway, want to see what happened when I made Yai Yai's cherries?'

'Yes,' I replied, suppressing a strong urge to hug Jason hard. It wasn't me, I wanted to say, it was you—you dragged yourself out of heroin addiction and turned yourself into a baker. I'm so proud of you, Jason! I wanted to say, but didn't because the moment had passed.

He brought me some bright red cherries on a dish. I picked one up. It was as hard as rock and as bright as a Christmas decoration.

'I seem to have made the first cherry toffees.' Jason bit one. So did I. They tasted fine.

'I like the taste,' I said. 'You could use them to decorate a cake, on the top.'

'Yeah,' he said, drooping. 'But that's not actually what I wanted. I wanted glacé cherries, like the bought ones but not made of plastic.'

'Come down to my flat, I've got a book of preserves recipes. You can try again when you get some more cherries. Are you happy with your cake recipe?'

'Try,' said Jason, producing a beautiful little cake. It smelt fruity. He cut it; the crumb was even and the cake was moist but not wet. I bit and savoured. Wonderful. I guessed at some ingredients.

'Candied peel?'

'I candied it myself. But that method doesn't work on cherries, you get glup. Cherry-flavoured glup, but glup.'

'And did you use brandy?'

'Rum. Golden Jamaica rum. Mrs. Dawson gave me the bottle, she says she doesn't know anyone now who drinks rum.'

'It's a wonderful cake,' I assured my apprentice.

'Except for the cherries, which aren't there.'

'Come on, I've a kilo of cherries you can have, get you back on the horse. And if you can spare some of the cherry toffees, I'm sure someone will like them too.'

Much cheered, Jason packaged some of the glassy cherries, checked that Bunny was secured in his cage—he had cleared his plate and now seemed to be considering an afternoon nap—and followed me down to Hebe. There I located the preserves text, which has three recipes for glacé and preserved fruit, and I surrendered my own personal kilo of fresh cherries.

'No plans for the weekend, then?' I asked him. He often worked at Mistress Dread's dungeon as an Igor.

'I been invited to rehearsal,' he said reluctantly. 'By Rowan.'

'You'll like that,' I said. 'Take the cake and you'll be very popular. And pay no attention to the skinny blonde. No one else does.'

'All right, Corinna,' he replied, took his cherries and the book, and left.

Horatio was reminding me that a little smackerel of something in the late afternoon was provided for in his charter of animal rights. I went inside to find him some cat treats. Lately my life seemed to have been overpopulated with my furry brethren.

Chapter Eight

All poor men and humble,
All lame men who stumble,
Come haste ye, nor feel ye afraid

KE Roberts (trans.)
'All Poor Men and Humble'

Daniel came back after an hour or so to find me contemplating the contents of the fridge.

'Shut the door, you're letting the cold out,' he told me. 'As my mother used to say. I've got the messages. Did you know you can retrieve text messages from a SIM card even after they have been sent? Otherwise it just gives you a list of numbers, which is going to take some messing about and comparison best done by two people. Fortunately this can be carried out in the coolness and privacy of our own home.'

'Hmm,' I agreed.

'Corinna?' He waved a hand in front of my face. 'Excuse me, lady, is Ms. Corinna Chapman home?'

'She is wondering what to have for dinner,' I answered.

'And the possibilities are…'

'A big salad,' I said. 'Or several little ones. Steak? Chicken? It's all frozen.'

'Or we let our fingers do the walking,' he suggested, 'and order a feast from the Thai restaurant. Or do you fancy Chinese?'

'I suddenly have a yen for curry puffs,' I replied. 'And coconut rice and satay chicken…'

'I'll ring them,' said Daniel.

◇◇◇

Dinner was very satisfactory, but I was disturbed by the weather and worried about Brigid, so instead of watching a DVD or listening to my new Vaughan Williams CD, we divided the text messages from the numbers called and began comparisons.

I have always had a facility for figures, so it wasn't hard for me to find the patterns in the long lists of numbers.

'She called this one every day,' I said, quoting it.

'That's Manny's number,' said Daniel.

'And this one every week or so,' I told my darling, reading off the numbers.

'Unknown—we'll have to find out who that is.'

'And this one rather irregularly.'

'Her sister Dolores.'

'And this one eleven times.'

'Lifeline,' said Daniel.

'Oh, dear.'

'As you say, *ketschele*.'

'This one several times.'

'School friend Melissa Thomas from the text sig. We'll need to talk to her,' said Daniel. 'I've never heard her spoken of by anyone in the case. No one thought Brigid had any friends.'

'And the last she called…three times.'

'Another unknown. All right. Here are the text messages. Do you speak text?'

'No,' I told him.

'It's easy,' he replied. 'Just think of shorthand. Here's the first to one of the unknowns. "*C U soon heart B*". Pretty obvious, *nu?*'

'Following you so far,' I said cautiously.

'Then she says "*must C U soon heart B*".'

'Increasing level of urgency,' I commented.

'And the final text to Unknown is "*U R cruel gbye 4 ever*".'

'Poor girl. Well, we need to find out who this Unknown is. Shall we call him Swain?'

'I'd call him Bastard,' said Daniel. 'Or Cad.'

'Cad will do. What about the other Unknown?'

'Texted every week or so. Rats.'

'Rats?'

'Numbers,' he told me. 'Only numbers. It must be some sort of code.'

'What does she say to her sister?'

'Chat,' he said. 'Just chat. Seems completely banal to me.'

'Let's hear it,' I said. 'Girls invented reading between the lines.'

'All right,' he sighed. The phone rang, he answered it, and there was that sort of conversation where the listener only hears 'Yes' and 'No' and 'I'll come right away'.

'Where?' I asked, as Daniel leapt to his feet.

'A contact of Sister Mary's repaired a boy who had been beaten up. In Collingwood. A week ago. And he had with him a heavily pregnant girl.'

'I'm coming too,' I told him. 'It's that or read all those banal messages.'

'It would be a help if you read them,' he said gently. 'And her online journal.'

'And so I shall,' I said. 'When we get back from Collingwood.'

He grinned at me, and phoned Timbo to bring the car round. One day I must find out why Daniel chooses not to drive. But not tonight.

After placating Horatio for our absence with a few cat treats, we were on the way to Collingwood. Again. And it is not my favourite suburb. It seems to me to be an uneasy fusion of nouveau riche and old poor, neither of whom approve of the other in the least degree. Also, I am instructed that I have to loathe their football team, for some reason. I have never understood sports.

Timbo threaded down Smith Street, which was loud with young persons getting really, really drunk. They also displayed a frightening lack of road sense, tippling out into the road and swaying back, centimetres from annihilation. This made me nervous. But I had insisted on coming along so I could not object.

'The fall of the Roman Empire,' remarked Daniel.

'Where are we going?'

'Timbo's trying to catch up with the hospital bus,' Daniel told me. 'We'll get off the main drag any minute now, if one of those drunks doesn't fling himself in front of us.'

'It's this way,' said Timbo. He had a God-given talent for driving cars. None of the bank robbers he had been persuaded into helping had cause to complain about their getaway vehicle. It was their tendency to get stuck in revolving doors which had done for them. Daniel swore that the reason Timbo didn't go to jail was that the judge had been laughing so much that he hadn't the heart to send the boy away. Also, in the case of those robbers, they were just not a massive threat to public order.

Timbo was right. We left the vomiting populace behind us and sneaked along dark, quiet, respectable streets. We stopped. In front of us was a very flash new bus. I was instantly envious on behalf of Sister Mary, who would not have recognised the emotion.

'Hospital bus,' explained Daniel. 'They cruise the streets looking for the lost and damaged and repair them. People who are too unstable or too scared to go to a public hospital and wait four hours. Has one doctor, several nurses and two heavies, one of whom is Ma'ani's cousin, Rui.'

Something huge hulked out of the darkness. A true shadow of the original. He was almost as big as Ma'ani. Distinguished from him by his shock of truly astounding peroxide blond hair, in cornrows with dependent beads. I doubted, however, that anyone told Rui that his hairstyle was effeminate. He grinned a watermelon grin.

'Hey, Daniel!'

'Hey, Rui,' replied Daniel.

'You must be Corinna,' said the behemoth, engulfing my hand to the elbow. 'That Ma'ani, he thinks you make the best bread. You looking for someone?'

'Your nurse,' said Daniel. 'Nancy?'

'Hey, Nance!' bellowed Rui into the bus. 'You all right now?'

'I'm all right,' said a tired voice. 'He didn't draw blood.'

She was cradling a forearm wrapped in bandages. An older woman in a nurse's uniform, complete down to the white shoes. She was lighting a cigarette and dragging in the smoke gratefully.

'Crazy bit her,' explained Rui. 'I'm out here making sure he don't come back.'

'He'd have to be really crazy to come back,' Sister Nancy told Rui affectionately. 'They all think we have drugs,' she told me. 'This one was high on ice, and that's a nasty thing. You're Daniel? I think I've seen your missing boy.'

'When? Where?'

'Last Saturday night—Sunday morning, actually, about four o'clock. Came out of the shadows. Beaten up. We reduced his broken nose; that'll heal itself if he doesn't get it broken again. Bruises and a cut lip, possibly a broken rib. Cut knuckles, too, he fought back. Spotty youth. But I remember him because he was a nice boy,' she said, absently caressing her bitten arm. 'He was very worried about the girl who was with him. Very young, very pregnant. Not visibly injured. Distressed. I suggested that he take her to hospital but he wouldn't, or rather, *she* wouldn't. Cringed away as though I had suggested an abattoir. Poor little brain-damaged mite. She was crying because she had lost her toy.'

'Crying for Bunny?' I asked.

'Yes, sad, isn't it? And someone had certainly taken advantage of her. The mentally challenged are so vulnerable to exploitation of all kinds. We see a lot of them. Of course,' she added with a chuckle, 'some of them bite back.'

'What did you do for her?'

'Had a talk with her. She said something very worrying. She said her mother had placenta praevia. She must have learnt the term like a parrot, poor thing.'

'Early placenta?' I guessed.

Sister shook her head, lighting another cigarette.

'It's a condition where the placenta detaches early. The baby doesn't have placental oxygen and it's still in the birth canal so it can't breathe. Can lead to a bad outcome.'

'By which you mean…' Daniel urged impatiently. She gave him a Look. Nurses specialise in that Look. It suppresses even the most belligerent. Daniel and I were suitably suppressed.

'The baby dies,' the nurse said flatly. 'Then, unless someone does something fast, the mother bleeds out. It's bad. She knew what it meant, too, said the boy had looked it up on the internet. Kids. Overinformed and don't know what to do with the knowledge. I told her to go to hospital, things like that run in families quite often. But she just cried and refused.'

'So what did you do for them?' I asked, as Daniel was still suppressed.

'Gave them vitamins, tonics, tickets for the showers at the rest centre,' said Nurse Nancy. 'The water's hot and it's a safe environment. They both went along in that direction, at least. They'll be open,' she told us. 'They're always open. I hope you find them,' she added, crushing out her cigarette in a little portable ashtray. 'The good boy and the poor little girl.'

'We'll find them,' Daniel assured her.

Back in the car and Timbo did amazing feats of pub-avoiding until we arrived at a low-key, two-storey brick building partly concealed behind a high hedge.

'Makes the neighbours feel happier if they can't see the clients,' Daniel said. 'And on a night like this the bushes might be more comfortable to sleep in, at that.'

The reception area was shabby, with worn grey industrial carpet on the floor and chairs upholstered in that sort of coloured plastic that is meant to be cheerful but which chips and cracks and becomes sordid in a week. The grey carpet contrasted beautifully with the ground-in Twisties and a wet, disinfected patch where some biological fluids had been spilt. There was no air conditioning and it was very hot inside. A thin young man hurried up to greet us.

'Daniel!' Everyone knew Daniel, it seemed. 'Looking for someone?'

'Pete, hi. Spotty boy and pregnant girl, may have appeared half-witted, last Sunday morning.'

'Oh, yes.' Pete rubbed a bald spot which seemed to be growing as we spoke. This man ran on nervous energy. 'Nice boy. They had a shower. I even managed to give the girl some of those free shampoo samples. Got them some fresh clothes. He'd been in a fight. Couldn't get them a placement together so they left. Trouble was they didn't have alcohol or drug problems, so I couldn't send them to the specialist placements, not that there's a lot of them. They just had nowhere to go.'

'Any idea where they did go in the end?' asked Daniel.

'I directed them to one of the cheap hotels. I got the impression that they had a little money. Here's the address,' said Pete, scribbling it down. 'It's a bit of a hole, but it's shelter.'

'Thanks,' said Daniel, and we went back to the car.

'To the hotel?'

Around a few more corners and down a fetid little back alley where the car barely fitted and I hoped we wouldn't meet anything coming the other way. We stopped outside a crumbling old terrace house called—I swear—the Hotel Splendid. I put my hand on the door and Daniel snatched it away.

'I'm not taking you there, Jason would kill me,' my darling said very firmly. 'You are staying in the car with the doors locked—you hear, Timbo?'

'I hear,' said Timbo, swallowing his mouthful of bacon and cheese crisps.

'Give her a few of your chips, I'll be back in a moment.'

Daniel took off his loose jacket, put his wallet and keys into my hands, and stalked into the Hotel Splendid as though he was going into action in the Gaza Strip. I wouldn't have tackled him. He is tall and slim and dark and when he wants to can extend an aura of menace three paces all around him.

'What's wrong with this place, Timbo?' I asked.

'Filth like you wouldn't believe, syringes on all the floors, nappies, dead dudes, it's gross,' Timbo replied. 'Druggies. They steal from each other and beat each other up. And other stuff.' He shifted uneasily in the car seat. 'Have a chip?' he asked.

I took one. I was unable to identify either bacon or cheese in it, but it was salty. The car was cool but the street outside was baking. No refuge, I thought, not even from the weather. No home, no safe place.

The final frightful touch was that someone in the Hotel Splendid was playing those dreadful Christmas carols from a boom box. And so it was to the tune of 'Have Yourself a Merry Little Christmas', crooned by some benighted female, that Daniel came back, scrubbing his hands together. He stopped at the boot, which Timbo opened, and wiped his palms with disinfectant tissues.

'Not there now,' he told me as he got in again. 'According to the loathsome owner, they were there very early Sunday morning and left without staying—now that I can understand. If I wasn't a pacifist I'd clear out the people in there and torch that place. It's a public health hazard. And so is the proprietor,' he said in an undertone. 'Him I would lay gently on top of the pyre.'

I had never seen him so angry. I put a hand on his arm.

'Erk?' I suggested.

'I might even go so far as to say "euw",' he agreed.

'Home?'

'Nowhere else I can think of tonight,' he said, relaxing a little. 'Home, Timbo, please.'

And we went home and we went to bed. Sunday I was going to read through a lot of messages from one girl to another, for which I felt very unprepared.

This must have been worrying me, for when I woke at four I could not get back to sleep, what with Horatio nestling on most of my pillow and Daniel occupying a lot of my bed. First I looked up St Helier. He was the first saint of Jersey. A hermit and sixth-century martyr. Apparently he was killed by robbers to whom he preached the Gospel. Stern literary critics, those bandits. His feast day is the sixteenth of July. Still wasn't sleepy.

So I went out onto the balcony and heard singing: sweet, sweet singing, from the roof, perhaps.

> *Joseph was an old man,*
> *And an old man was he,*
> *When he courted Mary*
> *In the land of Galilee.*

> *Joseph and Mary walked*
> *All in an orchard good,*
> *Where grew cherries and berries*
> *As red as any blood.*

This was a Christmas carol, but I was prepared to make an exception in its case. Medieval English, perhaps, which made it scan awkwardly in modern English. They must be singing it for Jason, donor of the cake and the rest of the glassy cherries. Which was nice of them. They had added some more voices. A very rich, strong tenor was rather dominating the sopranos, which was all to the good. I hoped Jason, with his techno and indie tastes, was enjoying the concert.

> *Then up spoke Mary,*
> *And she spoke meek and mild:*
> *'Pluck me one cherry, Joseph,*
> *For I am with child.'*

> *Then up spoke Joseph*
> *In answer most unkind:*
> *'Let him pluck you a cherry*
> *That brought thee thus with child!'*

Ah. Pique from the husband. Which was what could be expected even now. The night was turning to morning. I went in and got a drink. Ice and lemon and gin. I sat down in the chair next to the indestructible green leafy things Trudi had planted in my big pots.

Then up spoke the baby
All in his mother's womb
'Bow down, bow down, you highest trees,
That my mother shall have some.'

Then bowed down the highest tree
Unto his mother's hand,
and Mary cried, 'See, Joseph,
I have cherries at command!'

There was triumph in that cry. She might be embarrassed by a surprise God-given pregnancy but she was not without power. This was the Mary of the Magnificat, where generations would rise up and call her blessed. The Mary who declared: 'He hath showed strength with his arm : he hath scattered the proud in the imagination of their hearts. He hath put down the mighty from their seat : he hath exalted the meek and humble. He hath filled the hungry with good things, and the rich he hath sent empty away.' Just like me to remember the part of Evensong concerned with food.

My drink tasted wonderful. The voices came down from heaven like a cool shower of silver. I couldn't remember the rest of the story. What would the divinely cuckolded old man do now?

Then up spoke Joseph:
'I have done Mary wrong;
But now cheer up, my dearest,
And do not be cast down.'

'O eat your cherries, Mary
O eat your cherries now.
O eat your cherries, Mary
That hang upon the bough.'

Good man, Joseph! I cheered privately. Somewhere a window went up. I hoped the singers would get a chance to finish the carol before Mrs. Pemberthy objected. They did, but it was a narrow squeak.

> *Then Mary plucked a cherry,*
> *As red as any blood,*
> *And Mary she went homeward*
> *All with her heavy load.*

'Who's making all that noise?' shrieked Mrs. Pemberthy, making a lot more noise than the singers. Her strident elderly-parrot-with-indigestion voice jarred on the velvety night and the cool music and I swore.

Then, as the singers were made mute and Mrs. P continued to scold, I drank the rest of the drink. There was always someone, I reflected, who wanted to ruin the moment.

'And Mary she went homeward, All with her heavy load,' I hummed to myself. Where in this dark city was our little Mary, freighted with her dangerous and very heavy load?

Another window opened.

'Mrs. Pemberthy,' said Mrs. Dawson in her iciest voice, which caused my own cubes to tinkle in my glass out of sympathetic resonance, 'I was enjoying the music, but I am not enjoying your tirade. Consider them reproved,' she ordered.

Mrs. P is a little afraid of Mrs. Dawson. She humphed and slammed her window shut. The concert, however, appeared to be over. I was about to take my glass inside when I saw a strange shadow under the light in Calico Alley. I leant out. Not a human. Four-legged, though. Casting a very odd, long-eared shadow.

I sighed and went in to find some sandals and the keys to the bakery. I hoped that we had some raspberry and rosewater muffins left over. Snuffling at the door of Earthly Delights was Jason's most fervent fan and muffin gourmet, Serena.

Chapter Nine

Now every beast that crops in field
Breathe sweetly and adore.

Eleanor Farjeon
'Our Brother is Born'

I left Daniel a note. It is never nice to wake up without the person you went to sleep with, especially in his profession. When I opened the outer door of the bakery, the donkey put her head in, allowed me to caress her soft nose, and uttered a short, demanding *whuff!*

'All right,' I told her. 'But there aren't any muffins left. They all went to the Soup Run. You'll have to make do with bread and rosewater.'

Serena, by her stance, indicated that as long as it had rosewater in it, she would be content. I sliced my one remaining loaf, which had been overlooked in the packing, and sprinkled it with rosewater and a little sugar. This she accepted out of my hand and munched thoughtfully. Then she backed a little, stamped her foot, and asked for another.

'All right,' I said hurriedly, hoping that she wouldn't bray and wake Mrs. Pemberthy again. I cut this slice of bread thicker and poured rosewater onto it. This was sufficient, the animal indicated. That was the right sort of ratio of rosewater to bread. She mumbled my sleeve briefly, blinked her long-lashed eyes, and walked as serenely as her name down Calico Alley into Flinders Lane.

'Hang on,' I told her retreating tail. 'You shouldn't be wandering around late at night all by yourself. Someone might steal you. You might be hit by a car!'

Serena did not care. She kicked up her heels and set off at a brisk trot and was soon out of sight.

The Mouse Police, woken from their sleep on the flour sacks, demanded breakfast. I fed them. Then I took the loaf, locked up the bakery again, and went upstairs to make myself some toast. I wasn't going to get back to bed, and I was hungry. Toast and honey would be just as acceptable as bread and rosewater. And, of course, some coffee.

I got back into the apartment without waking Daniel. Horatio drifted into the kitchen to request his statutory dab of my butter. He never asks for more than one. It's like Danegeld. The city was silent, the whole of Insula was silent. Sunday morning. Lovely.

I didn't even want to crunch my toast too loudly. The coffee was excellent and I sipped quietly. Horatio ate his cat nibbles with impossible discretion.

Which is when someone began banging on the bakery door, of course. I grabbed a slice of bread and ran down the bakery stairs. The caller was, naturally, Mr. Pahlevi, angry, red-faced, panting, and about to start yelling. I didn't have any backup this time. But I was in my own bakery and in no mood to be affronted.

'She went that-a-way,' I pointed.

'Why didn't you stop her?' he yelled.

'Because she got away,' I told him, direct into those strange flat black eyes. 'Here…' I poured rosewater over the bread. 'Take this with you, and tie her up tighter tomorrow!'

For a moment I thought he was going to slap me, and my hand closed on the broom handle. He was going to get a serious belting with it if he showed fight. But he took the bread and ran down Flinders Lane, and I bolted the door behind him with a great deal of relief. Mrs. Pemberthy had not woken. I just could not deal with her at this hour. And a homicide trial cuts into your reading time.

I went back up the stairs. It was odd to be so awake when I didn't have to work. I put on the desk lamp and drew over the pile of text messages between the sisters. Now would be a good time to read them.

The first one said *How goes it Little Sis?*, and that rather set the tone for the rest. I had told Daniel that girls read between the lines, but there didn't seem to be any space in these communications for subtlety.

Sale at DJ pity we cant go, said one.

Dad pain, said the next. I could agree with that.

Awful trouble climb up tnt, pleaded another. This must be news of the pregnancy. Dolly must have been able to climb up to Brigid's prison.

Talk to S at sch, commanded another. Sister, perhaps? Putting herself into the hands of a strong-minded nun might have been the best that Brigid could do. But she hadn't.

Bring maths hwork up & I'll fix, promised another.

Hate Rev P hate him. Fell aslp X3 nites.

And so it went. The messages were dated. Nothing but lamentation and homework and the distasteful demands of their religion. I read them all, starred the ones which directly preceded the escape, and put them aside.

Perhaps a little nap might be good. I snuggled in beside Daniel, placed my head firmly on my very own pillow before Horatio got back, and closed my eyes. I was cool. I was relaxed. And I remained obstinately awake until I was suddenly obstinately asleep and was woken, at ten, by the sound of the doorbell.

'They're pretty good,' Daniel was saying with his mouth full.

'But not right,' insisted Jason. Cherries again? I yawned my way into the parlour.

'Have a taste, Corinna.' Jason offered me a plate on which reposed some pretty good glacé cherries. I inspected one carefully.

That strange translucence, yes. A little sticky, certainly. I bit it and got a mouthful of the most glorious cherry taste.

'And the syrup will make great tarts,' said my apprentice. 'But I reckon they're still a bit chewy.'

'Perhaps,' I said, marvelling at Jason's quest for perfection in all things culinary. 'Try them in one of those nice little cakes. Then you can buy some more cherries tomorrow and try the other recipe. Want some coffee?' I asked, sitting down and pouring myself a cup from the filter pot.

'Nah,' said Jason. 'I'll get myself a Coke later. Did you hear Mrs. Dawson squish Mrs. P last night?'

'Certainly. One of the best all-round squishes I have ever heard.'

'The singing was nice,' said Jason. 'I don't know why she had to stop it.'

'Because it was nice,' Daniel commented. 'Want some breakfast, Jason?'

Silly question. Jason was born hungry and had been feeding his inner famine ever since. 'Your choice of eggs, tomatoes, bacon, English muffins?'

'All of them,' said Jason.

'Sounds wonderful,' I concurred. 'You toast the muffins, Jason, and tell us about the singers. There was an extra voice or two last night, I fancy.'

'Yeah, old dude with a beard. Also a Russian bloke. Two more girls, Janeen and Emma. They're having a carol concert and they can't work out what to sing. Britten or Vaughan Williams. I never heard of 'em but they're real famous musical dudes. I took the rest of the failed cherries and that small cake to rehearsal and they sang me a cherry tree carol. It was nice.'

'I heard it,' I told him.

Daniel was frying up a storm. His time as a short-order cook had not been wasted. He could frizzle bacon, fry eggs to exact parameters and singe tomatoes faster than anyone I had ever met. Horatio demanded, and got, his statutory bacon rind. He likes to play with it and chew it and store it under the kitchen table for later resumption of games. The last is the only undesirable part of the routine.

Jason's muffins popped and he began to butter them. There was something on his mind apart from cherries. I guessed at what it might have been.

'How have you been getting on with Bunny?'

'Oh, all right. I've never had a pet before. He's eating the rabbit pellets and I found out he loves celery. I thought it would be carrots. But it's celery. He sits up and holds it between both front paws and nibbles it like he's playing a flute. It's sort of cute. But he spends a lot of time asleep or washing his face and ears.' Jason ducked his head and imitated a round brushing motion with both hands which covered his face and ruffled his hair. For a moment, he looked just like a rabbit, morphing into lagomorph in a way which would only have seemed usual to the *Fortean Times*.

'Good,' I told him. 'Poor Bunny has had a hard time. If the vet hadn't put that frozen bottle of water into his crate he might have died of heatstroke. Rabbits can't handle heat.'

'Yeah, it says in this bunny book I bought. *The Wonderful World of Pet Rabbits* by Christine Carter. I'm reading it,' he told me proudly.

Well, it wasn't worries about Bunny which were concerning my apprentice.

'So Bunny is all right,' I prompted. 'What's bothering you?'

'Rowan's girls,' he said slowly. 'They're mad keen on all this vegan stuff.'

'Yes, I know. My parents were the same. Only prepared to eat an apple if they had a signed suicide note from the tree. But there's no harm in them.'

'These ones are animal rights. I just didn't like the way they talked. About Bunny. And Horatio. They said the Mouse Police were exploited and companion animals were wrong and the best thing they could do was…'

'Hmm?' I prompted again, as Jason dried up.

'Put them out of their misery,' he said. 'But they aren't miserable, are they?'

'Ask Horatio,' I suggested, as food arrived on the plates from Daniel's pan.

Jason took me at my word.

'Are you unhappy, Horatio?' he asked, as Horatio sped past him, flicking the bacon rind, catching it, shaking it, and then sitting down for a brief chew. 'Didn't think so,' said Jason, and grabbed for a knife and fork.

I was just breaking the yolk of my second egg when Jason got up, put his cleaned and polished plate into the sink, and took his leave. The bunny book, apparently, said that rabbits should be allowed to exercise and he was off to bunny-proof the bathroom for this purpose. I wished him luck. In my experience an animal which really wishes to do something objectionable, such as shred the newspaper you are trying to read, will do so unless firmly locked into another room. And even then Bunny might chew through the door.

I gave up on that part of the newspaper, folding it so that Horatio could sit on it and wash his bacon-greasy whiskers. Which was what he had had in mind all along. For an exploited animal, he was doing rather well. Then again, a wealthy Roman might say that about his Greek-reading slave...

The wind was picking up again. I hate north winds. I sipped my (hot) coffee and read the less miserable bits of the paper as visible around tabby paws. Then I found a pencil and the other pages and Daniel and I started trying to do that dreadful general knowledge crossword which reminds me what an ignoramus I am.

'*Turkish premier, 1980,*' read Daniel.

'Haven't the faintest.'

'Me, neither. How about *Old Iranian word for tenant?*'

'You're making this up!' I accused.

'No, really,' he protested. I read over his shoulder. It was a very nice shoulder, muscular and warm...But we have a rule of at least going through all the questions, as though it was a quiz, because only once have we even come near finishing that crossword.

'No, Daniel, I do not know the old Iranian word for tenant,' I confessed, dropping a kiss on his neck.

'*Southern American stew with okra*,' he read. I clasped my hands. I might actually know this one!

'How many letters?'

'Five.'

'Gumbo!' I crowed.

'Fantastic. It fits, too. Okra. Now there's an unnecessary vegetable.'

'Slimy,' I agreed. 'Greeks love it, too. It's a vegetable thickener when you can't use eggs because of religious reasons.'

'Then why not use cornflour or rice?' he asked reasonably. 'No need to introduce okra into an otherwise unobjectionable dish. *Legendary Rumanian King.*'

'No idea.'

'Me neither. *Title of Estonian prince?*'

'Nope,' I said. 'You know, I really am an uneducated woman.'

Daniel grinned. 'Not as pig-ignorant as me. Any more coffee in the pot?'

'I'll make another. One cannot have too much coffee. Go on,' I said, getting up and filling the kettle again.

'Oh, really,' said Daniel. 'I don't know where they get all these questions! *Flowering tree of the genus Tilia*, four letters, third letter *m*.'

'We know that one! Trudi planted it. The lime. She wanted to be *Unter den Linden*. If the summer doesn't slay the poor little thing she's got a reasonable chance in a few years.'

'And we can sit under it and read Coleridge, "This Lime-Tree Bower My Prison". He did go on, though,' remarked Daniel, filling in the four hard-won letters.

'Poets are like that. Have some more coffee. What's next?'

He boggled briefly, then read, '*Diamond-shaped plane figure with four equal sides and no internal right angles. That ought to be a rhombus.*'

'Well, isn't it a rhombus?' I asked, ransacking my mind for the remains of my geometry.

'A square is just a term of a rhombus,' he said.

'Does rhombus fit?' I demanded, pouring coffee.

'It fits,' he said.

'Then put it in and don't press your luck,' I instructed.

He grumbled, but put it in. '*One of the spellings of the ancient Sumerian god of war.*'

'Sorry, my Sumerian isn't what it was.'

'*Established the Botany Department at Queensland University in 1893.*'

'Not the faintest.'

'*Floral emblem of the American state of Wisconsin.*'

'No,' I said sadly.

'Only a few more to go, thank God. In four letters, *Shade of brown.*'

'I know that. It's ecru, which it isn't, as ecru is ivory, but let it pass.'

'And here is another old favourite,' Daniel told me, biting the end of the pencil. '*Otherwise known as an etui.*'

'How many letters?'

'Six, with an *f* at the end.'

'Hussif, which is of course short for housewife, which is a little package of sewing things to repair uniforms and so on. Therese Webb collects them. Is that it?'

'That's it,' he said, giving the pencil a final munch before he slipped it back into the pencil case and turned to the sudoku, which he always—heroic man—does in biro.

'We did no worse than usual,' I observed, and found my novel. I was rereading Jade Forrester's memoirs. The first time through I had been so enthralled and horrified that I hadn't taken in any fine detail. I was just chuckling at her description of her foray into cross-dressing—tweed coat with leather elbows, white shirt, khaki trousers and army boots with steel toes—when the doorbell rang. Horatio woke and cursed, then resumed his nap. Poor exploited beast.

There was no one there when I opened the door but a leaflet lay on the doormat (a rather fetching coir mat from Oxfam). When I saw that it was from Against Domination Over Animals I took it between thumb and forefinger and laid it on the table. I knew about opening those leaflets from animal-rights people. Pictures of tortured animals made my stomach turn and proved indelible in the memory. I tried not to see them if I could avoid it. Moral cowardice, thy name is Chapman. Daniel looked up, his eyes abstracted, staring into the esoteric field of numbers.

'What's this? Junk mail?'

'From our student friends, I suspect. Can you bear to look at it?'

'Do I need to?'

'Just tell me if I can read it without throwing up.'

'For you,' he quoted Uncle Solly, 'the world. No, this is all text, and my, what drivel it is. You can read it—if you wish,' he told me, and dived back into the puzzle.

So I did, and drivel was too kind a word. Eating meat, it appeared, was responsible for all the problems of the world. War. Famine. Climate change. Menopause. Illiteracy. Blimey.

Daniel completed his puzzle, said 'Diabolical? I think not. Well, Corinna?'

I replied with another quote. From *King John*, which just proves, as Bertie Wooster would say, that Shakespeare was a very clever johnnie.

'Zounds, I was never so bethumped with words since first I called my brother's father dad. God, Daniel, I hope no one actually believes all this.'

He took the pamphlet from me and read a few paragraphs. He snorted. Horatio awoke again, gave him a severe look, and removed himself to the couch where a respectable cat could catch a few Zs without rude interruptions from the hoi polloi. Thus, incidentally, freeing up the rest of the newspaper should I have the nerve to read it.

'I see, meat-eating is responsible for Palestinian/Israeli con-flict. Because both Islam and Judaism ritually slaughter animals in a horrible way, we therefore wish to slaughter each other in equally horrible ways.' His eyebrows rose higher until they were almost into his hair.

'And that's the sensible opinion page,' I said. 'Read the medical news!'

He did. Then, very deliberately, he screwed up the pamphlet and flung it accurately into the wastepaper basket.

'There ought to be some sort of law against that kind of misinformation,' I said lamely.

'Too hard to frame,' he said. 'Nasty minds they have. And that was directed to young persons. Nice layout, pretty fonts, different colours…'

'And uses the old established hellfire method of scaring people into good behaviour.'

'Always worked in the past,' said Daniel.

'Has it?' I asked in turn. 'And you a member in good standing of those children of Israel who, as I remember, backslideth like a backsliding heifer.'

'My ancestors were rather known for disobedience, for which they always received a great heavenly foot from above,' confessed Daniel. 'Ho for the golden calf and bring back the fleshpots of Egypt. But we did give the western world a great gift,' he added, pulling me close and kissing my shoulder.

'What was that?'

'Guilt,' he told me. 'That's what this pamphlet will do. Might not turn people off meat but it will make them guilty about eating it. Of course, they are right, as Meroe will be the first to tell us,' he said, as the doorbell rang again and, coincidentally, Meroe appeared. Pamphlet in hand. Steaming around the edges of her ecru (as it happened) silk shawl. It was embroidered with bursts of yellow sunflowers which did not match the wearer's mood. She slung the shawl onto the couch (and over Horatio, who was not having the restful afternoon he had anticipated) and snarled, 'Have you read this…this…'

'Yes,' I said, to save her from trying to find a suitable expletive in English, not her first language.

'Sit down,' said Daniel companionably. 'Join the indignation meeting. I object to the politics, Corinna objects to the medical news. What is your objection? Can we offer you a nice glass of water or tea or—'

'Brandy,' said Meroe, breathing heavily. 'Then maybe some chamomile tea.'

I broke out the brandy and poured her a generous slug.

'I left Kylie in charge of the shop,' she said. 'She's still interested in the craft.' She took a deep gulp of the brandy and held out the glass for more. 'What is my objection? Simple. You know that I never eat meat. You know that I strive to make as little impact on the world as I can, to recycle, re-use and repair, to walk rather than ride. I was doing that forty years ago, when these…idiots…were not born.'

'We know,' I assured her.

'It is true that a lot of hunger and trouble would be either alleviated or prevented if everyone ate just vegetables and no one ate meat,' she told me, very earnestly. 'Meat animals are inefficient. Pasture uses a lot of water. Killing things to eat them is barbaric. This is well known.'

'Yes,' I said, one of the barbarians, filling the witch's glass again.

'So why are you so upset?' asked Daniel gently. 'They are saying all those things.'

'Mixed up with absurdities! The message ought to be simple. Eat more vegetables, less meat. Gradually wean the world off this cruel diet and these cruel practices. Explain patiently that we will cut down our karmic debt by being kind and compassionate to the other animals, of which we are just one species. Put across that the world is a goddess, Gaia, and she made us, and if we continue to try her patience and exploit her generosity she might just see how the earth looks without humans.'

'Cleaner,' I said.

'Greener,' said Daniel.

'And much, much quieter,' concluded Meroe. 'Some tea, Corinna, please. I must be calm. I am going to reason with those young persons and I must do it calmly. They are overstating the case, making it absurd. Their intentions might be noble but they are making all of us who try so hard to not bruise the feelings of the Goddess look like fools. Who believes such things as eating meat gives your children Attention Deficit Disorder? That eating meat starts wars? Pah!'

Entirely calm in no way whatsoever, Meroe threw down the pamphlet and sipped at her chamomile tea. I had not seen such a magnificent fit of righteous wrath for years. I was meanly glad that I wasn't going to be on the receiving end of it.

Our witch finished her tea, thanked us politely, removed the silk shawl from Horatio (who had decided that it made adequate bedding and had to be soothed and picked up very carefully so that he wouldn't lay a claw to the priceless fabric) and went out.

'Fireworks expected,' I commented to Daniel.

'They have it coming,' he said comfortably.

And he went on with the other sudoku, and I went back to my cross-dressing Jade Forrester. Silence, for a change, fell, except for the ever-present wind outside. And the doorbell rang—again.

'Now what?' I asked crossly. I hauled the door open with unnecessary force and Goss almost fell into my arms. She was crying like a fountain. In her hand was a half-eaten cold dough-nut and there was sugar all round her mouth. This decoration on a girl who only ever ate sugar-free everything, even chewing gum.

'Goss?' I said, bringing her inside and helping her to a chair.

'Can you feel them?' she demanded, pulling up her T-shirt and exposing her breasts. Daniel hastily took his sudoku into the study but Goss had not even noticed that he was there. I was amazed, but I did as she asked. I palpated gently over the small adolescent breasts. Her skin was like satin and the breast tissue, such as it was, was soft and natural. I patted her and pulled the T-shirt down.

'They're fine,' I told her.

Goss sobbed aloud and gulped at another mouthful of greasy doughnut.

'They're starting!' she said.

'What's starting? Come on, you don't want that doughnut. Drink this.' I administered more brandy—the bottle was emptying fast in these trying times—and put my arm around her.

'Lumps! You get breast cancer!' She sobbed again but she drank the brandy.

'From what?' I asked, still fogged.

'Eating meat!' she said. 'It was in this pamphlet!'

I tightened my hug and began to explain, very carefully, that no one had any proof that eating meat gave you breast cancer and that her breasts were perfectly lump-free and very decorative and she should not believe everything she read in pamphlets.

And as she calmed and drank her drink and accepted, finally, a tissue and then a glass of pineapple juice, I hoped, in my dark and vengeful soul, that Meroe was giving Against Domination Over Animals five or six different kinds of hell. And I couldn't think of a better person to deliver it. They were going to be very lucky if they didn't get to personally experience the life of that portion of the animal community which sits in damp places and goes 'redeep'. And they deserved it.

Chapter Ten

When fishes flew and forests walked
And figs grew upon thorn,
Some moment when the moon was blood,
Then, surely, I was born.

GK Chesterton
'The Donkey'

I have to go to bed early on Sunday because it's the dreaded four am start on Monday, so Daniel and I dined modestly on cheese, salad and the remains of the alcohol. He had made efforts to trace the missing phone callers. I had made a note to buy some more brandy. And cherries, of course.

No noise from below or above. The quiet was a little unsettling. I hoped that Meroe had turned them all into frogs. Toads, rather; frogs are quite cute, and endangered as well. Goss had finally calmed down and we had escorted her home to the soothing company of her cat, Tori, who had taken in the situation in one swift feline glance and demanded food and attention and hugs and had reinforced this by tangling around Goss' racehorse ankles. I'm still not sure how such a small elegant creature can actually manage this—surely there isn't enough cat to actually wind around ankles?—but she did it and Goss sat down by the fridge to feed Tori cream and recover. Shame to treat such a vulnerable young woman like that. I had it in for Against Domination Over Animals. All of them, including Rowan. Even if they did sing so beautifully.

Four am. Somehow it was worse on Mondays, because of the holidays before it, but it was worse for everyone, I sternly reminded myself, worse for all those poor office peons, worse for all those of my fellow shopkeepers who rose to feed and tend them, worse for the whole Monday-hating world.

I staggered down in my caftan to put on the first mixings, a little early. The air conditioner was kicking in as I went down the bakery steps, greeting me with a friendly blast of cold. The ovens roared into life. Fire and ice, I thought, what was the theory? Velikovsky, *Worlds in Collision*? I really needed more coffee if I was going to think philosophically this early in the morning.

The Mouse Police bounced awake, displaying the night's vermin harvest of four dead rats and a couple of big moths. I rewarded them with kitty dins, disposed of the deceased and washed my hands. Mixers on, yeast seething, coffee pot on, coffee!

I sat down in the baker's chair to drink it. And found myself contemplating, not 'what would the world be like without humans?' but 'what would my life have been without companion animals?'

Sadder. Colder. My parents were not affectionate and Grandma and Grandpa Chapman, who had adopted me, were not demonstrative. Also there had been school, which was a living hell. But there had also been Randolph, my mongrel sort of kelpie cross, who had done nothing for his whole harmless life from squeaking puppy to venerable old codger except sleep at the foot of my bed, miss me when I was gone, wait for me to get home, accompany me on those long miserable adolescent walks where I wished I was dead, and lick my face whenever I would let him because he liked the taste of tears. I could complain to Randolph about school where I could not talk to Grandma, because she was paying so much money for me to go there. I could confide in Randolph and he would never, never tell.

His only vices had been an inordinate greed for cheese, which he would even steal out of the shopping basket, and a habit of destruct-chewing thong sandals. When he died I had cried for three days. Tears still came to my eyes when I thought of him.

And during my unhappy marriage there had always been cats—because James hated dogs. He didn't like cats, either, but they were easier to ignore, though Mistinguette, a silver-grey tabby with a cynical turn of mind, would always seek out and steal small objects of his, like one cufflink or a cigarette lighter, and stash them under the fridge for future reference. It was very hard to fish anything out from under the fridge. When I divorced James and went back to the house to clean and move the furniture, I was amazed at the collection in that big square patch of greasy dust. Olaf and then Mistinguette had been companionable, beautiful, soft to stroke and to sleep with, affectionate when they felt like being affectionate. A little censorious when they felt that I was not living up to their standards. I looked at the Mouse Police, Heckle and Jekyll, crunching their kitty dins with gusto. A black and white pair; rough company, perhaps, but agreeable. In the old days they would have made very good ship's cats. I could see them swaggering off the ship in Balboa, looking for mates and boasting about the fight they had won with the pirates in the South China Sea. And I considered Horatio, that purring gentleman with his immaculate white front, a pleasure to look at and to hold.

No, without companion animals, however wrong, Corinna would have been sadder and lonelier. They decorated my life and I was lucky to have them.

Jason came in, dressed in his baker's whites, saluted the quarterdeck (i.e., me) and asked 'Orders, Cap'n?'

'Better make rosewater muffins, Mr. Midshipman, and maybe we should freeze a few for the future. Your devoted fan Serena came and demanded some yesterday morning and I only had rosewater and bread to give her. And put cherries, raspberries, a big bottle of brandy and rosewater on the shopping list. The rye is on and the pasta douro is ready, I'll just go up and change. You can let the Mouse Police out. You have the helm, Mr. Midshipman.'

He saluted again and I left the vessel *Earthly Delights* to him as I climbed up to put on my overall and bring down the brie for his experimental cheese muffins. I do not deserve him, either.

Daniel was still asleep and I didn't wake him. He had a list of things to do today, including a lot of interviews. Whereas I made bread, that was what I did, and I went downstairs again to do it.

I was just trying a brie muffin—scrumptious, gooey in the middle and crispy on the top—when I heard hoofs. I exchanged glances with Jason as he took the tray of rosewater muffins out of the oven and pried one loose, waving it in the air conditioning jet stream to cool it down. But instead of a benevolent grey furry face looking in through the door there was the flowered hat and pin-sharp eyes of Mr. Pahlevi. Pin-sharp nose, too, which wiggled at the end.

'Good morning, lady!' he said to me. 'You got any of them rose cakes?'

'Good morning,' I replied. 'How is Serena?'

I grabbed a muffin and slipped out past him. I found the donkey laden with her panniers, each one now filled with bunches of flowers. I had seen such beasts of burden in Greece, the only sensible way of carrying things through the narrow streets of, for instance, Mykonos. Serena greeted me politely. I slipped an experimental finger under some of the straps. None of them seemed to be chafing. She was fragrant with tuberoses, lilies and orchids. I gave her the muffin and she scoffed it. I stroked her satiny ears.

'She's all right,' Mr. Pahlevi assured me. 'We get flowers when the market opens, then sell them fast; flowers don't last in hot weather. Then we walk back to stable. Now, rose cakes, lady?'

I sold him three of the cooled muffins. He fed Serena one and kept the other two. She allowed him to lead her down into Flinders Lane.

The paperboy flung his payload at me, missed, and biked off before Heckle could do more than meditate revenge. I allowed the Mouse Police back in past my ankles and found Meroe with her basket, staring after the donkey.

'That's your Serena?' she asked. 'Do you know the man?'

'Mr. Pahlevi,' I told her. Meroe whisked herself and basket inside and shut the door, hard. Then she slumped down in my chair and gulped the remains of my coffee even though she seldom drinks coffee. She was very pale. She needed time to pull herself together so I addressed Jason.

'Jason, do me a favour and put on another pot of coffee? How are the rest of the cakes coming along?'

'Grouse, Cap'n,' said my apprentice. 'How was the cheesy one?'

'Fantastic. But the ingredients cost a fortune. Too expensive for the shop.' His face fell. I hated to disappoint him. I had to come up with something and I did. 'I was thinking—what say we do a fancy platter, like we do with sandwiches, for executive Christmas parties? One mouthful, easy to eat. Little exquisite muffins, say brie, ham…'

'Bacon,' Jason corrected me. 'Crispier. Zucchini and mozzarella, carrot and apple, walnut and blueberry, perhaps some spicy ones, like your fave Thai curry puffs? Cheese and sweet chilli sauce? And choccie ones, and rosewater and raspberry, Christmas pudding, drunken apricot…'

'All of those,' I told him. 'We've already got orders for sandwiches. The Stock Exchange party is next week—they've been asking about your muffins. Make up a price list and a menu and we can email it to them. And if you do the work, you get half the fee. And I buy the ingredients.'

'Sweet!' He remembered his role as Hornblower. 'I mean, aye, aye, Captain! Coffee ready, Cap'n!'

'Pour a cup for Meroe, then, and steady as she goes, Mr. Midshipman. Carry on.'

He saluted again and turned back to the ovens. I watched Meroe heap sugar into her coffee and gulp it down scalding.

'Better?'

She nodded, made a magical gesture in the air and sat up straighter.

'Anything I can do?' I asked. It does not do to force the confidence of a witch.

'Does he come here every morning?' she asked.

'Serena does. The donkey. She's a rose addict and Jason makes these amazing rosewater and raspberry muffins. She's got away from her owner a couple of times, so now he's decided to just buy the muffins. Donkeys are very determined beasts.'

'Yes. I once knew a donkey who loved roses.'

She didn't say anything else. Meroe, when she has nothing to say, says nothing. I got on with chopping the dates for Jason's oasis muffins. This took concentration because they had been soaked in orange flower water, which made them soft and slushy. After a while I abandoned the knife and just squished them between my fingers, harvesting the stones.

Jason had racked the cooked bread and was putting the next load into the oven when there was a tentative knock at the Calico Alley entrance. At this, Meroe picked up her basket and actually ran up my inner stairs into my apartment and slammed the door. Jason looked at me. I shrugged.

'Whatever,' he commented, and opened the door.

There was Rowan, barely visible behind a huge bunch of irises.

'Came to say I'm sorry about my friends,' he mumbled.

'Your friends are not your fault,' I told him. Then, as he just stood there, red in the face and melting with embarrassment, I asked, 'Are those for me?'

'For Goss,' he said. 'I met this man and donkey and I thought maybe she might forgive me if…'

'I think she might,' I said. 'But she got a severe shock. You shouldn't hand out misinformation like that.'

'I didn't…I mean, I wouldn't…Meroe said…I'm sorry…'

'All right,' I said. Poor boy could probably go on like this for hours unless someone rescued him. 'Goss won't be up yet. Come in and have a muffin while you wait?'

'No, thanks, Corinna, I just wanted to say…I don't think there is anything wrong with companion animals.'

And he blushed himself out, laden down with herbage. Heckle, Jekyll, Jason and I looked at each other.

'Anything for a weird life,' said my midshipman eventually. 'What about carrot and walnut?'

'How are you going to make little muffins?' I asked.

I should have known that he would have thought of that.

'Simple, just allow for the shorter baking time and use these little muffin cases. I've been trying them. Burnt the first ones to a crisp. Now I reckon I've got it about right.'

'Good. Nut combinations are popular. Pecans? Pine nuts?'

'I reckon we've got enough nuts around here this morning,' he muttered.

I had to agree.

Fortunately the rest of the morning was as usual. Kylie came into the shop. She reported that Goss had stopped probing her bosom for lumps and was reclining on the couch with Tori, watching a few *Sex in the City* DVDs. I tried one of the oasis muffins, scented with orange flower water, juicy with dates, and topped with orange icing and crystallised peel. Superb. Customers lingered in the shop, unwilling to go out into the heat again, which made it crowded but meant that they added a little extra something to the parcel or bag while they were waiting. The carrier arrived to take away the restaurants' bread. The racks began to empty.

Mrs. Dawson purchased four of the oasis muffins and told Jason they reminded her of Egypt, pyramids and exotic places without the accompaniment of beggars, sand and mosquitos. She had invited the Professor to lunch and needed sourdough for her smoked salmon and cream cheese sandwiches. Mrs. Pemberthy made Jason bring her bread to the door because I meanly refused to allow her rotten little doggie Traddles into my nice clean shop.

The Hollidays came in to advise that they were going on— as it were—holiday, and promised to send a postcard from Queenscliff. Goss and Kylie were looking after Calico, their cat, mother of Tori. I wished them bon voyage with muffins. Trudi bought two loaves, one for herself and one for the pigeons she attracts to the roof, hoping thus to persuade a kestrel to nest there. So far this has not worked but occasionally Lucifer tries to catch a pigeon. He's fast, and if he had not been on a harness would probably have flown one to the ground.

Therese Webb bought several loaves of the pasta douro for her craft luncheon. She and Jason exchanged ideas about sandwiches for vegetarians, in which they both became engrossed.

'Not grated carrot and sultanas again,' said Therese.

'Please,' said a voice from the door. 'Not grated carrot and sultanas.' The speaker was Janeen, the Soup Run medical student and one of the singers. I wondered that she could possibly associate herself with that pamphlet.

'What, then?' asked Therese, who had not been privy to the argument about the pamphlet and probably hadn't read the pamphlet. She only tends to read knitting patterns and Tolstoy.

'What about roasted peppers and onions and eggplant, lots of different sorts of tomato?'

'Sounds good,' said Jason judicially.

'Cucumber, hummus, baba ganoush, grated beetroot, any cheese but goat's cheese?' pleaded Janeen. 'Cream cheese and walnut, my favourite.'

'Good,' said Therese.

'Grouse,' said Jason. 'Have a brie muffin?'

'No animal products?' she demanded.

'Well, except the brie,' he said. 'I make the savoury ones with olive oil. No butter.'

'Thanks. Some butter is mixed with lard or GM canola.' She shuddered at the thought, then bit the muffin, which produced the right expression on her thin fanatic's face. She actually smiled. She was quite pretty when she smiled. Jason, who had shuddered at the idea that he might use butter made of anything else but one hundred per cent butter fat derived from milk, smiled in turn.

'I'm going to the deli,' Therese told us, and took her wheelie basket away.

'What can we do for you, Janeen?' I asked. I was still not impressed with that pamphlet.

'You're cross with us,' she observed.

'Certainly am. You nearly scared Goss into a conniption. You, a medical student, ought to know better.'

'I didn't see it,' she said. 'I only read the thing this morning. After the local witch descended on us and nearly cursed us last night.'

'You had it coming,' I reminded her.

'I know. Most of us aren't idiots, really. Sarah got a delivery of them from America and thought it would be a good idea to spread the message.'

'Wrong message,' I said flatly.

'Yes. Sorry. Really, I am sorry,' she insisted. 'Perhaps we can make it up to you? What about a little concert?'

'I'll think about it,' I told her. 'I'll ask the others. Did you come for some bread?'

'Loaf of wholemeal,' she sighed. I wasn't going to forgive her yet. Jason, who is a sucker for people who appreciate his cooking, gave her change and watched her go out, her thin shoulders sagging.

'She really is sorry,' he told me.

'Perhaps,' I said.

'Meroe cursed them?' asked Kylie, agog.

'No,' I said. 'She just nearly cursed them. If she had really cursed them, they would not be buying bread.'

'But catching flies with their tongues,' guessed Kylie.

'Indeed.'

'Euw,' she commented.

Then we sold more bread. The Pandamus family at Cafe Delicious have invested in a slushy machine which produces a very creditable granita and Jason did a cold drink run for Kylie and me. Grapefruit granita almost reconciles me to summer. Just not quite.

Quite soon it was lunchtime and the bread walked out the door. Summer equals salads and sandwiches and for both you need bread. I lunched on Greek salad, one of the world's great meals—crispy cucumber, onion and tomato, luscious feta. Jason dined on moussaka (first course) then beef stifado (main course) then five scoops of different ice cream with wafers (dessert). And a bottle of Coke. Kylie averted her eyes and nibbled an undressed stick of celery and three cherry tomatoes.

By the time two o'clock rolled around I was pooped. I loaded the sack for the Soup Run, cashed up and left the banking for Kylie, left Jason with the cleaning and trailed up to my apartment. I was intending to have a wash and perhaps a nap, if Daniel had gone out. Which he had. If he was staying—and I hoped fervently that he was—we were going to have to get a bigger bed. With Horatio and Daniel there just wasn't room for me as well. Meroe was not there. She must have just been passing through. Why was a stout-hearted witch afraid of Mr. Pahlevi of the pin-sharp countenance? Had she known Serena before? What, in fact, was going on?

As I had no answers, I washed and changed. I missed the luxurious baths of yesteryear, before the Big Dry. Ah, I could imagine telling someone's very bored grandchildren twenty years hence, in the old days I used to have a full bath every day! And they wouldn't believe me, having been cleansed from childhood with a wet washer and a cup of warm water. There isn't water like that, they would say, and what's more there never was. Such is history.

Sky blue and indigo caftan, shucking the overall. Sandals instead of the strong heavy baker's shoes. Bliss. I made myself a cool lemon drink and found Jade Forrester again.

She was excellent company for a cool day inside. But even Jade's fascinating narrative couldn't prevent me from gently falling asleep on the couch, with Horatio before me on the coffee table, where he appreciated the coolness of the glass top on his furry tummy. And, very strangely in view of the pace of events at Insula lately, nothing happened to wake me until Daniel kissed me and it was six o'clock.

'I've got salt beef and salads from Uncle Solly's,' he told me. 'Come and eat, *metuka*, I have to go out again in a moment.'

'How was your day?' I murmured, coming slowly to the surface.

'Confusing. I talked to Melissa. Well, I tried to talk to Melissa. All she says is "whatever". I can't work out if she is an idiot or afraid of something.'

'Could be both,' I said, spooning out Uncle Solly's famed creamy potato and mayonnaise with spring onions.

'I suppose,' said my beloved, piling pickles onto his salt beef on pumpernickel. 'I probably should have loosed Goss onto her. How is the poor girl, by the way?'

'All right,' I told him. 'Almost convinced that she isn't going to die today.' I told him about the repentance of poor Rowan and the apology delivered by Janeen. He paused halfway through a gherkin.

'I forgot to tell you. The freegans called to leave you a present.' He ate the pickle and rummaged in his satchel. The present was a used paper bag, carefully smoothed out. On it someone had written in bright blue calligraphy *Old Brewery Site.*

'Cryptic,' I said.

'Isn't it just?'

'What, do you suppose, this means?' I persisted, removing the gherkins and holding them out of reach, in order to capture his attention. Daniel considered the question.

'Possibly it is a freegan joke. Possibly it is a mistake. Possibly it is the hiding place of our fugitive couple.'

'And so…' I dangled a gherkin near his mouth.

'I'm going to wander around there tonight,' he said. I posted the pickle, which he crunched hastily—presumably in case I changed my mind.

'But first,' I told him, 'we have to see the Lone Gunmen. They left you a message. They have something to tell you about those phone numbers you wanted them to trace.'

We concluded dinner with iced tea and went down through Insula to the lurking place of our very own resident computer experts. Hephaestus was the smith of the gods in the Good Old Days when a deity was likely to manifest himself in every passing bush to every passing shepherdess. He was crippled and cruelly treated, poor Hephaestus, illicit child of Mars and Venus. None of those things applied to our nerds, unless the crippling was social. They really didn't get on with people, except other computer nerds. In fact, when we knocked at the door, we were greeted by a man in a T-shirt which read DON'T BE AFRAID, YOU'RE AMONG GEEKS HERE. And otherwise only a rather inadequate pair of torn boxers. Not a pretty sight.

Rat blushed pink and retreated behind the door. Taz, who has the most savoir faire, opened it, letting us in and crushing his housemate against the wall.

'Come in!' he invited. He himself was wearing a fetching sarong with purple hibiscus on it. The flat was clean enough, as they employed a cleaner. We had demanded that they do so after the smell had made Mrs. Pemberthy sick. That was to be expected, she being highly sensitive, as she says herself, but it had also made her rotten little doggie, Traddles, sick. Once it had been drawn to their attention that their deep midden of old pizza boxes and half-empty Coke cans and very antique under-wear was rendering them prone to prosecution under the toxic waste laws, they had acted. More swiftly, perhaps, because Del Pandamus was threatening to thump them because Hephaestus is located next door to Cafe Delicious and the stench was ruining his customers' appetites. They had hastily employed a cleaner who came every week. A woman who must have demonstrated that she was proof against conditions similar to that of Scutari hospital before Miss Nightingale arrived. A purge of appalling proportions had ensued. The rubbish men had to be specially bribed to take the suppurating stuff away. Since then her once-a-week visits served to keep the premises on this side of squalor.

No one could do anything about their tastes in food, of course, which inclined purely toward junk. If it didn't have chilli sauce in it, they weren't interested. Unless chilli sauce could be poured onto it. There were three of them, the Lone Gunmen, named after the nerds in the *X-Files*: Taz, who was relatively respectable; Rat, who was presently trying to get himself, his rat-tail hair and his boxers out from behind the door without indecent exposure; and Gully, who was the most plump and the most affable. Gully's mum came every week and collected their dirty clothes, returning them pristine enough to get chilli sauce on again. Another one of our humble heroines.

But what they didn't know about computers, their use and misuse, you could put in your eye without any impairment of vision. They had narrowly escaped being charged with an interesting collection of computer offences by offering free help to the Victoria Police Electronics Unit in any little computer puzzle they might encounter. I used to do their accounts. They made a reasonable living from selling games and operating systems, supplemented with appearances at a nightclub dressed as witches (yes, it is confusing, but that's life in Insula). Lately they had taken to opening the shop only when they felt like it and their lights burnt all night. I had wondered what they were doing, and hoped that it was sort of licit. They wouldn't like prison, which seldom has wireless broadband.

'Daniel!' exclaimed Gully, looking up from a search for the last crumbs in a bag of corn chips. 'We've got those phone numbers for you.'

'Legally?' asked Daniel, taking the piece of paper.

'Of course, it's all on the web somewhere, you just have to know where to look. We know where to look. But we're still running that code. Rat's dedicated a whole day's run time to it and we aren't getting anywhere. It must be a one-time or a book.'

He said this as though describing a strange and arcane piece of technology. The Lone Gunmen don't read a lot.

'Have a chip,' offered Rat, now clothed in heavy winter-weight jeans. He had the look of a man who wasn't going to take them off any time soon. I took one of his corn chips. I bit it. Bad idea. It was, naturally, chilli-flavoured.

'Give it another couple of hours,' Taz offered. 'Since you're an old customer.'

'All right, boys, thanks,' said Daniel.

'You've been busy,' I said as casually as I could. 'Working all night. Something special on?'

'Facebook,' said Taz, just short of a gloat.

'Facebook?'

'People put all sorts of information on Facebook,' Gully explained, as though talking to a very small and stupid child. I tried not to be offended. Compared to them, I was a small and stupid child. 'And then they grow up and regret talking about how much they fancied their English teacher and—boys do this all the time—how often they came that morning while they were in the bathroom. Or how big their…well, you know.'

'Euw,' I said, quoting Kylie.

Taz rescued his embarrassed friend.

'Or the information is false—put on by someone else. And there's no way to remove it. You don't want to spend your whole life with a freely available picture of yourself vomiting over a dog at a buck's night, for instance, which is the one I am working on at present. Or with a blue bow tied around your…well, you get the picture.'

Taz was silenced in his turn. They really were maidenly. It was a charming trait.

'Or with the slogan *Cathy is a slut* or *William has herpes*,' put in Rat. 'Only way to get the info off the net is to employ the very best hackers—i.e., us,' he said with justifiable pride. 'We can't keep up with the demand. We've brought in Taz's little bro and his buddy for the easy ones. But Taz's mum won't let them work at night. Actually we were going to ask you for some investment advice,' he added.

'Certainly,' I said. 'Stay out of property and buy super-annuation—I can direct you to a very good accountant. Isn't that Facebook thing the poison-pen matter you were working on, Daniel?'

'Yes, and I must say that the Lone Gunmen came to the rescue with great dispatch. The client is delighted and the money is in your account. However, they still haven't found out who did it.'

'Matter of time,' Taz assured him. 'He or she will go online again, and then they will fall into our little trap, and then we will have them! Ah ha ha ha!' He began to emit big villainous manic laughs until silenced by the stares of the others.

'Sorry, channelling Dr Phibes there for a moment. That all, Daniel? Only we have to get back to work.'

'That's all,' said Daniel, and we refused the offer of another corn chip and left Hephaestus. Our own apartment seemed so spacious and cool in comparison.

There being some time available until I had to go to sleep and Daniel had to go hunting in the old brewery, we made good use of it. I eventually went to sleep with a mouth swollen from kisses as sweet as honey.

Chapter Eleven

Deck the halls with boughs of holly,
Fa la la la la, la la la la

Trad.

Four am is such a ghastly hour that I didn't really notice that Daniel had not come back until I had fed Horatio, sipped away two cups of coffee and eaten my sourdough toast with cherry jam.

Something was missing from my apartment, I thought vaguely. Furniture? All there. Horatio? Under the table retrieving yesterday's chewed bacon rind (and I had the nerve to criticise the Lone Gunmen's housekeeping). Ah, yes. No Daniel. I checked the spare bedroom, where he sometimes crashes if he doesn't want to risk waking me. Nothing but the heaps of junk which are usually there. Ergo, he had not come back here last night after searching the brewery. He must have gone home to his own little flat. Ah, well, I was not fit for company early in the morning, anyway. Into the baker's overall and solid shoes, down the stairs, Mouse Police, litter tray, wash hands again, put on bakery coffee pot, greet Jason who was scowling furiously over several small red objects.

I was getting a little tired of Jason's titanic struggle with the glacé cherry. So I barked, 'Mr. Midshipman!' and watched him jump.

'Sir!' he saluted. 'Think I've almost got them now, sir!'

I examined the little red sphere. Translucent. Shiny. Yielding but not soft. I bit. Tasted very good. But…

Jason anticipated me as I tried to form a sentence which wouldn't offend him.

'I know,' he said, throwing up his hands. 'I know! I've made a real genuine plastic cherry!'

'Jason,' I began, 'it's a good cherry. A very good cherry.'

'But it's like the bought ones!' he wailed.

I was not in the mood to indulge anyone's tantrums, including my own. I put a hand on his distraught shoulder and shook him lightly.

'Enough of this. Midshipman, we have bread to bake. Tomorrow—not today—you can buy some more cherries and try another recipe. If it's any comfort,' I added, as we hauled out sacks and began measuring flour, 'I once made a perfect commercial tomato soup out of totally fresh ingredients. I have never been so disappointed. But I got over it and so will you. That's an order!'

'Aye, aye, sir,' he mumbled.

We mixed. We baked. The morning grew lighter outside in Calico Alley. I was listening for hoofs, but Serena's supply of rosewater muffins must have been secure. Heckle and Jekyll nosed out for Kiko's tuna scraps, then nosed back, beating the paperboy. He never even slowed when taking the sharp right into Flinders Lane these days, knowing how I felt about people who maimed innocent cats. Therefore it was not surprising that there was a yelp, a howl, and the crash of a bicycle hitting the cobbles.

'Break out the first-aid box, Jason,' I told him, and went out to the scene of the carnage.

It was, of course, poor Rowan on his morning run who had been flattened by the bike and was actually wounded, while the paperboy was uninjured except for his pride. I hauled the bike off the student and helped him, once more, into the bakery, to sit in the chair again and be tended. I told the paperboy that if he rode at that speed down my alley one more time I would have the law on him and he went away, the back wheel wobbling and a whole city full of papers to deliver. Which just about served the little ratbag right, though that didn't help our fellow tenant, who had re-scraped his shin and skinned the other knee. He was also much begrimed by contact with the unswept cobbles and looked upset.

On the other hand, Heckle was sitting on his foot, licking his nearest injury, and was radiating comradely piratical affection. 'That's the stuff, m'lad,' you could hear the evil-minded rogue cat saying. 'Only next time, pink 'em in the plexus with a cutlass.'

While Heckle was shivering his timbers and Jason was rescuing the bread, I was mopping blood and dust off Rowan. He regained his breath and tried to smile.

'You know, I'm beginning to wonder if all this exercise is really healthy,' he quipped, which was a pretty good quip for six am, delivered by a boy with a heavy black and white cat on his foot.

'Coffee, Coke, water or tea?' asked Jason. 'Muffin or roll?'

'Water,' said Rowan automatically, then grinned an unexpected wild grin. 'Coke,' he said.

'Don't worry, we won't tell on you,' Jason assured him.

'In that case,' said Rowan boldly, 'is that bacon I can smell?'

Well, that was a surprise. Jason turned out his tray of experimental bacon and zucchini mini muffins—a mouthful of delight, each one—and put two into Rowan's hand. The one which didn't have damaged knuckles. 'I miss bacon most,' he said sadly. 'And salami.'

'All the preserved meats,' I commented, drying his knee so that the bandaid would stick.

'Smoked salmon, beef jerky, ham, Uncle Solly's salt beef.' Jason sang it almost like a litany. 'I'd hate to give them all up. Why did you?'

'Have to do something,' said Rowan through his mouthful. 'Planet can't afford us. Also, my grandfather used to eat steaks, terrible steaks oozing blood, and he'd cut off bits for me, and then he and my dad would make me eat them. And if I was sick they'd make me eat more.'

Just remembering this, the boy's face was as white as milk and his eyes seemed very old. He gulped his Coke. Jason patted his shoulder. I patted the other shoulder.

'Can't think of a better recipe to make a vegetarian,' I said. 'There you are. Heckle, get off his foot, please.'

Heckle looked at me. He knew his name, all right. However, he declined to take any notice of my polite request. This was his old shipmate he was tending.

'No, he's fine,' said Rowan, caressing the ticket-punch ears. 'He's a good old cat. And he likes the taste of blood. I don't. Anyway, if he drinks my blood, he won't go stalking out into the night, waylaying innocent victims…'

'The curse of the cat!' said Jason, delighted. He loves horror movies.

'Eyes alight with demonic fire, he slinks out of a respectable bakery and finds his prey on the dark streets of a city called… Melbourne,' Rowan went on.

By the time that Meroe and Mrs. Dawson came past, arm in arm, the bakery was rollicking. Jason had taken instantly to work songs when I had taught him 'Deep River' on one memorably bronchitic morning. Rowan, naturally, knew all of them, and managed to sing whatever part we weren't more or less covering.

When Meroe and Mrs. Dawson joined in a spirited rendering of 'Swing Low, Sweet Chariot', I was sure that Mrs. Pemberthy was going to fling open her window and shriek at us, but we never heard a word out of her, though we did hear Traddles barking.

Possibly, Mrs. P recognised the voices, and didn't feel like exposing herself to another squish from Mrs. Dawson.

The coffee pot being on, we all had a cup of our chosen beverage and a muffin from one of Jason's experimental trays. I realised that I was happy. My fellow inhabitants were glowing with harmony. The coffee tasted wonderful, Jason's drunken apricot muffin was superb. When Goss arrived to open the shop, she thought we must all have been imbibing far too early in the morning.

'Like, Corinna, you're partying hard!' she reproved.

Mrs. Dawson patted her cheek.

'There are other reasons for singing, thank God,' she told her.

The party broke up. Rowan limped off to Perseus, his apartment, to recover. Jason went back to considering new sub-forms of the species muffin. Meroe went to open her shop, the Sibyl's Cave. Horatio descended to Earthly Delights to take his throne near the cash register and greet some old familiar clients.

'How are you feeling, Goss?' I asked as lightly as I could.

'Like, all right, sort of,' she said. That didn't tell me much. 'I had breakfast,' she added. This was good. Goss reverted to a complete fast when she was miserable.

'Good,' I told her. 'Can you make up a couple of platters when you've got a moment? Jason is cooking those little muffins for a corporate party.'

'Do it now,' she offered. 'Those little muffins are wasted on all those suits.'

'Go to it,' I encouraged. There were always spoiled or slightly burnt muffins for the assembler. I hoped she might eat a few. I turned away to tidy the ranks of bread in their metal racks and heard the door open with its little tinkle.

'Do you have vegan bread?' asked someone just appearing in a shaft of sunlight, like an angel.

She wasn't, but she was beautiful. Reed-slim Sarah with her mermaid hair arrayed around her. It fell to her waist in a golden cascade. I was in no mood for her.

'I can do you spelt,' I said. 'Low gluten. No animal products.'

'Thank you,' she said. Had she come to apologise, too? Horatio looked at her and turned his head away in a pointed snub which she did not notice. I fancy that Sarah didn't notice much that didn't support her views.

'Four-fifty,' I said, and held out my hand for the money. She rummaged in her jeans pocket. Designer jeans, I noticed.

'I'm right, you know,' she told me.

'That must be nice for you,' I said.

'But maybe I should have read those pamphlets before I gave them out,' she temporised.

'And maybe a merry round of "ring and run" isn't the height of moral courage,' I replied.

She toyed with her hair. She wasn't looking at me anymore. She was looking at Jason. And Jason, thunderstruck, was looking right back at her. Sarah smiled a Mona Lisa smile that I just wanted to belt with a baguette. Seduce my apprentice, would she? The hussy!

'Come up to rehearsal tonight?' she cooed at him. He nodded, unable to speak. Then the vision of loveliness left the shop.

There was really nothing I could say, though I wanted to warn him about reed-slim fanatics and I could not imagine what she wanted with Jason and it couldn't be good, so instead I asked, 'How is Bunny?'

Jason still exhibited the blithe indifference of the recently smitten.

'Oh, he's good. The bunny book said that I should lie down on the floor next to him. Bunnies like to snuggle but they don't like to lie on your lap like a cat does. So I did and he hopped up beside me and sniffed me a bit and then he just lay down. We're getting on fine,' he said, still exalted.

'And your muffins?' I asked, sniffing in my turn.

'Oh, shit!' He ran back into the bakery.

Just what I needed. A complication. Horatio twitched an ear. He was right. We had bread to sell.

'Oh, and we need to put up the decorations,' I called into the bakery.

'Ooh,' came back Goss' voice. 'Fantastic! Have you got some groovy ones?'

Groovy, my lord; I missed out on groovy the first time and now it is back—and I've missed out on it again. Still, I am not feeling robbed about that. There are a lot of other words for 'good'.

'Very groovy,' I yelled back. 'I got some from Mrs. Dawson and the rest online from Oxfam. They just arrived.'

'Corinna, what's wrong with Jason?'

'I don't know, what's he doing?' Luckily, there were no patrons in the shop at present.

'Standing in front of a lot of muffins and looking stupid.'

'It's all right, he's just fallen in love with a blonde goddess.'

'What, the skinny blonde bitch?' demanded Goss.

'Moderate your tone for a young man in his first infatuation,' I told her, going to the door. 'Have you done those platters yet?'

'All done.' She showed me artistically displayed muffins, carefully set around with sprigs of Christmas greenery (edible: you never know with corporate parties, and I didn't want anyone to develop holly poisoning and sue the shop).

'Lovely,' I said sincerely. 'You have a real talent for design. Why don't you tag along with Cherie next year when she goes to RMIT and does that fashion and fabric course?'

'Might,' said Goss. 'Our acting career hasn't taken off yet and Dad will pay the fees. He'd love it if I went back to school.'

'Well, there you are,' I said, far too soon.

'But I wouldn't,' she said. 'I'm too old.'

'Cherie's older than you,' I told her, than abandoned the subject before it became a sore point. 'Come advise me where to put all these lovely things.'

Jason was packing his muffins into boxes for the fridge, carefully, though his eyes were still abstracted. I had preferred him when he was obsessing about glacé cherries, but that just shows, as the Professor would say, the vanity of human wishes.

Actually, decorating the shop was quite fun. Goss has an excellent eye for where things will look their best. We hung the ice-drops and the glittering balls where they could not be knocked or broken by a careless shopper, and the plastic snowflakes from Guatemala and the other delicate things from the ceiling. The Oxfam crib sat on the counter. It was made of solid carved wood and probably wouldn't fracture if it fell. There were the animals who attended the birth of the child: the ox, the ass, the sleeping dog, the sheep and goats, the chickens and the ducks.

'Invented by St Francis of Assisi,' said a cultivated voice. It was Dion, our professor, the most charming and erudite man, except he won't explain the joke about the little doll in the bottle at Meroe's shop. One day I shall pin him down and tickle him until he tells me.

One day. Not today. He came in under the swag of artistically crafted ivy and holly, which hung so low that it brushed his white hair.

'St Francis of Assisi?' Goss asked, speaking from her shoeless height atop the counter.

'He wanted the Italians to be nicer to his friends the animals, so he reminded them that Christ had been born in a stable, because there was no room in the inn,' said the Professor. 'He built the first one—you know, Corinna dear, my memory really is failing—yes, it was in Greccio, I believe, in about 1223; St Francis set up a manger in the snow in the mountains of Umbria. Then, of course, the painters started painting it, and soon everyone had a wooden—this is a very nice piece of carving—or a pottery or a painted manger to remember, or perhaps I mean appreciate, that the first attendants of the Christ child were animals, and the first visitors were shepherds…a lovely idea.'

'It's hand-carved,' I said, caressing the wooden curve of the ass' ears. 'Mrs. Dawson lent it to me.'

'It all looks very seasonal,' he said, pleased.

When his wife of many years left him all alone in the world, the Professor had sold his house and most of his possessions (except his library) and had bought his apartment in Insula outright. He had required Dionysus to be decorated in proper Roman fashion and had commissioned a lot of Roman furniture to be especially made for him. Insula, for instance, has the very first and probably only example of the Roman television and DVD player cabinet. He lined the walls with bookshelves (Western, because he has only a few scrolls) and moved in to complete his study of Juvenal, comforting his broken heart with red wine, cultural activities and lunches with his old friends on the faculty. He naturally acquired me and the other Insulae as friends. And then Nox arrived in his life, a small black kitten with a whim of iron, who has him firmly under paw. But she is very nice to him as long as he does not come between her and anything resembling a prawn. I have seen her leap off high shelves onto the delivery man's tray if there are prawns on the pizza. The advent of a determined little black furry missile always makes the delivery person drop the box and then Nox is free to hunt and guzzle. But otherwise she is a benevolent despot and has even been seen—but not in this weather—parading the roof in a rather fashionable red harness.

Lately, I have wondered about Professor Dion's relationship with Mrs. Dawson. They seem to get on very well and she is a widow in the same way he is a widower. Both of them were happily married for a long time. But they are both so old, and in any case it is none of my business. I shook myself.

'Bread?' I asked.

He smiled benevolently as Goss jumped down from the counter and dived back into the bakery for more loaves.

'I am having a little gathering at Christmas,' he told me, 'for people who do not have any interest in the festival, or who perhaps might feel a little lonely, as I would. If you and Daniel have no plans, perhaps…'

'Accepted,' I said promptly. 'Let me know the time and what I should bring. Thank you! Now, can I serve you?' I asked.

'If only you had asked that twenty years ago,' he mused. 'Yes, a loaf of the rye bread, please, if you have any left.'

'Jason!' I called into the bakery. No reply. Then Goss answered, 'Yes?'

'Rye bread?'

'One left,' she answered, producing it.

'Is something wrong with Jason?' asked Professor Dion, taking the wrapped bread and giving me a note.

'A blonde,' I explained.

He raised an eyebrow. His bright blue eyes twinkled. 'Ah, blondes,' he sighed reminiscently. 'Fundamentally not a good idea, but decorative.'

'He's fallen in love.' Goss was scornful.

The Professor patted her arm. 'Ah, my dear young woman, with youth of that age, inadvisable never means undesirable.'

And with that he left, carrying his bread, still not explaining the doll in the bottle. I would have to get back to him on that.

Where, I wondered, speaking of desirable, was Daniel? The day was marching on. I said so. Goss was still scornful. She was in a scornful mood.

'Well, duh, Corinna, you could always ring his mobile.'

'So I could,' I agreed. 'But if he's doing something secret, he won't want a mobile phone ringing to give him away.'

'He'll have it on silent,' she told me, 'or vibrate. If he's being sneaky.'

I rang the number. I got Daniel's voicemail, so I left a message, and then Goss and I went on to sell more bread, to utter silence from the bakery. Damn, I thought, I was going to miss the charming Jason who made glacé cherries and played Hornblower with me and called me Cap'n. I suppose it was too good to last. He was sixteen, after all. He had spent such a lot of his life being abused and then being a heroin addict that he must have missed out on his first crush. Now he had it.

The trouble was, apart from being a jealous old hag, that I could not see what someone like Sarah, with her model looks, would see in Jason, who was surely too young and callow for her tastes. Therefore that fundamentally untrustworthy young woman wanted him for something other than his body, his company or his sparkling conversation, and I didn't like it at all.

Neither did Goss, I could tell, but there was nothing we could do about it. I could hardly pin the girl against a wall and demand to know if her intentions were honourable. So we sold bread. And admired the light twinkling through our Christmas decorations.

And when it came time to cash up and shut the shop, Daniel had not returned, and no message had been sent to my own phone, which is switched through to the shop. Phone calls, yes, several, including Mr. Nobody who hangs up a lot, some peon from Bombay trying to sell insurance, and a real estate agent telling me that property prices were about to go up again, in defiance of all reason. And another corporate client requesting more of those amazing muffins for the board meeting. But not, as it happens, Daniel. Still, too early to worry about a full grown ex-soldier.

Just before we shut Janeen came in. She got the last loaf of the gluten-free. She wanted to talk and leant on a bread rack to do so, while I was trying to get the shop floor swept and would have preferred her room to her company, however loquacious.

'People don't have to give up meat,' she told me, moving her feet as I motored around her with the broom. 'Just meat produced by the present methods.'

'What other methods are there?' I asked. 'Meat is animals, produced by other animals. Sexual reproduction. They told me about it at school,' I added sarcastically, which made Goss giggle.

'And meat is murder,' she capped. 'But what if it was vat-grown?'

'Science fiction,' I said.

'No, really. The technology exists to take a strand of, say, chicken DNA, and suspend it in a nutrient solution. It will be immortal—there is no reason for a cell culture to die. It will differentiate, producing muscle and fat. Just not brain.'

'You know, I don't like the sound of this,' I commented.

Goss seconded my opinion with 'euw'.

'But then, you see the advantage, huge amounts of chicken flesh can be produced without killing a single animal,' she said earnestly.

I thought about this, leaning on my broom.

'So if I want to make *pollo cacciatore* I just go along to the… chemist's, I suppose, the laboratory, and buy a couple of kilos of living flesh with no mind.'

'Superchicken,' said Janeen.

'Ingenious,' I said, completing the sweeping and giving Goss the broom.

'It's a complete solution. Then people can be weaned off meat gradually.'

'You've forgotten one question about your superchicken—the most important question,' I told her, shoving her very gently toward the steps so I could close the shop. I was tired, even if she wasn't.

'What's that?' she said, clutching her spelt bread.

'What does it taste like?' I asked, and shut the door.

Chapter Twelve

*Behold the handmaid of the Lord. Let it
be unto me according to thy word.*

Luke 1:28
The Holy Bible

I was feeling out of sorts and grumpy so, after I washed and
changed, I took Horatio and my esky loaded with plastic glass-
ware, a bottle of gin, a sliced lemon and some tonic water to the
roof garden. There I was pleased to find Trudi taking a break
from gardening. She was sitting on the bench, reweaving a straw
garden seat. Therese Webb was advising.

'No, the tension has to remain the same—you don't need to
pull so hard, Trudi dear. No, Lucifer, we do not want to appliqué
you to the chair. Kitten chairs are so, so unfashionable. Though
your fur would match very well,' she added, for Therese sees the
world in terms of colour and fabric.

'Drinks,' I announced. I opened the cooler, mixed a g and
t for me and Therese and a plain gin for Trudi, who does not
like adulterants in her national drink. I watched Lucifer give
up on the chair and bounce over to touch noses with Horatio,
who greeted him politely, if not warmly. Horatio does not like
kittens but he is constrained by the Code of the Cats not to

hurt them. In any case, attempting to hurt Lucifer might easily disarray Horatio's whiskers.

'These students,' growled Trudi. 'I do not like them.'

'Oh?' asked Therese. 'Why? The music is nice.'

'Music is nice,' conceded Trudi. 'But they talk nonsense. They say I may not eat sausages any more—or rollmops!'

We gasped. Trudi without her rollmops was unthinkable. She bought catering-sized jars of them and they were her constant refreshment and companion, as was a definite scent of smoked fish. Which was all right, because I liked smoked fish, and I could think of worse perfumes. Lucifer also had developed a taste for rollmops and had been known to kidnap them practically out of his proprietor's mouth. Trudi nodded grimly.

'Yes, they are a tad fanatical about meat is murder,' Therese agreed. 'Did you see that leaflet?'

'Yes, and it frightened Goss into thinking she had breast cancer,' I replied.

'God, Corinna, the poor girl!' Therese was gratifyingly shocked.

I nodded grimly in my turn and gulped my drink. I could still feel that thin little body shaking with sobs.

'Rowan, he is all right,' conceded Trudi. 'He knows about plants. He came and helped me with the watering. Him, I don't mind. Nice boy. That girl Bec, she seems sensible. But the blonde…' She said something in Dutch which really didn't need a translation.

'Yes, I expect so,' I said. 'And she's seducing my Jason.'

'No!' said both my listeners.

'And I can't imagine why,' I confessed.

'Because she can,' growled Trudi. She opened her plastic box of travelling rollmops and offered them around. I took one and bit. Soft fish, hard onion, strong vinegar. Perfect with, as it happened, gin. Horatio scorned one, Lucifer stole one, and Therese politely declined.

'Yes, but she must want something from him.' Therese moved a little further away from the fish feast. 'What can Jason do—I mean, apart from the obvious?'

'He can cook,' I replied. 'But he was happy providing the refreshments anyway.'

'Maybe they have a special project,' said Therese, finishing her drink and giving me back the glass.

'Time we get on,' said Trudi, setting up the seagrass loom again.

I watched them repair the seat, idle and slightly fuzzy. Horatio curled up at my feet and appreciated the cool marble floor. The sun shone on the greenery. Presently I betook myself to the rose arbour, where the wisteria provided extra shade, and fell lightly asleep for an hour.

When I woke, the weavers had gone, leaving a repaired chair. Horatio was awake and standing on my lap, indicating strongly that it was time to go down to the apartment for his afternoon nap. I was disinclined to move. The air was still and heavy and full of sleep. Then I heard more voices—damn, the students had replaced the weavers. And I really did not want to encounter them again. I might be extremely rude, which would be unkind to the young and enthusiastic, as Daniel had said.

So instead of moving, I stroked Horatio into curling up on my lap again, and closed my eyes.

This meant that my hearing was sharpened. I was indulging in that most pleasant of vices, eavesdropping. And all without moving a finger.

'Vaughan Williams' *Fantasia on Christmas Carols*,' a rich, deep male voice stated. 'It's a wonderful piece of music and a lot of fun to sing.'

'Needs a very strong bass or baritone,' said Bec. I recognised her voice, definite and crisp. 'You know, where it begins "This is the truth sent from above…" The first ten bars are unsupported.'

'Yes, but we've got Rupe here, and Alexander, they could dominate any space,' said an unknown female.

'Or there's Benjamin Britten,' suggested a diffident male voice—that must be Rowan.

This suggestion was greeted with scorn.

'Oh, puhleeze, not *Wolcum Yole* again!' said the light cooing tone of Sarah.

'Britten is a pain,' Bec agreed. 'All right, then, we need a string quartet and a very strong bass/baritone. Got the bass, check. Anyone know a string quartet?'

'You mean, one which doesn't need paying and will do a Christmas concert for beer and charming company?' asked the rich male voice.

'Rupert!' exclaimed Sarah. 'Don't be so sexist!'

'I didn't say what gender the charming company had to be,' he evaded.

'As it happens,' said the other deep voice, 'I think I can find one. There are a lot of music students hanging out for a job. But we will need to pay them.'

'Okay, Alexander. We'll come up with something. Two carol gigs today,' said Bec, clearly the organiser of this group. 'Everyone got carol books? Concert dress with extra tinselly pin, provided by Sarah.'

'Where did they come from?' asked Alexander. He had a faint and attractive accent—Russian, maybe?

Sarah sounded pleased. 'That craft lady, Therese, she showed me how to make them. Aren't they cute?'

'If you make up a tray of them, we might be able to sell them,' suggested Rowan.

'A good idea. Janeen, how are your plans for our festival coming along?' Bec again.

'All right, if I can store stuff in Rowan's fridge.'

'Of course,' said Rowan.

'Then that's it. The mall at three, ladies and gentlemen,' Bec concluded. There were the sounds of getting up and collecting hats and finding bags.

I gave them time to get away before I moved. As they went they sang their little song to massed giggling.

Haarmann Pearce and Soylent Green
Vargas Fish and Sawney Beane.

Horatio was now insistent about going home, so I went.

No Daniel in my apartment, no message. I rang his phone and got voicemail again. Where was my tall, dark and handsome? Well, I still had the missing Brigid's diary to look through. I might as well do that.

With some reluctance, I opened the files and began to read. More complaints about Reverend Hale and his doctrine. I logged out of the blog and googled the Holy Reformed Temple of Shiloh. As I read, my eyebrows rose.

Jesus was a rich man? Jesus had a big house? If Jesus had lived now, he would have a Cadillac? Jesus hates sick people and cripples? *Stands to reason, brothers and sisters, that Jesus doesn't want to look at the world through blind eyes*, it said.

Funny, that was what I had always thought he did. I read on, boggling.

Jesus died and took on the nature of Satan? Then as Satan he threw down Satan? Then he rose from the dead as a man and thus we are all of the nature of Jesus? Wait just a moment. I might not qualify as a devout Christian, in fact I probably didn't qualify as a Christian at all, but I had sat through enough church services, quietly reading my Bible when the sermon became too tedious. That wasn't what it said in the book, was it? Wasn't Christ conceived as a man, because God wanted someone to experience humanity so that he could understand it, like the demigod Heracles before him? And that conception was all he needed to do to redeem us, apart from dying horribly? I remembered the Professor talking about it. Ave wipes out Eva, he said, meaning that the conception of Christ demolished the sin of Adam and Eve.

The website was confidential in that greasy, unreliable way of a man who is selling you a stolen car and picking your pocket at the same moment. *When God says to me, I am, I just smile, children, I just smile and I say, I am, too.*

Where was the Spanish Inquisition when we needed it? This was poisonous stuff. I felt quite shocked, and was also shocked to find that there were still things that I found—well, shocking.

Why did these people want to be Christians? Why take a reasonably satisfactory religion and deform it like this? Why not make up their own, as L Ron Hubbard had done?

I had a nasty taste in my mouth. I went to the bathroom and brushed my teeth.

Poor girls, to have to listen to this drivel endlessly. Not even the smarmy claims of universal love could make anyone feel better about the Holy Reformed Temple of Shiloh. I diverted myself with a fantasy of what their welcome would be like in hell. I pictured a very large and obscenely ugly demon saying, 'Come in, Reverend, your place in the pit is all prepared.'

It was getting late. Dinner. Horatio had kitty chow (the expensive fish one which he really loves) and I made myself a steak sandwich, as I had already thawed two steaks. I put Daniel's back into the fridge. No word. No message. And it was getting dark and I had to go to bed soon.

I read more of the diary. The poor girl knew that something dreadful was happening to her, but she didn't seem to know that it was pregnancy.

I'm swelling up, she wrote plaintively. *I asked Mum if I could see a doctor because I'm sure it's a tumour. She didn't want to hear me. Mum never hears what she doesn't want to hear. Two hours of Rev Hale's TV show today. Luckily I was thinking out a thing about functions. I know what my sister was doing. She was making up another story about Lucinda de Vere (she's eighteenth-century English, based in Bath). Or Giacommeta di Lupa. She's fourteenth-century Venetian, or is it Florence? I wish I had her imagination. While Rev Hale is going on about God in man, Dolly just flies off to the Doge's Palace. As she says, we have to sit there but no one can make us listen. But maths only takes me so far. Tomorrow I'm going to try chess problems. Sandy got me a book of them.*

Poor girl, I thought, wiping my plate with my last crust and clearing the table. The fourteenth century in Venice had been a very unstable and dangerous period. Much more fun than the twenty-first.

I was getting restless. I wondered if Uncle Solly, who had mysterious connections, had sent Daniel on one of his little missions. But no, one of the nephews or nieces who ran the New York Deli would have called me. Sister Mary might know. That meant waiting until midnight, because I did not know where Sister Mary hung up her habit and stored her sensible shoes. And I had to get up at four to run my bakery.

I tried the phone again. Still on voicemail. What if something very bad had happened to Daniel?

That thought sent a chill all through me. I shook myself and read the next diary entry.

I can't talk to Mum at all. Dolly agrees that something is wrong with me. I don't want to bother Sandra. She already does a lot for us that could get her fired. She gave Dolly a plate of oven-baked chips yesterday. I can hear the exercise bike going as Dolly tries to burn off those calories. It isn't fair, the way we are treated. It looks all right from the outside. Nice house, people would say. Nice clothes. At least Dolly's clothes would be nice if they weren't pink. Expensive school. They wouldn't be able to see how hard our life is. Hours of Rev Hale. No dinner if we argue. Virginity checks. Mum is a fanatic and Dad isn't here most of the time and when he is he is bored with all of us. He doesn't seem to like me anymore, either. The parents only smile at each other when they have meetings and gatherings and then only because the Holy Temple won't let anyone get divorced unless Rev Hale or Rev Putnam tells them to. It would be nice if they divorced. Except I bet we'd have to go with Mum. That would be worse. If it could get worse.

I had a strong sense of doom. Sometime, fairly soon in this diary, it was about to get much worse. Horatio settled down into his after-dinner spot for a snooze. I turned on the news, watched briefly, and was about to turn it off. Afghanistan, Darfur, floods in India. Disasters all over. Riot in King Street. Oh—wait! I snatched my finger off the off button.

'A mysterious band of graffitists have been active in the city for the past week,' said the newsreader, suppressing a smile. 'Their target is not a band or a political statement. Their tag is freegans and they correct spelling and change the position of apostrophes in public signage. Mr. Tregend, lapidary, of The City Rock's, was outraged to find that someone had scaled his roof and blacked out the apostrophe in his sign.'

I laughed aloud. Those freegans. Have to love them. That City Rock's sign had annoyed me for years.

'Mr. Gorgious, of Melbourne Art Hairdresser's, has had his apostrophe amputated. Inspector Clamp, of the Victoria Police, said that although some people might think that this was funny, it was still vandalism and would be punished if the freegans were caught on security camera.'

That would be right. I had seldom met police persons with a sense of grammar.

'The freegans are expected to deliver a statement tomorrow, according to an email received this afternoon. Meanwhile, police advise shopkeepers to lock up carefully and have their grammar checked by a reputable English teacher.'

The ABC did have a sense of humour. Bless them.

Considerably cheered, I read some more of Brigid's diary. We were approaching a time when her pregnancy must begin to show. I wondered how a girl in the twenty-first century who got such good marks for science could not know the mechanisms by which one became pregnant. But she seemed to have no idea.

I'm swelling up more, it must be some sort of cancer. Anna said I must be pregnant and asked me if Sean was the father and they all giggled. I hate them. As if I'd let that beast Sean anywhere near me. He dumped me because I wouldn't. And Anna would.

Well, that about did it for Sean, even though he was captain of the cricket team. Must be Manny.

Fortunately Brigid had other things to think about, like exams. The diary was forgotten as she completed her common assessment tasks and wrote essays. And got more pregnant, of course, until the moment when she had given up on her mother and decided to appeal to her father for help. A miscalculation of catastrophic proportions. The account of it must have been written several days later.

It isn't fair, it isn't true! I can't be pregnant! I can't! And Papa is so angry with me! I'm shut up here and can't go out and the school is being told I'm sick and will send and mark my work and I get taken to the exams under escort. I'm not allowed to speak to anyone. It isn't fair! Why is God doing this to me? Is it because I used to fall asleep listening to Rev Hale? And Mum just stares. I think she's gone mad. But they don't know I've got a second mobile phone. They never understood the internet. I'm not cut off from the world like they think. They won't even let Dolly see me. But Dolly's brave, she can climb out of her balcony window and up the supports to mine. She's just gone. She can't work it out either. It's not fair!

I had to agree. It really wasn't fair. Who, then, was the father of this child? Assuming that it wasn't a rampaging case of stomach cancer. Or beri-beri from the restricted diet. I read on.

Dolly says that I should look out the window this morning and there was Manny. He waved and smiled. He is a nice boy. I talk to him every day. He worries about how I am. His mum has lots of kids and he knows about babies. But at least they didn't stop me doing my exams. I was taken in the car right into the school grounds so no one would see me and the VCE coordinator, Miss Gennezano, let me sit in her little side office and do them, with a teacher watching. As long as it wasn't my English teacher watching the English exam it's all right. I haven't had anything else to do for months but work and I think I did all right. I think I aced the chemistry exam. And physics. And maybe maths and even the English wasn't as bad as I expected. So I do my exam and the car takes me home, and no one sees me. No one knows I'm there. Like a ghost. I used to like school. I'm so lonely. Miss Threadgold sat in my exams knitting and she has made me a shawl for the baby. I was so touched I cried and she hugged me. Mum's coming up the stairs. Later.

Poor little thing! She must have finished her exams and decided to run away soon after them. I wondered what the precipitating factor had been. I read on and found out.

Mum came. She says that when the baby is born she'll take it and say that it is hers. Then she'll take it to America to visit the Holy Reformed Temple of Shiloh and have it adopted there. Then I can recover and go back to school next year and need never hear of the baby again. I don't like this. I don't like this at all. What does she want with my baby? She could have had more of her own if she wanted another baby. She never even liked babies—we all had a nanny and then we had Sandra.

I got up and made myself a cool drink with lemon cordial. I didn't like this either. Brigid went on:

Well, I'm not staying. I rang Manny. I rang Dolly. She can give me all her money. It won't be much because she buys so many books but she can borrow some from Sandra. I'm not letting Mum get her claws on my baby.

I smiled. Suddenly that lump had gone from a possible internal cancer to a baby—and 'my baby' at that.

And that was all. She never made another entry. I shut down the computer and closed the lid. Now what to do? It was nine o'clock and I ought to be going to bed but I was unbearably restless. Nothing from Daniel. I wandered over to the fridge and discovered that I was out of ice cream. That would never do. I found some sandals, picked up my backpack, and went out into the night.

Melbourne is one of the safest cities in the world, if you avoid King Street late at night. All cities have places like King Street, where youths from outlying suburbs come in to lose all inhibitions, get sodden or roaring drunk, and start fights which end in police cells and sore heads and the occasional death. I saw nothing more dangerous than the singing drunks outside Young & Jackson as I walked at an even pace around the block and into Swanston Street, heading for the 7-11 and a tub of chocolate and cherry ripple ice cream which had my name on it. It was warm but not too hot. Melbourne looks very pretty in the dark. I had almost reached my target when I was swept up in a group of dancers. Patchouli and rose oil stunned my nose. Dreads or silky locks flying, shaved heads gleaming, skirts swirling, the freegans surrounded me and carried me along, protesting.

Protesting until someone said close to my ear, 'We're going to rescue Daniel,' and then I forgot ice cream, hauled up my long skirts, and danced with them, a modified form of the Zorba dance, which covers ground really quickly and doesn't give any impression of haste.

Which is all very well for the young and fit but somewhere around the top of RMIT hill I collapsed onto a street chair and puffed. They danced around me.

'Corinna, Corinna...' Someone was singing the Bob Dylan song after which I had been named. But there were new words. 'He's in the old brewery, just over there. Trapped inside, trapped inside! Gotta get the gate open, free him from his chains.'

'How we gonna do that?' I sang. 'What do you mean, chains?'

'We gonna dance there,' returned the singer, 'and make a mighty scene! If you get through the gate you can open it for us! And then we'll find him, and maybe the girl as well.'

'Deal,' I said, running out of Dylan. 'Guide me, o thou great Jehovah, Pilgrim through this barren land!'

'Right you are,' they sang in return, and I got up and we danced the rest of the way to the half-bulldozed, extensively ruined old brewery site, which had high chain-link fences all around it, and a very heavily weaponed security guard at the front.

We weren't going to the front; banging tambourines and beating drums, we danced along the street, amusing or offending the citizenry as we passed. Now I knew what it was to be a Hare Krishna and resolved to throw a few coins into their box when they next passed me.

Then we split, leaving most of the freegans to howl and hoot while three of us—the beautiful man and the tough girl in the army fatigues and me—crept into a cul de sac where we were confronted by a gate.

'Nigel,' said the beautiful man.

'Molesworth?' I guessed.

'Of course.'

'Ivanova,' said the woman in fatigues.

'Commander Susan Ivanova?' I asked. She must have been a baby when *Babylon 5* was on TV.

She nodded crisply. 'I was Nike, but they all thought it was a sports shoes, not the goddess of victory. So I chose Ivanova.'

'Good choice,' I agreed.

Strange company. But meanwhile, there was Daniel.

I can pick locks. I could have taken this one with my eyes closed. In fact, I did close them, so I could feel the fall of the tumblers.

The lock parted, the gate opened.

'Where is Daniel?' I asked Ivanova.

'Somewhere in the middle building. We've got torches. Come on. Quietly.'

And it had been such a nice slow uneventful day until now. I like slow and uneventful.

Chapter Thirteen

*Perhaps it is because of their own fierce
love of freedom that cats have always
shown a strange sympathy for prisoners.*

Beverley Nichols
Cats' A.B.C.

Luckily, I have never been afraid of the dark. I can see quite well
in it. Possibly this is because I spent a chunk of my childhood
without any artificial light. And the things in the dark were
nothing like as scary as the things in the light.

The gate silently swung shut behind us. Ivanova the military
girl and Nigel the beautiful boy and I crept into the shadow of
the crumbling red-brick building and conferred.

'He's probably in there,' said Ivanova. 'We can get to it by
sneaking along the sides of the buildings. Then we'll just have
to run the last bit and hope that security is still watching the
dancers. Hoping they'll do something illegal so they can arrest
them and get their hands on all that sweet female flesh. This way.'

I followed. What had happened to Daniel? It was not like him
to be taken by surprise. Unless he was concussed. Or drugged. I
thought of those clear eyes clouded with pain and dragged my
fingertips across the rough surface of the brick to provide a bit

of distraction. My nerves had now screwed themselves up to what Lady Macbeth called 'the sticking place' and I wanted to run and strike and scream, not sneak. I wondered what weapons I had. In my backpack, I had a Swiss army knife. I had a flask of water, a snack bar—useful if Daniel was hungry or thirsty, but not offensive, even though the snack bar was of that really impacted muesli. I had documents, money, a torch, a folding shopping bag, a packet of tissues, a notebook, biros and pencils, and—aha!—an aerosol spray can of Fern Forest Household Deodorant, which the grocery man had delivered instead of the pump spray and I had intended to swap. I didn't think I could stab anyone efficiently with the pocket-knife, or indeed at all, but I was betting that a face full of Fern Forest might distract the boldest. And they would smell nice, too. Not to mention that nice heavy torch which I hadn't had to use yet. I was following the pale patches on Ivanova's camouflage shirt. I wondered why the freegans were taking all this trouble to rescue Daniel. If this was some street-theatre freak of their own, I was going to be very cross.

Darkness and not a lot of noise. Scurrying of small feet in the walls. I wished I had worn more suitable clothes for creeping about ruins in the darkness. Something about the size of a pterodactyl passed overhead and I cringed. It hooted.

'Powerful owl,' said Nigel. 'Hunting possums.'

I checked for my heart, but it hadn't really leapt out of my breast.

We reached the edge of the ruin and looked across open space. Ten, maybe fifteen paces to the alcove in the red-brick construction which would hide us from the view of the guards while I, presumably, picked the lock. I shoved the spray can down the bloused front of my lacy top, grasped my pocket-knife in hand and, when Ivanova gave the signal, ran like the wind.

Screams of laughter came from the gate. There was no shout of 'Stop thief!' or whatever it is people shout these days. I was packed into the portico with Ivanova at my side bruisingly tight and I fumbled for the lock. There was a bolt. I drew it. Then there was a lock, and shaking and panting, I tried to persuade it to open.

It seemed to take years. It was rusty and unwilling to move. I dropped the knife. I found it after frantic scrabbling and tried again, wrenching the tumblers around by main force. I tried swearing, I tried cursing, I tried spraying some of my Fern Forest into it and it finally yielded. Then we dragged it open with a groan like the expiring moments of a very large dinosaur and Daniel was in my arms.

'Quick,' hissed Nigel, and we ran back across the open space, through the little cul de sac and into the nice legal street. I even locked the gate behind us.

Commander Ivanova stowed the torches in her bag and danced into the singing multitude without a backward glance. Nigel kissed Daniel and then me and joined her. The noise and laughter faded away. The freegans were gone like a dream. I was left holding my very own dear Daniel in my arms, wondering what had just happened.

Didn't matter. I started to walk us away, down the hill, toward Insula and safety. After a few paces a parched voice said, 'Have you got any money?'

It was so unexpected that I laughed.

'Yes, shall I get you a drink?'

'Buy me a Coke?' he asked, sinking down onto that identical street sofa on which I had reposed an unlikely amount of time ago. God, less than half an hour. I obtained the Coke, shaking myself down before I went into the cafe. I was a little blotched and bruised, but nothing serious, and my pretty boho clothes had survived intact.

Daniel drank a whole bottle of Coke without stopping, then absorbed all the water in my flask. Apart from being very dehydrated, he did not seem to be injured, except his hands, which were bruised and had a lot of skin knocked off. He was also very dusty, a ruddy powder of old brick. I wasn't going to ask him what had happened until he wanted to tell me, so I went back for some more fluids. After the third bottle of water he stood up.

'Food,' he said hungrily, through my snack bar.

'Steak at home or shall we stop along the way?' I asked.

'Corinna, I adore you,' he said. 'Steak at home. Hamburger to get me there.'

He ate the hamburger in three bites. I managed to grab a couple of chips before they too went the way of all flesh. He had obviously been imprisoned without food or water for all the time he had been away. But the food was doing him good. He walked more freely and faster, so that I had almost to run to keep up with his long legs. That steak was clearly calling him home.

He noticed that I was flagging and slowed down. A tram clanged past. It all seemed so ordinary. RMIT students, people from apartments walking little dogs, patrolling policemen, families with children whining for ice cream. Just Melbourne on a summer night.

'How, O Worker of Miracles, did you manage it?' he asked. 'To whom should I be giving supplications?'

'The freegans,' I told him. 'They gathered me up when I was just going out for ice cream and told me they were going to rescue you, so I went along to pick the locks. I'm good at locks.'

'You certainly are,' he said with deep admiration. 'How did they know I was in trouble?'

'I don't know. They work in mysterious ways. Are you hurt?'

He gave a rueful smile which made my heart turn over.

'No, just my pride. I couldn't get out. My phone is lost who knows where. And that building must have been the liquor store. No windows. Thick walls. Only one door, and it was bolted. I could have stayed there until I mummified. By the smell of the place someone already had.'

'Nearly home,' I said. 'Who shut you in?'

'Manny,' he said. 'Manny and Brigid. They found out that I am employed by her father, and before I had a chance to reassure them, Manny just shoved me into the store and shut the door. I fell backwards and by the time I got up I was locked in. I am so embarrassed.'

'Don't be,' I said. 'You're not a superhero. You're not supposed to expect the people you are trying to help to attack you.'

'Even though they frequently do,' he pointed out.

'Yes, even so. How did they look?'

'Rough,' he said slowly. 'He's worn to a shadow and she's so tired she can hardly move under her heavy load. They're dirty and they're hungry. And now they've gone, and God knows where. They'd been in the old building for a week at least. And now I've scared them away. Dammit!' He kicked an inoffensive tram stop.

'They may not have gone far,' I pointed out. 'In fact, they can't have gone far. You need some more food and some rest and then you can put out the word to start looking for them again. Come along,' I said, and he yielded to the pull of my hand on his arm.

I have never seen anyone eat like Daniel after a twenty-four-hour fast, not even Timbo or Jason. The steak vanished, as did three potato rösti and a whole pot of pasta bolognese with extra cheese, and he only started to flag when I produced more bread and more cheese and a rather good tabouli.

'That,' he said, drawing me into his embrace and kissing me with the tomato-flavoured kisses of his mouth, 'hit the spot. Never let me go out again without a spare phone. And a satchel. In which I will carry emergency rations and water. God, I was so thirsty!'

'They might have killed you,' I muttered into his dusty hair.

'Yes, but they didn't think of that, they just panicked. They didn't mean me any harm. But I couldn't get out. I tried to dig and the earth was as hard as stone. So I just sat there and remembered Sterne. "*I can't get out*, said the starling."'

He shuddered. When I picked up his hand I saw how the fingers' ends were torn. I kissed them better.

'If the freegans hadn't found you, I would have,' I lied. 'I was thinking of combing the brewery site, security guard or no security guard. And that would have been embarrassing indeed, telling a magistrate what I was doing trespassing on someone else's land.'

'True. Now, a shower,' he said, and I went with him to wash his back and various other parts. His clothes were stiff with dirt. His skin also. I smoothed it under my hands. My precious Daniel. I had nearly lost him.

What with one thing and another, I didn't get to sleep until it was almost time for me to get up again. And that added a whole new horror to four in the morning.

I rose and drank coffee, wishing I could inject it into the vein. I made more coffee as I fed Horatio and myself and when I got to the bakery I put the bakery coffee pot on.

Jason was not there. I swore and put on the mixers, dragging sacks of flour across the floor in a very bad temper. After half an hour I had everything humming and I sat down for another cup of coffee. My feet hurt after all that dancing and my baker's overall seemed constricting after my floaty clothes. Black dark outside and no apprentice. What had that Sarah done with him?

He arrived fully an hour late in time to drag the first load of loaves out of the oven and apologise abjectly.

'My alarm didn't go off,' he whined.

'Ah, but did you set it?' I asked cunningly. I do not do very cunning at five o'clock in the morning.

'I might've forgot,' he admitted. 'I was up late with the singers and...' there was a starry-eyed pause '...Sarah.'

'And what does Sarah want with you?' I asked.

He looked up at me from the floor. 'Why are you so pissed off? She was real interested in me,' he said, hurt. 'Wanted to know all about me. I reckon I'm going to try being a vego like her.'

'Good,' I said nastily. 'That means your choice for breakfast is bread. With bread on it.'

'Oh,' he said blankly.

'No ham, no cheese,' I added, grating cheese vengefully, as though it was a personal enemy. 'No eggs, no butter, no milk.'

'Maybe not as vego as all that,' he said hastily. 'Maybe just no meat.'

'Sensible,' I said. 'I was up late rescuing Daniel from durance vile and I'm very tired today, so help an old lady and grate this cheese for the cheese muffins, will you?'

He brightened a little. I repented of being so cross and ruffled his hair. He pulled away and smoothed his curls back into place.

'Yes, sir, ma'am,' he said, and took over the implement.

We made bread and gradually the daylight happened outside. The Mouse Police zoomed out into the alley and stood over Kiko at the Japanese restaurant for the tuna scraps. When they came back they were just ahead of Serena and her load of flowers.

I zapped a couple of frozen rosewater muffins in the microwave oven and greeted the donkey with affection. She stood so uncomplainingly under a solid weight of buckets. Water is very heavy. I waved the muffins in the air to cool them and she nickered and stamped impatiently. A flowered hat came into view.

'Good morning, lady,' said Mr. Pahlevi, handing me the money for the muffins. 'Hey, you know you got an evil woman in your building?'

I thought instantly of Mrs. Pemberthy.

'I know,' I told him. 'And there is nothing to be done about it until she dies of old age.'

'That'll take awhile,' he said. 'That Meroe, she's a friend of the devil.'

'Is she?' I did not feel friendly toward Mr. Pahlevi anyway, and traducing and slandering my friend wasn't improving my opinion of him.

'Black witch,' he told me.

'Go away,' I said.

'There are people who'd love to know where she is,' he insinuated. Was he asking me for a bribe? If so he had a sad penniless future to look forward to.

'And you're the man to tell them, eh?' I demanded. My fists were on my hips. Behind me Jason picked up the heavy slide we use to remove bread from the big oven. It would make a very handy weapon. I wondered what kind of dent it would make in the flowered hat. Quite a sizeable one, I judged.

'Maybe,' he said, sensing that this interview was not going as he had expected.

'Take your donkey and go away,' I said as menacingly as I could. 'Meroe has friends who will not appreciate you making trouble for her.'

He slid away from me, somehow seeming to become distant without actually moving, took the muffins, and led Serena down the alley into Flinders Lane.

'That wasn't nice!' Jason stuffed a ham roll into his mouth, forgetting his recent conversion to the cause of Meat is Murder.

'Certainly wasn't.' There we were in complete agreement.

'He shouldn't say things like that about Meroe!' protested Jason.

'That, too. I'll go and see her later, find out if he's a real threat or just flapping his mouth.'

'And if he's a real threat?'

'Then you get to smack him with the slide.'

'Wicked,' said my apprentice, with relish.

We seemed be friends again, Jason and me, and we went on with the baking in relative amity. I told him about Daniel being locked into the brewery building and he whistled.

'I slept there once,' he told me. 'Before they put up the big fence. Not a safe place. Didn't like the dudes who were crashing there. I used to stay in Flagstaff, feed off the Soup Run. They weren't good times,' he told me, gazing into his muffin mixture.

'These times are better,' I agreed.

He hugged me briefly.

'Muffins at five o'clock, Cap'n,' he informed me, and I felt so much better at the return of the old Jason that I almost forgot how tired I was.

Almost, as Uncle Solly would say, isn't quite. By the time Goss arrived to open the shop I was drooping and the bright day was hurting my eyes. Kylie, who had come downstairs with her flatmate, eyed me with concern.

'Like, Corinna, you look terrible,' she told me candidly. 'You partying hard?'

'Not so much,' I said.

'We can do the shop,' she told me. 'You want to go upstairs again?'

Hardly had the suggestion passed her lips, pearly with Dewy Rose lip gloss, than I was on the stairs and on the way out of the bakery. Sleep. What a wonderful idea. Jason was explaining about the rescue of Daniel as I ascended out of hearing. Horatio remained staunchly at his post, which he wasn't going to desert for such a paltry reason. Sometimes I feel that I cannot live up to his elevated standards.

Safely inside my own apartment, I tore off my baking clothes, shucked my heavy shoes and flung myself into bed next to the divine Daniel, who was still deeply asleep. I closed my eyes with great thankfulness. I did not deserve such excellent and enthusiastic assistants. I must think of something nice to do for them…

That was my last thought for some hours. Even an heroic consumption of coffee was not going to keep me awake. But I was not displeased when I woke gently to smell the god-like scent. Daniel had gone. Horatio had returned, which argued that it was afternoon. A thin ray of very bright light speared through a hole in my blackout curtains which I ought to mend before the day was out. Daniel, in the kitchen, was cooking something and talking on the phone.

I heaved myself out of the octopus-like embrace of my bed and sat up. I felt all right. Definitely awake. My clothes were in a heap on the floor. Standards slipping, Ms. Chapman! I put on a clean caftan. I had no plans to go anywhere today.

Daniel nodded at me and put another sandwich under the griller. Cheese and tomato, yum. He concluded his conversation and hung up.

'I have to get another phone,' he told me. 'Coffee?'

'Please,' I said. I examined him as he stood, naked to the waist, in the half-light. I had never seen such a beautiful back. His front was pretty special, too.

'I feel all right,' he answered my unspoken question. 'How about you?'

'I shamelessly handed over my bakery and livelihood to my apprentice and two assistants and went back to bed,' I told him. He laughed.

'Oh, yes. They were very pleased with themselves. They did the deliveries, sold out the shop, cashed up, and Jason should have finished the cleaning by now. He asked permission to borrow some of your old cookbooks. I said that would be all right. Some new project. Have a sandwich. I'm still starving.'

'Then you should not wait for yours,' I said, moving to take his place at the griller and constructing a few more sandwiches. 'Plenty of bread.'

'And I can recommend the bakery,' he capped. I wondered how my profit margin would cope with another Jason to feed but he only ate three sandwiches. They, however, were perfect of their kind; crisp bread, gooey cheese and well-cooked tomato. I also ate a cheese muffin and a strawberry one. They were not as celestial as usual. I hoped that love would not dim Jason's genius forever.

'Your plans for the day?' I asked my beloved. He stretched.

'I get to take today off,' he said. 'I'm stiff and bruised and still a little shocked and I wish to spend the day with my own true love, perhaps taking in a little Terry Pratchett.'

'Admirable plan,' I said. 'You can read to me as I mend the curtains.'

So we did that. We had tea at a civilised hour: real tea. Earl Grey. With scones. We were reading aloud to each other when the bell rang and there were Kepler and Jon, two of our favourite people.

Jon is tall and handsome. His red hair is greying now. He works for a charity which means that he spends a lot of his time in tropical hellholes, fighting off the leeches and avoiding death squads, bringing light, trade and clean water to the benighted and lost. His reward for this virtue is Kepler, a transcendently beautiful Chinese man who solves horrendous computer problems and who adores Jon with a very touching whole-hearted devotion, exactly matching Jon's. They are extremely sweet together. They live in Neptune. Apposite, in view of the amount of travelling they do. Kepler had been everywhere recently, taking pictures.

'Corinna,' said Jon, 'Kepler's photos are ready.'

'Come in,' I invited, clearing the table of cups and sewing materials and papers. 'Show me!'

They did as requested. Daniel smiled at them. They made a picture. Jon is so very Caucasian, and Kepler is exceptionally Asian. He favours flowing clothes and was presently wearing a completely outrageous pair of purple brocade pyjamas.

'Kep's been up all night,' explained Jon. 'Some fearsome North Korean virus. Which he defeated because his heart is pure. And you wanted to see the finished product, Corinna.'

I did. Kepler is a very skilled photographer and he had been taking pictures of Insula for some weeks. He was always popping up. Now he had had the photos made into a panorama, the tall building with its eight floors, with one iconic image for each apartment. They were never what one expected them to be, either. He had a wonderful eye. Mrs. Pemberthy had complained about him, demanding that she should edit her photo, but the one of her was merciful. It was a long-distance shot of a bent old lady caressing that rotten little doggie, Traddles, under the chin. Thus we got a figure of age and a portrait of the dog and didn't have to look at Mrs. Pemberthy, which was all to the good.

Jon had a bottle of champagne and I fetched some glasses. I leant the panorama up against my blackout curtains and sipped as I examined it. It was a marvellous piece of work.

There we all were. Beginning at the far right corner, Cafe Delicious. The cafe was crowded, people were talking and eating, and there were Del and Yai Yai in the middle, caught serving Greek coffee. The arc of the falling coffee was precise and beautiful. Del was scowling with effort, and Yai Yai was actually smiling.

Then there were the nerds. Kepler had managed to catch them when they were all playing some game. All the eyes were concentrated on one point and they looked alike, although they are actually very different.

The Sibyl's Cave was stuffed with magical stuff, and in the corner, sitting in her big chair, was Meroe enthroned, long hands lying flat on the armrests, and Belladonna stretched across the top like the ornament on the Isle of Man chess queen. Meroe was thinking deeply. Her eyes were closed. She was formidable.

In Earthly Delights we were all action. Jason hefted a rack of bread to one shoulder, I was wiping my hands on my overall, and Kylie was laughing at something which Daniel, lounging by the door, had said. Horatio presided from the counter. We looked busy and prosperous.

I took a gulp of my champagne.

'Wonderful work,' said Daniel.

'Thank you,' said Kepler modestly.

'Look, there's Kylie and Goss,' said Daniel, as we went up a floor. The girls were lying on their white couch in their pyjamas printed with little elephants, half asleep, each with her teddy bear on one side and Tori curled photogenically on Goss' lap. Kepler had caught their innocence and their sensuality. Whereas Mistress Dread, who runs a very strict dungeon, was attired in her plain tweeds and drinking tea from a porcelain cup, the Royal Doulton tea set on the lacy wrought-iron table. Professor Monk was talking to someone, expounding a difficult point, with one beautiful hand raised. His white hair and classical profile floated against his Roman frescos like a cameo. Andy and Cherie Holliday were cooking together. Cherie was chopping parsley, her father was stirring something in a basin, and Calico sat patiently on the corner of the table, waiting for tidbits. It was as compelling as a Vermeer Dutch kitchen.

'How do you do it?' I asked Kepler. 'You must see the world differently from the rest of us.'

He blushed. 'I don't really know,' he began. 'There is always something that catches my eye, to begin with, something that I know I want to convey. Meroe, for instance, she has a core of perfect stillness and silence. It's hard to see because she is always moving and talking and doing things. So when she sat down to think about a spell and Belladonna climbed onto the chair, she looked like the Isle of Man queen, and I caught it. The stillness.'

'I thought the same. What about Mrs. Dawson, then?'

Immaculately attired in evening dress, a long swoop of cinnamon crepe caught at the shoulder by a huge Minoan brooch, a wrap of superfine dark brown wool, she was standing with her back to sunset. The golden light flowed all around her. She looked distant, somehow, as though she belonged to an older world.

'I wanted the light,' he explained. 'I wanted the elegance of the dress and the drape of the shawl, and the blob of gold of the brooch, against the golden light. But I also wanted her feeling that she is in exile, far away from the world she used to rule. A little wistful, but very positive.'

'So it is,' Daniel agreed.

'Then, with Ms. Webb, I wanted the clatter of the loom and the craft, the skilled effort.'

He had it. Therese was weaving something green. He had taken the picture through the weft threads. Her head was bent, her hair escaping from its plait, her clever hands on the warp. You could indeed almost hear the clack of the loom. She was going to love her depiction, especially since Kepler had caught the expression of benevolent interest from Carolus, her King Charles spaniel, sitting on the workbench beside her.

Next came Neptune. What would Kepler do with himself and his lover?

It was adorable. Kepler in a flowing ankle-length dark blue Chinese scholar's robe, Jon in correct gentleman's evening costume, down to the white tie. Jon was seated with his hands on his knees, clasping a book. Kepler was standing beside him with one hand on Jon's shoulder and the other holding his camera. It was a Victorian family portrait—with certain differences.

'And with Trudi I wanted her gardener's patience,' said Kepler.

Through the blossom-laden branches of the linden tree, Trudi sat foursquare on a seat. Her elbows were on her knees. She sat like a man, legs apart, boots firmly planted. A seed catalogue was open on her lap and Lucifer sat on her shoulder, also staring into space. You could see new gardens growing, seeds sprouting, flowers unfolding, in front of Trudi's eyes.

Jason, wearing shorts and a tank top, was beating a mixture with a hand whisk. The basin was cradled in the crook of his elbow. He was smiling. His whole body was involved in the action; hand, arm, shoulder, torso. His background was the unaltered 1920s kitchen of his apartment. There was a rabbit sitting at his feet, leaning against his ankles. Its eyes were half shut and it appeared to be very content. Jason was a picture of youthful energy and enthusiasm.

'And Rowan…' Kepler just made a gesture.

Fast asleep, Rowan and his books reposed under a tree. He was lying on his front, legs outstretched, and his head was on a textbook. He was undoubtedly carrying out that ritual which says that if you put the book under your pillow some of the knowledge will seep into your head while you sleep. I had tried it myself. It never works. He looked about twelve, infinitely vulnerable.

'Where are we going to mount it? Can I buy a copy?' I asked. Kepler blushed again. I forced money into his pocket. This was a work of art and I really needed a copy. Then we ate some of my little ricotta and spinach munchies, of which I always keep a supply in the freezer. We toasted Kepler and his skill.

They know that I have to get up early so the two of them packed up to leave fairly soon. Among the displaced papers which I was putting back on the coffee table, Kepler noticed the code which even the nerds had not been able to break.

'You're playing chess by phone,' he commented. 'That opening looks familiar.'

There was a dead silence and he looked up, wondering if he had said something wrong. He still has an endearing humility which we really don't deserve. Kepler has better manners than most people I know.

'Kep, it's a chess game?' demanded Daniel.

'Yes. Of course. The character for the piece has been replaced by a number. c4 e5 is translated to e4 e5. Knight is N+6, K+5 Q+77 B+2 R+6 and so on. The pawn has no number, of course.'

'Of course,' I echoed, numbly.

'Well, goodnight,' said Jon, and the door closed behind them. Daniel dived on the code and began scribbling.

Chapter Fourteen

For he painted the things that matter,
The tints that we all pass by

Alfred Noyes
'The Elfin Artist'

Despite the amount of sleep I had already managed, I went to bed at the right time, leaving Daniel muttering and moving pieces on my chessboard. And I slept all night. When I woke at four on Thursday I was refreshed. Well, as refreshed as I usually was at that hour.

Daniel slept on. I did the ordinary thing—I like ordinary things. My toast was topped with apple jelly, which I had made myself because no one seems to make it these days. Daniel had left me a note that he would be back for lunch. He was going to talk to the O'Ryans and buy a new phone and other useful things. Then, he asked, perhaps I would come with him to see Manny's parents.

I thought that would be interesting. I myself had to see Meroe, and ask her about Mr. Pahlevi and whether I ought to ask Sister Mary to recommend a hit man.

Jason was in the bakery when I came down. I asked him if he had seen his portrait. He grinned.

'He's real good, isn't he, that Kepler? They were real good photos. Wish he'd take one of Sarah.'

'You could ask him,' I said unenthusiastically. 'You all right for the spelt bread?'

'Why are we making it?'

'It's low gluten without being no gluten,' I told him. 'Thus it will actually rise. Spelt is the wheat they grew in ancient Egypt, where they invented baking. And beer, of course. It's historical.'

'Right,' muttered Jason, unconvinced.

'No argument, Midshipman,' I barked, 'make it so!' and he saluted and complied.

We worked for a couple of hours, until the first sets of loaves were cooling and the second set were baking, and I had a cup of coffee and Jason had three onion rolls and a cheese sandwich with Gentleman's Relish.

'I'm going over to get some herbs from Meroe as soon as she opens,' I said. 'I thought we might make some herb bread. Haven't made any for ages. Very nice with salads.'

'It's going to be hot,' said Jason, opening the door to Calico Alley and letting the Mouse Police out. I heard Kiko or Ian put on Radio Nippon, which meant it must be six am. Jason was right. It was already scorching in the alley. Oh, goody. The air conditioning in the bakery was so effective that I hadn't noticed the outside temperature.

'Is it all right if I stay on today and do some experiments?' asked Jason. 'Only I need the big oven.'

'You're welcome to, and make sure you leave the cooler on,' I told him. 'What are you working on?'

'I'd rather tell you later.' He ducked his head. 'I'll feel like such a dork if it doesn't work.'

Glacé cherries again, I diagnosed. 'All right, Midshipman, just don't burn the place down. How are those Christmas cakes coming along?'

'Got ten to sell today, Cap'n,' he told me. 'Ingredients cost a packet, though. I can't put them out for less than fifteen dollars.'

'Fifteen it is,' I told him. 'If we have to reduce the price you'll just have to cut down on the fruit. Let's see how they go. Get Kylie to do a sign: "Super-excellent Christmas fruitcakes from a master baker."'

'I'm not a master baker,' he protested.

'Wanna bet?'

He blushed.

'Make sure Kylie wraps them in the moss and then the cyclamen paper,' I instructed. 'I'm off to see Meroe, can you cope?'

'Yes, sir!' he said.

'You have the bridge, Mr. Midshipman,' I ordered, and went out into the lane.

◇◇◇

The Sibyl's Cave is a grotto absolutely crammed with everything you might need for any kind of spell except voodoo dolls. Meroe instructs her clients that they must make their own dolls and cope with their own karmic backlash. There are sheep's bladebones and green ink for writing to Pan and seashells and azure stones and crystals of all sorts, occult jewellery and magazines, notes on astronomy and astrology and cards, jewels and runestones for telling every kind of fortune from tarot to the Babylonian Mother Cult. Today I had serious business and a puzzle and Meroe was alone. Belladonna was lying on her decorative back in the window, occasionally batting at some charms for success in business.

'Meroe, what is that doll in a bottle about?' I asked as I came in.

She answered me in a monotone.

'The Sibyl of Cumae was so reduced by time and fate that she fitted into a bottle, and they hung her up against the wall of the temple of Apollo. And when the boys teased her, saying, "Sibyl, Sibyl, what do you want?" she said, "I want only to die." It's a little joke between Professor Monk and me. Blessed meet, Corinna.'

A Wicca greeting. 'Blessed meet, Meroe, Bella.' It never did to ignore a witch's familiar. 'I came for some of your herbs for herb bread and to ask you what we should do about Mr. Pahlevi.'

'I'll get the herbs.' She vanished into the back of the shop. I waved a charm for success in love at Bella and she batted it back with a skilled paw. When Meroe returned with the white paper parcel she said, 'Sit down,' and I did so, removing a pile of Wiccan literature from the chair.

'When I was travelling with the Rom I was considered to be a half-breed,' she said abruptly. 'They did not accept me. Not entirely. I had skills and they could use them. But there were some who did not approve. One was this Pahlevi and his brother Roman. Some of the very conservative Rom consider that a witch must be a virgin and Roman decided to ensure that I was no longer a virgin and thus would have no power.'

'Goddess,' I said.

Meroe's voice was quiet and calm. 'On the way to my caravan, intent on rape, he somehow stumbled over a bear and the bear killed him,' she said. 'Pahlevi said I had cursed his brother. I said I hadn't because I had not been aware of his intentions—or I would have. The camp master decided that I should leave and Pahlevi should leave, and I came to Australia and have avoided him until now. Now he has found me.'

'And what should we do about him?'

'Nothing,' said Meroe. 'I am sorry about his brother but it was not my doing.'

'What will he do about you?' I asked, taking up my packet of fresh herbs.

'Nothing but blacken my name,' she said flatly. 'You need not be concerned, Corinna. Merry part,' she said inflexibly, and I had no other choice but to murmur, 'Merry part,' and leave.

I told Jason about this and he was not impressed, either.

'He won't just slag her off,' he said, mixing his muffins with a long spatula.

'Indeed.'

'Not if he thinks she killed his brother,' he added.

'Yes.' I laid out my big flat square of dough and chopped the fresh herbs into it. Yum. Essence of green. Mint, parsley, basil, a little coriander.

'I reckon we ought to tell Daniel. And Sister Mary,' he told me.

'I will,' I agreed. I rolled up the dough, slicked the ends together with water, and left it to prove before I sliced and baked it.

'All right, then,' said Jason, mollified.

The herb rolls smelt so magnificent when they were taken from the oven that I secured three for myself, then added another one.

The morning warmed and warmed toward hot. Curses. And some tasteless trader lost to all decent feeling had installed a loudspeaker and was playing those worthless Christmas carols at full blast far too near my door.

'If I hear "Santa Claus is Coming to Town" one more time, Jason,' I threatened, 'I shall scream.'

'Go ahead, Cap'n,' he told me. 'No one's gonna hear. I reckon we might shut the alley door and then…maybe we set up some interference.'

'What do you have in mind?' I asked suspiciously. He was smiling his sunny smile, which was ominous. Jason has a very black sense of humour.

'Just a little music of our own,' he said, smiling (sunnily).

'You are thinking heavy metal?' I asked.

'Sort of,' he replied.

'And you aren't thinking of a shotgun blast to the speakers?'

He looked horrified.

'Me, Captain? Use violence?'

'All right then,' I agreed.

Jason pottered about with my CD player and some electrical apparatus. Meanwhile, loaves and muffins got baked, the shop was opened by Goss, and people came to buy bread. The tinny music jittered along, advertising the merits of a ride in a single horse-drawn vehicle for those who had probably never seen a horse except at the races.

I don't know where he found the CD. I would have sworn it wasn't mine. But what came bellowing out of Jason's speakers, twice as loud, was music for committing homicide by. In other words, Wagner's Ring cycle, all huge chords, massive fugues, and voices belting out notes beyond what any human voice ought to be expected to reach.

The Nibelungen, it appeared, were back.

Trial by Wagner in no way resembles Chinese water torture. The assault is immediate and ferocious. However, after a while the ears grow numb. And all in all I would rather have a lot of Scandinavian people threatening each other with mayhem and doom than that sugary jingle jingle jingle.

Strangely enough, the customers seemed to quite like it. Several people sang along, and Jaye and Vic my old friends did an impromptu Ride of the Valkyries on the path outside the shop—there isn't enough room in Earthly Delights for extravagant artistic expression. Goss and I applauded. Jaye is taller and broader and Vic is smaller and thinner, Jaye is a femme and Vic very boyish, but they threw themselves into their roles with such enthusiasm that they looked like twins. They swooped and gathered the souls of dead heroes into their arms. I could practically see the horned helmets and the glitter of breastplates. They came in panting but pleased. They are vegetarians, I remembered, and I took the chance to ask them about my fellow tenants as I served them with herb rolls and seed bread.

'I wouldn't worry about them,' Jaye reassured me over the music. 'Every movement has its fanatics. We just don't eat our fellow animals, that's all. Not only is it good for us, it's good for the planet. It's not too bad. We still have wine and chocolate. And goat's milk cheese and figs. And we eat eggs and dairy. That would make us as bad as you, for some of the more extreme.'

'It's easier if you think of them as a religion,' Vic put in, hefting the bag full of bread. 'We are orthodox—in some ways...' She smiled meaningly at Jaye. 'Others are charismatics or enthusiasts.'

'I've got them, too,' I said, feeling overburdened.

They both hugged me. One cannot continue to feel downcast when hugged by such delightful women. They smelt, for some reason, of bluebells.

So I cheered up. When we came to the end of the first CD, the jingle jingle was silent, so we kept CD two in reserve in case it started again and went with quiet. I was starting to feel sort of guilty about this. 'And of course there must be something wrong/In wanting to silence any song' as the man who wrote 'Good fences make good neighbours' said. Who was he? Poem about stopping in the woods? Ah. Robert Frost.

Oh, well. Jason again requested the use of the big oven and I gladly left him with the cleaning. When Horatio and I arrived upstairs, Daniel was awake, clothed, and presumably in his right mind. It's always hard to tell with chess people because they mutter a lot. He moved a pawn and looked up at me. He smiled.

'The girl was good, really good,' he told me. 'Taking as her model the amazing Judith Polgár. When in doubt, she attacks. Her opponent is a mediocre player, but good enough to be worth beating.'

'Any idea who he or she is?'

'Not so far. I haven't got the results of the search back yet. Lunch?'

'Lovely,' I commented, sitting down to a big bowl of tomatoes with chives, Uncle Solly's potato salad with Thousand Island dressing and a plate of cheese and cold roast beef. Daniel allowed me to select what I wanted then started to wolf the rest.

'You still haven't caught up on your day of starvation,' I said. I like watching people eat. He nodded with his mouth full. I made myself a sandwich out of cold meat and Gentleman's Relish. Delicious.

There was lemon cordial to drink. This was to be a working afternoon.

'Timbo will be outside by now,' said Daniel.

'I'll change and be right there,' I said.

I put on my loose boho garments, adding a pair of thin black trousers underneath. My inner thighs had been scraped by that rescue. I added my biggest hat. Horatio elected to curl up on my bed, which Daniel had made, complete with hospital corners. God love him.

Timbo was indeed waiting. He gave Daniel a large bag, and started the car.

'To Footscray,' said Daniel, and gave the bag to me. I looked inside. It was full of old-fashioned sweets. Humbugs, mint leaves, jelly babies, boiled lollies, musk sticks. Lovely. I remembered some of them from my own youth. There was a packet of gummi bears and, my favourites, sour lemon drops, the expensive ones in a tin.

'The Lake household has a lot of kids,' Daniel observed. 'No money to buy luxuries. So I am bringing sweets; the parents will accept presents for the kids.'

'I remember Mr. Lake,' I said, recalling the red-faced men grunting and grappling, before Sister Mary put the mozz on them.

'That was out of character,' said Daniel. 'He's very worried about his son. You'll see. He's a shift worker; he ought to be home.'

'Oh, goody,' I said. I was not filled with enthusiasm.

◇◇◇

The house was shabby. It was in a line of similar houses which must have been built for the factories, perhaps, or the railways. It had last been painted during the reign of Paul Keating, but that didn't matter for the verandah had been enclosed and over it swagged, reading from left to right, a huge jasmine vine, a vivid bougainvillea, a wisteria and another flowery thing which I could not identify. This meant that the front door was in deep shade. On either side I could see hammocks and tightly made single beds.

The doorbell made a sad ratchety noise, but it summoned a large woman in a loose house dress. She stared at Daniel.

'Any news?'

'No, but no bad news,' he told her. 'And they were alive and well a couple of days ago.'

'Come in,' she invited.

The house smelt of fruit. Daniel introduced me and she shook my hand. Her own was as work-worn as mine. 'I'm Mags. I'm just making jam,' she said. 'Come into the kitchen.'

The house was full of children. Two boys were playing snap on the drawing room floor, assisted by a toddler who kept grabbing the cards. They were putting up with her with great patience, for boys. Mags continued on into a small kitchen full of steam and two very good small girls, who were splitting plums. A preserving pan was boiling on the obsolete stove. Ranks of jars stood in the oven, drying out and sterilising.

'We eat a lot of jam,' explained Mags. 'On toast and on scones and in pies. The bought stuff is expensive and who knows what is in it? Here, I know what's in it.'

'Fruit and sugar,' said one of the little girls. She was muffled under an apron and was clearly very proud of it.

'Good,' said Mags, inspecting the halved plums. 'Now Sue can fill the water jug and Ann can prepare the saucers for testing. I'll put these plums into the basin to wait for the next batch. Good work, girls.'

Ann, the child with the apron, dived across the kitchen and opened a cupboard. She took out three saucers and put them in the fridge, a disproportionate monster of a thing with a freezer at the top. It was, I noticed, stuffed almost as full as my own.

'And Sue can go out to help Daddy if she wants to,' added Mags. Sue vanished out the back door, where something barked a lot. 'Do sit down, would you like some tea?'

'No, just had lunch. I wanted my colleague to meet you. And Sam.'

'Delighted, I'm sure,' replied Mags.

'How many children do you have?' I asked. I had counted five so far.

'Two of my own,' she told me. 'Six others. Fosters. They send us the ones who have been abused. No one's going to abuse them here. They can get used to a man who isn't a fiend. And they seem to like being with other kids all the time, sleeping in the same room, which is good, because we haven't got a lot of space.'

I looked at her. She had mousy hair cut short with what I guessed was a pair of nail scissors, a broad face with small eyes and a wide mouth. She was almost as large as me. No one was going to give us fashion prizes. But her expression as she watched small Ann testing jam with religious care was meltingly tender.

'Not yet,' she told the child. 'It needs to crinkle when you push it. Soon. You got to be patient when you're a cook.'

'Is Manny coming back?' asked Ann.

'Yes,' said Mags with a steely note in her voice. 'Soon.'

'Indeed,' said Daniel.

I hoped it was true.

'Would you like us to go outside?' I asked. 'We're rather clogging up your kitchen.

'Just till I get this jam into jars,' she said, smiling at me for the first time. 'Tell Sam tea'll be ready soon. Fresh bread and hot jam, yum.'

'Yum,' repeated Ann.

Sam was waiting for us. He was looking in through the kitchen window at his wife and the child.

'She didn't talk at all when she came,' he told us. 'Then she started repeating things. Then she started talking for herself. Manny was real good with her. Poor little mite. Her mother tied her to a bed for weeks at a time and left her all alone. Never really learnt to talk. Only reason she didn't die was the dog. It's a scraggy old mongrel, but she adores it. Scamp washed her and brought her food. Treated her as though she was his puppy. Here, Scamp!'

Scamp rushed to his feet. He was a strange mixture of, at a guess, labrador and maybe German shepherd? He licked Sam's hand.

'Eats like a pig, though. And a terrible thief, we have to keep him outside when Mags is cooking. You're looking for Manny, eh?'

'I am,' I said.

He was examining me narrowly so I returned the compliment. He was a solid, stocky man with a red face, curly dark hair and work-ruined hands. His black singlet shifted a little, revealing milk-white skin underneath his mahogany weathering. Sue arrived and swarmed up him as though he was a tree. He cradled her carefully. She wrapped her arms around his neck in a choke hold. I smiled.

'You'll do,' Sam Lake told me. 'You want to know what Manny was like, why he left, eh?'

'Whatever you can tell me,' I said.

'Let's walk,' he said.

The backyard was largeish and crammed with growing things. Two children were carrying water to the large plastic barrel under a plum tree. They ranged in age from about four to about ten, and they had suitable pots, from a milk saucepan for the smallest to a bucket for the largest. Ropy tendrils of pumpkin writhed along the far wall, along with a large lemon tree and a few others. I wished Meroe or Trudi was with me. They would really like this garden.

Because it wasn't just vegetables and fruit. Someone had planted nasturtiums and they swarmed over everything. There was a bush of daisies. There were little plots which seemed less well cultivated, one of which had a bountiful harvest of radishes, and another of which had nothing at all except some dying lettuce.

'The kids can plant whatever they like but they have to water it,' he told me. 'Looks like Kane's forgotten again. You remind him, Susy?'

'He's cross,' said Sue. 'You tell him, Daddy!'

'All right, maybe later, when he comes home. Kane's got a job at the supermarket,' he explained. 'Bringing in the trolleys. It's a job,' he added. 'He has to get up and go to work every day. He's been doing it. He's doing real well. Manny was doing real well, too. Natural gardener, that boy. There's his tomatoes—look at them!'

I looked. Taller than me. Fruiting freely. There was a whole trellis loaded with cherry tomatoes, bowing under the weight.

'They look fine!' I agreed.

'Taste fine, too.' He plucked one, picked a leaf of basil, and gave them to me. I bit. Warm. Savoury. Gorgeous.

'We mostly live off the garden,' said Sam Lake, unwreathing Sue and putting her down. 'You can go and help with the watering,' he suggested. She scampered off. 'Poor kid, her step-father's doing seven years for what he did to her and her little sister, and it ain't enough. Took her six months before she'd even talk to me. That's Sue's little sister, carrying water, bless her. They rely on each other. Cruel to split them up.' I watched the children, bickering quietly because it was becoming very hot, replace their implements and go to ground under the lemon tree. Sam Lake went on, 'Manny's my natural son. Maggie had seven miscarriages, then Irene, then Manny. Manuel, his name is. After her grandfather. After that she couldn't have any more, and she dearly loves kids. So we're foster parents. Government pays us something for them.'

'Not a lot, I'm guessing.'

'If we were doing it for money it wouldn't matter how much we were paid, we'd be ratshit,' he opined, plucking a tomato for himself. 'Mags, she'd be sad without kids. Her mother had seven. Mine had five. I like them all right. I've got the afternoon shift at the factory, so I'm home in the mornings. I can help with breakfast and getting them off to school, though Mags has to do dinner on her own. Manny was quiet. Liked the plants. Talked to them. He was going to do an exam for a scholarship to the agricultural college. He would have got it, too. He wasn't dumb. He just hated school. Then this girl came along and he buggered off. You reckon he's all right?'

'Yes,' I said. 'Daniel saw him a couple of days ago and he was all right then.'

'That silvertail wanker,' he started.

'My opinion exactly,' I said, laying a hand on his arm.

'I shoulda knocked his block off,' muttered Sam.

'No, because what would the children do with you in jail? So, no one here has heard anything? Phone message? Text?'

'We only got one phone,' said Sam. 'It's in the kitchen. He hasn't rung. But I feel better about it now I know you're on the case. You're like Mags. You get things done.'

'Thanks.' I was very flattered. 'I'm a baker.'

'Working woman,' he grinned. 'Could tell from your hand.'

Mags called from the kitchen. 'Here we go,' said Sam. 'Bread and hot jam. Come on, kids!' he yelled, and the lurkers under the lemon tree raced across the garden.

There wasn't room in the kitchen for all of us, so Daniel and I took our treat into the garden. It really was lovely. The beds bristled with fresh leaves, tall sunflowers, spears which meant onions, perhaps? Two boys joined us, jam smeared all over their faces.

'You looking for Manny?' asked one, very gruffly.

'I am,' said Daniel.

'You tell him to come home and bring his girlfriend,' said the boy. 'Mags likes babies. He'd be all right here. I been here the longest. Tell him Talyn says come home.'

'I'll tell him, Talyn,' said Daniel. He and the boy touched knuckles. It was one of those masculine bonding moments.

I finished my bread and jam, which was very good, though the bread was commercial. I went back into the parlour and retrieved the big bag of sweets.

'Mags, we brought a present for the kids,' I said, and handed them over. Mags grinned. The kitchen inhabitants cheered.

'Good. Thanks. And you'll take a pot of jam? And you'll tell Manny that we love him and we want him to come home?'

'If I see him, I'll tell him,' I assured her.

I hated depriving the children of even a spoonful of their jam, but I had no choice. As we left, Mags was organising a trip to the library.

'Simple people,' said Daniel as we got into the car.

'As opposed to the complex and educated O'Ryans,' I said sharply.

'Yes,' he agreed. 'Nice people, the Lakes. Those kids are fortunate. They've got a lot of aunties and uncles, too. And they know that if anyone hurts them Sam Lake will punch the soul case out of them. He already did to the molesting stepfather who turned up to kidnap his daughter back. The local cops were very understanding and he didn't do any permanent damage. That's when the child started to talk again.'

'Sue,' I said.

'Yes. The older ones know how lucky they are and don't cause trouble.'

'Wonderful.'

'What they could really do with,' said Daniel, 'is an air conditioner. That house is murder in the summer. The kids sleep in the garden, under mosquito nets.'

'We must see what we can organise,' I promised. 'An air conditioner shouldn't prove too difficult to find.'

The trouble with the world is that you forget that there are good people in it. I contemplated the Lakes and wondered how many more people there were, doing the best they could every day, with scant help and no respect.

Probably quite a lot.

Daniel's phone chimed. It was a text message. It said: *were ok safe 4 now sorry Daniel Fr say yr ok.*

Chapter Fifteen

Madame Loubet, the proprietress and
cook, was of commensurate size. Like
many first-rate women cooks she had tired
eyes and a wan smile.

Alice B. Toklas
The Alice B. Toklas Cookbook

It was later. I had showered and changed and at last reduced my core temperature to something lower than the heart of a volcano. I was sipping a gin and tonic. Daniel had returned the text message with another which said *Talyn says come home Mags and Sam send love I would never turn you over to the O'Ryans How is Brigid?* but had not received a reply. He knew the number of the phone. It was his own.

'Couldn't you find them with the GPS chip in the phone?' I asked.

'I could, but I don't want them to run away again. I need them to start talking to me. Oh well, perhaps we could find the freegans and ask them. They'd know.'

'But would they tell?'

'There's another question. Nothing to be done at present. What's been happening in the mad, mad world of Insula?'

I kissed him on the ear.

'Oh, I haven't told you about Mr. Pahlevi. He's here on a revenge mission. He thinks that Meroe cursed his brother, who was eaten by a bear.'

'Even for Insula that is extreme. Did she?'

'Curse him? She says not. He was on his way to rape her to prevent her being a witch, as witches have to be virgins according to this tribe's mythos, when he fell over the bear and it killed him.'

'Just the Goddess protecting her own,' murmured Daniel, who seemed drowsy.

'I hadn't thought of it that way.'

'So even bears can wake up cross.' Daniel yawned. Horatio yawned also. So did I.

I shook off encroaching sleep.

'It's not all that funny—he's going around telling everyone that Meroe is a black witch and an evil woman.'

'But everyone knows that isn't true.'

'Mud sticks. Mrs. Pemberthy would believe it instantly.'

'Yes, indeed. We shall have to find a way to switch him off. Meroe doesn't believe he is a physical threat?'

'She utterly refused to be even slightly alarmed.'

'That isn't the same thing, you know.'

'I know. I think she's scared and won't admit it.'

I was now yawning fit to break my jaw. It was all Horatio's fault. A yawning cat is the most relaxing thing in the universe. They ought to be on prescription. I gave up. I yielded. I set the alarm to wake us at six for dinner, and fell asleep.

I woke up ravenous. There was a scent of cooking meat in the air. Pork, if I was any judge. Pork sausages, in fact. And me without a sausage in the house. I felt languid and disinclined to move from my cool apartment. I could always put on all those clothes again and go out to the supermarket, but they didn't have the sort of sausages I liked. Or I could send Daniel out to Uncle Solly's, though his sausages would not be pork. Much the best idea.

Daniel went out, taking one of the New York Deli's white canvas bags, stuffed with the three we had to return. I set the table, found the mustard, and poured myself a glass of cold crisp New Zealand sauv blanc. The light was flickering on the answering machine. I pressed the button.

'*Give up Shiloh or be damned to everlasting fire!*' shrieked a voice. No greeting. No '*Hello, Corinna, prepare for a nasty message, perhaps you had better sit down.*' Just a female, perhaps, voice, screaming. I saved the message. There were no others.

Slightly shaken, I gulped my wine, and was sipping another when Daniel returned, hot and sweating but loaded with provender.

'This way we don't have to go out tomorrow, either,' he told me, laying bundles on the table. 'They say it's going to be stinking tomorrow. It's already on its way. The Christmas shoppers are nearing meltdown. Here, Madame has three sorts of sausages, plus salads with the remarkable Uncle Solly dressings, salt beef, smoked chicken and, of course, pickles. And bagels. Baked cheesecake for dessert.'

'Terrific,' I said, and dived into the food. Smoked chicken bagel with shredded lettuce, cream cheese and onion, marvellous. Daniel accounted for more than half of the food and then looked sadly at the table.

'Oh, well, maybe there's enough leftovers for a little snack. On the other hand, pass me the last of that potato salad, will you, Corinna?'

'Pleasure. We can cook the sausages tomorrow. Do you have to do anything tonight?'

'I'm going out with the Soup Run at midnight to see if any of Sister Mary's people have seen our missing two.'

'Then before you go out we can have a nice evening, after I play you this creepy message.'

He grinned at me and kissed my onion-scented hand. I love the way he doesn't mind if I smell of onions. James, my ex-husband and major error, used to forbid me to eat them because he hated the smell. Of course, it was a useful way of keeping him away from me. I have always liked onions and during my marriage I rather specialised in them.

'Deal, so play me the creepy message.'

I played it. Daniel made me play it again.

'Man or woman?' I asked him.

'Sounds female to me. Pity your prehistoric answering machine doesn't record incoming numbers. Leave it on there, *metuka*. I didn't like that tone of voice at all.'

'Me neither. Shiloh? That's the lunatic sect the O'Ryans belong to called the church of something and Shiloh.'

'Holy Reformed Temple of Shiloh. Shiloh is in the Bible. He's the Child of Peace. Not a lot of peace in that communication,' he commented. 'Right, how about an episode of the new *Doctor Who*? I know you have to go to bed at eight.'

'*Doctor Who* it is,' I agreed, and settled down for a charming couple of hours before I had to sleep. The Doctor went forth to save the universe—again—from the Daleks—again—and the person seeking Shiloh did not ring back. Despite my nap, I slept well, and when I awoke Daniel was gone.

But there was the faithful Horatio, curled into a neat ellipsoid cushion of tabby and white. It unfolded and demanded breakfast, so I got up. Morning things happened. The phone rang and I let the machine pick it up. I don't answer the phone at 4 a.m.

'*Shiloh! Give up Shiloh or burn forever more!*' screamed my caller of last night. Making a note to google Shiloh the person when I had time, I washed, dressed, and allowed Horatio to follow me down the stairs to the bakery, which was full of smoke. Jason was visible by the open door, frantically fanning with an empty sack, and the air conditioner groaned, straining to clean the air.

I slammed the inner door in Horatio's affronted face and ran down the steps. Where was the fire extinguisher? Where, in fact, was the fire? Nothing seemed to be actually burning.

'It's all right, Captain,' yelled Jason. 'I was trying to dry something in the oven overnight and it caught fire. There's no danger. Just a lot of smoke.'

'Well, let's step out into the alley and let it clear,' I said. 'I hope you haven't set off the sprinklers, because that will put paid to baking until we get everything dried out.'

'I'm so sorry,' he said, tears of smoke and regret spilling down his cheeks.

'No harm done,' I replied, patting his shoulder. It was too early in the morning to be angry. The smoke was already clearing. Fairly soon we would be able to go inside.

'Where are the Mouse Police?' I called. Jason pointed. They had withdrawn themselves as far as the doorway of the Rising Sun Japanese restaurant and seemed to be determined to stay there until the fire was out or the restaurant opened, whichever came first. They might change their minds when they heard kitty dins rattle into the plates.

'All right,' I ordered my midshipman. 'Up on the ladder and start swabbing the walls and ceiling. Shouldn't take too long. Do the ovens need cleaning?'

'No, Cap'n, just that one,' he pointed to an open door. Whatever he had been cooking had been carbonised. I took the whole shelf and left it in the alley. It was still pitch dark but with any luck I might trap that paperboy later. The oven was all right, just needed to cool down. Smoke vanished and the smell started to disappear under enthusiastic applications of orange-scented cleaner. I felt that I might risk beginning the baking for the day and started loading mixers.

By the time I had all of them humming Jason had stowed the ladder and was helping me. He was the only thing in the bakery which still stank of smoke.

'Shower and clean overalls,' I ordered, and he vanished into the bathroom. I put the coffee pot on. The Mouse Police crept back, drawn by the smell of food. They gave me that look which means: we are seriously offended, and if you do anything like that one more time, we will exercise our right to withdraw our labour and move to a place where people appreciate us, i.e., as it might be, the Rising Sun, which might well have a rat problem which needs a solution in exchange for bulk tuna.

I stroked and sympathised, eventually eliciting a reluctant purr or two. I also had been shocked and I put sugar in my coffee and ate a leftover muffin. It was one of Jason's chocolate orgasms and I could feel it doing me good. Or harm, perhaps.

When Jason emerged, freshly clothed and cleanly scrubbed, I was in a forgiving mood. All that chocolate, probably.

'What were you trying to make?' I asked him, holding out a bag containing the leftovers from last night's dinner. He dived on the salt beef and salads and began to make Dagwood sandwiches, interleaved with gherkins.

'Beef jerky,' he replied with his mouth full. 'It was Sarah's idea. I prepared it all right, but I must have got the temperature too high or maybe the smoker was wrong. Perhaps the sugar caught fire. I nearly shit myself when I came in and found it all burning.'

'Yes, me too,' I commented, wondering how anyone's jaw could stretch to accommodate the sandwich he was building. 'So let's not do that again, eh?'

'No, it's a failure,' he sighed. 'I'll have to tell her that it doesn't work.'

'Sarah asked you to make beef jerky?' I said, amazed that I hadn't noticed this oddity before. 'But she's the vegiest of vegans!'

'Janeen got it,' Jason replied thickly, through a mist of mayonnaise. 'Some sort of experimental tofu-based protein, she said. I thought it seemed more like pork, myself. Pale and stringy.'

'Well, that explains why it didn't dry like meat,' I told him. 'Tofu is moulded and extruded and generally worked upon soy beans. Nothing like as dense as meat. You'll need a whole new set of recipes, and you'll be making them in your own oven, if you please. And do be careful, Jason—you've got that apartment by grace and favour and only while you keep it nicely. Set fire to it and you might be out on the street.'

'Yeah, Corinna, I know,' he replied, muffling a scowl in his sandwich. And I left it at that. I had hated being nagged. I wasn't going to turn into a nagger myself if I could help it.

After our little emergency we were late, so we leapt into a frenzy of mixing and baking and had no time for further conversation. When Kylie arrived at the shop I opened the door for Horatio. He stalked through the bakery and leapt onto the counter, tail twitching. Just so that I knew he was unimpressed. He managed to convey this without any trouble.

There was hardly any smell of smoke in the shop but I left the door open to air it out anyway. The hot wind tore inside and licked out the previous atmosphere in seconds. When I shut it again, the air conditioner whined with the effort of bringing the temperature down to a human level. Summer. Loathe it.

'No need to worry,' I said as my assistant wrinkled her adorable nose. 'Just a little experiment of Jason's which didn't work. He won't be doing it again,' I added, meaningly, to my blushing midshipman.

'Shit, no,' he agreed. 'I only got blueberry muffins today. I'll get up extra early tomorrow and make the fancy ones,' he offered.

I knew an apology when I heard one.

'Good work, Midshipman,' I said crisply. 'Carry on, miss.'

Both of them saluted. Oh, how I love being captain.

After that it was an ordinary morning. The faint smell of smoke was overtaken by the strong smell of baking. People flopped into the shop and stood under the air-conditioning vent, purring as they cooled down. Horatio unbent enough to allow his ears to be caressed by especially favoured customers. Even Jason's despised default blueberry muffins sold out. Kylie was telling me about the new ultra-neon yellow thongs she was going to buy and Jason was exuding relief that I hadn't screamed at him. I was wondering about textured soy-based protein. Hadn't someone already made it? Or was I thinking of nut-meat?

We sold out, cashed up and closed down about two. I took Horatio up to the apartment, Jason started the mopping, Kylie went off to the bank and then to the shoe shop and all was well with the world. After such a nerve-wracking morning, I did not go to the roof. I showered and changed and settled down with a cold glass of white wine and my Jade Forrester. Horatio had a comprehensive all-over wash to remove every trace of smoke from his fur and joined me on the couch. And so Daniel discovered us when he returned, looking rough from his all-night foray among the lost, stolen and strayed.

'I think I've found them,' he told me, and slumped into a chair.

'Good,' I murmured.

'And you'll never believe where they are,' he added.

'No?'

'But first,' he said, 'I want a shower and a change of clothes, a glass of that wine and a few hours' sleep. How are things with you?'

'Jason tried to burn down the bakery this morning but we put it out in time,' I told him. 'You look terrible. Shower first and I will be pouring the wine.'

'Darling,' he told me, and went into the bathroom.

I beguiled the time by looking up Shiloh. I knew it was in the Bible. Genesis 49:10, the prophecy given by Jacob to his son, Judah. 'Until Shiloh come, and unto him shall the gathering of the people be.' It also had a connection with Joanna Southcott, the eighteenth-century prophetess who had died giving birth to the putative said Shiloh (at the age of sixty-five: no baby had resulted) and whose ultimate prophecies were locked in a box inside another box, which twenty-four bishops were going to have to open when they really needed a prophecy. About now sounded good. Then again she had been firm about the ending of the world in 2004. Of course, it might have happened, and we hadn't noticed. I resolved to ask Meroe about her. Then I poured the wine as I had promised Daniel.

He emerged distractingly rumpled and sweet-smelling, drank the wine, kissed my shoulder, and somehow the matter of the missing children was shelved for the moment. I hadn't seen him for hours. I missed him.

When we emerged from our trance it was getting late and I had to go to sleep.

'I am meeting some of the freegans at ten,' Daniel told me, searching for his briefs. 'They said that they would introduce me

so the children won't be too scared. I'll let you know by morning if all is well. Meanwhile,' he kissed me again, 'sleep well.'

And I did. Morning brought no news. I went down to the
bakery with some trepidation, but nothing was burning. Jason,
in his clean overalls, was taking trays of tiny muffins out of the
oven.

'Good morning, Cap'n!' he saluted. 'Gourmet muffins in
train. Sourdough in the mixer. Pasta douro in the oven. Making
rolls, today, sir?'

'Why not? Practise your French twists. Was Sarah very cross
with you about the jerky?'

He gave me that stunned-mullet beam. 'No, she's so cool,
she said it wasn't my fault. Janeen says she's getting some more
and we can experiment with how to cook it. I reckon it needs
to be wet. Maybe sausages?'

'Might be good, as long as you put enough onion and stuffing
into them,' I said idly. 'I've never made sausages but I remember
our Italian neighbours used to have a sausage fest every year.
And one to make the tomato sauce, the one they call passata.
Base for most Italian cooking. You could mince your fake meat
finely, make rissoles out of it. Or put it into a risotto or a stew.'

'I think she was after finger food,' said Jason. 'Easy to eat.'

'Then what about little meatballs cooked in broth? Vegie
broth, of course. Or crumbed and deep fried. Try it out sometime. And make a tomato dipping sauce. One thing about
summer, there's a glut of good tomatoes. There's a recipe for
tomato sauce in that old vegetarian cookbook you borrowed.'

He nodded. 'Got leftovers?' he asked hungrily.

'Sorry, Daniel ate them all up. Have a cheese roll. Or two.'

I watched as he engulfed several cheese rolls and a bottle of
Coke (at this hour!) then went on to compound a new muffin.
I set out the catering trays of the elite little muffins, each one a
tiny mouthful of delight. I diverted one slightly scorched one to
sustain myself and accompany my second cup of coffee.

'This is fantastic!' I remarked after the first bite. Even if you
nibbled they were really only two bites. 'What's in it?'

'Coffee and walnuts,' he told me. 'I just used your filter coffee to mix it instead of milk. And chopped the walnuts very small. You like?'

'I could take it home with me and cuddle it all night,' I told him. Whatever the temporary effect of being in love, adoring Sarah had not managed to dampen Jason's essential muffin magic for long. 'I'll get on with the rolls, you finish the icing for the shop muffins.'

'Orange today,' he said, in a fluff of icing sugar. 'Candied the peel myself.'

We worked in silence for an hour or so, until Jason's icing was all spread and my rolls were in the oven.

'By the way, how is Bunny?'

'We're getting on real well,' said Jason, taking off his cap and wiping his forehead. Getting piped icing right takes severe concentration, especially if you insist on a little candied orange section in the exact centre of each one. 'I let him out for a hop as soon as I get home. He's worked out how to use a latrine like the bunny book says. Likes to sit alongside me on the couch and watch TV. Never had a pet before,' he said. 'It's ace.'

'Wonderful,' I commented and, with a pang, thought of Bunny's owner, and wondered if she had the space for a nice long hop, or a couch to stretch out upon.

Goss came in to open the shop, Horatio descended to the counter, the wind howled like a banshee outside and Earthly Delights was open for business. Jason had set up a separate account for his muffins and his Christmas cakes and he was cleaning up. As, of course, was I, even after I deducted the cost of the very good ingredients. And even though he had not succeeded to his own satisfaction in candying his own cherries.

'What are you going to do with your Christmas money, Jason?' I asked, although it was none of my business. He crumpled his baker's hat in nervous fingers.

'When you're shut for January, I thought I might, you know, just get a bus to the beach. I never had a holiday, not a real one. Some charity used to send the poor kids to Anglesea every year but I never got to go, I was always in trouble. Holidays were only for good boys.' He was imitating someone, screwing up his face. 'And I wasn't a good boy. In fact, I was a little deadshit.'

'But you're not that Jason now,' I said lamely.

'Yeah, so I thought, why not go and stay in a backpackers or maybe camp? Daniel says he'll lend me the gear. If I run out of money I can get a job as a cook. Fast food, greasies, I can cook all that. Might learn to surf. And you,' he leant forward to speak into Goss' beringed ear, 'will have to mind Bunny.'

'We can do that,' replied Goss, who was thinking about something else and, I am persuaded, hadn't heard what he said. 'Corinna, can I come in tomorrow as well? Only Kylie's got to get on with her Christmas shopping.'

'Of course,' I replied. Eek! Christmas shopping! I hadn't started! Or had I enough presents for all without going out? I always bought a stash of emergency presents at the January sales. I foresaw an urgent audit. Of course, if I knew what I wanted, the girls would be delighted to battle their way through the crowds to secure it. One did not get between a bear and its cub, a tiger and its prey, or the girls and a shop.

The morning went well. Jason went off to Cafe Delicious for a Trucker's Special breakfast. I ate another muffin. I went upstairs to change into my respectable shop clothes, a pair of light blue trousers and a dark blue shirt and comfortable sandals on my tired feet. The smoke from yesterday had left no trace. The shop smelt gorgeous, rich and spicy. People sniffed greedily as they came in and dived for wallets to secure one of Jason's fruitcakes. Small enough for a single person, thinly sliced big enough for a luncheon, great keeping qualities, and if you had unexpected guests, why, just break the seal on another cake and you had a party.

Carriers came for the restaurant bread and for the catering trays. Each one of those parties was an advertisement for the shop. Several people came in every day who had eaten a Jason muffin at a party and now wanted to secure a supply of their very own. They ought to be listed under addictive substances

in the Drug Act. I made up a basket for Meroe, all vegie: zucchini and tomato, fig and goat's cheese, roasted capsicum and
parmesan, orange, lemon, coffee and walnut, chocolate orgasm
and kama sutra and oasis. I was concerned about my witch and
the unpleasant Mr. Pahlevi.

Come to think of it, he must have run out of rosewater muffins by now. I wondered where Serena was getting her rose fix.
Possibly he was buying her roses. Somehow I didn't think so.

It was about eleven when Jason came into the shop and
whispered to me, 'Some dude's staking us out.'

I never ignore comments like that. Jason spent a lot of time
homeless and has not lost his hard-won street smarts.

'Where?' I asked, there being no point in whispering.

'Corner of the lane. He's been there since I let the Mouse
Police out. Suit,' said Jason.

I went to the front of the shop, ostensibly to rearrange my
decorations. Yes, a middle-aged man in a conservative black suit,
white shirt, black shoes. Short hair. A clipboard, which was a
nice touch. Might be making a traffic census or collecting for
a charity. But he didn't accost any of the thousands of people
using the lane as a short cut and he made no notes. I wondered
who he was. He was unlikely to be a gypsy. So he was probably
a devotee of the Holy Reformed Temple of Shiloh, wanting me
to hand over the child. Or watching to see if I would lead them
to the girl Brigid and her devoted Manny.

Over my dead body, I thought. Or preferably his.

'Yes, you're right, we have got a watcher,' I told Jason. 'He's
no trouble if he's only watching. Goss, I am giving you back
your phone,' I said. She gaped at me. Ordinarily I required that
they store their phone, turned off, on a high shelf while the
shop was open. There had been friction about this unreasonable
demand. 'I want you to key in the emergency number on your
speed dial,' I added.

'Already got it,' she said.

'You can leave the phone on in case we need it in a hurry,' I
said. 'But otherwise it's on voicemail, all right?'

'All right,' said Goss, laying the phone on the counter within reach. 'What do I do?'

'If that man in the black suit makes a single threatening move, you call the cops and lock the door. I don't think he will,' I added. 'I think he's just a watcher. Probably harmless.'

'But creepy,' said Goss. And Jason and I agreed with her.

But he made no move as the day went on. He must be sustained by faith, I thought, as the temperature outside rose like a lift. We sold out, leaving only meagre pickings for the Soup Run. I would have to replenish it with some supermarket bread, which was ironic, though the elderly clients preferred soft white bread as easier on their missing teeth. Goss took the banking and went to augment her Christmas purchases. Jason put in his earplugs, hooked his iPod on the front of his overall, and began the cleaning, well satisfied with the holiday money he had earned in one morning. The man in the lane had not moved. I was just about to escort Horatio to his afternoon nap when Daniel ran downstairs from the apartment, my backpack in his hand, gasped, 'Come on!', and hustled me out into the lane and into Timbo's car, where Meroe was also seated.

Chapter Sixteen

Fools! For I also had my hour;
One far fierce hour and sweet:
There was a shout about my ears
And palms before my feet.

GK Chesterton
'The Donkey'

I hadn't had time to catch my breath before Timbo roared off, heading north. I caught one glimpse of the suit dragging out a mobile phone before he was lost in a cloud of exhaust. It was too much to hope that we had disconcerted him for long.

'Where are we going?' I asked. 'Merry meet, Meroe.'

'Merry meet,' she replied sedately. She was dressed in her usual black skirt and black top. Today's wrap was a clear azure, unfigured. She had a basket on her lap.

'We've found them,' said Daniel, alight with purpose. 'I spoke to them last night. I just don't know how we're going to get them out.'

'Out of where?' I demanded.

'You'll see. We're being followed. Get a move on, Timbo!'

Timbo, spraying sugar from his interrupted breakfast of a dozen doughnuts, hauled the car around a corner, ran a yellow light, flung us under the nose of an affronted tram, and into the main street. Then he sped up.

I closed my eyes. When I opened them again, we were past the brewery demolition site and in a small lane beside a large apartment complex.

'Quick,' hissed Daniel, and we dived out as Timbo squealed the tyres and practically spun the poor car on its axis, leading any pursuit—I hoped—away. Daniel hustled me, Meroe and the basket into the deep doorway of the apartment. A car belted down the alley after Timbo and with any luck hadn't seen us stop. Daniel did something to the door and we were inside the building.

It was cool, modern and echoing. The colour scheme was pale grey and pale blue, colours which won't offend anyone. There was a desk and a room for a guard or supervisor, but there was no one there and some of the fittings were still enveloped in bubble wrap.

'You remember the glut of office space we had in the nineties?' asked Daniel. 'The developers turned the offices into apartments. Now there's a glut of apartments. The freegans know how to get in, and how to fool the operating system into supplying them with electricity and hot water. Not a secret they are willing to share, by the way. They never stay more than a month, which is when the bills start to come in, and they never cause any damage. Sometimes takes them hours to find the discarded cleaning materials they need to keep the place tidy, they say people hardly ever throw out cleaning materials.'

I thought about this. It was true. I only ever threw out empty bottles, and then into the recycling bin. But we were wandering from the topic.

'So the freegans let our two into an apartment?' I prompted.

'Yes, it's nice and clean, has a shower, it's air-conditioned and they'd be safe. There are some people living here, mostly overseas businesspeople who aren't curious about their neighbours. Come on,' he said. 'We shouldn't linger in the foyer. It's a glass door.'

'But they can't get in,' I pointed out. Meroe laughed.

'Neither they can,' she agreed.

'Upstairs,' he said.

We followed. I was still bemused by the speed of events. The stairwell smelt of fresh paint. We went up two flights and emerged into a pristine corridor. The silence was deafening. Daniel knocked on the door of 205 and someone on the other side whispered, 'Daniel?'

'It's me, open the door,' he replied.

'Who's with you?' The voice was hard with suspicion. 'I can hear people.'

'Meroe the witch and Corinna the baker.'

'My dad says you're all right,' said the voice, and the door opened.

So here was our fugitive from that crowded house in Footscray. He still had spots. But otherwise he greatly resembled his mother. He had the same air of brisk efficiency and the same mousy hair and small, clever eyes.

'Corinna.' I extended a hand. He shook. His hand was solid, muscular and calloused.

'Blessed be,' said Meroe, and patted his cheek. He took a step back.

'I'm Manny,' he told us. 'Brigie's in here.'

Meroe went in to see the young woman, shutting the door firmly behind her. Daniel and I examined the flat. It was spacious and largely empty. The kitchen, one of those really expensive ones, had been augmented with a box for a table and a couple of cushions.

'You want some tea?' asked Manny. 'I can do tea.'

We accepted tea and Manny put the kettle on. A sense of dread was growing on me. I shook myself.

'This looks cosy,' I said for something to say.

'So nice and cool,' Manny replied. 'We can have a shower every day, twice a day. Brigie gets real overheated. Freegans found us a big old chair and she's been sleeping in it. She can't lie flat anymore. And we can wash and dry all our stuff. Freegans found us a lot of food. It's been ace.'

Jason's word. How strong had this young person been, to elude pursuit with the added burden of a pregnant, gently reared girl to protect? The bruises from his nasty encounter in Collingwood had mostly faded. I was lost in admiration.

'Daniel says you found Bunny and he's all right,' Manny said.

'Yes, presently hopping around my apprentice's flat and in the rudest of health.'

'That's good. Thanks! Brigie's been real upset about Bunny. He ran away when we got jumped and I couldn't find him any-where. I was afraid he'd be stew by now, or that some fox'd get him.'

He poured tea into one china cup, one plastic cup and one large mug emblazoned with *World's Greatest Grandpa*. Grandpa had not appreciated his present, it seemed. Someone had put in the correct apostrophe with a black felt pen. This must be freegan loot. No one else would do that.

'Bunny hopped downhill to the Collingwood Children's Farm and was identified by his microchip.'

'He's a bright rabbit,' said Manny.

'Certainly is.'

We sipped tea in silence. It was Earl Grey. Manny took his with long-life milk fished out of a big cardboard box on the counter. Therein were also tins and packets and a collection of fresh fruit and vegetables, a paring knife, two saucepans and a frying pan. Those freegans were efficient.

'But what are we going to do?' Manny asked suddenly, grasping Daniel by the arm. 'You can't keep her family away from her.'

'You watch me,' said Daniel.

'Really?'

'Trust me,' said Daniel. Manny stared into his eyes. Daniel stared back. One of those Clint Eastwood moments which infuriate women to screaming point.

I had heard the door open and Meroe was beckoning me to come in. I left the boys to their unspoken conversation.

'This is Corinna,' she introduced me to a girl lying back in a big chair. I dropped to one knee beside her.

She was beautiful still, though so tired that the heart ached to look at her. Black smudges underlined her blue eyes. She was clean. Her hair had been recently washed and plaited to keep it off her face. She still had her exquisite beauty but the swelling of her belly was almost a deformity. Her wrists and ankles were swollen and looked sore, the skin shiny. She was wearing a freegan-supplied white crimplene maternity dress of hideous cut which someone must have been very glad to discard.

'Hello, Brigid,' I said, taking her hand. She gave mine a little squeeze and then the exhausted grip fell away.

'Bunny?' she whispered.

'Bunny is fine. He's living with my apprentice until you can come back and get him.'

'That's good,' she whispered. 'I was so worried about…'

Then she drifted off. I raised my eyebrows at Meroe.

'We have to get her to hospital fast,' said my witch. 'I've just massaged her belly with mint oil and that child is moving to be born. Any time. She told me that she wet herself about an hour ago. That was her water breaking. She's already in the early stages of labour.'

'No!' the girl roused herself. 'Not hospital! My mother…'

'No, no one is going to come near you, not if I have to personally fell them with a bedpan,' I assured her. 'You can trust Daniel and Daniel has a plan. Don't upset yourself.'

'You trust him?' she appealed to Meroe.

'Yes,' said Meroe. 'I trust him. I'll come with you. I won't leave you.'

'All right,' the girl assented.

No time to lose. I went back to the male half of the situation and reported. They had stopped staring at each other and were drinking tea while Daniel made phone calls.

'We need to go to hospital now,' I said.

'Right now?'

'Yes, really, right now—Meroe says so.'

'The trouble is…' said Daniel.

'What?'

'Well, we were going to have a freegan escort,' he told me. 'Like the escort that got me out of the brewery site. But last night the freegans got into a bit of bother with the police and most of them are in jail.'

'What happened?'

'They were dumpster diving outside a supermarket and the night packers called the cops,' he said slowly. 'The patrol turned up and the freegans danced around them delivering their lecture on how much food is wasted in Melbourne every night. They probably would have been all right even then if Nigel hadn't wreathed the nearest cop in sausages. And kissed him.'

I laughed, even though the situation was not funny. Daniel and Manny were standing near the window and I looked out.

'They'll be released later today, I expect, because what are the cops going to do with them?' Daniel went on.

'But we can't wait until later,' I said. And pointed. 'And the situation has just got more complicated.'

Down in the alley there were men in suits. At least four of them. Watching the door.

'And more,' said Manny.

There in the street were several roughly dressed men and a donkey.

'Lord, the gypsies. They must have followed Meroe.'

Meroe joined me at the window.

'Yes, that's Pahlevi and his brothers.'

'Why are they carrying a bucket?' I asked.

'It's full of holy water and various herbs. They want to throw it over me. I am expected to sizzle and boil away.'

'Like the witch in Oz? "I'm melting, I'm melting?"' asked Manny with interest.

'Just like that,' affirmed Meroe.

'And will it hurt you?' asked Daniel.

'Not unless I get hit in the eye with a clove of garlic.' She smiled grimly.

There was a silence. Brigid moaned. Manny chewed fingernails. I ordered my mind to think of something. It obliged.

'I'm remembering a Flambeau story,' I said. 'We might be able to do this. It will take split-second timing, though. First we have to get Brigid downstairs. Then you have to be prepared to be drenched,' I told Meroe.

They listened to my exposition. There were few questions. This was either going to work, or not work. Manny packed the things he would need, Meroe took up her basket and I donned my backpack. Then we carried Brigid to the lift and emerged into the immaculate foyer. Meroe flung her azure shawl over Brigid's head so that it should not get soaked and we surveyed the crowd. Gypsies to the right. Men of God to the left. Serena in the street, idly chewing. Daniel at the door, opening it.

'Go!' I yelled, and we hauled the poor girl to the door and then several things happened at once.

Meroe ran into the middle of the suits and grabbed one around the neck, embracing him. Manny and I heaved Brigid toward the donkey while I grabbed up the buckets of water and the few remaining flowers from the panniers and threw them at the gypsies. The gypsies, with a collective howl of rage, grabbed for Meroe. One of the Men of God punched a gypsy. One of the gypsies returned the compliment. Meroe danced in between the suits, just out of grabbing range, teasing her exorcists.

Once I had emptied out the panniers, Manny and I hoisted Brigid onto Serena's back and I shook the leading rein.

'Come along,' I told the donkey. 'There's a precedent for this.'

Manny on one side, Daniel on the other, me in the lead, Brigid hanging onto the harness, we began to hurry along Rathdowne Street toward the Women's Hospital. We left the sounds of the cultural studies lesson—that gypsies do not tolerate being thumped, even by men in suits, when they were on an important magical errand—behind as we scuttled along. I didn't dare run, even if I could have run that far, but Serena had an easy lope which ate up the distance and she did not seem distressed by the weight. I suppose that, even pregnant, little Brigie didn't weigh much more than six buckets of water.

She was managing gamely, head bowed under the drape of blue silk, one hand on her belly, one hand clutching the harness. We slowed a little as no one was pursuing us, though there were shouts of 'Son of Peace! Shiloh!' from the alley.

'All right?' Daniel asked me. 'I ought to go back and rescue Meroe.'

'All right,' I told him. It was all right. My plan had worked. Just like in the Father Brown story. Let no one tell me again that reading detective stories was frivolous. Flambeau, a criminal, had fooled two sets of policemen into arresting each other. I had set two antithetical groups together and used Meroe as the bait.

I hoped she was all right. I hoped that Mr. Pahlevi hadn't ensured that the bad witch would sizzle by using, say, battery acid instead of water in that bucket. But Daniel was looking after Meroe and I was leading a donkey down Rathdowne Street. A donkey carrying a pregnant girl, attended by the devoted.

We were getting away with it. It was exhilarating. People we almost ran down did not object but threw coins and compliments. They thought we were a Christmas pageant. And so, in fact, we were.

Serena cooperated with splendid aplomb. Her ears were forward, her pace was deft. She seemed to be trying not to jolt her rider. We climbed the hill without trouble from the donkey, though I was panting and so hot that I thought I might burst into flame. Brigid was clinging like a monkey. Manny was shouting encouragement to the donkey and me.

'Come on, Corinna! Come on, Serena! Hang on, Brigie! Good girls! You can do it!'

We crossed the road with the lights to the tooting of appreciative horns and carried our burden right through the double doors and into casualty.

The triage nurse did not flicker an eyelash. Triage nurses have seen everything. We unloaded Brigid and she was hustled away into an examination cubicle. As the established donkey wrangler, I reversed Serena with some difficulty—every child in the department had flung themselves at her—and took her outside. There I fed her all the flowers which remained in her panniers. After this the children took over and supplied her with a frightful selection of sweets, some pre-sucked. As I was thus engaged, Daniel ran past me with a soaking Meroe by his side. He was licking cut knuckles. I tethered Serena to the stork sculpture and went in to find out what was happening.

Meroe was drying her hair with a hospital towel. As always she had complete self-possession, even soaking wet and bedraggled. No one ever challenged her right to be wherever she was. The sister summoned a wheelchair and Brigid, Meroe and Manny were borne off into the depths of the hospital. Daniel and I, panting and very hot, were left at a curiously loose end. We embraced briefly.

'It worked,' my darling congratulated me.

'So it did,' I said. 'What do we do now?'

'The nurse said it would be hours before she has any news.'

'Shall we go home?' I asked.

'Let's shall.'

So we went outside, unhitched our donkey, and walked her back to Earthly Delights, where there were a lot of rosewater muffins with her name on.

Chapter Seventeen

A virgin most pure as the prophets do tell
Hath brought forth a baby as it hath befell
Trad.

Daniel drew first go at the shower in my apartment, so I stayed in the alley with Serena. The problems of what to do with the heroic donkey were compounded when she was discovered by, first of all, Kylie and Goss, returning hot but sated from their shopping expedition, and then by the choir.

Serena had devoured several hastily defrosted rosewater muffins, half a bucket of lukewarm water, and I was feeding her some leftover carrots from Jason's carrot cake experiment when both girls arrived, squealed with joy, flung their bags into the bakery and then flung themselves at the donkey with a delighted cooing such as is heard from one dove who has just been reunited with its favourite other dove after a long absence. Serena stood up to this very well, allowing them to stroke her silky ears, kiss her nose and straighten her straw hat, which had rather suffered from the pace of events in Rathdowne Street recently. I handed over the rest of the carrots and went in search of some more supplies. Fortunately I had just ordered in a lot of celery and leafy greens and the outer leaves of the cabbage seemed to be just what Serena liked. For what she had just done, she was entitled to wade knee-deep in the produce of the whole Victoria Market.

When I returned loaded with leaves, the confrontation in the alley was advancing nicely toward total war.

'What are you doing with that donkey?' demanded Sarah. Jason was with her, and Rowan, and several other people in severe black and white, carrying folders. Carol singers, I presumed. Bec looked cross, Rowan nervous, Jason agonised and Janeen fascinated. The others looked bored. This must have happened with tedious frequency before.

'I'm feeding her cabbage,' said Goss with complete truth. 'What does it look like I'm doing, girlfriend? And what business is it of yours?'

Goss was on the warpath. Kylie joined her on the front-line.

'Yeah, what she said,' she agreed.

'You are exploiting the labour of that innocent beast,' declaimed Sarah. 'Just like she does with those miserable cats!'

I had seen enough fights for one day and I wanted a wash, a big drink with lots of ice, and total silence. Now Sarah had included me in her denunciation, it was my fight, too, so I stepped in beside the girls.

'You are going away,' I ordered. 'While you are going away, *now*, you might consider that without the Mouse Police I would have to use poison on the rats, which is cruel, and might endanger the organic status of your spelt bread. And secondly, without the labour of animals, the farmers would have to use machines in order to grow your vegetables, which would greatly increase their use of scarce and polluting fossil fuels. Off you go.' She started to retort and I held up a hand, moving very close to her and speaking into her beautiful, impassioned face. 'No, no, shut up, I don't want to hear it. Go now, and avoid arrest. Stay one more moment and I call the cops.'

'Come on, Sarah,' urged the large, bearded bass. 'I'm melting out here. Come and get a nice cold glass of perspective and soda.'

He winked at me as he went past, holding Sarah's arm, and there was a discreet mutter of applause as the choir filed past on their way, I assumed, to Rowan's apartment.

Serena had not twitched an ear. The girls huffed out their breath, exchanged a congratulatory high-five, and tore up more cabbage.

Time passed. I was so heated and grimy. Daniel replaced me, all cool and damp. I went upstairs to get my wash and change my clothes. I showered lavishly and scrubbed my hair. I greeted the affronted Horatio and fed him. I sat down for a moment, just until I cooled off enough to dress again, and must have fallen asleep. An indeterminate time later, I woke. Daniel was kissing me and it was beginning to get dark.

'What happened to Serena?' I asked urgently.

'A very crestfallen and apologetic Mr. Pahlevi reclaimed her. He admits now that Meroe is not a black witch and he says he is sorry. And he understands why we borrowed Serena and promises that he will not mistreat her. He even collected up all those strewn buckets. He had a black eye but assures me that the other bloke looked like he'd been run over by a truck. It's Thursday dinner. Want to go?'

Usually I missed Thursday dinner, where all the tenants gathered for a meal and to discuss the week's doings and iron out any problems before they festered. But tonight I was rested, clean and cool. What's more, it was Mrs. Dawson's turn to provide, and she always had dinner catered by Le Gourmet. Not to be missed. I donned a loose purple gown, made of silk which Jon had brought me from Jogjakarta and constructed by Therese in return for some accounting advice. Daniel put on a pair of brief denim shorts and an Amnesty T-shirt, in which he looked edible.

We dine in the garden if the weather is clement, but this howling north wind was not even within a hundred k's of clement. So we descended to the vault. This was the girls' name for the basement of the old apartment house, where meals had been prepared when the place was serviced, meaning that you had your meals in the in-house restaurant or they could be delivered to your apartment by dumb waiter. Those were civilised days. I would love to be able to order a meal and have it delivered to my rooms, all hot, without having to work out how much to tip room service. I suppose the nearest equivalent is pizza delivery. It isn't the same, however.

We floated down into the vault to find that both Goss and Kylie were there, along with Jon and Kepler, Mistress Dread, Therese and Trudi, and Rowan was sitting next to Jason. Professor Dion and Mrs. Dawson were there, in fact everyone except the holidaying Hollidays. Even Mrs. Pemberthy wasn't going to miss a meal from such a famous restaurant. Despite having to put up with our company. Only Meroe was missing, still attending on our birth. The first course—a delicate cold watercress soup—was already on the table as we sat down.

'Why's it green?' asked Goss, sotto voce.

''Cos it's watercress,' confided Kylie. 'Almost no calories if you don't eat the cream.'

'And not a lot if you do,' observed Mrs. Dawson. She was wearing a charming trouser-and-shirt ensemble in ivory linen, on which I just knew she wasn't going to spill green soup. Around her neck she had wound a strand of pigeons'-egg-sized amber beads which went down below the table and must have belonged to a flapper ancestor. I could see Mrs. Dawson in 1920s clothes, knees rouged, stockings rolled down, doing an energetic Charleston. Meanwhile the soup was excellent.

On being reassured that it was not made with chicken stock, Rowan sipped dubiously. Then he cheered up, as did Jason. Rowan seemed very conservative about food, except muffins. Even Mrs. Pemberthy was drinking the soup without complaint. This could not last.

The next course consisted of several compounded salads, cold vegetables and cold meat. Even though the temperature in the vault was quite acceptable, even to me, one did not feel like eating hot dishes on such a night. Mrs. P complained that the cold made her teeth ache. I knew this for a fib, for china teeth do not ache. Or if they do you can put them in their glass of water to ache all by themselves. Jason and Rowan were talking about Bunny.

'But he likes to chill, see, same as me; we both stretch out on the sofa and watch Ainsley Harriott DVDs. He's happy with me,' Jason was arguing, which did not impede his colossal absorption of cold chicken, of which he is very fond.

'Wouldn't he be happier in the woods with his little bunny friends?' said Rowan.

'What, in Holland?' scoffed Jason. 'He's a Dutch rabbit. Someone here would shoot him or he'd get carchesi…calesi… you know, that rabbit disease. I figure, we brought him here, so we have to make him happy. Besides, when he's unhappy he scratches my ankles. I notice.'

This struck me as sound philosophy. We caused Bunny to be born. Therefore he was our responsibility. Something which could have been gainfully learnt by Jason's alcoholic mother and his absconding father. Or my hippie-dippies who nearly let me starve to death because Father wanted to feed me soy milk. There weren't a lot of people around who were taking responsibility.

I ate some superb rare roast beef, bitter rocket and mayonnaise which had never seen a jar, and tried to adjust my mood. After all, we had rescued Brigid and her baby. I ordered myself to cheer up and poured a glass of wine.

Mrs. Dawson was saying something about Rowan's father when the boy burst out, 'Don't talk about him!' and she was momentarily surprised. Then she leant across the Professor and patted his arm.

'My dear,' she said, 'my father was a pig, just like him. I hated him until he had the good taste to die before my first child was born. I loathed the man. You are not at all like him.'

'I'm not?' quavered Rowan.

'Not at all. We don't have to grow into copies of our parents, you know. I was very fond of my mother, she was a good woman and a good wife but I never heard a peep out of her through that whole marriage. I was not going to have the same life as she had.'

'Me neither,' I put in. 'My parents were complete nut cases.'

'And mine were mostly missing,' said the Professor sadly. 'Working very hard.'

'My parents were wonderful,' said Mrs. Pemberthy combatively. 'Of course, I didn't see much of them, my sister and I had a nurse. Then a housekeeper, of course. Then I married Mr. P.' And the less said about that the better.

Daniel put in, sounding a little shocked, 'I am very fond of my parents, but they are in Israel and I am here and we are happier like that.'

'You know what I think of my father,' began Kylie.

'And mine is worse,' Goss chimed in. They both took more pilaf, defiantly.

Rowan was looking puzzled but had relaxed. The conversation veered off to the weather. I ate a rough country terrine made of truffled pork with thyme and forgot about talking. Except to ask for more toast. Daniel poured us both a glass of a severe, flinty red. It went very well with the rich terrine and the even lusher chicken liver pâté with which I followed it. We had found that these meals worked best when everyone could just eat what they fancied, so they tended to go, one soup for an entree, a large number of dishes for the main course, one dessert, cheese, fruit and coffee. This catered for both the bird-like nibblers and the heroic trenchermen, like Jason.

'We haven't heard any singing lately,' said the Professor to Rowan. 'Are you planning any more concerts?'

'Carol rehearsals are over,' said Rowan. 'But tomorrow we start on the Vaughan Williams, so you should be able to hear us.'

'Noise!' objected Mrs. Pemberthy.

'You can always shut your window, my dear,' advised Mrs. Dawson, something I would never have dared to say. Then again, I wouldn't have called Mrs. P 'dear' for any price. 'Much the best thing anyway, in this very disagreeable weather.'

'I like it,' said Mistress Dread, resplendent in corset and fishnets, for she was going out directly after dinner to her select dungeon. 'Better than listening to, for instance, a horrible little dog yapping.'

'This meat's real good,' said Jason hurriedly. He liked Mistress Dread and didn't want Mrs. P to make another of her endless complaints about her. 'What is it?'

'It's pork,' I told him.

'I thought it was. Much more like that protein tofu stuff. I don't know why Sarah said it was like beef.'

'Probably hasn't tasted either,' I said.

Jason agreed that this could be true and we finished the meal with, in my case, a glass of orange flower muscat and some parmesan and quince paste.

I went up to bed, Daniel went off to spell Meroe at the hospital, and peace, unusually, reigned in Insula…

Until four o'clock in the morning, when the alarm went. And the phone, at the same time. I groped and stumbled. Horatio removed his tail from danger with a fine angry whisk. I grabbed up the phone and listened.

'Born!' exulted Daniel.

'Really? How's Brigid?' I blurred.

'They've got her on a drip, she's exhausted and malnourished, lost a lot of blood. The baby is fine. All is well.'

'Wonderful,' I said, waking up a little, but only a little.

'I'm staying around to make sure there's no trouble with parents,' he told me. 'See you later.'

'Fine,' I said, put the phone down, and went to wash, brush my teeth, and drink coffee. No one should give me news of any sort, especially good news, at four in the morning. I just don't have the wherewithal to react. I did the morning things and allowed myself an extra cup of the divine fluid. The baby was born, Brigid was being cared for. That was good news. I should be very pleased about it sometime soon.

Jason was already in the bakery, frowning at a recipe book while mixers rumbled. Like Winnie-the-Pooh, long words bother him. I did not offer to help. He would ask if it was important.

Just as the bakery coffee pot was coming to the boil, I noticed a large figure wearing a monk's robe sitting in my chair. It was the bass with the white hair and beard. I was about to ask when he gave me a carefully lettered piece of cardboard with one hand and held his finger to his lips with the other. I read it without commenting aloud.

Hello. My name is Rupert. I am making a soneme, a soundscape, of your bakery. Your apprentice let me in. Kepler said you wouldn't mind. I won't get in the way. Just go on as usual. The process will take a couple of hours. Thank you.

I shrugged. Rupert grinned. Jason left the book with a last puzzled shake of the head and stood to attention.

'Cap'n on deck!'

'How goes the ship?' I asked.

'Had to buy some bread for the Soup Run, sir. Drafted out today's muffins. Broke the eggs for the challah.'

Jason is very proud of his skill in breaking eggs with one hand. A skill I never mastered, by the way. Challah. It must be Friday. The week had rather run away with me.

'Carry on, Midshipman,' I said, waving a Picardian hand.

After a while—the bakery really is very busy—we forgot about Rupert. He had a rare quality of repose. I suppose it comes from spending his whole life listening. When Jason returned from his breakfast and Goss opened the shop, he drew a deep breath. Horatio obliged with a delicate mew. Rupert switched off all his apparatus and then laughed aloud.

'That was so interesting!' he exclaimed in his deep, curiously precise voice.

'Rupert?' I asked with extreme scepticism.

'I have always admired Prince Rupert,' he said, uneasily.

'You're a freegan, aren't you?' I accused. He smiled. He had the most beautiful sapphire blue eyes.

'Used to be. Getting too old to sleep on floors and eat out of bins. But it was fun,' he said reminiscently. 'They really are the only free people. But beds are nice. And money. And work, too. I'm a sound man. You can tell, can't you?'

'No shit,' said Jason, packing little muffins into their flat boxes.

'Sound is never appreciated. Objected to, if it increases into noise. Silence is becoming increasingly rare, especially inside people's heads. Music, news, information is being continuously fed into their mistreated ears. God knows how many will have any hearing by the time they are thirty-five. Also, the microwaves from mobile phones are cooking their brains.'

'What is a soneme?' I asked.

'It's a sound picture. I take the ordinary noises of industry—in this case, the mixers rumbling, the hiss of steam escaping from the loaves, the clang of the oven door—and mix it with the human sounds, speech, the mew of a cat, footsteps, hinges creaking. Even the brush of overall material on flesh and the little, little noise of rising bread.'

'I've heard that one,' I told him. 'A small noise, indeed.'

'You can buy endless sonemes of running rivers and gentle streams and birdsong,' he said, smoothing his short white beard. 'But I can make a symphony out of ordinary sounds—morning in the city, cars hooting, people walking past—and they are both illuminating and comforting. At the moment mine sell best to prisoners. Stay-at-home parents. They are played to people in comas. Anyone who misses the everyday world.'

'And someone pays you for them?' asked Jason scornfully.

Rupert grinned at him. 'Just as someone pays Kepler for his panorama of Insula.'

'Fair call,' I said. 'Have a cup of coffee and a muffin. What are today's muffins, Jason?'

'Mandarin and pecan, honey and cinnamon, lemon and poppyseed,' sang Jason.

The bright blue eyes lit up.

'One of each,' he said hungrily. 'But don't bother about the bread, please.'

Aha. A fellow Winnie-the-Pooh fan. For that he should have all three. But when I handed them over he insisted on paying for them.

'I'm not a freegan anymore,' he reminded me. 'Sonemes are my calling. The rest of the time I write maths CDs for schools. It's a living. How is the lost girl?'

'Delivered safely,' I said. 'Resting.'

'Oh, that is good news,' he replied.

I agreed that it was and went into the shop to give Goss a mandarin and pecan muffin. I got one for myself, too. They were superb.

Rupert took his leave. He had an appointment to record Therese weaving. I hoped that Carolus, her King Charles spaniel, would put in a small (but royal) bark. I felt that Horatio's voice, right at the end of the recording, had added something extra to the soneme. The Mouse Police seldom spoke, reserving their energy for hunting. And eating. And sleeping, of course.

The gourmet muffins walked off in the arms of a PA from the Stock Exchange. I noted down the orders for the fruit and veg for tomorrow's treats. Plus a lot of sugar. Jason must have decided to revisit the glacé cherries. He had better get a move on or they would go out of season. Every year I swear I will make blood orange marmalade, and every year I forget until the blood oranges are gone. Fortunately Therese didn't miss them and the jar of perfectly pink jam only cost me an hour's work on one of her endless tapestries.

But I had serious business. I had done my census of presents in my head and had come up short. Getting the three remaining Christmas presents meant that—gasp—I would have to brave the heat, crowds, jingles and so on and go out again. And I ought to do it soon. Goss could mind the shop. She, of all people, would understand.

Accordingly, I dressed in what amounted to combat gear, took the hated mobile in case Daniel rang, and, jamming on my straw hat, marched out into the throngs.

They looked so miserable. That's what worried me. This was supposed to be a feast of joy and jollity and the practitioners looked like they were shopping to avert the imminent execution of their nearest and dearest. Still, with a background like mine, what would I know?

I fought my way onto the main drag, where there were sweating Santas, clanging trams, screaming children, and no air whatsoever. Diving into a big shop at least meant that there was some semblance of cool and, if I stuck to the 'extremely expensive' counters, not too many people. I made my purchase of very fragrant gardener's soap, scrub and hand cream and stuck the gift-wrapped box into my bag. The air was full of exceptional perfumes. I leant against a display and breathed deeply, which was a cue for three nice ladies to pounce and hand me slips of cardboard with the latest scent sprayed upon them. I accepted them all. I put them in my jumper drawer to keep away moths. But these were all too sweet to please me. I liked the sophisticated French perfumes by Guerlain. Which, on my skin, instantly reverted to Coles Bargain Counter. It was unfair.

I found the Roman bath oil for the professor in the same place. I knew that he soaked his aged bones in sybaritic spas and this bath oil was compounded of the same herbs the Romans had used. And, come to think of it, had brought to England, bless them; mint, basil, all my favourites were Roman imports to keep the troops as happy as possible in a land where it rained all the time and dulled their harness, rusted their swords and depressed their mood. This oil contained sage and mint and ought to do our Ancient Roman's body the world of good.

The cookbook I wanted for Jason, one written in simple language, meant that I had to find an escalator and rise through the building. Noise, children, people consulting lists, I was glad I didn't have to go near the toy department. It must be hell up there. I wished there was an equivalent to Hamleys, the famous London toyshop: five quiet floors of excellent toys, and so big that even gangs of children got subdued in it and stopped yelling (unless, of course, their parent was obdurate in the matter of toy purchase, when a tantrum is de rigueur). I had spent happy hours in Hamleys, trying out different games and kissing teddy bears, and had never seen anything to upset me.

On arrival in the book depository I was directed to the toy department as the book I wanted was written for children.

Damn. Up again, rising through heated air, into the stockyard fug of the Christmas Crèche. More dead ducks, I assumed, more miserable stock. I did not want to look at them, moral coward that I am. So I looked.

Just as bad as before. The calf mouthed hay that I was pretty sure it was too young to eat. The sheep looked dazed, though that is pretty normal for sheep. The ducks were very unhappy, tucking their heads under their wings and hoping they would wake up somewhere wetter. It was more likely to be a roasting dish. The chooks were panicking, running away from the grabbing hands and losing feathers by the moment. More bald chickens for the pot at closing time. The goats chewed and sneered. They, at least, were all right. I found a few carrots in my shopping bag, which was the only one I could find in the bakery when I made my stern resolve, so I managed to decoy the donkey over to me. She nudged me gently. She was dark brown, with the same long-lashed eyes as Serena. I stroked her and told her that soon it would be Christmas and after that she got to go home, and almost anywhere, even carrying flowers for the repentant Mr. Pahlevi, would be better than here. At least Serena was a well-fed and cared-for and valued member of a team.

'What's your name, darling?' I asked the donkey. She had a headstall on, and an engraved name tag which said *Diligence*. It was a good name. A Quaker name to match her peaceable nature. I fed her the last of the carrots as a flying wedge of snotty-faced moppets attacked us, and Diligence shifted unhappily as they leapt under her belly and grabbed for her tail. Another contingent was swinging on her ears. I moved away as a feckless parent held up a frightful child to the donkey's back.

I hoped Diligence would kick, but she was too used to turning the other cheek…

I got Jason's book, which seemed to be very useful. Lots of new things he could experiment with, solving the problem of his limited literacy. Then, as I was leaving, I looked back at the crèche and the mistreated animals, wishing there was something I could do. I thought of Beverley Nichols' vision of the zoo animals freed in the night exacting revenge on the spectators. Each of those crude undisciplined children needed a good kicking, followed by their parents who hadn't taught them any better. Then Diligence and the goats could move on to the owners of this shop…

Then I saw something which remained with me on the long trail downhill and into the street and all the way back to Insula.

What was Sarah, the vegan of vegans, the Vegie Queen, doing talking on such friendly, even intimate terms, with the man who supplied the animals for the crèche? She had laughed. She had patted his arm. And this a man who mistreated animals, even as he supplied them for a festival and, moreover, exploited them rotten?

It was a mystery.

Meanwhile, I intended to have ice cream. I had never got my cherry ripple and chocolate, so I bought it on the way home. There are deeds which demand a big drink with umbrellas in as a reward. And there are deeds which demand ice cream. Christmas shopping demanded ice cream, and it was going to get it.

Chapter Eighteen

The sexual life of the camel
Is stranger than anyone thinks;
At the height of the mating season
It tries its luck on the sphinx.

Trad.

Horatio did not approve of ice cream. His view was that cream should be cool but not cold and he objected to the way the stuff melted on his immaculate nose. I gave him some cream while I spooned out my treat. I had shucked the straw hat, slipped off my sandals and good clothes, and was cool again. Jason and Goss had finished up the banking and my working day was over. Where was my Jade Forrester, where was my cool drink? A little reclining was indicated. The mobile had not rung while I was braving the Outer Limits of Xmas and there were no texts. Things must be all right at the hospital. The choristers were rehearsing. The words that came through the wall, however, were very rude. Who would have thought that people would still be singing 'The Sexual Life of the Camel' (or, as Terry Pratchett interpreted it, 'The Hedgehog Song') in the twenty-first century?

'…comparative safety on shipboard,' the voices assured me, 'is enjoyed by the hedgehog alone…'

I ate my ice cream. I drowsed. The indecent songs continued. Daniel, having missed the 'rude songs sung in pubs' part of my university education (quite the most amusing part) was puzzled to catch, as he came in, the strain of a traditional MUFS item.

'See the dingoes in leather jackets, see their Harleys ride (vroom vroom vroom) through the tunnel in downtown Paris, the night the Princess died.' Then the chorus howled triumphantly: 'The dingoes did the Princess in, the dingoes did the Princess in...'

'What are they singing? I thought I knew that tune,' he commented. 'It's "The Lion Sleeps Tonight".'

'Was. Let me introduce you to the Melbourne University Falsetto Society, aka MUFS, purveyors of terrible lyrics in the worst possible taste to the gentry for many years,' I said sleepily.

'Oh, rugby songs,' he said, interested.

'And we don't need to have the rugby. How are things at the hospital?'

'Good. Well, pretty good,' he temporised. 'For the moment. Coffee?'

'Coffee,' I agreed, getting up. 'You must be worn out. Whom have you left in charge?' I felt sure that the freegans would approve of that 'whom'.

'Meroe has a witch friend amongst the midwives,' he said, slumping down and rubbing his eyes. 'There seem to be witches everywhere. Not that that isn't good,' he added hastily. 'Fine women, all of them. She's looking after Brigid. Who is recovering very fast. Manny hasn't moved from her side. He, however, called his mother. So the secret is out and I am expecting trouble as soon as the O'Ryans hear the news.'

'Who will they hear the news from?' I asked, waiting for the kettle to do its stuff.

'Once a secret is known to one it is known to all,' he quoted. 'Old Yiddish proverb.'

'That is true, isn't it?' I realised. 'Some form of osmosis, possibly—diffusion through a semi-permeable membrane,' I explained. 'I remember it because of the words. I can also tell you about endemic dicotyledons. Actually, I can't tell you anything about endemic dicotyledons, except that they have two seed leaves, but the phrase is instantly memorable, don't you think?'

Daniel was looking at me. I made the coffee. I gave him a selection of slightly singed muffins. He ate them with suitable expressions of delight. I wondered what we could do to prevent the O'Ryans descending on the hospital in force and just removing Brigid. In her weakened condition she surely wouldn't be able to do much about it. Manny, however valiant, was only a boy. The O'Ryans were rich and influential and he was poor. Bugger. I went over and looked out the window.

'Our watcher's back,' I said. 'I forgot to tell you about him. He's harmless. And I bet he's melting inside that heavy suit. They could at least have given him a hat. A fedora would have been quite appropriate.'

'Anything on the answering machine?'

I pushed the button. The same female voice shrieked, '*Shiloh! Give up the Son of Peace!*' over and over until the time ran out. I shivered.

'No, I don't like it either,' said Daniel. 'However, the hospital won't make Brigid see her parents if she doesn't want to. I have told the nurses very forcefully that the O'Ryans are not to go near her. Meroe's friend will reinforce that. It's when she has to leave that the fun will begin.'

'Fun,' I said scornfully.

'Come and sit down, *metuka*,' he said kindly. 'Sufficient unto the day is the evil thereof.'

And he leant his head on my shoulder and fell neatly asleep. I hugged him for a while, then shifted him by degrees to the pillows of the couch. Poor Daniel, selfish Corinna! He'd been up guarding the baby and the mother all night. He slept beautifully, neither snoring nor drooling, his eyelashes a black line on his perfect cheek.

The least I could do was to guard his sleep. Horatio and I curled up with him. I read the Jade Forrester, recalling 1991 with some horror. Horatio dreamt, I assume, of Memorable

Meals, for he was licking his whiskers in his sleep. I bet it was the morning when he had secured all that smoked salmon for himself. I had left it unattended on the kitchen table. After I had got it out from behind the fridge it wasn't fit for anyone else to eat but Horatio.

Time passed. It started, at last, to get dark. I was in the mood for cooking so I got up carefully and prowled the kitchen. What to make? I was sick of salads. How about a good strong curry? No. What, then? I had lamb chops, didn't I? Well, then, what about good old-fashioned lamb chops, mash and three veg? And for dessert, what was left over? Half a banana cake, already made from aged bananas, in the freezer. Misc fruit. In the liquor cupboard, a drain in the bottom of the sherry bottle but—aha! A half bot of Stone's Green Ginger Wine. All right then, trifle it would be.

Because I was not in a hurry, I did it all properly, with no shortcuts. I cut the cake into slices which I soaked in Ginger Wine. I made a jelly with gelatine, ginger syrup and pineapple juice. I made a crème anglaise with three eggs. I whipped a lot of cream. I chopped glacé ginger. When I assembled it, it was a work of art. Horatio and Daniel slept on, though Horatio woke briefly to assist me with the whipping of the cream.

And the voices sang, at intervals, pub songs of my youth. Through the Wild West show echoed the agonised cry of the OoMeDoodle Bird. Agostino Agostella proclaimed his own form of relaxation. Strange noises came from the chandler's shop. The woodpecker song was just getting to 'remove it' when they broke off and sang, in perfect four-part harmony, the little ditty which I had first heard:

> *Haarmannn Pearce and Soylent Green*
> *Vargas Fish and Sawney Beane.*

What was that song about? It wasn't the 'Twinkle Twinkle Little Star' of my childhood. Who was Sawney Beane? Sounded Scottish. I was just rinsing the last of the glacé ginger syrup off

my hands, preparatory to googling all the names, when the singers knocked off for a rest, Daniel awoke hungry and we began
to make dinner.

It was a lovely dinner. It is important, Meroe said, to enjoy
good things when they happen, because otherwise you might
miss them, and the Goddess would be displeased. Outside
it was hot and humid, the screaming wind having departed.
Inside it was cool. The sun was setting in cream, gold and blood
orange streamers—sometimes nature has no taste. The chops
were grilled so that the outsides were just a little burnt and the
insides still pink. The mash was smooth and cheesy. The little
Evian carrots reposed in their puddle of honey glaze. The rocket
salad was bitter and restorative, leafed with slices of green apple
and dressed with lemon juice and oil. I found steak knives and
the pepper. We listened to Vaughan Williams as we ate. Lovely.

When I proudly brought out my trifle, Daniel groaned.

'Oh, that's too much!'

'I know,' I said. 'But it's impossible to make half a trifle.
What say we share it?'

'With whom?' he asked. The freegans would be proud of his
grammar, too. 'Just a spoonful, please.'

'Someone will turn up,' I assured him. 'If they don't, I will
carry it up to Jason.'

'Maybe Bunny likes ginger,' he agreed. He tasted. 'Wonderful,'
he told me. He had a spoonful more. 'Oh, by the way, I've found
the chess man. The one who was playing chess with Brigid on
the phone?'

'Really?' He didn't seem to matter much now that we knew
where the girl was. I said so.

'On the contrary,' said Daniel. He licked his spoon and laid
it down. 'Since I am assured that Manny is not the father of
Brigid's baby.'

'What? Who assured you?' I was astounded.

'Manny and Brigid. Brigid refuses to tell anyone who the
father is.'

I was so astounded that I didn't reprove him for ending a sentence so inelegantly. Then I thought through the implications.

'Oh, no, Daniel, you don't think one of those vile reverends…'

'Seems most probable, except I doubt that Brigid would protect them.'

'She would if she thought they were going to claim the baby and take it away from her. Shiloh, Child of Peace, and all that.'

'Indeed.'

'But that means Manny has put his job and his safety in jeopardy all this time to help and protect her and she isn't carrying his baby?' I protested.

'That's so,' said Daniel. The trifle, which had soured in my mouth at the thought of those rapist hypocrites, sweetened again.

'He really is a good boy,' I told Daniel.

'And she really, really loves him,' Daniel replied. 'So, this chess player. He's one of the singers. The extra tenor. Michael. He's here tonight. Saw them outside.'

'Then why don't we ask them all in for dessert?' I suggested. 'Plenty of trifle and we can allow for Sarah.'

'Perhaps Horatio will bite her,' he laughed.

I hoped he would, but I knew that my aristocat would never soil his teeth on such as Sarah. Still, he might discomfort her. Cats were very good at that. I rang Jason and received a rapturous acceptance. Eating Jason's food must have given them a high opinion of the Insula cuisine and I hoped I could live up to it.

They came in a group and spread themselves all over the parlour. They were hot and tired and a little hoarse. I got out the lemon cordial made to Grandma Chapman's recipe and made jugs of icy drinks. Daniel got out the wine for those who indulged. Most did, except for Sarah, who lounged splendidly on the couch, long tanned legs over one arm, hair trailing. She was a stunning advertisement for a vegan diet. She refused trifle indignantly because it had cream and eggs in it, and I offered her a plate of (bought) gluten-free biscuits. They were also deliberately chosen—by me, with her in mind in case I ever had to feed her—as fruit-free, chocolate-free and taste-free. The others dived in enthusiastically. Bec licked her spoon with delight.

'Fantastic!' she said. 'That hint of pineapple juice just takes the extra sweetness off the ginger syrup. The base is banana cake, isn't it?'

I began to exchange recipes with Bec and Rupert, who liked cooking, and Janeen, Alexander and Michael, who liked eating.

Janeen, I noticed, was nibbling a little trifle, even though she too was a vegan, or so I understood. She smiled wearily at me, still small and meek.

'Sometimes soy cream just isn't the same,' she told me. 'And I'm going to be up all night at the hospital. I'm in emergency surgery—in the operating room,' she said proudly.

'Congratulations,' I said.

'It's all life and death,' she said in her small voice. 'So I like singing and sometimes I award myself a treat.'

'Works for the freegans,' I said, pleased that my trifle had tempted away a true believer. Ancient Egyptian courtesans must have felt that about seducing the desert fathers. I have always believed that what tempted Saint Anthony was not a naked lady but a naked roast lamb. With mint sauce.

'Sometimes I wish I could go back,' she confessed. 'They all have assumed names, you know. G'Kar, Vir, Nigel Molesworth, Nikabrik, the Mouse, Jadis, Kryten, Sir Thursday, Miles Vorkosigan. Lord Powerscourt, Phryne Fisher, Prince Caspian, Gordiamus the Finder, Trufflehunter, Agatha Raisin, Anita Blake. Kay Harker, Mr. Green, Father Brown, Roseanne, Henrietta and Katydid. Cat Chant and his boyfriend, Tonino. Even Lord D'Arcy, Angel and Belladonna, Princess of Cats. Vila, he could get through any fence or lock if he was scared enough. All our favourite characters. Can I have some more trifle?'

'Certainly.' I supplied some. The trifle was running out. But I had a lovely apricot crumble that just needed to be popped into the oven if the evening looked like extending. 'What was your name?'

'Xena,' she said softly. Anyone more unlike the warrior princess could not be imagined, which was, of course, the reason for the aliases. I dared anyone to laugh but no one did. Rupert hugged Janeen. I knew him now. He wasn't the dashing Prince Rupert. He was Rupert Bear. So much more comfortable to have around the house. I gave him the last of the trifle.

Daniel had lured Michael, a tall, good-looking boy with a vaguely piratical air, to the chessboard for his opinion on a game he was playing with Kepler. Kepler was, of course, going to win. Kepler always did. The interest, Daniel told me, was watching how he managed it. I will never understand games. Why not read a book? The others began to talk about a new vegan restaurant and I eavesdropped on Michael and Daniel as best I could.

Horatio helped. He decided that the one person in the room who did not adore him was Sarah. On her an impression must be made. So he ascended the sofa, sat on her artfully displayed hair, and dug in all his claws. As long as she didn't move, she was fine. If she jerked her head away, she might be bald. I think she was afraid of animals. She froze. I didn't say a word and the others didn't seem to notice. Content, perhaps, with not receiving another lecture on their own wickedness in eating my trifle, product of the arrogant exploitation of innocent chickens and cows.

'They do an artichoke, brazil nut and tahini schnitzel that you just have to taste to believe,' enthused Bec. 'Orange ras-el-hanout dressing with sesame seeds and roast beetroot.'

'I loved the trifle—though this is also a very good trifle,' said Rupert hastily. 'It was, as I recall, made of rosehip, champagne and raspberry with honey and lavender ice cream. For some reason they had a lot left over. That was a very good night. So is this,' he said, hoping that I was not offended.

'No cook is offended by another cook's skill,' I said. 'Or shouldn't be. Eh, Jason?'

'How do you make a schnitzel out of nuts?' he asked.

While the group was explaining the process to Jason, I listened to Daniel and Michael.

'You're a good player,' Daniel said.

Michael shrugged his shoulders. 'I like chess. It's unemotional. I mean, no one gets hurt and upset about chess.'

'Is that why you played phone chess with Brigid?'

'Do you know how she is?' he asked eagerly. 'Rupe says that she got to hospital and had the baby after all. And there was a baby, which I did wonder about.'

'You did?'

'Well, look, I never met her, not in person, I've got enough on my plate what with Bec and Sarah; keeping them both happy, I mean, takes a lot of energy. I didn't need another girl. Ours was purely a chess relationship,' he proclaimed.

Daniel must have raised an eyebrow. Michael took a long gulp of his lemon drink. Then he asked plaintively, 'Look, have you got any beer, if we're about to have a D&M?'

Daniel broke out the beer, more wine was poured, I stuck the apricot crumble into the oven, the room rearranged itself. Now the conversation had broken into three parts. One was Bec talking to Jason about vegan food. One was Rupert and me and Janeen. The choristers were all ignoring Sarah's plight. I didn't see that I should notice it until she asked for help. We sipped the crisp white wine.

'Sometimes they all seem very young, don't they?' sighed Xena.

We three were keeping an ear on the D&M when Jason noticed Horatio's prisoner and prepared to convince my imperious cat that loosing his claws from Sarah's hair would be noblesse oblige. He lifted Horatio, correctly, forward, and unhooked the talons. Sarah, freed, sat up, shook her mistreated coiffure, screamed, 'I hate you!' at Jason, leapt to her feet and left. Abruptly. Slamming the door.

'Ooh dear, temper, temper,' said Rupert. 'Now where are we going to get another soprano at this late date?'

'Katie?' suggested Bec. 'It's all right, Jason, she does that sometimes. We like to take her down a bit. She's such a princess. Come and let's reward this excellent companion animal.'

Jason, shocked, went along with Bec to show her where to find the cat treats. Bec and Sarah, both lovers of this gangling youth? You just never really do know about people.

Meanwhile the wine was good and the discussion about replacement sopranos was good cover. Michael had an Australian accent and a nice, soft voice.

'I've got a mate who's a maths teacher, I like playing chess, he gives my number two mobile number to people who like playing phone chess. It's different from face to face, you get time to think about your moves. I've got four games on the phone at the moment. I don't even know the gender of two of them. Playing on the internet you have to declare if you're a girl and people can get nasty. You can get flamed. I used to sign myself in as a girl to flame the flamers as a public service. There's some weird dudes in the chess world.'

He emptied the stubbie in one draught and took another.

Daniel sipped his beer and nodded.

'So a phone game with one person is a good option for the shy ones. This one called herself Brigid from the start. So I knew she was a girl. Probably. See previous comment about weird dudes. Then we used to chat a bit, you know, after a month or so. She asked me what I did, I told her about Sarah and Bec, she told me about her shitful rels and crazy church—she needed someone to talk to, right?'

More beer went the way of the first stubbie. Daniel nodded again. This D&M process didn't require him to say much, I noticed.

'She was a good player!' Michael exclaimed. 'Fucking brilliant. Played like the best girl players, lots of aggression. I showed one game to Bec and she said that Brigid was fierce and desperate. She's clever, Bec.'

'Yes,' said Daniel.

'Knows stuff, Bec does. Thinks. Now Sarah, she doesn't think, she's just sure she's right, and if you argue with her, she flounces off or gets mad. She's real dark on your Corinna. Nearly wet myself when she told her off in front of everyone just when she was getting into one of her raves.'

'You don't seem to like her much,' Daniel commented.

Again the boy shrugged. And grabbed for more beer.

'She's been strange since she got into this vegan stuff, her and Janeen. But she's too clingy to run with the freegans, like Rupert did. And she and Bec...I don't know...'

'Brigid?' Daniel hinted, trying to get Michael back onto the topic.

'Yeah, well, as I said, we used to chat a bit while she was thrashing me at chess, and she told me she was sick, and I asked what was wrong. And she said she seemed to be pregnant, had no idea how it happened. I thought, why do I always end up with crazy chicks? Sorry. Ladies. Women. Like I said, I never met her.'

'Indeed,' said Daniel.

'Got enough trouble,' mumbled Michael, and drank more beer. I was glad I had laid in supplies of light, or we were going to be carrying Michael home.

'What's a D&M?' I asked Rupert.

'Deep and Meaningful,' he told me. 'I'm a little worried about Michael. Too much success with women, too soon. Not good for such a young man.'

'If Bec heard what he just said, and relays it to Sarah,' I replied, 'I think success is going to be the least of his troubles in the near future.'

'We will have to replace her, and if we have to replace Bec as well it would be better to find a less...complicated set of relationships,' he agreed.

The apricot crumble was eaten. Herbal tea, cherry brandy and coffee was drunk. The choristers departed, issuing an invitation to attend rehearsal in the roof garden and a promise of a return feast to come. Jason went with them.

The room was suddenly empty except for a lot of cups and glasses and beer bottles. I gathered them all up for washing while Horatio sat on the couch and purred. There was a strand of golden hair caught in his front claws.

'Pleased with yourself, eh?' I asked him as I straightened the couch around him.

He purred a brief agreement.

'Well, that was illuminating,' said Daniel.

'But not agreeable in conclusion,' I said.

'Yes. I'm pretty sure that Michael isn't the father, and he was the only outside candidate. Sean dumped her because she wouldn't kiss him.'

'Bummer,' I sympathised. 'Let's leave the washing up and go to bed.'

There seemed nothing better to do, so we did.

Chapter Nineteen

Tomorrow shall be my dancing day;
I would my true love did so chance
To see the legend of my play,
To call my true love to my dance

Trad.

Saturday morning brought no alarms. I like that in a morning. Daniel and I stayed in bed indecently late, then had coffee and croissants and read the newspapers (which were uniformly depressing) and tried the crossword again. Saturday's is do-able. Sunday's is impenetrable. We got the Saturday one out. A triumph! The CD player gave out pavanes and galliards. It was lovely. Despite the trouble in the world, the plight of Brigid and a strange uneasy feeling I was getting from the choristers, it was cool and civilised and cultured in my parlour at ten in the morning on that Saturday. I was just thinking of finding some clothes and getting dressed when the doorbell went, and disclosed, when I opened the door, Meroe, Kylie and Dolores.

'This is a surprise,' I said, allowing them to enter. 'Nice to see you, Dolly. How did you get away?'

'I just went,' she said. 'I'll be in terrible trouble when I go home,' she added matter-of-factly, 'but that doesn't matter. I'm always in trouble, I don't worry about it. I had to see Brigid and the baby.'

'And you have seen them?' Daniel was putting on the coffee pot again and was pouring a liqueur glass of green Chartreuse for Meroe, who looked like a tragedy queen who had been dragged through a hedge backwards. She sagged onto the couch, took the glass, and drank it off as though it had contained water. Even though she knows that alcohol damages the chakras. And when Daniel refilled it, she skolled it again. Then she raked her fingers through her hair and greeted Horatio.

'The baby is so cute,' said Dolores. She had shed her pink persona. Perhaps Kylie had lent her some clothes. She looked like any other young girl, in jeans and an indie T-shirt. 'Brigie's very worried. She looks terrible. She thinks Mum is coming to take the baby away, like she said she would. Can I have chocolate milk?' she added, as Daniel displayed the contents of the fridge for her choice.

'And that lemon stuff for me, please,' said Kylie.

'Your mother has no right to Brigid's baby,' I told Dolores. 'It's born of her body. It's hers.'

'My coven friend had another sister who is minding the situation for the moment,' said Meroe, who was clearly listening though her eyes were closed. 'What happens when she leaves the hospital is the difficulty. There are watchers from the Holy Reformed Temple of Shiloh all around.'

'I know,' I said. 'But so far, apart from when you hugged them, all they have done is watch.'

'You hugged them?' asked Dolores, horrified. 'I'd as soon kiss a snake.'

'A good analogy, though snakes are innocent compared to those men,' said Meroe. 'Food of some sort, Corinna? Salty, if you can manage it. I didn't hug them out of affection, but to embroil them in a fight with my exorcists so that Brigid could escape.'

I explained and Dolores and Kylie laughed in admiration as Daniel assembled and cooked a grilled cheese and tomato sandwich and cut it into four triangles so that Meroe could eat it easily. I joined him and we made a few more sandwiches, and then a few more until we ran out of ingredients. Our audience was ravenous.

'You're so brave!' exclaimed Dolores, accepting a sandwich in her turn and beginning on it as though she had not eaten for days. Perhaps she hadn't. And she had better stock up for the future when she was confined to barracks at home.

'It was nothing,' said Meroe, who was sitting up and looking much more alive under the influence of cheese sandwiches and Chartreuse. It was designed originally as an elixir of life, after all. 'Corinna, what will become of them?'

'Manny and Brigid? I don't know. They'll need somewhere to live. They're too young to marry, anyway, unless both parents give their permission—and I can't see your parents doing that, eh, Dolly?'

She shook her head. Her mouth was full.

'Manny's mum would love a new baby to care for,' said Daniel. 'She's very good at babies.'

'But the O'Ryans won't let her keep the Child of Peace,' I said.

'They've got lots of money,' said Dolly. 'They could afford to buy Brigid a house. They could afford to give her an allowance. And me, too,' she added sadly. 'I'd have a room that wasn't pink and time to write and no need to hide everything. And I'd never have to listen to Revs Hale or Putnam ever again—*ever*.'

There didn't seem to be any way out. Then I heard someone knocking very respectfully on my door and I went to see who it was. How were all these people getting into Insula past that expensive security system?

A very different Mr. Pahlevi was there, hat in hand.

'Lady,' he said. 'You seen my Serena?'

'No, but the bakery isn't open today,' I told him. 'Have you looked in the alley? She might be waiting outside the bakery door. She doesn't know it's Saturday.'

'Not there,' he said, drooping. Even his flowered hat seemed depressed.

'If she does arrive here, where shall I send her?' I asked.

He pressed a card into my hand.

'You call me,' he said. 'I'll come right away.'

I promised that I would call, and closed the door.

'Anyone seen a donkey?' I asked the gathering as I came back inside.

'Serena? She's missing?' asked Kylie.

'Serena's gone walkabout. Probably in search of roses. You know how she is about roses. She's a very self-possessed creature,' I assured Kylie. 'She'll be all right. But call me if you see her.'

'All right,' she agreed. 'I'm taking Dolores home now.'

'Was your father very distressed that Brigid was missing?' I asked.

'Dad? He's never been that interested in us. I mean, we're at the end of a lot of sisters and brothers. Mum's mad to find her. But she won't find out from me,' said Dolores. 'Not if they don't feed me for days. I have a stash. And Sandra's a lot nicer these days.'

With that they took their leave. Meroe stood up and stretched until I could hear her joints crack.

'I need a bath and I need to reconnect with my familiar,' she said, which meant that she needed to spend a reasonable time stroking Belladonna, her cat. And staring into space, which was something Meroe did a lot. And, who knows, she might find a solution.

We escorted her to her apartment and then went back to our own. Daniel wanted to watch the cricket and I wanted to finish the sewing on a rather nice embroidery for a Christmas present, so we were booked for a quiet afternoon. Fortunately I like cricket too, enough to share a sofa and not object to the voiceover like I do with football or racing. Cricket commentary is mostly quiet and calm, with only occasional screams of outrage or triumph. Horatio also likes to watch cricket. Occasionally he is overcome and leaps down to trap the ball under his paw. I have always wondered what I should do if he came away from the screen with a little man in his mouth...

Daniel watched and I sewed, sitting under my light, while the city went on with Christmas and the day wandered toward lunch. I love Saturdays. They are open-ended. I do not have to get up early and I don't have to go to bed early. My only day and night of total freedom, to spend as I like.

I heard the choristers go out, singing. Poor things had a hard life. Singing songs about the deep midwinter in these temperatures in full concert dress could not be easy. I heard Mrs. Pemberthy open her window and snort. I heard Carolus barking as Therese took him for his afternoon walk. The rest of Insula was sunk in Saturday peace. There ought to be more of it.

I drew the last stitch flat, double looped the thread and cut it off. Finished! In these troubulous times it was a feat to have actually completed anything. I pottered off to the kitchen and found—ironies were rather mounting up—that I had run out of bread. I usually have a couple of emergency loaves in the bakery so I called out where I was going to Daniel, engrossed in the screen, and he waved a hand to signify that he had heard.

The Mouse Police, always glad to see a visitor, bounced up and down at the alley door, insisting on an outing. I opened it. They bolted out, through the marching tread of Christmas Shopping feet, heading toward the Rising Sun Japanese restaurant. I idled about the bakery, checking on the sourdough, totalling the grocer's bill, waiting for my feline assault force to return. I could have left the cat door open but I was worried about their safety with all those feet and wheels. It was nice to have nothing to do in the bakery, too, provided that the greedy moggies didn't take so long obtaining their tuna that I found myself something to do. If you have your own business, there is always something you could be getting on with...

Then I heard singing. Rhythmic chanting, in fact, with little drums and finger cymbals. I hadn't heard the Hare Krishnas in years and walked into the lane to see them.

They weren't Hare Krishnas. In a long dancing line of tatters, army uniforms, ballgowns, frilly aprons, combat fatigues, rags and feathers, Greek tunics, emo black T-shirts and gypsy skirts came the freegans, chanting 'Hare Wombat! Hare Wombat! Wombat, wombat! Hare, hare!' in the approved style. 'Marsupial consciousness!' one called. 'You can't start a war if you never come down from your tree! Carry your baby in your pouch! Eat gum leaves! Dig in the burrow of love! Live in the burrow of love! Hare wombat! Hare Wombat!'

I was enchanted. After the dancers came a long string of fascinated children, harassed parents, and an opportunistic girl with a bicycle-driven barrow selling ice cream and cold drinks. I ducked into the bakery, grabbed the petty cash, ran up to her and handed over a small wad of cash. 'Ice cream and drinks for all the freegans,' I told her. She wiped her eyes and pushed back her ice-cream hat and I knew her. It was, in fact, my rickshaw courier Megan, lately working the Soup Run, now moonlighting for the weekend. She grinned at me.

'Corinna! Aren't they fun? I'm cleaning up following them, I'm almost sold out. Fair enough that they get a dividend. I'll stop them here in the shade.'

'How are you going to stop them?' I asked, as the dancing maniacs proclaimed the joys of life in a tree. She grinned again and made a megaphone with her hands.

'Freegans! Freebies!' she yelled.

Immediately the dance coiled around toward us until we were standing in the middle of a crowd of hot, sweating and exhilarated freegans.

'Ice cream,' I said. 'Drinks.'

'Thanks!' they said, and selected and distributed the remainder of Megan's load. Soon all of them were munching and slurping. When the cargo was all gone, they broke off chunks of ice and smeared them on hot foreheads or tucked them into overheated bosoms. Jadis, Queen of Charn, asked me, 'Is all well with Brigie?'

'Yes, safely delivered. But she's trapped in the hospital. Her parents want that baby and they want Brigid back.'

'To lock her up again?' asked Ivanova crisply.

'I'm afraid so.' Several other freegans joined their commander.

'Thanks for the drinks,' said Nigel. He was wearing a fetching blue-flowered toque, just the thing for Her Majesty's garden party circa 1950. 'And don't worry.'

'Why?' I asked, as the finger cymbals snapped, the drums beat, and the dance began to move again.

'Hare wombat! Hare wombat! Wombat, wombat! Hare, hare!'

And they were gone, with their train of children and one puzzled patrol policeman, who was sure that they were doing something illegal and had sent his colleague to a quieter place to enquire, by radio, exactly what it might be.

I went back to the bakery. The Mouse Police had returned and were settling in for a little day-long nap. Obscurely cheered, I took the extra rolls and a loaf of leftover challah and went upstairs again.

The cricket was finishing up for lunch. I made salad sandwiches. I found my next project. I was having such a nice day.

And it turned into a lovely afternoon, full of quiet industry, with no visitors. Then a not-so-quiet and lusciously erotic night. I had had Daniel to myself for twenty-four hours, and I felt fine.

So when I woke to the sound of hoofs in the alleyway at dawn, I just assumed that Serena would wait for me and rolled over and went back to sleep. I thought I had heard something cluck or possibly quack, but presumed it was a dream. Lots of things made a sort of bird noise. And after a late breakfast, when I opened the alley door for the Mouse Police, there she was, grey and calm, waiting for the bakery to produce rosewater muffins.

I would have to get Jason to make a stock of them, I could tell. Serena drank half a bucket of water with her muffin, then stamped for another, which I gave her. She did not have panniers today. She just wore a headstall which was clearly her nightwear. I unlooped a section of light rope which Megan sometimes used to secure loads and threaded it through the ring.

'Sorry, darling, but you really shouldn't be alone in the big city,' I told her. I rang Mr. Pahlevi. Then I found the bottle of rosewater and sprinkled some stale wholemeal rolls. We were out of muffins.

Meroe came down the alley, carrying a basket, and I recalled the selection of muffins that I had frozen for her when the pace of events meant that I could not deliver them.

'Meroe, could you mind the donkey while I go and get your muffins?' I asked. 'I mean, can you handle seeing Mr. Pahlevi again?'

'Certainly,' said Meroe, taking the tether and stroking the donkey between the ears. 'Merry meet, little sister.'

Serena nosed her. I climbed the stairs to my own freezer, noticing that Daniel was stirring, and went down again to deliver my present. Meroe and the donkey were perfectly in harmony, I saw. They had trapped one of the ubiquitous suits in a corner of the wall and the alley. Meroe had a raised hand and Serena, backing up, was all prepared to kick his lights out.

'You will leave this watching,' snarled Meroe. 'You will leave now.'

'It's God's will,' he stammered, switching his terrified glance from Meroe's hand to the donkey's hoofs.

'Then God will provide,' she told him. 'If I see you here again I will call the police. And I will put a nice little curse on you,' she hissed. 'You will itch and itch and never stop itching until you die screaming, tearing your flesh. Lice,' she purred, getting closer. 'Fleas. Bedbugs…'

He broke. He scuttled round the corner like an insect and was out of sight in moments.

'I am tired of their surveillance,' she told me, allowing Serena to turn again.

'Oh, so am I, and aren't you glad Mr. Pahlevi didn't see that? He might douse you again.'

'I am not going to actually curse him,' she said. 'His own fear did the work. For me? How very kind of you.'

'My pleasure,' I said, handing over the packet. There are days when I do not know what to say to Meroe and this was one of them.

Presently my witch went back to Belladonna and, just as I ran out of rosewater, Mr. Pahlevi arrived and very humbly took the rein from my hand, undid and returned my rope, and led Serena away without a word or a slap for her unaccountable absence. I did wonder where Serena went, when she was on the loose.

The nearest rose garden, probably. If this brutal summer had left us any roses to bloom.

And Sunday went quietly on. Daniel read Pratchett aloud as I finished up all my presents, for this week would give me Christmas Eve, Christmas Day, and the end of work for four weeks. I had not even thought what I might do. Would Daniel have to stay in the city? Could we find Horatio a sitter and run away together?

Then again, where else did I want to be other than here?

All was calm and bright in my apartment, though the chaos was growing outside, until Daniel's phone rang around four pm.

I could hear the voice shrieking from where I sat.

'What's happened?' I asked, prepared to start stiffening my sinews.

'Brigid's gone,' said Daniel. 'That was Meroe's witch friend; she and Meroe are at the Sibyl's Cave and want to come up for a cup of tea and a conference.'

'Fine,' I said, getting up to put on the kettle. I really would have to get some serious groceries delivered on Monday. I was running out of everything. I put out the pad to write a full list which I could then email. Stalwart persons would then haul it all the way up to my apartment, only asking money in return. I found the box containing a variety of herbal teas but the witches, when they arrived, demanded brandy and tall, icy glasses of lemon cordial.

'It was very strange, and I don't know if you have an explanation,' said Meroe, introducing Kate, witch name Abraxas. She was short and plump with a bun of white hair and twinkling blue eyes, looking like the sort of midwife whom everyone would prefer. I noticed her hands as I supplied the drinks. Small and very strong, with clipped nails, the skin red with years of antiseptic. She didn't look at all like a witch, but most of them don't.

'Thank you, dear,' she said in a nice cosy grandmotherly voice, then downed her brandy in a gulp and held out the glass.

Daniel refilled it. He was always careful around witches, not wishing to indulge a misplaced sense of humour and end up sitting in a pond going 'ribbet'.

'Phew! I thought I'd seen it all. And now,' she added, sipping this time, 'I have.'

'What did you see?' I had to know.

'I was in the child's room when her parents came in, pushing the nurses aside, demanding that she get up and bring the baby. I pressed the panic button for security but they're slower than a wet week. Brigid started to cry and Manny stood in front of her and Mrs. O'Ryan hit him—just like that—she belted him across the face and he fell. Then the two of them, with two henchmen—don't look at me like that, Meroe dear, you know they were henchmen—just picked up Brigid and the baby and started to force their way out of the hospital. But by then there were doctors and nurses and a lot of people milling around so they had to shove and Brigid was screaming for help and I couldn't get to her because of a great lump of an orderly standing there in front of me like a…lump. Not helping.'

'We get the picture,' I said.

Abraxas took a long gulp of her cold drink and blinked.

'They progressed to the stairs with the poor girl screaming all the time and me trying to get through and the rest of them behaving like sheep, when the most amazing thing happened. The henchmen got her and the baby to the foyer, where the reception desk is, when in through the door came a parade of people all wearing different costumes. I thought they might be clowns to entertain the mothers but there were no red noses. They were chanting. Nonsense.'

'Hare wombat?' I guessed.

'Yes, dear.' She turned her very bright eyes toward me. 'Was this your arrangement?'

'Not exactly,' I demurred.

Abraxas resumed her narrative.

'Manny caught up with the O'Ryans and hit Mr. O'Ryan with a bedpan and knocked him down. Then the…clowns, I should call them, were upon them and all around them. The henchmen were confused and put Brigid and the baby down. Brigid kicked several shins, grabbed the baby and twisted out of their grasp. And when they tried to grab her the clowns began doing some sort of mime. The leader would shout "Monotreme!" and they would all wriggle and swim along or sort of stump with their fingers held spread out over their heads. They were good, their platypus and their echidna. I was reminded of some Koori dancers I have seen. Matter of belief, perhaps. I always thought that such was the explanation for werewolves and those African leopard men.'

'Quite. What happened then?' I asked, pouring more brandy. We were getting low on brandy, too. Abraxas looked worried and chewed at her thumbnail.

'Mrs. O'Ryan was stranded over my side of the throng and I used a Word on her, Meroe. I know we don't like to do that, but I had to stop her in her tracks. She was the driving force.'

'Perfectly correct, sister, and very restrained of you, Goddess have mercy,' said Meroe. 'I threatened to curse one of those watchers only this morning.'

'Well, that's all right, then. The Word held her for a minute or two. The leader shouted "Macropods!" and they all started bouncing like kangaroos. Mr. O'Ryan and the henchmen got rather trodden on, I'm glad to say. The kangaroos must have found the terrain lumpy underpaw. When they all bounced out of the foyer, Manny, Brigid and the baby were gone.'

'I wonder how difficult it is going to be to reward the freegans?' asked Daniel.

'I bought them a lot of ice cream,' I told him. 'Food is always acceptable.'

'That's their name? Freegans?' asked Abraxas.

'That's them,' I said.

'The Goddess' blessing on the freegans and may they flourish and be rewarded,' said Abraxas prayerfully.

'Amen,' I agreed. 'Nigel did tell me not to worry.'

'What a getaway,' said Daniel. 'But it does not solve the underlying problem, you know. Brigid and the child Shiloh.'

'Didn't a certain person not two metres from me tell me that "sufficient unto the day is the evil thereof"?' I demanded.

'And that's true,' said Meroe. 'Come, Abraxas, you could do with a cleansing ceremony, if you had to use a Word.'

'Thanks for the drink, dear,' said Abraxas, getting up. 'We just thought you ought to hear it from our own lips, or you wouldn't believe it.'

The door shut behind them. We were silent for a space. Then Daniel asked, 'What's a Word?'

'I hope I never find out.'

'Indeed.'

'You never did get to see the baby,' he said wistfully.

I had to tell him. It was my dreadful secret: the one thing a woman Must Never Say, even now. One can confess to all manner of interesting fetishes, one can change gender, one can declare a passion for the Prince of Wales or George Bush and only attract a moderate amount of denunciation. But I had something much worse than that to tell him and he had better know now.

'I don't like babies,' I confessed.

'Really?'

'And I don't like children,' I completed my confession.

'You don't have to, you know,' he told me.

'You don't understand! I don't like pictures of small children! I don't coo over other people's rotten slobbery offspring! I find the creatures egotistic, noisy, and lacking in interest until they grow manners! I don't like children!'

'I understand,' said Daniel carefully, seeing how much in earnest I was. 'That's allowed. That's all right. You don't have to have anything to do with them. And I have no intention of having any, so it doesn't bother me.'

'You don't want children?' I asked, almost in tears of relief.

'No,' he said. 'This is no world to bring them into. Tell you what,' he said, lifting my chin and kissing me.

'What?' I quavered.

'Let's have cats instead.'

And we laughed, and drank the rest of the brandy, and went to bed.

Chapter Twenty

Bring me flesh and bring me wine,
Bring me pine logs hither.
Thou and I shall see him dine
When we bear them thither.

John Mason Neale
'Good King Wenceslas'

Four am and I hoped that, in view of the recent history, it would be a nice boring day full of hard work and baking. I had emailed the list to the grocer last night and I left Daniel asleep to rise in due course and welcome in the heavies bringing the boxes of food. I had even managed to run out of things which one always has in the back of a cupboard somewhere, like molasses and rolled oats. That would have been those Anzac biscuits, of course. Coffee. Feed Horatio. Monday. But this week would end with a feast and after that, rest. I was shutting Earthly Delights for the month of January. I had agreed to bake bread for the Soup Run, just for the Soup Run, and on lazy days I might even buy it. The prospect was intoxicating. I had not had a holiday for three years, except for a nervous week when the Health Department had closed the bakery, and that wasn't at all restful.

Cheered, an overalled and booted Corinna went down into the industrial-strength air conditioning to find Jason already taking some of those wonderful little fruitcakes out of the oven. They have to rest for twenty-four hours in their tins, doused with good-quality brandy, before they can be packaged. The air smelt fruity and winy, very pleasant.

'Cap'n on deck!' He jumped to his feet and saluted.

'How goes the ship?' I asked.

'Steady she goes, sir.'

'Carry on,' I ordered.

Then we mixed and pummelled and baked and cooked. Jason had a recipe for a cake called barmbrack that he wanted to try, which was why he was so early. I did the bulk of the ordinary bread. It rolled into the oven pallid and came out shiny. I had decided to do a little experimentation of my own and tried, once again, to make croissants. I had the original French recipe, the best butter, the finest flour. But they still disappointed. Perfectly good croissants, yes, but not the ones I remembered from the artisan *boulangeries* of Paris.

Megan arrived early for the shop bread, just as the Mouse Police returned, smelling of tuna scraps. Heckle took a good look at her rickshaw and decided it would be too hard to tip over. He hadn't taken down a runner for weeks. I hoped he might have run out of vengeful feelings about the paperboy who had caused his tail to be abbreviated, though I didn't think this at all likely. But lately there had just been too many people on foot for him to practise his trick. He would have been trodden on in his turn, which was not part of the joke at all.

I paused to think glowingly of Mr. O'Ryan and his henchmen falling under freegan feet. I bet they hadn't enjoyed being bounced on by all those people channelling macropods. The freegans were slender, but there were a lot of them. I hoped the bad guys were bruised to the bone.

And Meroe's curse had worked. For the first time since Thursday, we had no uncomfortable sentry suit on the corner, sweating into his white shirt. The morning had already improved.

Megan and I loaded a huge amount of bread. I asked her where the freegans were hanging out when not dancing their Hare Wombat dance.

'Down by the river, as far as I know,' she replied. 'The old men are complaining about them still. You knew I work the Soup Bus every month or so, didn't you? I was on it last night, with Ma'ani as heavy. That Sister Mary, she's a very persuasive woman.'

'She certainly is,' I agreed.

'On the other hand, I noticed that you have Janeen visiting,' she said, tying up the last load with Serena's rope. 'Good luck with that.'

'Why?'

'She gives me the creeps,' said Megan frankly. 'I'm glad she's not my doctor. She's got a hungry look. Cut off your leg and eat it, my Irish grandpa used to say. Well, I'm off. Look out for your tail, puss.'

And she went. Horatio descended to the shop, Goss arrived, the Mouse Police sought their flour sacks for a well-earned nap, and Jason and I kept baking, at full stretch, as Kylie agreed to take over the shop tomorrow so that Goss could finish her Christmas tasks.

'She has to find presents for all these horrible old aunts,' Kylie told me.

'Lavender water?'

I was about to recommend Potter & Moore, when Kylie added, 'They're all real fit and go in for mountain climbing and stuff.'

And I left Goss to her fate. She would manage. The girls have a genius for shopping.

'So I'm going to Mum's and poor Kylie's going to her dad's, because it's his turn, and she hates his new girlfriend. And she isn't all that keen on him, either. I don't know why he's making her go; he never really paid much attention to her until they split. It's like that with men,' said Goss in her most sophisticated tone.

'Yes, poor Brigid's father didn't seem very interested in her,' I said, as I reached into the oven for another set of loaves.

I clanged the tray down to dislodge the loaves and slotted it into the washing-up rack. 'That's the last of the shop bread, thank God. Let's open the door.'

'There's a queue,' Goss told me, and I fled upstairs to change my work clothes for something fit to be seen. One of Jason's slightly overfilled jam muffins had exploded all down my front, making me look like a minor cast member of *CSI*. Four days before Christmas and either a shop is doing well, in which case it is hell, or it is doing badly, which is worse.

Earthly Delights was doing well and Goss and I were run off our feet. I let Jason go out for his breakfast—otherwise the poor boy might have expired before two pm—but Goss and I only achieved two ten-minute breaks all day, and that was by shoe-horning Jason into the shop while we went into the bakery to sit down. Even Horatio was weary. But we sold bread, cakes, muffins, rolls and everything we had except the fittings and the curtains.

Then Jason, who is as strong as a donkey, got out the cleaning things. Goss and I walked to the bank, because we were so tired we were afraid that either of us, alone, might just sit down in the gutter and cry. I escorted Goss back to the lift, gave her a fifty-dollar bonus, and told her to soak her feet in hot water. That was what I was going to do.

I realised, as I plodded into the bakery again to collect Horatio, that all my shopping, tons of it, would be piled up in my kitchen waiting to be put away, and I quailed. I would at least have to find the things for the freezer before they melted. My ex never put things away. I just couldn't face it. I was, as Grandpa Chapman would have said when Grandma couldn't hear him, like Barney's bull: buggered.

But with my furry assistant I slowly ascended the stairs. Courage, Corinna! My head was thumping and my feet felt like lead. Then I opened the door and found that 1) the shopping had all been put away, 2) there was a hot bath with bath foam already run, and 3) the gorgeous Daniel stood ready to provide me with a large drink, compounded to a secret recipe of his own. He called it a Baker's Bracer.

I flung myself into his arms and burst into tears. How did I deserve such a gorgeous man?

He detached me long enough to ply me with the drink, which tasted like iced pineapple juice and various other tropical things. Orange, maybe? Coconut milk? I drank it. I bathed in luxury. I was put to bed and I fell asleep instantly, glowing with gratitude.

And I awoke just as grateful. Daniel had gone out, leaving me a note. My feet had recovered. It was four am and time to get my act together for a day which would be as hard as the day before. This time, I boiled an egg for my breakfast. I made sandwiches for Kylie and me. I took the big picnic thermos and filled it with ice and lemon cordial. We were going to be prepared.

Jason seemed little the worse for a day which would have crippled a carthorse. He had been up all night, it appeared, making muffins and many more Christmas cakes. He wanted me to draft a note which would tell the customers to douse the cake in either good brandy, sherry or orange juice for a couple of days so that it would keep. I did so as the ovens came on and the air conditioning roared. The weather had been stinking now for four days straight. I liked this planet much better before there were people on it. And all the hydrocarbons were in the ground where they belonged.

My plans worked. Now we knew that we were not going to get any respite, we organised to take time off, we ate sandwiches, and we survived much better. We were coining money. This time I escorted Kylie to the bank in case anyone thought we might be worth robbing, because we were. However, the day was free of anyone in a balaclava and we walked back through the heat only exhausted, not partially slain.

I gave Kylie a bonus. She just nodded and got into the lift. Horatio was waiting at the door into my apartment. Jason was not getting on with the cleaning, but putting a series of little patties into the big frying pan.

'Just want to try these out,' he said to me. 'For Sarah's rehearsal. We're all invited. I'm making munchies.'

'What's in them?' I asked, not very interested.

'That textured vegetable protein stuff, mashed potato and spring onions and so on. They ought to be like little fritters and there's a tomato and chilli sauce. She's using Rowan's computer to do a menu.'

'Right,' I said, plodding toward the stairs.

'And she's expecting us all to come,' he added.

'Right,' I repeated.

Too much to expect the same service as the day before. Daniel was not there. But the makings of a drink were set out on the counter, together with a plate of Uncle Solly's salt beef on rye. A Baker's Bracer, I learnt, was composed of orange and pineapple juice, tonic water, coconut liqueur and Cointreau. Horatio and I washed, lunched, drank, and lay down for a nap. I set the alarm to wake me at six. Tonight, at least, I would like to see Daniel and have dinner. Only two more days of this, and we would stay a whole day in bed, only getting up (possibly) for meals.

When I woke at six Daniel was still not there. I defrosted a serve of something indistinguishable under the ice. One thing I must do when I had time was unload the freezer and retrieve all those labels which hadn't stuck properly. The dark mass turned out to be a good meaty, creamy beef stroganoff. I ate it with bread as I could not be bothered finding the noodles and cooking them. Jason tapped at the door. He had a tray in his hands.

'Thought I might bring you some dinner, Cap'n,' he said cheerfully.

'Come in,' I invited. 'What do you have there? Coke in the fridge,' I added, confident that there was.

'I got lots of vegan nibbles,' he said. 'Hummus, tzatziki and beetroot dips. Crudités,' said Jason, pronouncing them correctly. 'Baked tofu nuggets with crushed nuts. Little vegie meatballs cooked in vegie stock. Corn cakes. Lentil loaf with walnuts. Not them meat patties. They didn't work properly, so I'm going to make sausage rolls. Bit hard, no cream or eggs, no milk, no gluten—this soy stuff is strange. But have a taste, Captain!'

I had done many things for love, including watching nine hockey games, so I prepared to taste the nibbles and not lie more than was proper.

And actually they were quite tasty. Nothing to object to at all. I suppressed the thought that what the lentil loaf needed was a big slab of blue cheese. Jason watched me narrowly as I ate one of each category, which was quite enough after all that beef stroganoff (with cream).

'No, they're very good,' I told him.

'Ace. Knew I could rely on you, Cap'n, even if you are a meat eater. I'm going back now to do the fruit things. And the sausages rolls. Cold's best for this weather, that's good.'

'When is this concert?'

'Tonight,' he said. 'At eight. In the roof garden.'

'Right,' I said.

He took his tray and went back to the kitchen. I was at a loose end. Finally I decided I might do my email. And from thence, idly, and then with increasing horror, I googled the words of the little song sung to the tune of 'Twinkle Twinkle Little Star'.

Haarmann Pearce and Soylent Green.
Vargas Fish and Sawney Beane.

Haarmann, it appeared, was a murderer. So was Vargas. So was Pearce. He was the convict who walked out into the wilderness with companions and was recaptured alone. Albert Fish was a degenerate who murdered children. Sawney Beane was a (possibly mythical, I really hoped so) bandit who haunted Scotland, had an incestuous tribe of appalling children and grandchildren, and was executed in a style which matched his murders in brutality.

They were all cannibals. Pearce said that he preferred human flesh because it 'tasted like pork'. And when I found out the meaning of Soylent Green I was out of the apartment on my way to Jason's apartment with the speed of terror.

Fortunately I was in time. Bunny was flaked out on the couch. Without much argument, Jason handed over the little packets of textured vegetable protein given to him by Janeen. Possibly he, too, an experienced cook, had been uneasy about them. I let him keep the stuff which came in the box labelled *Tempeh*. I carried my horrible little package home and lodged it, enclosed in three separate plastic bags, in the freezer. After a moment's thought, I took the parcel out again and stuck on a label which said, simply, *Poison*.

Then I made myself a nice cup of tea, which I deserved. I thought about being sick, decided that I was not so weak, and drank my tea.

When Daniel came in at seven I was quite calm. We ate an omelette with smoked trout and drank a glass or two of white wine. We dressed in garments suitable for a concert in the open air in Australia: my loose boho skirts and blouse and Daniel's shorts and shirt. We doused ourselves in insect repellent. I made a few preparations of my own, and then we ascended to the roof garden, where all was in readiness for the concert.

Trudi had soaked the garden in her hoarded grey water, then rinsed it in fresh water, so that it smelt divine. The ground steamed slightly. We joined our fellow tenants on wicker chairs set out in a half-circle around the opening of the grotto of the goddess Ceres, which had seats for the musicians and space for the singers. I looked around. Mrs. Dawson was present, wearing a dress made apparently of two pieces of ochre cloth, tacked together at shoulder and wrist. It was patterned with dark brown trees rising from the hem. Outrageous and only she could have worn it. The Professor was in attendance upon her. Jason was staring at the spot where Sarah would shortly appear, in rapture. Trudi and Therese were talking about plant fibres. The girls, in skimpy floaty gowns, looked uncomfortable. *Is this going to be boring?* would have been in the thought bubble over their heads. Mrs. Pemberthy was sitting in the furthest chair, not speaking to any of us, which was a mercy. Jon and Kepler, an educated audience, were reading the program notes. The Lone

Gunmen—Taz, Rat and Gully—had not come and had not been expected. Mistress Dread, in her 'Pat' persona, was wearing a linen walking costume, circa 1912. Meroe was wearing a bright scarlet shawl, which might or might not have been a good sign.

And I was not in a mood to appreciate Vaughan Williams, great composer though he was.

Daniel put an arm around me.

'What's afoot, Sherlock?' he whispered into my ear.

'You won't believe it,' I whispered back. 'Just come with me when I corral the singers after the concert.'

'All right, *ketschele*,' he said agreeably. 'We have the Vaughan Williams first, to put us in the mood, then carols, then supper.'

I did not reply. I was rehearsing in my head the fine stinging words I had in store for certain young persons to be delivered not two hours hence, and I did not want to let go of my outrage, which was enlivening me.

But when the unsupported tenor began 'This is the truth sent from above', I was caught up in the music. The string players were used to playing together and managed well, even in the open air with mosquitos zooming down to bite them in mid-cadenza. The melodies were all familiar, the singing was very competent with only a few minor hiccups, and I was swept away. When the first half finished, I had difficulty dragging myself back to the present.

But I did so, accepting a cup of herbal tea and an almond biscuit and listening to the girls exclaim, 'It's all right! Not boring at all! Who'd ha' thought?' All around me the audience were smiling. I saw the singers exchange glances of complete relief. It had worked. That was the hard bit. Now there were carols, and they had been singing them for weeks.

We sang 'Good King Wenceslas', 'O Come All Ye Faithful', 'In Dulci Jubilo', 'God Rest Ye Merry, Gentlemen'. It was lovely. We clapped and cheered. We got an encore of 'Past Three O'clock'.

Then it was time for supper, which was to be laid out in the temple. Chairs were shifted, a trestle set up, and Jason and Sarah went down to Rowan's apartment to fetch the food. I waited until Jason came back and then sent him down to my apartment to bring the makings for sangria which I had left on the bench.

'So these are all vegetarian?' asked Mrs. Dawson, allowing the Professor to fetch her a small plate with a selection of olives and a slice of lentil bread. Everyone took some of the nibbles. I was watching the singers. Alexander was talking on a mobile phone. Michael was discussing chess with Jon and Kepler and seemed unworried. Bec was talking tulip culture with Trudi and deploring the drought. Janeen looked small and meek, as she always did, but Rowan was sweating more than the weather required and Sarah was alight with excitement. And when I caught Rupert stealthily walking away with the plate of Janeen's textured protein sausage rolls, I called them to the side.

'Rowan, Janeen, Sarah, Rupert, might I have a word? In the apartment, if you please. Sorry to take your singers,' I said to the gathering. 'Urgent food conference. Come along.' Daniel squeezed into the stairwell to make sure that no one broke and ran back to the garden. I waited as Rowan opened his door and we all went in, including Rupert and the sausage rolls. He did not know, of course, that I had taken Janeen's ingredients away.

'The others are very young and stupid, but I would have expected better of you,' I exclaimed.

He shifted uneasily, a very embarrassed bear.

'I wouldn't have let it happen really,' he protested. 'But they were so urgent about it, and…'

'You wanted to see if they would go through with it,' I concluded.

'Well, yes. I mean, it's the ultimate taboo, isn't it?'

'That's the trouble,' I told him. 'Can you imagine what effect your little sideshow might have had on civilised people like the Professor and Mrs. Dawson, who aren't young and might collapse? You stole the human flesh from the operating room disposal bin, didn't you?' I demanded of Janeen. 'And you had such fun tantalising us, singing your little nursery rhyme— "Haarmann, Pearce and Soylent Green, Vargas, Fish and Sawney Beane". Snickering at the idea that all the stupid mundanes had to do was google the names and they'd know what you were up to.'

'They deserved it,' cut in Sarah self-righteously. 'They eat flesh and wear leather and have no compassion.'

'Oh, such as the compassion you showed Jason,' said Daniel. 'You found out all about him, you know he's a recovering heroin addict, and you used him to make your filthy sausages.'

'He's a boy. He'll recover,' she retorted, and Daniel grabbed my hand just in time. I have never wanted to slap a human so much in my whole life.

'Soylent green,' I said, as calmly as I could. 'Harry Harrison story. The world is so short of food that the only available protein is soylent green, and that is made of people.'

'It's a solution,' said Janeen, speaking for the first time.

'Jonathan Swift in his cruellest satire said the same thing,' I told her. 'His Modest Proposal to solve the famine in Ireland was for the Irish to eat their own children.'

'It's a way out!' she said with mounting fervour. 'What else have we in huge quantities but people? They breed and breed so that the earth cannot support them. They're protein. It would be better if everyone stopped eating meat, but if they have to eat meat, then they can eat each other! Otherwise we are all going to starve!'

'Sit down,' Daniel ordered. 'Shut up.'

She had really upset him, I could see. So could Janeen. She sat.

'Give me the pamphlets,' I said. Sarah, scared at last, gave me a posting box. I took one out. It was lettered in bright red on a black background.

'You have just eaten human flesh,' it proclaimed. I could imagine how this would have affected Mrs. Pemberthy. Or me, for instance. I read on. The pamphlet suggested that if you couldn't stomach human meat, how could you eat cow's flesh, or sheep's? From the same publisher as the last one, which had convinced at least one young girl that she had breast cancer.

'I'm willing to make you an offer,' I said.

'What?' asked Rupert. 'We'll entertain any way out of this terrible situation. Yes we will, Janeen. You studied all this time to get barred from the medical profession as though you had the plague? You want a career as a vegan model, don't you, Sarah? They'll never employ a cannibal—that's not the sort of diet anyone wants to put in the *Women's Weekly*. Rowan's father will put him out on the street and I—I should have stopped this weeks ago. But I never thought you'd actually go through with it. What are you offering, Corinna?'

'Those sausage rolls are made of tempeh. You are now going to eat them as I watch. I have the human flesh in my freezer and I will dispose of it. You will not breathe a word of this fiasco to Jason. You will, in fact, compliment him on his cooking and be very, very nice to him. I will take this vile propaganda and get rid of it. The matter will be ended there. If I hear of anything like this happening anywhere you might have been, I will reveal this to the *Herald Sun*. You can imagine the headlines...'

They shuddered. They could imagine. Rowan grabbed a sausage roll, shuddered again, and ate it. Rupert scoffed his and wiped his beard. Janeen ate, and so did Sarah. I smiled at them.

'Right. Now, if I told you that I lied and you have just eaten human flesh, how would you feel?'

Rupert gave me a twinkling look and patted his stomach.

'Full,' he said.

Sarah just beat Janeen to the bathroom. We heard a fugue of retching.

Rowan gave me a startled look.

'You aren't sick?' I asked. His freckles stood out on his white face.

'No, because you weren't lying,' he said.

'Come up to the party again,' I said. 'Sangria for all.'

Rupert gave me a large hug.

'Thank you,' he said. Gesturing toward the bathroom in which painful recriminations were now echoing, he added, 'for all of us.'

Escorted by a grim Daniel, I took the pamphlets down to my apartment, and then carried them and the packet marked *Poison* out to the rubbish skip in the alley. I flung them in. The lid closed with a pleasantly final clang. I washed my hands with rose geranium soap and we returned to the roof garden.

It turned into quite a good party after that. The sangria went down well. Daniel gave up on the niceties and mixed it in a clean plastic bucket. Jason had made, bless his heart, several trays of vegetarian delights which were greatly appreciated. He had invented a little egg and herb pie which was good enough to sell in the shop.

'It's olive oil pastry,' he told me. 'Just have to keep it cold enough. Try the cheesy one.'

The cheesy one was also pretty good. Jon and Kepler produced a lot of little munchies, also meat-free—ricepaper rolls, dim sum, interesting mushrooms wrapped in wonton wrappers—which they had been preparing ever since Rupert had asked them to provide some Asian delights. The sangria, made of cask red, was ice cold and just the thing for a hot night, though Trudi insisted on her usual tipple, gin. I had a new one for her to try, Hendrick's, which she said tasted just like gin used to in the good old days before her national drink got so lily-livered. And Trudi insisted on her rollmops.

When Sarah and Janeen came back from their epic emesis, they were determined to be good. They did not recoil from Trudi's fishiness. They hugged Jason and told him he was a wonderful cook. They even ate one of his cheesy tarts. They drank sangria, although that was perfectly acceptable in any case.

Then they all started to sing and we sang with them. The stars came out. The musicians had gone—musicians do not perform for free if they hope to be professionals. But we only needed voices. I suspect they were singing so well from sheer relief. Only Janeen and Sarah were fanatical enough to really carry out such a dreadful plan. Rupert was indulging a diseased sense of humour, and Rowan, Michael, Bec and Alexander did not figure in it. But they sang like angels, all of them, and even Daniel began to forgive them. I didn't know what terrible events in his own or maybe his people's past of which this had reminded him, but he had been greatly shaken. I hugged him as the voices rose to the stars.

Bring me my bow of burning gold!
Bring me my arrows of desire!
Bring me my spear! O clouds, unfold!
Bring me my chariot of fire!
I shall not cease from mental fight,
Nor shall my sword sleep in my hand,
Till we have built Jerusalem
In England's green and pleasant land.

The Professor wiped his eyes. Mrs. Dawson was in tears. So was I. The girls fluttered. Sarah reached out an arm and drew Jason to her side. Rupert stood forth and bowed to the company with an elaborate eighteenth-century flourish which matched his white hair and beard.

'Ladies, gentlemen,' he said. 'Thank you for a wonderful evening. Merry Christmas, and good night.'

And we applauded them as they left.

Chapter Twenty-One

Ein feines Kindelein liegt in dem Krippelein...
beim Öchslein und beim Eselein

Praetorius
'Psallite'

Four am. Rise and shine but not for much longer. I rose, ate, drank, all the usual stuff. Today we would sell out the shop, because today was Christmas Eve, tomorrow was the actual Christmas itself, and after that it would all be forgotten until October next year. Now all I had to be prospectively annoyed about was Easter and even that was several months away. I just hate festivities, and this one grates on me like cake crumbs in bed. As you might have gathered.

But there you are and there we were. I had hired both Goss and Kylie for the day and we would work until we had nothing left to sell except possibly the Mouse Police, who were non-negotiable as employees.

By what Meroe would call the special mercy of the Goddess, it was quite cool outside as I released Heckle and Jekyll. The Rising Sun was also closing for January. They were just going to have to go cold tuna on the Southern Ocean endangered species until February.

Jason was looking ragged. The pile of cakes, the baskets of muffins, the stack of loaves testified to his industry. Surely we could never sell it all. It was a mountain of baking.

'Have you been to bed at all?' I asked severely.

He pushed back his cap and wiped his forehead, leaving a streak of flour.

'Not really, Cap'n. Couldn't sleep. Thought I'd catch a few Z's this afternoon, maybe. It's the concert tonight.'

'So you shall,' I said. 'How is Bunny?' I added idly, as I slid loaves into the oven.

'Oh, he's…he's fine,' stammered Jason, who is really a very bad liar considering his history. I wondered what had befallen that self-possessed rabbit, but we were busy, and got busier. Goss turned up at seven, when there was already a queue outside the shop. Lots of people had left their Christmas shopping to the last moment, hoping that it would miraculously solve itself. It hadn't, and now they wanted not only bread and cakes, but Earthly Delight's biscuits, wrapped in cellophane: Bosworth jumbles, hermits, molasses cookies with crinkled edges, Anzacs, ginger-bread boys and girls, dogs and cats, ducks and geese. Shortbread in the shape of santas and half-moons and trees, decorated with silver cachous on red and green icing. Jason was developing into an adept with icing, which was not my favourite medium. We also sold out the glacé fruit, the fig and apricot dainties, the coconut-covered dried fruit rolls, the little Christmas cakes and mince pies and, of course, the muffins, pies, loaves, rolls, even yesterday's not-quite-right croissants.

I hastily stuffed a big bag full of bread and dainties for the Professor's luncheon party and stashed it in my apartment, where it could not get sold by mistake. At eleven Horatio indicated that he found all this commerce just too fatiguing and retreated to the sofa for a restorative nap. I sent Jason up to his own bed at twelve, when we were beginning to clear the shelves. Earthly Delights produce went out in pockets and handbags and string bags, all wrapped in our own cyclamen and moss-green tissue paper, presents for people who were hard to suit: aunts and distant cousins and post persons, and perhaps even to rescue an exhausted family cook, already wondering what to do about a turkey which was too large to go in the oven, from trying to bake cakes as well. It went to drinks parties and after-dinner coffee and the family lunch, and to placate screaming children there were Jason's plate-sized cookies studded with Smarties, his gingerbread zebras, his jam fancies. There wasn't a lot of room in the shop and it was shoulder to shoulder all morning.

Goss and Kylie were at their best in this situation. Always a smile, always a joke, slightly shaky on the change but the machine did that for them as it rang and chimed like Christmas bells. I noticed that the girls were keeping up their strength, which was excellent news. Goss was dipping into a box of slightly failed fruit rolls, Kylie was nibbling lopsided shortbread trees where the icing had slipped, as icing has a habit of doing if you are too impatient, which I always am. I reserved some of packets of bikkies for my own presents, including one for Megan, who came to pick up the last load of bread for the year.

'Been good,' she said, taking the package and giving me her new card in exchange. 'I'm doing ice cream for the summer. What's happened to your watcher?'

'I hope,' I replied, 'that he has melted.'

'I hear you,' she said, wished me a merry Christmas, and sped away.

My fellow tenants also made their final purchases. Meroe fell in love with the coconut macaroons. My gamble on making a lot of chocolate crackles had paid off. People cooed with nostalgia and bought them all. Juliette from the chocolate shop Heavenly Pleasures brought us all little boxes of Best Assorted, though mine was coffee truffles, my favourite. Juliette reported that she would also have to close, probably before noon, as she had not a sweet left in the shop and was presently entertaining bids to sell her apprentice, George. I told her to raise the price. George's character had improved, he made good chocolates, and he was very pretty.

I had not thought that we could possibly sell that ziggurat of cakes, but we did. And the mountain of muffins and the stack of bread. At one o'clock Goss, Kylie and I looked at one another over the last three gingerbread ladies, took one each, and closed the door on Earthly Delights for the year.

Even then there were pitiful tappings at the shutter as we poured our coffee and sat down to nibble our biscuits and catch our breath. There was silence for a few minutes. Coffee. Gingerbread. Silence.

'These are really good,' said Goss after a while. 'Really spicy.'

'Most people don't put enough ginger in them,' I said absently. 'Well, that was a morning, wasn't it?'

'Fun, though,' said Kylie. 'Christmassy.'

They looked at each other and giggled. Something was up, but I was too tired to bother about it.

'It's been good,' said Goss. 'Working for you, Corinna. We okay for the new year?'

'Certainly,' I said. 'Do you want to come back?'

'Sure,' they said, and giggled again.

'Well, then, I'm going to start the cleaning,' I said. 'Poor Jason's pooped.'

'We can help,' Kylie offered, unexpectedly. 'You do the banking and we'll start the washing up.'

This was unprecedented but it was probably Christmas spirit. People did go strange at this time of year, buying presents they couldn't afford for people they didn't like. I heard the clash of trays and the roar of water as they did as they had promised.

The banking added up to so great a sum that I was nervous as I went out with the money in my backpack. I almost called up to Daniel to escort me. But I hadn't far to go and no one was interested in me; one does not expect a tired woman in a flour-spattered apron to be carrying any real money. In which you would be wrong.

Relieved of the cash, I dawdled back through the shuffling shoppers. End of the year. I hadn't really noticed it in previous

years because I had been so tired and so broke. Now I was afflu-
ent and I had Daniel. Things had greatly improved.

In fact, I was almost home and actually humming 'In Dulci
Jubilo' under my breath when a tall man in a white shirt and
dark suit grabbed my arm and swung me around to stand face
to face with a thin woman.

Very thin. She was almost skeletal. Her hair was blonde by
intention and cut in what Professor Dion calls a South Yarra
bob, straight to the shoulders and curled in at the bottom. Her
clothes were modest, with long sleeves and a decorous hemline:
a linen suit in pale blue. Her makeup was impeccable, but her
eyes, now, those eyes were blue and perfectly insane.

I shook the hand off my arm.

'Corinna Chapman?' she asked. Her voice was hoarse, as
though she had been screaming.

'Who wants to know?' I demanded rudely.

'I'm Mrs. O'Ryan, Charlotte O'Ryan,' she told me, in that
accent which grates on my nerves. The St Katherine's chirp,
the one which says, 'I'm just a little girl, don't hurt me. What
does poor little me know about nuclear physics? You gweat big
man you!'

'So?' I returned.

'You know where my daughter is. I want her and the child
back.'

'Then want must be your master,' I said, and started to walk
away. The man grabbed again. I grabbed in turn and bent back
his thumb. He winced in a most gratifying fashion. 'If you want
to use that hand again for the next six weeks, you'll keep it to
yourself,' I snarled. He looked shocked. The Holy Reformed
Temple of Shiloh was not used to female resistance. They
considered all females to be nothing but breeding machines,
anyway, to keep silent and do the housework and care for their
husbands, adoring them as close to God. I had read their disgusting literature.

'Please,' said Mrs. O'Ryan.

'I don't know where she is,' I said, softening slightly.

'I don't care where *she* is,' said Mrs. O'Ryan. 'She is only the vessel. Where is the child, Shiloh, the Son of Peace?'

'I don't know that either. Your husband might.'

For the first time I felt that there was an actual thinking person behind those china-doll eyes.

She shook her head. 'My husband? Why?'

'He's the father of the child, isn't he? It isn't the boy who has been guarding and protecting your daughter, I know that.'

She blinked. The tall man rubbed his mistreated hand. I was about to turn the corner into Flinders Lane and get out of this nasty situation when she said quickly, 'Yes, yes, Don is the father, now where is the baby?'

'Not so fast.' I had noticed that hesitation. 'If it isn't your husband, who is it?'

'Do you need to know?' she croaked.

'No, it's none of my business,' I agreed, and started to move away. As I took a pace or two, I put it together. The 'virginity' tests. Falling asleep listening to the Rev Hale. Her mother monitoring her menstrual periods. Surely not. Surely not even fanatics would be capable of something this loathsome. Even those mythical Satanists that the FBI could not find would choke on this notion.

I turned back. Acquaintance with Daniel, Sister Mary and the Soup Run clients had broadened my mind. Now it was so broad that it resembled one of those blasted plains Milton was so good at describing in *Paradise Lost*.

'You didn't,' I said. I really couldn't believe it. A mother inseminating her own daughter to give birth to the child of a shyster evangelist? Ridiculous, Corinna. You have been working too hard lately.

Mrs. O'Ryan just stared at me.

'We should leave this godless company,' said the tall man. I could tell I wasn't going to get a Christmas card from him, unless it was one which ticked.

'How did you do it?' I had to ask, even though I knew I wouldn't like the answer.

It was as though I had startled her into confession.

'It came in a sealed frozen package of biological material from the Reverend himself,' she said, hands clasped in awe. 'I put her to sleep three days in a row in her fertile period. It almost didn't work!' She giggled. It was the most grotesque thing I had ever seen. I felt sick. 'It was the last dose which did it. She is and was a virgin throughout, as the prophecy requires.'

'Why did you pick Brigid?'

'She's a better specimen than the other,' she told me flatly. 'Slim, comely, just as the Father requested.'

'So he knew about this?'

'Of course. He is divinely guided,' she replied, with perfect self-assurance. 'Then she ran away, then we couldn't find her, and now...she has the Son of Peace, and we need him! I have the passports ready. I can leave at any moment and carry him to his Father on Earth. Then shall the eyes of the blind be opened...'

I had had enough, and more than enough. I addressed the tall man. 'Take her home and call her doctor to give her a good sedative,' I told him. 'I have no knowledge of the whereabouts of Brigid or the baby. And if I had, I would never tell you—never. You're insane, and you're criminal, and...'

I had nothing else I could think of to say, so I walked quickly away. I fell into the bakery and slammed the door and bolted it and dropped the night bar as well. The girls paused in mid-mop and stared.

'Someone did try to rob you?' demanded Kylie, wiping her wet hands on her sopping bosom. They had rather overdone it on water and disinfectant. The air was redolent of Pine-o-cleen.

'No, just an unpleasant encounter...Well done, ladies, that is a nice job. Here is your Christmas bonus.'

'Merry Christmas!' they chorused, and I let them out through my apartment. The bakery door was staying barred. Though I did unbolt the little cat door, in case the Mouse Police wanted some air in the early morning. I was not going to be rising at four am for some time.

◇◇◇

Or so I had thought. When the shot rang out at four am, Daniel's army-trained reflexes had him out of bed and into a pair of shorts and sandals and at the door, listening, before I woke properly.

'Car backfire,' I insisted.

'Pistol shot,' he replied.

'No, don't be silly…' This was beginning to resemble a scene from *Romeo and Juliet.* 'Oh, all right.'

I hauled myself to the floor and found my own sandals. We opened the door. Insula was silent, as it usually was at that hour. Then, gradually, I could hear voices coming from under me. Not from my bakery, which was locked as tight as a drum. Therefore, from…

'The cellar,' said Daniel. 'I think I'll just creep down and find out what's happening before we call the cops.'

'All right, but you aren't going alone,' I insisted.

'Fair enough. You take the phone, it's on speed dial, just press this button. Stay behind me,' said Daniel, and as he was the expert on creeping up on people, I agreed.

The front door was wide open. I left it open. We might have to get out in a hurry. The voices were coming from the cellar, all right. They sounded angry. The lift was not a good option, as it might deliver us into the middle of a gun battle. So we slipped down the stairs. Daniel could move like Horatio. I just tried not to clump. There was a dim light below. When we reached the bottom, we were transfixed.

There, in front of me, was a Christmas crèche in real living colour. There was the deep hay, the Virgin Mary cradling the child, there was Joseph leaning protectively over her. There was the baby ox and the baby ass, and the only surprising note was the freegan T-shirt of St Joseph and a large Dutch bunny stretched out at the Virgin's feet.

We had found Brigid and Shiloh, the Son of Peace. And so had the enemy.

Frozen against the stairwell, almost within touching range of Daniel, was Rowan. Lined up against the Holy Family were Charlotte, her husband, Don, and three men in black suits with white shirts. And guns. One was carrying, incongruously, a child's safety capsule to go in the back of a car. It was blue.

'Give us Shiloh, the Son of Peace,' said Charlotte.

'Or what?' demanded Manny.

'Or I'll have them shoot you,' said Charlotte. She might have been discussing a charity luncheon. 'Both of you. The baby is born, we don't need Brigid anymore. She was but the vessel as are all women.'

'This looks bad,' I mouthed to Daniel. He nodded, eyes searching for a way out. The moment stretched and broke.

'No,' said Manny.

'Hang on,' said Rowan. He was so terrified that he was shaking, which was reasonable. 'You're Americans, aren't you? You can't carry guns in Australia like this, a gunshot will make the whole building call the cops. You can't just shoot people.'

'If it is God's will,' said the tallest man (and I hoped his thumb still hurt), 'then it will be done.'

Then I thought of something. I nudged Daniel and asked a question. Then an idiotic bloom of a laugh started in my solar plexus and strove to be free. I motioned Daniel back as I strode forward into the path of the guns, which was the only thing which sobered me.

'Me again,' I said to Charlotte.

'You again,' she said. 'As you see, I have found the Son of Peace, and he is mine.'

'Brigid?' I raised my voice a little. 'Show them the baby. Strip the child and bring it forward and show them their Son of Peace.'

Brigid looked confused. She didn't really know me.

'All right,' said Manny. 'Go on, Brigie.'

Brigid put the baby down and stripped off gown and nappy, then wrapped it again and brought it forward to the men with guns. The baby began to cry. As Brigid turned, exhibiting the child to each man, each one bowed his head, put away his gun and turned and went out of the cellar. Charlotte dived forward to see what they had seen.

The child was red and ugly as are all babies, though some hair was on its head. Its little body was fully displayed. One could see the eyes travelling down the ribby chest to the genitals, and note what was missing. Curves. A cleft. No penis. Brigid's baby was a girl.

I hadn't even asked about the gender, because I am not interested in babies. I had assumed, as Charlotte had assumed, that the child conceived in such a manner must be a boy, must be Shiloh. And here was a girl baby, a frail vessel, a failure. I started to laugh.

Then, deserted by her allies, Charlotte clawed the baby from Brigid's grasp, dropped it into the safety capsule, and ran like the wind.

Daniel ran after her but Rowan was ahead of him, long legs flashing in the semi-dark, up the steps and through the foyer and into Flinders Lane. Charlotte was desperate and fast, and she would probably have got away if Heckle, nursing old injuries, had not chosen that moment to issue from the cat door and avenge his missing centimetre of tail one more time.

Charlotte came down with a bone-breaking crash. Rowan was just close enough to catch the baby capsule before it hit the cobbles. Then time stood still. Rowan righted the capsule and opened it.

From inside came an aggrieved wail.

Heckle licked his paw and washed an ear with a satisfied expression, sneered lightly, then returned to the bakery, tail as straight as a taper.

Sheer relief made me laugh, which made Daniel laugh, which dragged in Rowan. Mrs. Pemberthy opened her window and screeched, 'Is that you drunks again?', which made us laugh more.

Finally we hauled Charlotte up. I held her with her hands behind her back and was rather hoping that she might fight. We returned to the cellar. Rowan carried the baby to Brigid, who examined the baby all over in the manner of a mother cat before redressing her and placing her in the basket which was doing duty for a cradle. Manny embraced them both.

'Now,' said Daniel grimly, 'if you will just sit Mrs. O'Ryan down over there, Corinna, and you sit here, Mr. O'Ryan, we shall have a conference.'

'How many charges, do you think?' I asked Daniel as they complied.

'Oh, at least eight—sexual penetration of a minor, rape, using a drug to procure sexual access, assault occasioning serious injury, assault with a firearm, assault in company, kidnapping, false imprisonment…ten years' jail, I think.'

'Fifteen,' I said.

'Split the difference,' he said generously. 'Twelve and a half.'

'Wait a moment,' said Mr. O'Ryan. He was looking battered, as those who are hopped on by a whole tribe of freegans often do.

'Not to mention the aggravating factors, like breach of trust,' Daniel continued. 'Did you tell Brigid how the Child of Peace was conceived, Charlotte?'

'Just now,' said Brigid. I had not heard her speak before. She had a calm, quiet voice, which was amazing, considering the circumstances. 'No one believed me that I hadn't…that I hadn't. You know that? They all nagged me all the time: who is the father? They all thought I was a liar and a slut. You did that to me,' she told her mother. 'And you let her do it,' she said to her father.

'Well, now, we have a negotiating position,' I said. 'What do you want to do, Brigid?'

'I'm not sure, what are my options?' she asked coolly.

'We can call the cops and get everyone involved arrested, and then there will be a trial and your parents will probably go to jail.'

'But then it would be in all the papers,' she said.

'Yes. And the social services might not let you keep the baby, if you are unsupported until Manny gets another job. Or we can offer your father the rich man's traditional way out of trouble.'

'What's that?' asked Manny.

'Money,' said Daniel. 'Shall we say, purchase of a house, to be chosen by you, services of suitable carers or nurses, rooms for your sister Dolly, living allowances?'

'Sandra,' said Brigid. 'Sandra would come. I miss Sandra.'

'She misses you,' I told her.

'Manny, what do you think?'

They went into a huddle, the baby in the middle. I realised that the traditional blue and white of the Virgin Mary was a long white broderie anglaise nightdress and Meroe's azure wrap, which had gone into hospital with Brigid. I also realised that the presence of the animals explained the girls volunteering to clean and using so much disinfectant to cover the stockyard smell. It also explained Jason's equivocation about Bunny. They had all been in on this scheme. But that could wait.

'How did the heavies get in?' I asked Rowan.

'I was coming back from the concert, and they stuck me up at the door,' he said. 'I was sure I was going to drop the baby!'

'But you didn't,' I told him. 'You don't do everything wrong, Rowan.'

'No, I don't, do I?' he asked. This thought brought a smile. 'That cat Heckle,' he said. 'He used to trip me on purpose, didn't he?'

'Yes,' I said, and explained about the paperboy and the missing piece of tail.

Meanwhile Mr. O'Ryan had not moved or said a word. Charlotte appeared dazed, which was good. I got up and went to examine the animals. The calf was the calf from the department store crèche, though now it was being fed milk from an oversized bottle. The ducks and chickens were those ducks and chickens, though the ducks now floated in the filled rinsing trough, heads under wings, and the chickens were asleep on an improvised roost. And the donkey was Diligence, advancing in hope of more carrots. Those vegans had liberated the animals from the Christmas display and hidden them in my cellar. I did wonder what had happened to the goats and the sheep. I asked Rowan.

'They weren't meant to be here at all,' he assured me. 'But the man Sarah had arranged, his truck broke down on his way back from taking the goats and sheep to the farm, and he couldn't get back in time. He'll be back in two days to take them away. We couldn't leave them there, Corinna! They were suffering!'

'Yes, they were, and as long as you can keep Mrs. Pemberthy out of the cellar it will be all right,' I said. 'They were suffering. I was wishing there was something I could do, and you did it. Ah. The conference is beginning again.'

The Virgin Mary produced a notebook—this was a very modern crèche—and wrote busily. Then she handed it to me. Daniel and I read it over. Seemed reasonable. A house. Sandra and Sandra's salary. School fees. A car and driver when required. Rooms and allowances for both Brigid and Dolores. Daniel's fees. Nothing for Manny. I queried this. I am an accountant, after all, as well as a baker.

'Not me,' said Manny proudly. 'I'm going back to work. I'm going to win that scholarship.'

'Contingency fund, then, to pay fees,' I said. 'Just in case you don't. You've had a rather interrupted study vac, you know.'

He smiled for the first time. He had his mother's smile.

There was a note at the end of the list of demands. It was in capitals and bold and underlined.

AND CHARLOTTE O'RYAN IS NEVER TO SEE EITHER OF HER DAUGHTERS DOLORES OR BRIGID AGAIN.

I gave the notebook to Mr. O'Ryan. He squirmed. I stared. Daniel stared. Rowan stared. Brigid and Manny glared. The baby whimpered.

'And if I refuse?' he said, making a feeble effort to bluff. 'This is all just on your word, you know.'

'Didn't you know there's a security camera at the front door?' Daniel asked. 'Where you and your appalling wife will have been recorded entering as trespassers with three armed men and Rowan in captivity?'

And that was the end of the negotiations. He agreed to all of it. Then he took Mrs. O'Ryan away. She had recovered a little and was now mumbling complaints about the way God had cheated her.

I asked Brigid if she would rather stay in my spare room.

'Oh, no,' she said softly. 'I'll stay here with Manny and Bunny and the gentle beasts. I like beasts a good deal more than I like people,' she said, resuming her place in the hay next to the manger. Manny lay down beside her. Bunny curled up at her feet. He was one happy rabbit.

We tiptoed out and left them. And it was Christmas Day.

Chapter Twenty-Two

Full royal gifts they bear for the King
Gold, incense, myrrh are their offering.

Peter Cornelius
'The Three Kings'

Daniel and I hugged Rowan farewell and went back to our apartment. On the way I called him on a matter of fact.

'Daniel, there is no security camera at our front door.'

'I know,' he said. 'When you bluff bluffers, it's best to bluff big.'

'I'll keep that in mind,' I told him. We went to bed and fell asleep again. When we woke about ten I said, 'I had the oddest dream,' before I realised that it was, in fact, the case that the cellar was a scene that would have made St Francis of Assisi write us a special canticle.

'That was strange,' said Daniel. 'And I'm not familiar with the iconography.'

'It had it all,' I assured him. 'The Virgin in white and blue, the baby ox and the ass, the manger for the child. Admittedly the rabbit was not canonical, nor the T-shirt or the notebook, but otherwise, all it lacked was angels.'

'And wise men, I understand,' he said as he went to take a shower.

We were invited to the Professor's luncheon, so we ate a little toast for breakfast and idled the morning away. I gave Daniel the T-shirt I had painted for him: THE MESSIAH IS COMING. LOOK BUSY. He was not offended. I had wondered. I received a bottle of that delightful Badedas bath essence which someone from America had obtained for him. A menu had been pushed under the door and we studied it.

CHRISTMAS LUNCHEON
Kir royal
Antipasto
Little vegetable delights

White wine
Ham with quince glaze
Turkey with cranberry jelly
Pumpkin, walnut and parmesan terrine

Red wine
Roast beef with horseradish
Hazelnut loaf with pine nuts and chickpeas
Salads: potato, spinach, bean

Iced Christmas pudding with cream

Dessert wine, liqueurs
Glacé fruits and nuts
Coffee

'If I had a belt, I'd loosen it,' Daniel commented.

'The Professor is doing us proud,' I informed him. 'So just eat a bit of everything, or he'll be living for months on the leftovers.'

'Not while Jason is in the world,' he replied, and he was, of course, right. I collected my gift of Roman bath oil and the other things and we rose in stately fashion to the Professor's apartment on the third floor.

We were greeted by Mrs. Dawson, which was a surprise. She was wearing an ochre top and a marvellous wraparound skirt, tied on the hip. It was made of a soft cotton material with paisley and swirly patterns in long stripes of dark brown, green and cream.

'My children are away,' she said. 'My son's gone to Queensland with his family and my daughter is in Hobart—she hates the heat. Merry Christmas! Come in!' She ushered us in and handed us each a tall glass full of kir royal, champagne and crème de cassis.

Meroe was there, nibbling Jason's little vegetable muffins.

'You understand that this is merely a Christian ceremony planted on the smoking remains of a pagan one,' she informed me fiercely.

'I understand,' I said. 'But you can still eat the food.'

'Certainly,' she said. 'Even pagans can do that.'

'I got your menu,' I said to the Professor, kissing him on the cheek. 'Here's a small token of my affection, and I can't see us eating all that provender.'

'And mine to you,' he said, kissing me in turn. 'And I think we shall manage.'

He put into my hands a translation of Ovid's *Ars Amatoria*, addressed to me and Daniel, though he 'didn't expect that we needed any instruction'.

Therese gave me my apron, emblazoned with NEVER TRUST A THIN COOK in white on green and I handed out the other things I had made.

Daniel had the simplest idea. He had just printed a lot of little certificates, good for 'four hours work'. It was a lovely idea in a building full of people who were getting old, or who didn't know how to hold a hammer.

Trudi gave everyone a tulip bulb, which she then collected back to plant for us. Mrs. Pemberthy did not, she informed us, give presents. But she took my lavender bag with flowers embroidered on it anyway. Small black Nox was discussing a plate of finely chopped smoked salmon. That cat was a fish fiend and this was her Christmas present.

Jon and Kepler had bought lengths of the most luscious fabric for all the men, and wine bottle openers for all the ladies—a fine distinction, I thought. Mistress Dread, I was informed, had gone home to an unsuspected daughter. People were laughing. This was not the sort of Christmas I was used to…No arguments? No feuds?

Of course, as writers from Wodehouse to Saki have known, the essence of a happy gathering is to have a Mrs. Pemberthy, whom everyone dislikes. This smooths over any little difficulties in the social round. She was doing such a good job that I took her another glass of champagne.

Mrs. Dawson had even provided a plate of doughnuts for Daniel's Hanukkah celebration. She thought of everything. He kissed her hand, a little greasily.

I drank the white wine—a fine sauvignon blanc from the colder bits of New Zealand. I ate an artichoke heart and a few slices of salami. Crackers were pulled. I put on my new apron. Pleasant carols were playing softly. Even Meroe was humming along. She had given me a packet of her wonderful hangover cure, a tea which smelt like old cricket pitch but rectified the unbalanced humours almost instantly. Jason was serving drinks, glowing with conscious virtue, knowledge that he had produced the perfect glacé cherry, and the prospect of holidays.

'Now we have all had our private party,' said the Professor gravely, 'I found all these hungry people in the cellar this morning, so I invited them to lunch.'

In came Rowan and Michael, Bec and Sarah, Janeen, Rupert and Alexander. They were escorting Manny and Brigid and the baby. I observed that someone had given Brigid new clothes. That, I guessed, would be Kylie and Goss. The girl, now wearing a pair of khaki trousers and a loose green top, no longer had iconic force. But she was a brave girl and Manny was a remarkable boy and we loaded plates for them of the roasted and the seethed and the beautiful salads.

Sarah, informed that the raw crudités and the hummus, the lentil loaf and the olives, nuts and fruit were for her, ate them without complaint or lecture on the rabidly carnivorous nature of the buffet. She even had a glass of wine. The others hopped into the food as though they had been starving since childhood.

'This is fantastic,' blurred Rupert through a mouthful of roast beef. 'Did you cook all this, Prof?'

'No,' he said. 'It was provided by my most gracious friend.'

He indicated Mrs. Dawson. We applauded and she bowed.

'It was the least I could do for such excellent company,' she said, and accepted another glass of a strong red wine from the Flinders Ranges.

Manny ate like he was starving. Brigid allowed Trudi to hold the baby while she collected a feast for herself. Jason, besotted, offered her a plate of fruit bread. Barmbrack, also called St Brigid's bread. Sarah had been discarded for a safer object of devotion. I was delighted.

Naturally, there were presents for the baby. Meroe had told everyone—except me and Mrs. P—that she would be at the feast. Professor Dion gave her a little gold locket which had belonged to his daughter. He touched her forehead and murmured an ancient Greek blessing. Translated, it said, *Welcome to the grain-bearing earth.* Therese enveloped her in a beautiful bunny rug on which she had hastily appliquéd a brown and white Dutch rabbit with a benign expression. Meroe obliged with a jar of her emollient, made of lanolin and just a faint scent of herbs, sovereign for preventing nappy rash. Mrs. Dawson gave Brigid a necklace of rose beads, compounded of rose petals and smelling very sweet, because she said that no one ever gave the mother presents and she had done all the work.

Then the singers obliged with a carol in honour of the baby. I had never heard it sung before but it was the carol performed by the field mice in the Mole's little house, and it had always touched me deeply.

Villagers all, this frosty tide,
Let your doors swing open wide,
Though wind may follow, and snow beside,
Yet draw us in by your fire to bide;
  Joy shall be yours in the morning!

[...]

And then they heard the angels tell
'Who were the first to cry Nowell?
Animals all, as it befell,
In the stable where they did dwell!
   Joy shall be theirs in the morning!'

I was feeling strangely giddy, as though I had drunk too much wine, though I hadn't. I was feeling, Mrs. Dawson informed me, Christmassy, as was only proper. I was exhilarated, like Ebenezer Scrooge post-ghost. I wanted to hug the whole world.

I sat down, in case I actually tried this. The food was wonderful. I peeled another slice from an ambrosial ham and ate it with a slice of my own bread and a strong mustard piccalilli from the Dawson Grandma's recipe. Meroe, of all people, said, 'Merry Christmas!', and I lifted my glass and Jason filled it and kissed me. And we toasted Christmas and mercy and charity and compassion and even the vegans joined in.

There were things I would have to do soon. Find the freegans and fill them full of good things, for instance. Make sure that Mr. O'Ryan kept to his bargain. Perhaps help Brigid find a suitable house near the Lake establishment. Feed Christmas raw tuna to the Mouse Police and Christmas smoked trout to Horatio, who doted on smoked trout. Pay Jason his holiday money and give him my mobile phone so he could call for help if he had to. Things to be done.

But for the moment all I had to do was be happy. Someone asked Brigid if she had named the baby yet.

She smiled very gently and told us that she and Manny had picked out a name already if the baby was a girl. We asked what it was. She held out the sleeping baby.

'Her name is Serena,' she said.

After that I had a toast of my own. I raised my glass again and quoted Tiny Tim.

'God Bless Us, every one.'

Recipes

Glacé Cherries

The oldest recipe turned out to be the best. Thank you, the Goodman of Paris.

> 500 g cherries
> 500 g sugar

Stone the cherries and put them in a heavy-based saucepan. Cover them with the sugar and leave overnight. In the morning bring them slowly to the boil and stir frantically to make sure that the fruit does not stick. Cook for about 10 minutes. You will see the cherries turn translucent. Take them off the heat and leave them for two days in the syrup. They will absorb a lot of it. Then remove them from the pan, drain, roll them in caster sugar and put them on a wire tray in the sun to dry. Or in the bottom of a very cool oven. Don't package them until they are really unsticky. The leftover syrup makes fantastic sorbet—just freeze it.

You can use this recipe to glacé anything—except, possibly, potatoes. For apricots, peaches, and so on, douse the fruit first in boiling water to remove the skins, and then stone and quarter them.

If you miscalculate this recipe you will get toffee cherries, which luckily are also delicious. Use them as decoration and try again.

Glacé Fruitcake

This is a good family Christmas cake recipe. It also looks very pretty. If you don't glacé your own fruits you can buy some very good ones.

> 300 g mixed nuts (pistachios, almonds, brazil nuts, macadamias, whatever you like)
> 600 g mixed glacé fruit (pineapple, peaches, figs, apricots, cherries. Include some sultanas if you like them)
> ¾ cup plain flour
> pinch salt
> 1 teaspoon cinnamon
> ½ teaspoon baking powder
> ¾ cup brown or raw sugar
> 2 eggs
> ¼ cup brandy or rum
> 1 teaspoon vanilla essence
> extra cherries to decorate and ⅓ cup warmed apricot jam for the glaze

Preheat the oven to 160°C.

Grease a 20 cm cake tin and line it with baking paper.

Mix nuts and fruit together, then add flour, sugar, baking powder, cinnamon and salt, and stir until combined.

Mix eggs, brandy and vanilla together in a separate bowl, then add to the flour mixture.

Mix until it is all more or less mixed, calling in members of your family to stir and make a wish.

Plunk into the tin and bake for as long as it takes—about one and a half to two hours. Test by poking it with a skewer. Allow to cool in the tin.

When cool, either pour another measure of brandy over it and shut it in a tin, where it will keep for a long time, or pour warm apricot jam over the top, stud with extra glacé fruits and serve.

Vegie Delights

Every vegetarian has been to a restaurant, sadly, where there is only one vegetarian option and it is always roast vegetable lasagne. While there are good, even superlative roast vegie lasagnes, some variety would be nice. It is as though a chef will expend endless effort on a meat dish, but not think a vegie one is worthy of his consideration. This is, however, changing.

I recall the complaints of some of our group on the Women Writers' Train (note appropriate use of apostrophe—plural women, plural writers) when the nice ladies who made sandwiches for us had only one vegie sandwich and it was always sultana and grated carrot. And hard-core vegans would have to live on baked potato in some towns, which is not a good diet even if you are pure.

The world is full of gorgeous vegetables and all you need is a nice friendly organic grocer (like my own, Pompello, which is a social centre and recipe exchange as well) and a good cookbook. Borrow an armload of vegie cookbooks from the library and see which one makes you hungry as you read. I like *The Cranks Recipe Book*. Remember also that most of the world looks on meat as an occasional treat and try lots of different cuisines. Try a different vegetable. I recently found fennel, which is gorgeous as a salad with fish. And boiled my first globe artichoke. And peeled my own broad beans…And if you find you don't like the veg when you have prepared and sauced it properly, then put it in the compost, where it will be appreciated by the worms.

Try a cheesy vegetable muffin. If you want to make mini muffins, watch the cooking time. They seem to singe easily.

Topping

>   1 small onion, peeled and sliced
>   1 zucchini, grated
>   1 clove garlic, crushed
>   2 tomatoes, chopped
>   ½ red capsicum, chopped
>   pepper and salt

Gently fry the veg in a little olive oil until soft but not brown. Cool.

Muffins

>   2 cups self-raising flour
>   ½ cup grated parmesan
>   2 eggs
>   1 cup buttermilk (if you have no buttermilk, use sweet milk with a squeeze of lemon juice and add 1 tsp baking powder. The buttermilk is a raising agent, oddly enough)
>   pinch of salt
>   ¼ cup olive oil

Preheat the oven to 180°C.

Mix the flour and parmesan in one bowl. In another bowl mix the eggs, oil and buttermilk.

Pour the wet ingredients into the dry ingredients, mix gently, drop into a 6-cup muffin tray, then top them with the cooked vegetables. Alternatively you can stir the vegies into the muffin mix, but this can turn out soggy. Even so it tastes very nice.

Cook in a moderate oven for 25 minutes or so until it springs back when poked. Perfect cocktail savouries—you can do yourself harm with the cocktails and good with the little muffins.

Cordial

My grandma made gallons of this (a gentler beverage than her ginger beer, which gave 'spritzig' a meaning closer to 'blast radius') and it is a good way to quench the thirst without all those optional added chemicals. Any citrus fruit will do. The citric and tartaric acids are both natural substances, like the pectin used in my jams.

> 8 lemons or equivalent in grapefruit, oranges etc.; juice of all and grated rind of three
> 1 kg white sugar
> 8 cups boiling water
> 1 tablespoon tartaric acid
> 2 tablespoons citric acid

Mix all ingredients together until sugar dissolves. Bottle and seal. To serve, dilute one in four with water or soda water or, as a special treat, mineral water. Wonderful with gin...

Afterword

The best book on pet rabbits in Australia is definitely *The Wonderful World of Pet Rabbits* by Christine Carter. Order one at www.petrabbitworld.com or email me if you want my copy. I would like it to go to a good home.

Beverley Nichols wrote the best books on cats, *Cats' A.B.C.* and *Cats' X.Y.Z.* They have been reprinted by Timber Press at www.timberpress.com. You will notice Nichols' correct use of the apostrophe. A wonderful thing in these parlous ungrammatical times.

The carols come mainly from *The Oxford Book of Carols* and the choristers' standby *Carols for Choirs 1* (known as 'the green book'), both from Oxford University Press. 'Villagers All' by Kenneth Grahame was set to music by David Greagg.

Anyone who likes is welcome to email me on kgreenwood@ netspace.net.au

To receive a free catalog of Poisoned Pen Press titles, please contact us in one of the following ways:

Phone: 1-800-421-3976
Facsimile: 1-480-949-1707
Email: info@poisonedpenpress.com
Website: www.poisonedpenpress.com

Poisoned Pen Press
6962 E. First Ave. Ste. 103
Scottsdale, AZ 85251